# Bloom books

Dear reader,

This is it. The final installment of the story. (I get teary-eyed just thinking about it!)

So much has happened since chapter one of *Gild*. Auren's life went from a single cage to two big worlds, and she's gone through so much. I'm incredibly proud of her.

Auren's journey has always been about opposites: day or night, light or dark, healing or trauma, powerful or powerless, flying or falling, and Annwyn or Orea. With every flip of the coin, she's made choices to become the person she is.

Now, she has to make sure she remembers that.

The rest of these characters will have to remember what's important, too. They've been walking uphill for a long time, and I'm excited to finally show them reaching the top. And while their views may be different, they all stand at the same precipice. The same spot where they will either fall…

Or fly.

Finishing is bittersweet, but I'm so happy to let these characters have their end. Thank you for coming on this journey with me. I've been able to tell this story completely and thoroughly, with laughter and tears, with love and grief, while giving everyone their time and their voice, and it's all because of you that I've been able to do that. I am grateful from the bottom of my heart.

I hope like hell that you enjoy
*Goldfinch*.

# GOLDFINCH

## RAVEN KENNEDY

Bloom books

Published by Bloom Books, an imprint of Sourcebooks
P.O. Box 4410, Naperville, Illinois 60567-4410
(630) 961-3900
sourcebooks.com

Cataloging-in-Publication data is on file with the Library of Congress.

Printed and bound in the United States of America.
VP 10 9 8 7 6 5 4 3 2 1

# About The Book

## THE MYTH OF
## KING MIDAS REIMAGINED.

This compelling and dark adult fantasy series is as addictive as it is unexpected. With romance, fae, and intrigue, the gilded world of Orea will grip you from the very first page. Be immersed in this journey of greed, love, and finding inner strength.

*Please note: This book contains explicit content and dark elements that may be triggering to some. It includes explicit romance, mature language, violence, grief, suicide, death, reference to a stillborn birth that occurs off page, death of mother and child during childbirth, and death of a creature. It is not intended for anyone under 18 years of age.*

*This is the final book in the series.*

Remember, you are stronger than the dark,
and you have the wings to fly.

# CHAPTER 1

## SLADE

The beasts are antsy, talons digging into the cobblestone, sharp eyes on the sky. The soldiers know the risks, but the animals know the energy, and every single one of them is sensing the nerves, the suspense, the bloodlust.

They always do, when it's time to go to war.

Beside me, chunks of black rock litter the ground like a heap of scattered coal from Queen Kaila's earlier arrival. The black obelisk is now ruined and splintered.

Crumbling. Just like my fucking patience.

I want to leave now. I've hurried to ready myself, to ready my Premiers and my Wrath, and I need to get going.

My mind keeps spinning, gut twisting with this new truth that Lu brought. That the bridge of Lemuria is unbroken. Remade. Connected to the fae realm.

*How the fuck did they rebuild the bridge? How does Seventh Kingdom even exist?*

When I flew over Seventh years ago, all that was left was a fissured and freezing land of white and gray. No people. No animals. No cities. Just emptiness within the clefts. The only thing that seemed to remain was a lingering echo from the magic that had pierced through it like a shattered mirror.

I remember the wrongness of that echo. It reminded me of the scent that loitered after burnt food had been tossed away. A lingering unpleasantness that didn't let up.

All that was left at the edge of the world was nothing. Nothing at all.

My father—The Breaker—broke that bridge hundreds of years ago, long before I was born. Powerful magic that made him the crown's greatest ally. Made him famous and wealthy.

And now, someone or something took that broken bridge and *fixed it*.

I don't know if my father is involved or even if he still lives. I don't know who ordered this invasion into Orea, and I don't know the state of the bridge itself.

But none of that matters. All that matters is *her*.

I now have a way to get to Auren. I've failed to open a rip, failed to fulfill my promise to find her, but now, there's hope.

My rotting heart aches more incessantly. Pulsing in tune with my adrenaline, except instead of a beat, it just thrums,

*go go go.*

Go to the bridge. Go to Annwyn. Go to her.

My hand delves into my pocket, my fingers twisting around Auren's scrap of ribbon.

*"I will find you. I will find you in that life. I fucking promise you that. But you have to go. Please, baby."*

The memory of my cracked plea haunts me. So does the way she'd said my name. The way she'd looked at me, with pure devastation.

My heart throbs with pain that seems to emanate from two different sides. Left and right, up and down, inside and out.

I can't wait any longer.

Releasing the ribbon, my gaze searches the dark courtyard, the surrounding torches casting off an orange glow through the night. I see Ryatt organizing his handpicked Elites, the profile of his face lit up by the torch flame.

He's motioning toward a pair of timberwings, while a few Elites fix the straps of the harnesses. Between every pair of beasts are the reins of a carrying compartment, woven from thick leather and stiff rope. War panniers. Able to hold soldiers and weapons for the timberwings to carry between them as they fly.

Not the most comfortable way to travel. Also not the quickest since the beasts will be weighed down. But it's a tried-and-true method used for centuries during Orean battles.

Thirty-six riders on thirty-six timberwings—that's eighteen pairs. Per pair, that's five elite soldiers carried in the war panniers. That's one hundred twenty-six soldiers we can fly in with us to try to ready Ranhold for invasion.

One hundred twenty-six. Against thousands of fae.

But our plan is to head straight for Ranhold, to ready Fifth Kingdom's army, and for me to strike the fae with my magic. Meanwhile, our Elites and King Thold's will do everything possible to stop them from advancing.

*Give Orea a chance*, my brother begged me. So that's what I'm doing.

I reach Ryatt, and when he sees me, he dismisses the soldiers he was talking to.

"How much longer?" I ask as soon as we're alone, very aware of the impatience tingeing my tone.

Ryatt is in full commander leathers, his expression stoic and professional. "I'm still waiting on six more Elites, and the smith should be bringing up the weapons within the next hour.

The kitchens are readying the ration packs as well, and King Thold is also preparing—"

A growl scrapes up my throat. "This is taking too long."

He gives me a look of exasperation. "I'm going as fast as I can. I'm trying to get everyone ready for you to leave at first light, but preparation takes time."

"I don't have time," I say, harsher than I mean to. I know my brother is working his ass off to get us everything we need, but even their quickest is too damn slow.

With an impatient glance around the courtyard again, I see how far off we still are from leaving. Some timberwings haven't even been fitted with their saddles yet.

*go go go go go*

I can't resist this push anymore.

"I'm going ahead."

Ryatt's brows lift in surprise, just as Lu and Judd walk up to join us.

"You're leaving right now?" Lu asks as she stops beside me. There's no missing the tired circles under her eyes.

"I can't wait. I need to move. I can't stand still a fucking second longer."

"I'll go with you," she immediately offers, but I shake my head. She might be too stubborn to admit it, but she needs a few hours of rest before she gets back on a timberwing again. It's been barely five hours since she got here and told us about the fae attacking Highbell.

"No," I tell her. "Go get a few hours of sleep and then leave with the rest of the contingent."

"But—"

"That's an order, Talula."

She scowls at me. "Don't pull that shit with me." Her tone is sharp, but I don't miss the flash of relief in her eyes. She really does need some fucking sleep.

When she looks over and sees that Judd's grinning, she

slams her forearm into his stomach, making an *oof* escape him.

"Hey!" he complains. "I wasn't the one to call you by your whole name! Why'd you hit me?"

"Because of that dumb smile on your face."

"My smile's not dumb," he defends as he rubs his stomach.

Rolling her eyes, she looks back to me. "One of us should go with you."

"You'd only slow me down," I reply. "Argo is the fastest timberwing. If I can travel on my own, I can get to Ranhold quickly without having to wait on anyone. Since Ryatt is staying behind to command the army here, that means I'll need you and Judd to lead the Elites and help King Thold with his group too. They haven't traveled through Fifth often. You two know the quickest path and how to handle the elements. So does Digby." When she still looks dubious, I add, "Besides, you'll only be half a day behind me."

"And once you reach Ranhold?" she asks.

"I'll tell the new King Fulke about the threat and make sure he readies his army. Then I'll drop as much magic as I can against the fae. After that, I'm heading straight for the bridge."

I can see that Lu still doesn't like the idea of me going alone, but she bites back whatever argument she might have. That's how I know how exhausted she really is.

"I'll see you at Ranhold," I tell her. "Now get some sleep, Captain."

"Fine," she relents before turning to Ryatt. "Make sure someone sends for me when it's nearly time to depart."

Judd opens his mouth, but without even looking at him, she points at his face and tells Ryatt, "*Not* him."

Judd grins again.

Ryatt smirks, shaking his head. "Don't worry, I'll send for you."

5

Lu nods and then looks back at me. "Be careful," she says, dark brown eyes solemn.

"I will be."

As she walks off, I see her stop and talk to Digby before heading inside. I glance at Judd. "Go let King Thold's guards know to alert him that I'll be flying ahead."

"Will do." He gives me a salute. "See you in the shitty snow kingdom. Next time, let's try to have a war on one of the warmer continents, yeah?"

"Sure," I say dryly.

As I watch Judd lope away, an abrupt pain in my chest makes me grimace, and I press my fingers over my heart. Ryatt's attention narrows on me. "What's wrong?"

"Nothing," I quickly reply, dropping my hand.

"Slade…"

"I just need to go, Ryatt."

His lips press together in a hard line, but he nods. "Okay. I'll get them moving as quickly as possible so they're right behind you."

"I know you will."

My brother walks with me as I head for Argo. He's easily spotted amongst the other beasts because he's larger, and he currently has his bark-colored wings shoved out and his face twisted in a snarl. He's playing a game of dominance, ensuring he has a twenty-foot radius surrounding him, and snapping at any of the other timberwings who dare set even a single talon too close. Still, he's a lot friendlier now than he used to be before he nearly died.

"Territorial beast," I mutter as I stroke him on the side.

He blinks at me unrepentantly. Then he turns his head, and his demeanor changes instantly. Snarl gone, tense form going lax.

I look over to see the little girl, Wynn, skipping up to him. Her sister is right behind her, both of them out of their

Second Kingdom religious gray robes and instead wearing colorful dresses.

Wynn tosses her arms around Argo's neck as soon as she reaches him. He bends his head around her in what I think is a timberwing's rendition of a hug, nuzzling into her curly black hair.

When she pulls away, she looks up at me. "Does he have to go to war?" she asks, her big brown eyes teary.

I can't help but feel guilt at her sad tone.

"I'll keep him safe."

She sniffs, and her older sister, Shea, places a comforting hand on her shoulder. "Wynn just wanted to say goodbye. She became very attached to Argo while she healed him during our trip here."

Flicking my gaze up to Argo as he nuzzles against her, I smile. "He's obviously become quite attached to her as well."

When I hear Wynn's sad sniff again, I crouch down in front of her and meet her eyes. "Argo has let me be his rider for a very long time," I tell her. "He loves flying, and he's very fast. He's going to be just fine."

"He got hurt with you before," she reminds me, honest accusation in her young face.

Shea's fingers tense. "Wynnie," she reprimands.

I shake my head. "No, your sister is right. He did get hurt with me." I glance back at Wynn. "I give you my word that if things become too dangerous, I will send Argo back." I hold out my hand. "Deal?"

The girl takes my hand and shakes. "Deal."

"Good," I say. "And I also wanted to personally thank you again for healing Rissa."

She squirms a bit, like she's feeling shy. "You're welcome."

Rising back to my feet, I look to Shea. "You've received everything you need?"

"More than. Thank you, Your Majesty," she tells me before looking down at her sister. "Come on, Wynnie, time to go. The king is very busy."

Wynn looks at me. "You'll really make sure he isn't hurt again?"

"I promise."

"Okay," she says with a nod. Then she hugs Argo one more time, and the two sisters walk away, hand in hand.

I glance over at Ryatt, and my brother nods, already knowing what I'm thinking. "Don't worry, Isalee and Warken are making sure they're well taken care of. And don't tell him I told you, but Osrik bought them their own house in the city. A nice one, right on the river. He doesn't want the girl to know it was from him though."

"Doesn't surprise me."

"You know him," Ryatt says. "Os never wants people to know if he's done something nice."

"If he heard you say the word *nice* in the same sentence as his name, he'd punch you in the gut."

Ryatt smirks. "Probably."

Turning, I start checking over Argo's buckles one more time, ensuring my pack is secured. Then I swing myself up onto the saddle and glance down at my brother. I can see the nervousness in his expression, even though he hides it well. Everyone is nervous. After centuries of fae being gone from this world, this isn't a threat Orea ever expected to face again.

"Keep Argo *and* yourself safe," he tells me, tone going quieter so no one else around will hear.

"I will. And I'll take out as many of them as I can before I head for the bridge."

"I know you will. Fight fire with fire, and fight fae with fae," he says with a small smirk before his expression grows serious again. "Orea definitely has a chance with you on our side."

"Not just me. Orea has a chance because of *you.*"

He swallows hard, and guilt hits me again, because I can see how much my words mean to him. I should've been saying these things sooner. Should've given him this position a long time ago. I was so used to being his older brother and protecting him, that I stopped him from being able to step into the role of a protector too.

"Send word as soon as you get to Ranhold."

"I will," I reply.

If we need to mobilize Fourth's army, he'll be ready.

There are so many other unsaid things between us, but there's no time. Instead, we share a drawn-out look, and then I give him a nod. "Lead well, Commander."

He bows at the waist. "I'll protect Fourth with my life."

That's what I'm afraid of.

"You'll find Auren and our mother," he says, not an inch of doubt in his voice, because he knows I won't settle for anything else. "Be careful," he murmurs.

"You too, brother."

My grip tightens on the reins, and my chest tugs with both emotion and pain.

But the pull to get to Auren tugs harder.

*go go go go*

With one last nod to Ryatt, I nudge Argo with my heel, and he lifts us into the night sky. The other timberwings on the ground screech at our departure, envious that we're on the move.

My pulse jumps—leaps—because *finally*, I'm on my way. Finally, I'm heading toward her. And although pain throbs in my chest and I can feel my veins pulsing with poison, I ignore it. Because I'm going to her, and nothing, not even this rotting fucking heart in my chest, is going to stop me.

# CHAPTER 2

## SLADE

Argo goes upward to gain altitude, the dark of the night enveloping us like a shroud. Below, my brother lifts his hand in a shadowed send-off.

I face forward again when we pass over the moat, leaving my castle behind as we fly toward the city. The capital is dotted with streetlamps and lanterns that hang inside the bobbing boats where they drift up and down the rivers. Every flickering flame reminds me of just how many people live in Brackhill alone. People that I'm responsible for.

*Let it topple.* That's what I told Ryatt about Orea, and I meant every word. But that was before an outside threat broke in.

I could see it in Ryatt's eyes. The accusation. Buried deep, but there. The army invading Orea is *my* species. My people. He didn't say it aloud, but I could hear it all the same. To some degree, it's my responsibility to protect Orea against my own.

*Give Orea a chance.*

*Get to the bridge.*

Two birds, one stone. I can pass by Ranhold, and then head straight for Seventh. It will only add a handful of hours to my travel, half a day at most as I dump power there to deter the fae. Then I can get to the bridge.

I hiss through my teeth as another twinge of pain surges in my chest. It arcs down my veins, shooting through the roots of rot in my arms. I flex and fist my right hand, trying to shake the sensation off.

It doesn't go away.

But I grew up enduring pain, so my tolerance is high. My father didn't allow anything less. If I can put up with what he meted out, I can push through for Auren.

As if in challenge, the rotting organ in my chest throbs harder, but I grit my teeth.

*Push the fuck through.*

I re-grip the reins as we pick up speed, and soon, Brackhill City and the castle disappear behind us. Argo must sense my urgency, because he's flying like he's racing the night.

And winning.

We're eating up the distance, and at this rate, I know we'll make it to Ranhold in record time. Thank fuck.

Through the night, we fly over Fourth Kingdom. My eyes stay peeled, my teeth gritted. All I can do is count the seconds between the throbs of pain. It drums in time with the incessant push to hurry.

*go go go go*

I can't open a rip, no matter how hard I try, but I can get to that fucking bridge.

I have to.

Right before dawn, Argo spots a flock of birds mid-flight. He drops out of the cover of the clouds, attention locked on his prey. They don't even see him coming until he's swooping down, scooping two of the winged creatures up into his wide maw. The sound of their shrieks is cut off by snapping bones and a litter of feathers.

I lock in my knees, bracing as he swoops for a third. "Argo—"

Intense pain slams into me so abruptly that I jerk in the saddle. The sensation pitches brutally into my chest, stealing my words. Stealing my vision.

It clutches me as sharply as Argo's teeth snap through those bones. Except it's happening with my fucking *heart*. Lancing it through, bleeding me out.

I lurch on the saddle, body falling forward. It feels like I'm being sliced open in the middle of a sea, and a whirlpool of poisoned water is pumping into me. I jerk my gaze down to where the pain radiates, and my eyes widen.

My rotting heart has started to *swell*.

It's lifting my leather jerkin. Making it distend outward with dizzying agony, and I realize what's happening.

It's about to burst.

*No.*

My heart is choosing *now* to give out on me? Right when I finally have a way to get to Auren? When I'm finally on my way?

I'm not dying. I fucking *refuse*.

But my body seems to have other ideas.

My heart is filling my body with poison. It feels like hot, acidic rain pouring in, flooding it past capacity, washing out all my blood and stinging every vein.

I look at my wrists and hands where my rot has pumped in. Every inch of visible skin is riddled with so many black lines it nearly overruns my flesh.

I lose the ability to hold on. My grip slips off the reins, body jerking as I slam against Argo's back, unable to sit up, unable to do *anything*. I feel more than see Argo curl his head around to look at me, and then there's a deafening roar as I start to slip sideways.

*Fuck!*

Panic pounces, limbs flailing as I start to fall.

I jerk to an abrupt stop as the straps holding me to Argo's saddle cinch, keeping me seated, though they strain with the stretch.

The saddle starts to twist over Argo's middle as my body tips until I'm hanging off his side. This one strip of leather is the only thing keeping me from plummeting through the air.

The pain is unimaginable.

Argo roars again and tries to twist his body to get me back where I'm supposed to be. But I can't move. I'm paralyzed from the spasms, can feel the poison leaching up into my neck, my cheeks, my eyes…

Darkness blotches my vision just as I feel Argo dive.

My stomach hits my throat as we speed through the air. The leather strip twists, making me pitch backward as it slips, and I get torn off the saddle. The only thing still connecting me to Argo is the single strap wrapped around my waist.

If the leather were to snap…the buckle to fail…

Pain spreads out like bolts of lightning through my entire body.

*Fuck fuck fuck*—

I might be dead before we hit the ground.

The air whips at me, jerking my body left and right as Argo continues to roar. Continues to dive.

I'm streaming behind him like a flag caught in the wind, and then the strained strap on the saddle *snaps*.

Without the tether, the air whips me away like a leaf in the wind, and instead of being pulled down with intention, I start to truly fall.

I fall and fall, staring up at the dark.

I have a moment to wonder if this is what Auren felt when she fell through the rip. If this is my punishment for sending her in there alone. I gasp and flail, terror fisting me.

I'm falling.

*Dying.*

Heart about to burst through my chest, rot ready to rupture.

Body ready to slam into the ground.

I brace myself.

But just before my inevitable crash, Argo dives down and catches me with his feet, talons circling around my arm and leg. I wince from the pressure, but within seconds, he's dropping me again, and I thud against solid ground, rolling and skidding across wet grass and spongy soil before coming to a stop.

I land half-slopped into a bog, my entire right side drenched in muddy water.

The pain wants to debilitate me, wants to keep me hostage, but I fight past it. Remind myself of what I've endured at the hands of my father.

*Move.*

*Move move move—*

A roar rips from my lips as I fight against the anguish for control of my body. Mud threatens my airway, but I command my body to obey anyway. Reaching one arm up, I grip hold of the grass, straining as I pull myself up.

The pain is all-consuming, my vision still stained with spills of ink, but somehow, I get my knees under me and manage to crawl out of the muck, grip by grip. Then I drop and roll onto my back, dripping in sweat, shaking all over, ready to fucking puke.

I move my hands down and rip open my coat and leather jerkin, exposing my chest. My heart looks like it's ready to explode. Like a massive blister full of pus, except it's singed brown and leaking roots of black.

Not fucking good.

I can see every vein that leads out of it pulsing, pumping more poison into my system. Instead of the rotted lines staying contained to my upper chest and arms, I'm absolutely covered in them, breaching down my stomach and hands, even blackening my fingernails.

I'm riddled with so many that it doesn't even look real.

Argo nudges me on the arm, making distressed noises low in his throat. He lowers himself, urging me to get up, so I lift my hand and reach the strap around his neck.

But before I can attempt to pull myself onto his back, my body convulses. I lurch backward, breath stolen from me as the torment reaches a crescendo.

And I know.

This is it. I'm dying.

But my life doesn't flash before my eyes. She does.

Auren floods into me, memories consuming me entirely. There aren't enough, not nearly enough. But I see them. Feel them. Hear them.

The little moments. Like when I'd watch her without her even realizing it. Taking in the side of her face while she ate, watching her walk up the stairs, seeing her smile at something Judd said. It's the sound of her voice as she told me her truths. The scent of her hair when she laid upon my chest.

It's the big moments too, when she was entirely too magnificent for this world. When she made everyone else seem small and dull in comparison. Her vengeance and her strength and her kindness and her light.

I was always meant to find her. To see her.

This can't be it.

This can't be all.

A rasping breath cuts out of me, tines dragging against my ribs with a clatter. "Auren," I gasp out. As if she can hear me. As if I can say everything I need to say.

Moisture gathers at the corners of my eyes, shedding the misery of my failure. Of everything I'll never get to see her do. The little and big moments I'll miss. I wanted them all. I wanted to see and experience and have all of her, forever.

And now I can't.

Misery drenches me, while rot starts gushing into the ground. Argo whines. My heart slogs.

I stare up at the swarm of branches from the twist-root trees, slunk in this bog, while my heart pumps out a poison that's killing me.

I choke as it reaches my lungs and infects my breath.

My heart is so distended now, it sits like a stone over my chest, rising like a hunching creature ready to tear free.

But still, I try to fucking fight.

Because I will always fight for her. For as long as I can.

My entire body shakes, limbs numb, pain encompassing, but I force movement anyway, because I will not give up. I will not give in.

If this is the moment that I end, I will end with my fight for her.

As long as there is breath in my lungs and a heart in my chest, I will fight for her with everything that I am.

I growl, my throat tearing open with the determined sound and spilling out into the air, making birds explode from the trees.

With desperate struggle, I turn. Shove my knees beneath me. Pump my arms up, and then strain to reach Argo's strap at the back of his neck. All of it a battle between life and death.

Do not give up. Do not give in.

*Fight for her.*

I pull myself up, head swimming, vision bolting, legs threatening to give out. But I clench my fists around the strap, and I fucking stand.

"Auren. Need—to get—to her," I pant through gritted teeth.

Neck twisted around, Argo blinks at me, whining low in his throat. But stubborn perseverance hooks into my voice and yanks the resolution out. "I'm going to find her. Fucking get to her…"

The pain in my chest reaches a poisoned peak, and I suck in a thin breath that has my lungs ringing with warning that it might be my last one.

I can't take in another. I try, but I *can't*.

Panic consumes. My eyes go wide and wild as black spots block my vision. The agony in my chest is about to burst my heart, and I know my fight doesn't matter anyway because *this is it*—

And then, everything changes.

I'm suddenly hit. Not with pain, not with death. But with *her*.

Something shifts. Death pauses.

I suck in a breath, feeling her in my inhale.

It's as if she's standing right here next to me. No—even more than that.

It's as if…

Her scent floods my air. I can taste her at the back of my tongue. Feel her warmth consuming me like a fire consumes a forest. It starts to eat up every toxic limb and rotten root that exists within me.

Her flame, her sun, it blazes. Delves into every crevice, burning away every pinch of polluted blood. It swarms around my near-bursting heart, and I feel her essence grab hold. Fist me in her light.

And then something deep inside of me suddenly… collides.

# SLADE

I gasp.
I can scent her.
Her warmth. It consumes me.
My knees buckle.
My rotting heart suddenly swells.
*Bursts.*
Something shifts.
My two sides…they *mend*. Something else tears free.
Scales erupt over my chest, bursting from what I thought
was my dying heart.
A roar sounds in my ear. Souls tether.
My aura pulses.
Changes.
*I can feel her.*

# AUREN

I gasp.
Breathe.
The air of Annwyn. The air of Orea.
I pitch backwards.
The beast and the seed surge.
*Combine.*
My back heats.
Rot delves. Not with death, but rebirth. *Life* tears free.
Two souls reach out. Clasp. My ears echo with two heartbeats.
With a bonded song.
My aura flares.
Changes.
*I can feel him.*

# CHAPTER 3

## SLADE

I know what this is.

I'm not sure exactly *how* I know, but an innate understanding fuses with my fraying consciousness.

I'm on my knees and heaving breath, my body trembling as an age-old magic floods through me. This is magic born when existence first bled into Annwyn. Magic that is rare and coveted and revered.

*This is a päyur bond fusing.*

As soon as that realization enters my mind, my entire body flares. Black tendrils sift off my skin like smoke, swarmed with golden rays that shine amidst the inky black, flocking around my body in rippling streams.

I stare at my hands, my arms, watching the black and gold drift off me like steam from a hot spring.

It's our auras. Mine and hers, mixing.

The päyur magic ripples. I feel it within me, like someone shoveling up my entire foundation and packing it in with Auren's essence.

Our souls are now bound together. Our lives forever connected. Our magic entwined.

It means that she and I are a match fated by the goddesses. It means that we have been given the greatest gift ever bestowed on a fae.

It means that she's mine.

Elation fills me as much as the magic does. Stunned, all I can do is stay kneeling on the murky ground.

I feel her magic pulse through me, the warmth of it filling my limbs. My rot dumps into the land, but streaks of gold, like gleaming ribbons, run through the black roots.

This power that stretches over the land also stretches through me. I feel it swim through my depths and rush into my chest.

I feel her burn. Her *light*.

I jerk my eyes down to my torn shirt, gaze locked on my distended heart. My teeth grit with the growing heat of the burn as sweat pours down my face. The heat is nearly unbearable, and yet, it feels like it's burning away all the bad, like cauterizing a wound.

The skin over the bulge starts to itch, making me flinch with its intensity. I have to scratch it. The urge is compulsory. Lifting a shaky hand, I reach down, and the moment my fingertip skims against it, the itch sizzles. Then the browned, sickly skin starts to curl and flake away like burning parchment.

The itch isn't satisfied. Not at all.

My finger presses down further, hooking in, taking chunks of more dead layers. I dig it all out, dig it away, like molded bits of bread being ripped off and tossed onto the floor. Faster, frantically, needing this sensation to be sated, I keep going. I watch as each piece peels off, a lighter brown than the layer before, all while my chest continues to burn.

I peel away one last flake with a hiss, and it finally stops itching. The spot is no longer bloating, and I blink down at it, breathing hard.

Without any more of the dead skin, I don't see a rotting, blistering heart. Instead, something else has grown beneath all those flaked-away layers.

Right here, over my heart, is a scale.

A *golden* scale.

I pull in a sharp breath, just before I reach down to feel it. Yet the moment my fingertip touches it, I explode.

Not my heart, but *me*.

Spikes and scales burst out of me in a violent rush that tosses me back. The spikes along my forearms, the ones down my spine, the ones above my eyebrows. I cry out as they pierce through my skin so fast that blood streaks from the punctures.

The countless rotted veins spread throughout my body start slithering wildly, like serpents racing away, just as my fae fangs drop down. My cheekbones feel scraped raw when my scales appear, and my ears pinch, the tips sharpening.

I remember what it felt like when I first tore in two. When I was forced to fight my father with raw power, and when the world ripped open. I remember what it felt like when that same power somehow ripped *me* in two.

But this...this feels like those two parts of me are smashing back together.

It's euphoric. Agonizing. Like needles sticking soul-deep, thrashing a thread through my entire being, and binding me back together again.

Two halves combining into a whole.

But when I feel the last stitch merging me...something *else* suddenly surges up.

Argo cries and flings back when shadows suddenly lunge out of my body. And it's not my aura. This is something else.

The vapor is as black as night, save for a ring of light around the edges that's unmistakably gold. It billows out of me like an odorless smoke.

I try to move, but I'm caught in this surge of magic. The smoke gathers and thickens, streaming out of me and pulling all my breath with it. More scales tear across my chest like a slashed wound from predatory claws, peeling away my skin in the process.

Sweat slicks down my face as I lift my head, watching as those shadows start to gather. Coalesce.

They come streaming out of my body and land upon the ground, making Argo back up even further.

I strain to sit up, to see…

The smoke takes form.

I suck in a breath of shock at what I see. It's as tall as I am when standing, its vapor dense and rippling. When I realize what shape it is, my mouth drops open. My eyes widen.

"What…the…*fuck*."

A face looks out at me from billowing darkness. A face of power and viciousness. A face that hasn't been seen in Annwyn for hundreds of years.

A dragon.

A fucking *dragon*.

The same curved black spikes that are on my body are also on the dragon's. Four on each front forearm, six down its back, a row of stubbed ones arcing above each eye—just like mine.

The dragon is formed from the shadowy smoke that streamed out of me, but the wicked sharp teeth seem dense enough to bite. The layered black eyes clear enough to hunt for prey.

The creature has a sweep of gold scales along its silvered cheeks, with more down the chest like gilded armor. Each scale is as wide as my hand, brighter than the flare around my shadows, making the smoke creature gleam in the dark. It looks like something out of a nightmare. Something that can't possibly be real.

Except it is.

It turns to me, iridescent eyes blinking, and its gaze makes my blood run cold. The hair on the back of my neck lifts as it opens its mouth, flashing its coal-black fangs.

Yet just as quickly as it appeared, it dissipates. Like someone blew away a plume of dust. Just like that, its form and its magic fade away.

And I fade with it.

The last thing I see is Argo taking flight high above me, sending birds to burst out of the trees and aim for the sky. I slump back on the ground, and my eyes fall closed, submitting to the dark.

But inside of that dark, I feel Auren's fire continue to burn.

# CHAPTER 4

There is something chomping, digging, *writhing* in my mind.

I want it out. I want all of it *out*.

Sweat breaks over my skin as I feel my body slump. Feel hands catch me. My ears are ringing…but the sound feels far away.

*I* feel far away.

*What is happening?*

I don't know. There's no clear thought, no clear memory I can cling to. I'm blowing in the wind.

"Auren!"

I blink around blearily, lost, confused. I can't hold my body up. There's a man yelling, looking right at me. Tan skin, black hair, brown eyes, a wound on his arm. He looks frantic. Terrified.

*What's wrong?*

I'm flooded with panic, though I don't know the source. My head is pounding. Sharp smacks that make my eyes sting.

"Leave her alone!" the man shouts before he tries to surge forward, and then he blows out a big breath that seems to glimmer…

The hilt of a sword is slammed against his temple, and he's instantly knocked unconscious.

Another person cries out. "Wick!"

My eyes follow the sound to a woman who's lurching toward the slumped man, her fingers scrabbling down his arm. Something flickers along his wound.

Strange. I thought there was a flash of gold there…but no, his wound is bright red with blood.

The sensation of something tunneling through my mind makes my whole body shudder.

The woman is wrenched away from the man, pushed onto her knees by someone dressed in armor.

Soldier?

Wrong…this feels wrong…

The soldier yanks her back by her orange-tipped hair, exposing her throat. I try to get up, but the hands holding me tug on my arm, and I cry out from debilitating pain.

*Why am I in so much pain?*

"Vulmin filth," someone spits.

I blink through the tears in my eyes. There's a man wearing a crown standing over the kneeling woman.

My stomach twists and twists so much it's going to get knotted in place.

"You are a traitor to your species," he spits venomously, and she starts to shake. "You don't deserve to call yourself fae."

He nods, and someone moves, blocking my sight for a second. It all happens so fast I don't see until it's done.

Until she's *screaming*.

A soldier has a dagger in his hand that now drips with blood. The woman is sobbing, her arms still held back, but her ear…the top half is now missing, a chain left to dangle from her lobe as blood pours out.

"Emonie!" A man with blue and white hair behind her shouts her name and tries to get to her, shoving at another armored soldier.

One second, he's trying to get to her. The next, there's a sword poking out through his chest. He looks down at it, like he's surprised to see it there. Bright teal eyes lift up to me, and then he falls.

Doesn't get up.

Blood blooms. Rivulets seeping out onto the ground.

More screams.

I'm in a dream.

A nightmare?

As if the horror is contagious, I look past him. Beyond. There are more bodies. Unmoving, drenched with spilt blood.

The word comes up, floating forward.

Dead.

That's what they are. They're *dead*.

My twisted stomach swells, the knots bloating with bile.

Then the three of them are dragged away. The unconscious man, the sobbing woman, the dead one whose blue eyes are shut and red blood still flows.

Where are they taking them?

I struggle, even with the pain, because maybe I can wake up.

I *need* to wake up.

But hands clamp over my ears, and sharp nails dig into my skin. Though there's a deeper digging that goes past my skin, past my *skull*.

Holes.

So many holes left from the hostile burrowing, making the throbbing in my temples amplify even more.

*What is happening to me?*

I try to shake my head, try to clear it. I can't latch on to anything but perforated haze. The digging writhes down my ears, making me shudder.

I need it to *stop*.

My body jerks so violently that I manage to dislodge the hands at my ears, manage to yank away from the one holding back my arms.

A snarl tears through the air, and I realize belatedly that it's coming from me.

Then something wet slicks from my hands, and I look down to see liquid gold pouring onto the ground. Inside of it, the thinnest black roots writhe. My gaze gets stuck to it, attention transfixed.

Either he moves very fast or my mind is moving very slow, because suddenly the crowned man is before me, and he holds something sharp against my throat.

There's a flash of a different crowned man…a different blade…a pain at my throat as I was held back.

My head swims.

Someone is behind me. Touches the back of my neck. I hear him make a noise—maybe in surprise? I start to turn my head, but his hand pulls away as quickly as it came, and I'm distracted again by the crowned man in front of me.

"I should kill you, Turley scum, and be done with it," he seethes at me, his eyes glaring.

More holes burrow.

Should I feel fear, as the sharpness of his blade settles against my vulnerable flesh? Should alarm bells peal at the trickle of hot drips tickling out?

I don't know what to think. I don't know what to feel. There should be something solid in my head that I can grasp onto, but there's just…a sieve, letting everything trundle out. Past and present trickling.

Is this here? Then? Now? Never?

*Why can't I wake up?*

Another man steps up from behind me, coming around to my side. A patch covers his right eye. There's red cloth tucked in front of his throat, but my neck is the one bleeding.

"Look at her, Your Majesty," he says smoothly. "A gilded Turley. Everyone who sees her will realize what she is. She is the symbol that the rebels have been squawking about."

"So I'll slit her throat here and now!"

The one-eyed man shakes his head, even as the sharpness digs into my throat like the stinger of a wasp. More dribbling. Landing on my collar, freezing my swallows.

"King Carrick, look at the power you could wield through her. You could ruin the rebels *through* her. Don't give them a martyr. Give them a *mockery*."

The sharp threat against my neck stops digging in.

Holds still.

My heavy eyes drag up to stare at the man with the blade. He's staring back at me, his eyes hard as stone. Both in appearance and demeanor. The crown he wears is like a boulder ready to topple and crush me with its weight.

"A mockery…" he repeats.

"Yes, Majesty. Flaunt her. With your memory fae's magic, make this Turley a spectacle. A laughing stock of this so-called symbol for rebellion. Make her kneel to you and show them all what a traitor she is, and you'll make their insurgence fail. Without her, the Vulmin will have nothing to fight for. You'll cut this uprising off at the knees. Don't waste her. *Use her*, and you will be that much more powerful."

*Use her.*

Those words echo down the hollowed-out pits in my head, not just in his voice, but in many. So many saying that very same thing.

*use her use her use her use her use her use her*

The sharp blade peels away from my throat. In its place, there's a hand at my ear. A cold, slick something digging into the canal.

I sway, head drooping. Can't hold it up.

The crowned man—King Carrick—stares down at me, and now, there's a twisted smile curving along his taupe face. His skin looks hard enough to crack. Beneath his feet, lined gold is hardening into stiff puddles. I can see the reflection of the one-eyed man within the gleam.

"She's much more valuable to you alive. Look at this magic alone."

They both look down at the gold spilling off my hands and pooling on the ground.

My own reflection looks distorted. I can't quite see me.

"She's *malleable*, Your Majesty. So make her into whatever you like."

Something wet peels from the corner of my eye. Splashes upon my shirt. I don't know why.

The pain in my body, the hollows in my head, they win against the adrenaline and confusion.

And I?

I slump. Plunge.

Because this is what it feels like to fall into the pitted, overwhelming dark.

And yet…somewhere in these shadows, there are veins of black that don't succumb, but that *spread*.

# CHAPTER 5

I blink.

Stare.

Hands curled in my lap. Bare feet against the cold stone floor. The wall feels rough against my arm where I lean against it, and I stare at the single window of green stained glass. It's the only pretty thing here, but it's covered with bars.

A woman's voice speaks. "Did you hear me?"

My head lifts.

Heavy.

*Did you hear me?*

The question echoes—not in the room, but in my ears.

"Yes."

The woman in the room with me—Una—cocks her head. She has hair that grows in blocks. The sections are perfectly symmetrical squares, making her scalp look like a chessboard. Her tan skin is speckled with freckles of blue. Eyebrows are two flat lines and brown—the same color as her blocky hair.

Square hair, circle freckles, lines for brows. The shapes on her are overwhelming.

But it's her eyes that are the most unnerving. Blue stripes cut down through the irises. Just like the bars on my window.

I don't like her.

When she comes, she says she's healing me. But I think she might be lying.

"What did I say?"

With great effort, I fix my attention on her. She sits on a stool right in front of my pallet bed, leaning in close.

Always so close.

"You said I am loyal to King Carrick."

She nods. "That's right."

An echo of pain thuds through my arm, my ribs. As if it's remembering broken bones and bruises. Lingering trauma. Every time I breathe or move, I expect it to hurt, but it doesn't.

"You were a traitor, but you have changed your ways. You owe the king your life. You are loyal to him, aren't you? Ready to prove yourself?"

I nearly flinch from the hard nudge in her voice.

"Yes."

My voice is clustered. Caught. Like every word is getting stuffed into this already small dungeon cell.

"Do you remember being a traitor? Do you remember turning yourself in so you could beg for mercy from your king?"

Beg?

I feel my brows pull together as I try to pick my way through my mind, but there are too many holes. I keep stumbling. Keep tripping over them.

My eyes drop to the cuff around my ankle where its cinched over the leg of my pants. My feet are bare and dirty, but the cuff is a smooth, drab gray. It looks almost like colorless dirt packed beneath glass. It makes my skin itch and drags me down with a burdensome weight.

*I begged for mercy?*

Una's lips purse with impatience at the question I've muttered aloud. "Of course you did. You're a traitor, and if you want to live, you *must* do better."

"Yes."

I must do better.

"Focus on how merciful King Carrick is. How much you want to please him," she orders.

*How much I want to please him...*

There's an echo, like a bell after it's been rung. The impact of the clang *just* out of reach.

My eyes drift to the window. The color drawing me in.

Deep green. The color soothes me.

Una makes a noise. "We must try harder, mustn't we?"

My head is so very heavy with the nod. My tongue the weight of a brick, though it still drops out a word. "Yes."

"Yes," she repeats. "Never fear. I am very good at what I do. I will get you there."

She scoots her stool even closer and lifts her hands. I tense. "No, please—"

Ignoring me, her palms clasp over my ears, making me shudder, while something inside of me shudders too. My back stiffens, muscles locked up. Nearly paralyzed.

"Repeat after me."

My eyes get caught in the net of her gazing stripes.

"I was a traitor."

My lips follow hers.

The digging goes deeper, and in those holes, I see myself. See myself falling at the king's feet, begging for mercy, telling him I was wrong as lightning streaked across the lavender sky.

No...not lightning. It was a crack. In a ceiling. In a wall. A house *breaking*...

There was thunder, but it ripped out like a scream.

I close my eyes, feeling something squirming within the

dark, emptied depths of my mind, trying to shove up through the hollows.

"Focus," Una snaps.

Her voice pulls me in, while something else oozes out.

"Repeat after me," she commands again, her voice droning.

My mind flashes, the squirming stops, and I see myself bowing for the king. The memory shoves in, presses down, trying to fit into the gaps.

"I was a traitor."

My voice melts with hers, eyes opening.

"I turned myself in."

Her fingernails dig deeper against the sides of my head.

"King Carrick is merciful. He will let me live if I atone."

My lips lash out every word. Monotone. Filling up every available space, gorging on it, near-bursting. Stuffing into my pitted mind with forceful shoves.

"I am loyal."

*Loyal.*

"I am beholden to his benevolence."

*Beholden.*

Her striped eyes bore into me, fingers digging into my ear, caterpillars munching through my forgetfulness. Filling up the holes with dirt that doesn't seem to fit.

"I am lucky to be here."

*Lucky.*

That word gets caught in the dripping ceiling. Swells and sticks.

Lucky?

"Yes, very lucky. Most traitors are killed. You have agreed to make yourself useful to the king and do whatever he asks."

I nod again, though I can't blink past the murk.

Una's hand drops from my ear. The digging stops. The shudders subside. My muscles slowly relax.

"Do you remember?"

I open my mouth but shut it again. That frown digs in deeper.

"Do you remember?" she presses.

I'm staring through that green window again. Binding to the color. It reminds me of summer grass. Of a shadowed forest. Of—

Overwhelming grief suddenly crashes over me, with waves too big to withstand. Grief and an undertow of panic rise up. My frantic eyes fly back to Una as I lurch forward and grip her arm. "I'm supposed to do something." My fingers dig in. Squeezing. *Desperate.* "I was supposed to do something!"

When she just stares at me, I try to jump off the pallet bed, but Una's hand stills me. "Yes. What you need to do is prove yourself. You need to serve your king."

"But…"

Her striped eyes narrow. Making another line that digs between her eyebrows. "That's all you have to do," she says sternly. "Please the king."

I frantically shake my head, my heart racing. "No, no, no. I was supposed to do something else. Someone…there's someone…I…I can't…"

Una slaps me.

Hard.

The strike across my cheek flushes with a throbbing sting, freezing me in place.

"Stop this fighting! Give in," she shouts through her teeth, her gaze livid.

I stare in shock, mind reeling, confusion boiling over.

*There was something…*

Her palms clamp viciously over my ears, squeezing so hard I panic that she'll crack my skull. I try to scrabble away, but she won't let go.

There isn't just digging that I feel this time. There's a

*swarm.* Things squirming, slithering, eating their way through. I go slack. Droop like a dying vine as I'm inundated.

*Infested.*

I don't know when I shut them, but my eyelids peel open again when Una's hands leave my ears to cup my face as she forces me to look at her. Her touch is cold. Like she stowed her hands in a patch of snow and rooted through the frozen grains.

I'm floating. I wonder if I can float right past the bars of her eyes. Right through the ones on the window too.

*Bars? Why are there bars?*

"You're Auren Turley."

Yes. That feels right.

That's the *only* thing that feels right.

"I am Auren Turley."

"You will serve the king."

That must be right too.

"I will serve the king."

Her hands drop. A sigh does too.

She gives me a look of irritated pity, but with all the shapes on her, I can't help but notice the dark circles now under her eyes. "Sleep, Auren."

*Rest is best when sleep is deep…*

The holes in my head shake.

She leaves, and I watch the solid stone door scrape shut. Hear a lock click.

Bleary-eyed and hollow-headed, I scoot back on the pallet bed, tucking my knees in front of me and clasping them with my curled arms. I rest my pounding skull against the wall and let out a shaken breath.

My gaze drags back to the window.

I feel like the color is something from a dream. Or maybe *I'm* in a dream, and that's why it all feels so strange. So…flat. Missing something.

Missing *everything.*

Through the tinted glass, I see the faintest trace of a star glittering in the void. One speck of light within all that dark.

"There was something I was supposed to do," I whisper to it.

It doesn't say anything back.

"There was something…"

I wish I could remember.

"Maybe this is all a dream."

Yes. This is a dream, so I just need to make myself wake up.

A voice from somewhere whispers to me. *You have your own light, little sun. So you must carry it with you when it grows dark.*

I want to cry, because it's grown so very, very dark.

Sadness waters my lids, so I let a single drop fall down my cheek. And that star that I've been watching falls down the face of the night, matching the descent of my tear. Leaving nothing but darkness behind.

I close my eyes, and my lips move in a voiceless whisper that only the sky can hear, with words that somehow materialize on my tongue.

*When tears are like starfall, when bleak is like night,*
*We remember the dawn that will bring back the light.*

When my eyes open again, my gaze becomes steady. Strong. A breath pulls in and blows out. That green view grounds me.

I blink away every bit of moisture as I stare at the empty spot where the star fell, and something in me pulls taut.

My face sets with determination. Something down my spine hardens.

This void in the sky, this void in my *head*…it won't defeat me. I won't let it.

I might not know anything else yet, but I do know this truth with innate certainty.

My name is Auren Turley.

And I am stronger than the dark.

# CHAPTER 6

## RISSA

Dragging the comb through my hair, I scrape out the knots, tangle by tangle. It's taken a very long time to brush it out, all of it already dried from my bath. My arm aches, but when I finally get the last snarl loosened, I sigh in relief.

I check myself in the mirror on the vanity table before me, shifting my head left and right as I peer into the glass. Both mirror and table are quite plain, the wood painted black like all the rest of the furniture in this room. It makes it look as if everything is always in shadow.

Speaking of a shadow…

My eyes snap to the darkened bulk that suddenly walks into my room. My heart leaps, but I can't fool myself and say it's because he startled me. It's because ever since I woke up, my heart has been doing those leaps every time I look at him.

It's very aggravating.

Setting the comb down, I send him a look of accusation as I eye his reflection in the mirror. "Don't you knock?"

"No," he grunts out.

The big oaf of a man blunders in, letting the door slam shut behind him.

My nose wrinkles as I watch him stomp toward me. "Great Divine, have you always stepped that *loudly*?"

Osrik stops and glances down at his booted feet, as if he might stop and ask them. "I'm walking normal," he says with a shrug.

"You practically stampeded," I say snappishly.

He looks up at me then, and though I try not to, I get stuck in his brown gaze. Stuck, like an insect to sap, with no hope of escaping.

*Am I going to be trapped forever?*

There's been an intensity to him since the moment I woke. It's obvious *something* has changed. It's like we were both reading the same book, but he went ahead and finished it before me. It feels like he's just waiting for me to catch up, watching me flip every page, staring at me as I go word by word.

"Didn't take you for a reader," I mumble.

"What?"

"Nothing." I clear my throat. "Like I said, you need to knock. You can't just come and go into my private room as you please."

Especially looking like *that*. He looks masculine and broody, as if he's just finished training some soldiers before riding a horse and then chopping down a tree.

Every single one of those images of Osrik flits through my mind, making butterflies skitter through my stomach.

I wonder if he does chop wood? Maybe I could be near a window to watch...

"Yes, I can," he retorts before setting down a trunk I hadn't even noticed he was carrying. It lands with a thump at his feet, the brass handles clinking. "Clothes for you."

I try very hard not to watch the way his arms flex, bare and on display from where his sleeves are cut at the shoulders. "Thanks, but no, you *can't*—"

Before I can finish, he leans over and spins my stool around so we're face-to-face. My breath pauses, and I'm caught in those eyes again.

"Yes, I can." We're inches apart, but he watches me like he's closer. Like he's all the way under my skin.

And he is.

Not that I'm going to admit it.

But I was told he stayed by my bedside every single day—nearly every single *minute*. That he was so devoted to me he barely ate or slept. That sort of bedside vigilance goes way past simple attraction.

Doesn't it?

His voice drops down and scrapes out with the grim look on his face. "You were almost dead, Yellow Bell. Hours ago, I was fucking saying *goodbye* to you."

There's a lump in my throat the size of his fist, with emotion I haven't been able to unstopper. Haven't been able to clear away.

When I opened my eyes from my deathbed, Osrik was staring at me like I was a ghost. Like I was a gift. Then he buried his face into my hair and wrapped his arms around me and made me feel something I haven't ever felt before.

Safe.

Which is funny, considering I was dying, until, suddenly, I wasn't.

My thoughts keep veering back to Auren, because unlike me, I don't know if *she's* safe. Osrik told me what happened after I was stabbed. How she was taken, how King Rot went to save her. Now she's a realm away, apparently.

And a *fae*.

Admittedly, I'm not sure I truly believe him. Then again…I saw her use that gold magic. It certainly seemed otherworldly.

Being awake feels more like a dream. Like all of this isn't real. I'm still trying to make sense of everything, trying to settle into this new normal. It's as if the entire world changed that night I was attacked.

The flashback of that blade stabbing into me flickers through my mind, and I shudder unintentionally from the phantom pain.

Osrik's eyes drop down to my chest, but not for the usual reason that men look there. He's staring at the edge of the scar that's visible over the top of my nightdress. I follow his gaze, my finger grazing the healed slice. It's tender, and my chest twinges a bit, but other than some overall achiness, I feel fine.

Physically, at least.

It's emotionally and mentally that has me all mixed up. The reason for which is right in front of me. I need to stop this now before he scrambles my mind even more.

"I didn't die," I tell him, my tone defensive. "So you can stop this."

His gaze lifts to mine and he cocks his head. "Stop what exactly?"

I motion between us. "I know what this is. You felt guilty. That's why you were at my bedside night and day. You felt guilty that I was attacked, because you're the captain of the army and in charge of the security of the castle and I was hurt. But I free you of that burden of guilt," I say, forcing my tone to stay even. To not crack. "It wasn't your fault. So you can stop hovering over me. I'm perfectly fine now, thanks to that girl who healed me. You don't need to worry about me anymore. Consider me out of your messy hair."

A foul frown creases his face. "There were so many fucked up things in that little speech, I don't even know where to start."

I rear back. "Excuse me?"

He sighs, as if *I'm* the insane one. I worry about the sort of people he's spending time with if he's this bad at judging mental stability.

In one fluid motion, he reaches down and plucks me from my seat, making my heart leap in surprise as he carries me across the room. "What are you doing?" I demand as my hands go around his neck, fingers tangling in the long length of his coarse, dark brown hair.

Without answering, he sits down on the sofa in the corner of the room and settles me on his lap. My heart pounds so hard I can feel the bruising from the healed wound.

He holds me delicately, which is so at odds with his gruff strength. It makes my heart twinge for a completely different reason. The way he looks at me, keeping my gaze so thoroughly captive, it's like he's bound me with rope.

"I know things are a lot right now," he says, surprising me again. "Because we were fighting this thing between us, and then before we could set it straight, you were attacked and nearly died."

He chews out that last word like he wants to grind it to dust.

"But while you were fighting for your life, unconscious, I was very fucking *conscious*. I watched every minute of your suffering. But I wasn't sitting there just for fucking guilt. You want to know what I felt?"

"What?" I ask breathlessly, unable to even attempt to be snippy.

"So fucking devastated that I was going to lose you," he replies, stark honesty rumbling out of his gravelly voice. "That I was going to lose you before I could tell you that I love you."

Breath sucks in between my lips, my eyes widening as I stare at him. "*Love*?"

He pauses and studies my face like his dark brown eyes

are soaking up every inch of me. "Yes, Rissa Bell. I fucking love you."

My mind sputters, heart skipping. "But…we barely know each other. We've barely spent any time together," I say in a rush, looking around like excuses are going to start falling onto the floor so I can pick them all up. "We can't even stand each other!"

He smirks. "We like the fire. We each don't back down to the other, and we like it that way. So don't lie and try to act like we can't stand each other, because we both know that's not true."

My pulse feels like there are a thousand birds taking flight within every vein, fluttering all over.

"You almost died," he says again. "And I'll never fucking forget how close it was. Just like I won't waste any more time now that we've gotten a second chance. We can't fight this anymore, Rissa. I'm claiming you as mine."

I stare at him. Mouth opening and closing like a struggling fish. "Are you out of your mind? You can't just…*claim me*!" I say shrilly.

"I just did."

My back stiffens. "I am an independent woman. I decide who to be with."

"You'll decide to be with me."

My teeth grind. "You cocky son of a bitch."

"And *yours*."

"*Mine*?" I scoff and try to slap his hand away from my waist, but he pays the swat no mind, his touch still holding me. "What, you're mine until we have a real argument one day that *actually* pisses you off, where you get to storm off as your big captain-of-the-army important self, leaving me here to wait while you go and find a saddle at a brothel house to fuck?"

His expression darkens. "No," he growls. "I said I'm claiming you, and I mean it. You think I give a fuck if you argue with me? If you piss me off? You think I'd be such a piece of shit to go fuck someone else out of spite?"

"That's what men do to their wives," I spit. "Either after an argument or because they're suddenly bored of them, or just because they can. I know, because I used to *be* one of those saddles at a brothel house that they came to. I know exactly what men are like."

"Those are weak men. You think I'm weak?"

My eyes drop down to his arms, all rippled with hardened muscle. I don't even know when I started gripping them, but I know they're keeping me balanced. Keeping me upright. And I also know no one could ever look at him and say he's weak.

"I don't know what to think," I admit, shaking my head like I can clear it. I try to hold onto my defensive anger, but it slips off anyway. "I woke up and now all of this…"

He lifts a hand and gently smooths a strand of hair behind my ear, fingers barely brushing against my skin like he's afraid he'll scrape me. The gesture makes me want to cry. Makes me soften toward him even more. Then he pulls me forward until my head is resting against his shoulder and tucking me in.

Safe.

"I know, Yellow Bell," he murmurs.

He smells of leather. Of trees. Of dirt and sweat and musk. He smells all man and I thought I'd hate that, but after years of scenting the pompous perfumes of prettified nobles, I prefer the natural rawness of it.

"I'm scared," I whisper against his neck, fingers gripping his skin.

"I know that too."

A tear slips from the corner of my eye and drips down his leather shirt. "You can't love me," I tell him, my voice full of denial.

"I can."

No argument. No added detail. Just a vow.

"You don't want me really," I argue.

"I do."

"You won't always."

"I will."

*I can, I do, I will.*

His promises drum in my ears, and I want to trust them—trust *him*—so desperately. He isn't what I ever envisioned. He isn't what I thought I wanted. But my heart aches at just the thought of him suddenly not being here. Of him not wanting me anymore. The thought of leaving now, of finding some remote part of Orea to live alone, makes my stomach churn. I can't bear it.

*How did that happen?*

I lift my head so I can look at him, one last chance to see if there's any deceit in his eyes. There isn't.

"Are *we* a mistake?" I ask quietly.

He doesn't mock me. Doesn't get mad. Instead, he rubs my back with tenderness. "Like I told you before, you're the best mistake I want to make. Over and over again. For the rest of our lives. So what do you say?"

My eyes burn, and the feeling goes all the way into my chest, settling deep.

Emotions churn wildly, but I know the answer, know what I want, even though I shouldn't want it. Yet whatever happened between us on that deathbed has changed us, and I realize that he's right—I can't fight it anymore.

I don't want to.

I let out a breath and then reach up to grip his beard hard, making sure I have his attention and that he knows I'm deadly serious. "*Don't let me down*, Osrik. Don't you dare, *ever*, make me regret this," I demand harshly, delving into his brown gaze, sticking him just like he's stuck me.

The corner of his mouth twitches. "You threatening me, Yellow Bell?"

"I absolutely am."

I release his beard as his hands come up to cup my face. "*Good*," he says. "Because the two of us? We threaten anything that might try to tear us apart—including each other."

I swallow hard at the praise in his tone. "You won't let me down?" I press.

"Never, Rissa," he replies firmly. "I will never, ever make you fucking regret this."

My breath sucks in at the potency of his promise. Then I nod out a shaky breath. "Alright then."

He cocks a brow. "That's it? Just, *alright then*?"

My eyes narrow. "Is that not up to your standards, Captain? Would you like me to say something prettier? Perhaps you'll also request a foot massage or for me to dance around you in nothing but your vest?"

"Now that is a nice picture," he says, and my lips press into a hard line. "But no."

"No?"

"You speak and act and feel however the fuck you want."

That's not something a man has ever told me. It was always *do this*, *wear that*, pander right down to the smallest detail for a client. Being a royal saddle, there was no room for error. No space for a single slip. I had to be on, or I would be out.

"It's okay," Osrik rumbles. "Just be you."

I want to scoff, but I suppress the urge, because…maybe I truly *can* be me. Maybe with him, everything can be different. So instead, I fall into this impulsive wave of longing, and I lean forward and kiss him.

Because that's what I've wanted to do since the moment I woke up.

My kiss doesn't catch him by surprise. It feels like he's been waiting for me all along. His lips part for me, and they're surprisingly soft. I flick my tongue against the wooden piercing through his bottom lip and feel the texture of his scratchy beard against my face.

He cradles the back of my head with one hand and splays the other against my spine like he wants to prove he'll always be here to hold me up.

Kissing him is like the first sip of warmed mead during a snowstorm. He heats me from the inside out, making me want another gulp, another taste, more and more, even when I've drained the cup.

He makes me want to keep drinking him down forever.

"Rissa Bell…" he murmurs, lips pulling slightly away, even as I try to chase them down. "I will kiss you for fucking ever, but you just woke up from your deathbed hours ago and you need to rest…"

"I can't rest," I say, shaking my head. "I don't want to rest."

"What do you want?"

The question suspends in the inches between our faces, holding between our gazes.

*What do I want?*

I've asked myself that many times throughout my life.

What did I want when I was a young girl with dead parents?

To eat. To feel safe. My options were to find work or marry, and I didn't want to marry. Not after I saw what marrying did for my mother. Loneliness, arguing, and the occasional black eye.

So I became a saddle instead. There wasn't much else I could do, and since I was always told how pretty of a girl I was, I used that beauty to my advantage.

What did I want as a saddle?

I wanted to be the best, the most coveted. I achieved that and then traveled to more prestigious saddle houses. I got myself all the way from my tiny town to Sixth Kingdom's capital, where my beauty and skill in sexual pleasures landed me a contract as a royal saddle.

The top of the top.

What did I want then?

To be the most desired. The highest paid. Looked up to or envied by all the other saddles. Aside from Auren, I achieved that too.

I thought I had what I wanted because I was in control. I used my beauty and my body to better my situation. Until one day, I looked in the mirror and realized I didn't want any of that anymore. Didn't want to have to please anyone else but myself.

I wanted out, and because of Auren, I got out. Because of this big oaf, I was able to flee Midas's control.

What did I want after that?

To go as far away from the cold kingdoms as I could. To be alone, rich and glamorous, with no man around that I'd ever have to please for coin again. To live content on some remote palatial estate far from any saddle house.

"What do you want, Rissa?" Osrik asks again.

I shake my head. "I thought I knew, but…I want something different now," I admit quietly.

His eyes spark with interest.

My throat closes, jaw aching with emotion I keep trying to bite down on. "Don't make me say it."

I'm not a woman comfortable with emotions. I have no experience with having real, honest conversations with a man. If he makes me try to explain now, it will come out a jumbled mess, and I don't want this—us—to be a mess.

He looks at me like he's reading my thoughts through my eyes. "You don't have to say anything. I hear you anyway."

My jaw tightens around the wad of sentiment, nearly choking as I try to hold back tears to his perfect response.

"Osrik?" I whisper, and my voice sounds small. I've never let myself feel small around a man. It wasn't safe. But it is with him.

"Yeah?"

"I want you to do something for me that no one ever has before."

"What's that?"

Embarrassment tries to strangle the words, but I push through, my eyes meeting his. "I want you…to make love to me."

# CHAPTER 7

## RISSA

Osrik's dark brown eyes shine. He blinks several times, like he's trying to staunch the moisture there, and I see his own jaw work, as if he too is trying to chew down these emotions neither of us seem to be very good at feeling.

It's nice—knowing I'm not alone in that either. We're both feeling around in the dark, trying to find our way, but at least we're doing it together.

His answer is gruff and low and, for a man who claims to not be very good at words, also quite perfect. "It would be my fucking honor, Rissa Bell."

A tear threatens to slip from my eye, but I sniff and clear my throat. "My last name is Caddell."

"Your last name is going to be Ferox soon, because that's mine."

He abruptly stands up with me in his arms, making me

squeal in surprise, so it takes me a couple seconds to realize what he said.

"Wait a minute, I'm not marrying you!" I blurt out, staring at him aghast.

"Yes, you are."

He sets me gently on the bed, and I sit up, bracing my hands behind me as I glare at him. "I most certainly *am not*. Marriage is a cheat."

Standing at the foot of the bed, he smirks at me. "How so?"

He looks ridiculously good standing like that, but I'm not to be deterred. "It legally ties the woman to the man. Gives him all the rights and gives her none. Makes him seem respectable, affording him more freedom in the process, while the freedoms of the wife are limited even more."

"Okay, so we won't marry," he says with an easy shrug, as if I haven't just said what most men would consider blasphemy.

"Just like that?"

"I'll get you a ring. To us, we'll be married. Without any of the bullshit. It's just for us—for me and you. Think you can handle that?"

I feel shaky, my adrenaline not used to being flooded with so many feelings. Sniffing, I wipe at the corner of my eye and then straighten. "Well. I suppose that would be fine."

His gaze flashes. "Yeah?"

My heart flutters, though I keep my face impassive. "I *do* adore jewelry, and rings look quite nice on my fingers," I say, holding out my hand and wiggling my fingers.

He captures my hand in his, threading his thick fingers through each of mine, clasping tight as he bends one knee on the bed. Leans over me while I tip my head to look up at him.

"You'll wear my ring, Yellow Bell?"

I nod slowly, and the hunger that comes in his eyes makes

my stomach go hot. "Yes, but I hope being captain of Fourth's army pays well, because my taste is very expensive."

He chuckles, and great Divine, I do love how the sound seems to travel all the way down my back. "You get whatever you want, so long as I get you."

I swallow hard, and I feel like I'm filled with bubbles, ready to float right off the bed. I tug on his hand, pulling it to my waist. "Touch me."

The hunger in his eyes magnifies. He drags his hand up, cupping my breasts through my clothes, and it feels *wonderful*. "Are you sure you can handle me?" he asks quietly, his massive hands continuing to massage, to knead and grip.

"Are you sure you can handle *me*?" I retort as I let my head hang back, relishing in his touch.

What I don't say is that it's been a while for me, and before Osrik, it was King Midas. It was a job. It's *always* been a job.

An undercurrent of humor ripples through his chest. "If I couldn't, we wouldn't be here."

He's right. He's the only man in the world I think actually *can* handle me.

Reaching up, I make him drop his hold for a moment, while I slowly start undoing the buttons on my nightdress. His eyes drop, watching raptly as the fabric parts inch by inch. My cleavage is revealed, the curve of my breasts uncovered for his roving gaze. My chest has gone slightly pink, and every breath tugs at the fabric, making it nearly fall open.

Instead of pouncing, he fists his hands, continuing to watch.

So I part it the rest of the way, tugging off my sleeves, letting the nightdress drop behind me and baring myself to him, naked everywhere. His eyes flow down my body like water rushing over a parched ground. He soaks in every inch, making my skin go hot everywhere he looks.

Is this what real attraction feels like? Without the strings attached? It's quite…exciting.

And incredibly nerve-wracking.

"You're fucking gorgeous."

I've heard many men compliment my beauty in the past, but when it comes from Osrik, it sounds different. Feels different.

With heartbreaking gentleness, he skims his thumb over the healing scar that's cut across my heart. I can see the flicker of shadows in his eyes as he remembers me being on my deathbed, but I grip him by the chin, shoving his gaze back up to my face. "I'm alright. All healed."

Humming at my words, he lets his fingers fall from my scar to dip down to my nipple. He circles it, making it harden and pluck up at his undivided attention.

He groans before leaning in to kiss me against my neck, hand grasping my breast, palm scraping against the pointed flesh. "So fucking pretty and soft."

I may be soft, but he's hard—all over. His callused hands, his muscled arms…and especially the length bulking up the front of his pants. The sight makes my thighs press together in anticipation.

Leaning forward, I tug at the laces at the top of his tunic, pulling the strands loose. Then I strip him of it so that my own eyes can take in his impressive chest. His body is the largest and strongest I've ever seen.

My fingers come up to trace over the dark hair covering his upper chest, before dropping down the planes below his defined pecs, and then even further to his thick, rock-hard middle.

His skin is marked with old scars, some faint, some deep. All of them cut into his tan skin like words carved into wood. Telling a story of hurts and heals, of time spent and blood spilled.

"Pants," I tell him, snapping my fingers before I point at the delicious lines disappearing into his trousers.

I want to see all of him.

The corner of his lips tilts up, hands dropping as he undoes the laces. In an incredibly sexy move, he stands and kicks off his boots, letting them land with a heavy thump.

Then he lets his trousers fall, and my eyes widen on his cock. "All that is Divine and blessed…"

I have seen thousands of naked men. I have seen just about every shape, size, and curvature there is to a cock. Osrik is *huge*. Girthy. With the perfect flared head and a length that makes my stomach clench. And that vein—I don't know what it is about that stretch of pulse along his shaft, but it makes me want to run my tongue over it.

"It'll fit," he says, as if he thinks I'm intimidated and that's why I'm staring.

And I *am* staring.

Am I slack-jawed? Utterly preposterous. I was a professional for goodness' sake.

My eyes yank up to his still smirking face. "Oh, I know it'll fit. It's just that you're a man who's actually big *everywhere*," I say with open appreciation.

He shrugs. "I'm a big man, so I have a big dick."

"That's not always the case, and yours is quite impressive."

Laughter blows out of him. "Yeah?"

"Honest to Divine, the biggest one I've ever seen, and I've seen *many* naked people."

His smirk drops. "Don't talk about seeing *many* others, or I might ask for every single name of every single man you've seen so I can fucking kill them all."

I hum. "That would be a lot of men. Some women too."

"My jealousy doesn't discriminate, and I'm thorough."

My smile is so wide my cheeks ache. For some reason, I

like the possessiveness he has for me, because it doesn't feel cruel or overbearing. It doesn't feel like it comes from a place of anger or insecurity, but from a place of protective devotion.

"Well, then…prove how thorough you can be," I say, my tone seductive as I finally let my hand trail over his erection. It's hot to the touch, and I trace that vein all the way to the root, where I let my fingers drift over the hair at his groin and then cup his balls. He growls under his breath, the sound filling me with thrill.

Hand curling around his girth, I squeeze, making him jolt out another throaty noise as I stroke up and down once, twice, three times. A bit of precum beads out, and I dip my fingertip to catch it.

"How do you want me?" I purr before I sit up on my knees. I drag my fingertip tantalizingly between my breasts, spreading the bead of his moisture all the way down to the juncture of my thighs. "On my back so you can play with my breasts as you fuck me?" I demonstrate just that as I lie down. "Or do you prefer me like this?" I say, twisting over the mattress until my knees are beneath me, arms keeping me upright. "Taking me from behind as deep as you want, gripping my hair and watching my ass bounce with every thrust?"

I look at him over my shoulder, ready for him to tell me how he wants me, ready to please him, ready to perform.

"Come here."

Surprised, I turn back around, brow arched as his knee braces on the bed and he leans over me. Heat travels from his body to mine, his scent filling my nose. His hard, heavy cock calls me to reach out and grab it again. To stroke and caress and see what other noises this beast of a man will make with my touch.

"You don't have to do that," he says.

I pause. "Do what?"

"You don't have to play a part, or check with me, or gauge my wants like it's your job to please me. I just want *you.*"

Instant defensiveness rolls down my stiffening spine, but he grips my hand before I can pull away. "Hear me, woman," he rumbles. "With me, you aren't a saddle. You're just you. That means you do whatever the fuck feels good for *you*. In whatever position *you* want. I'll take you from behind, from front, backwards, forwards, upside fucking down. I'll slam you against the wall or be fucking sweet in a tub. Don't worry about pleasing me, because I promise, I'll enjoy every second of whatever we're doing, however we're doing it, because I fucking love you. You get me?"

My heart pounds. How can his words make me feel both small and incredibly powerful at the same time? This feels like a chastisement, but also something so sexually liberating. My mind can't quite decide if I want to argue or not.

Then he asks, "How do *you* want *me*, Yellow Bell?"

And I can't be mad at that.

There's heat all over my body, and a vulnerability that chases it with chills. I think for a moment, feeling his steady grip in my hand. He doesn't rush me. He lets me sort it out.

No other man. Osrik is like no other man I've ever been with.

Tentatively, with my pulse racing, I let go of his hand so I can grip him instead by the shoulders, and then I *yank*. He lets me move him, which I'd never be able to do by my strength alone, and I position him until he's the one on his back, and I'm kneeling over him. My chest rises and falls, excitement and nervousness pushing against my ribs.

This feels new—like sex is some unknown thing to me, which is ridiculous. And yet…perhaps it's not so ridiculous at all. Because this isn't just sex, is it? This is *intimacy*. And I'm very, very new to that.

I move up and shift my leg over until I'm straddling him. He rumbles low in his throat, eyes latched onto my pussy. His hand moves to it, fingers skimming down my slit and stroking.

*That means you do whatever the fuck feels good for you.*

His words echo, urging me to do something I've never done before. I take his hand and guide him right where I want him, showing him without words exactly how I like to be touched.

I press his fingertips flat against my clit, moving him in a circular motion before going quicker and quicker, my own fingers pressing over the tops of his, guiding him, and he follows.

Unlike most men, Osrik doesn't get a bruised ego, nor does he try to take back control or ignore my quiet direction. He follows *my* lead, looking thoroughly pleased to do so.

"You like that?" he rasps out.

My head tips back, eyes fluttering closed as I simply let myself enjoy it. "*Yes.*"

"Your gorgeous cunt is wet. Getting my fingers covered."

He's right. Wetness *is* coating him, some of it even getting on my own fingers, ropes of delicious fire stretching from my clit and spreading throughout the rest of my body. His touch is perfect, and I let my hands drop with a moan, while he continues exactly as I showed him, not moving away or changing pace.

I brace my hands on his thick thighs and let myself rock with his motions.

*Great Divine, this feels good.*

My hair tumbles down over my shoulders, my body tightening all over.

"What else do you like?" he asks, his voice as deep and as hungry as a growl.

"Dip your finger into my pussy," I whisper.

One thick digit drags from my clit, and he hooks it

inside, opening me. Even his finger feels thick, making me practically salivate at the sensation.

"Fucking hell, you're soaked and tight," he says before pumping into me. Again and again. Hooking that finger and rubbing against my insides while his thumb goes back to stroking my clit.

It feels amazing, but I'm not ready to come. I'm still climbing, yet to arrive at the peak. But I'm thoroughly aware of the seconds ticking by. Of the time he's spending touching me. I don't want him to get frustrated or discouraged. So my body picks up on my hurried cues. It's habitual.

My lips part and I cry out, a throaty moan filling the room as I pretend to orgasm. It sounds scandalously sensual. It sounds perfect. It's the same lusty cry I've made thousands of times before.

And Osrik...stops.

My eyes flare open and I look down at him. "What's wrong?"

His lips are pressed together in a hard line, his tongue messing with the wooden piercing on his bottom lip with visible aggravation. Before I can ask again, he swings me up and around like a rag doll, until I find myself lying over his seated position, ass up, head down over the side of his legs as he sits at the foot of the bed.

"What are—"

*WHACK!*

His palm comes down on my bare ass with a startling crack. I try to push on his leg to sit up, but his other hand clamps down on my back, pinning me in place.

"What are you doing?" I screech indignantly.

"You faked your pleasure," he grumbles, and then he spanks my ass again.

I cry out, and while it's not overly painful, his hand is large enough that the strike stings the entire cheek.

"Vow to me now, you will never fake it again."

I jerk my head around to glare at him. "You pompous, brutish, son of a—"

*WHACK!*

I squirm, the heat of the spank suddenly shooting right down to my pussy. He's not hitting me hard, but he's hitting with enough force that it makes my ass jiggle, makes the sting spread.

But the sting and the warmth *blooms*, feeding into an intense arousal.

I like it.

I'm *irate* that I like it.

"Stop!" My demand comes out as a moan, which makes my face heat with embarrassment, my anger surging even more.

"You stop first."

"The absolute nerve of you!" I holler. "I wasn't faking!"

*WHACK!*

"You were. Admit it."

I don't.

So he rains down smack upon smack upon smack. Until my stubborn ass is on fire. Until I'm like a spitting cat, ready to claw out his eyes. Not because of the pain, but because he's so thoroughly in charge of me admitting my lie.

Until finally, I give in.

"Okay! Fine! I faked it!" The words come out in a sputtering scream, and he stops instantly.

I'm trembling all over, from the biting pain nipping at my ass cheeks and also from the liquid desire thumping through my core. I'm so turned on right now, so dripping wet, I think even his wide girth could slip in without trouble. But gods, am I *mad*.

"How pissed are you?" he asks.

"Oh, I'm *fuming*."

The hairy giant has the audacity to chuckle. With me still bent over his knees, my entire ass emanating heat, and wetness coating my thighs.

The absolute bastard.

"I didn't give you more than you could handle," he tells me before smoothing his rough hand over my smarting bottom. "And I wouldn't have done it if your body wasn't telling me it was exactly what you needed," he adds, dragging his finger down to my throbbing pussy.

I whimper out loud. I can't help it. The spanking sparked me to flame. "Asshole. Keep touching me."

He chuckles again. "I will. Just tell me you're not going to fake it anymore. Not going to rob yourself of your own pleasure because you're worried about mine or worried about me getting impatient." With his demand, his fingers delve. Spreading me open, making me suck in a breath. "I'm not going to get fucking impatient," he tells me, just as he shoves a finger into my slick entrance.

The noise *squelches*. It's humiliating how wet I am. My entire body feels like it's caught on fire, but he quenches that embarrassment when he groans, like he thinks it's actually the sexiest sound he's ever heard.

"How could I ever get impatient when I'm seeing you? When I'm touching you?" he grinds out, swirling his finger for a second before he takes it out. I look up to see him suck his finger into his mouth, licking my juices clean off with a satisfied groan. "How could I get impatient when I'm fucking *tasting* you?"

He twists me until I'm sitting on his lap, chest to chest, though my ass is saved because each of my thighs is on the outside of his, my bottom hovering in the space between his legs.

"You don't fake with me. You not ready to come? Then that's fucking heaven for me because it means I get to keep touching you." His mouth comes down, beard scraping against my neck. "Get to keep tasting you." Those lips press against mine, making me taste my own arousal with decadent wickedness. "Get to keep fucking you…"

Pulling back, he looks into my eyes. "Now *take your pleasure, Rissa.*"

His command is like a release all its own. A bubble of pressure suddenly popping and expelling an excited bliss.

I grip him hard, making his cock jump in my hand. I stroke up and down, watching his face, delighting in his expression of craving. Then I shove him back, and he goes easily, his weight making the bed shake as he lands.

Straddling him once more, I drag one of his hands to my waist and the other to my clit. "Touch me."

He does. Exactly the way I showed him.

I grind over his cock, and the sensation of his hard, hot length beneath me is erotic. Exciting. Every time I shift my hips, teasing him and dragging my wetness over him, he lets out a groan and watches me with rapt attention.

"Fucking perfect," he tells me.

"Not quite…"

Reaching down, I wrap my hand around his width, fingers not quite meeting. With excited flutters in my stomach, I lift up, lining him up with my entrance, and then I slowly, slowly sink down.

*Great Divine…*The stretch is unbelievable. I wasn't lying when I said he's the biggest I've seen, and certainly the biggest I've ever had. My body works to accommodate him, and I close my eyes, letting myself slowly descend, letting myself feel every single inch until I've dropped down all the way and I'm so full I have to remind myself to breathe.

I look down at him, and he's watching me like he never wants to look away.

Then, I start to move.

Slowly at first, getting him coated in my wetness, working myself up and down, rocking back and forth. I test every movement to see what I like. To see how he feels best in me while he keeps dragging his touch over my clit, making me even wetter, even hotter.

"You feel…"

"Fucking perfect," he finishes.

Yes. Exactly that.

My hips roll as I grind myself into him, against him, and every nerve ending is lit up like lanterns. I'm hot all over, like I could combust into flames. But I need more.

"Flip me," I order.

He does it in a heartbeat, moving me so easily it makes my stomach jump. Then I'm beneath his powerful body, and my legs are curled around his hips. He thrusts into me, making my eyes roll back with pleasure so that I barely even notice the stinging of my ass as I'm pressed into the mattress.

I reach down and rub my clit with one hand and cup his balls with the other, my breasts bouncing with his movements as I moan and writhe.

"*Fuck.*"

He leans down and sucks my nipple into his mouth, lathering it with his tongue, then moving to the next one and dipping his mouth between both. His tongue is hot and exploring as his cock drives in and out of me.

"Harder…" I moan.

He doesn't just start fucking faster. He knows exactly how to drag in and out with his deliciously slow, hard strokes. The breath explodes from my lungs with every snap of his hips, going so deep with his massive cock I swear I can feel him all the way up to my ribs.

His powerful thrusts jolt my body up the mattress until I nearly hit the headboard, but he just drags me back down, one hand hitching up my hip so he can angle me further. So he can get even *deeper*. So he can make love to me with a fierce and devastating rhythm.

I don't just fall over the peak. I explode out of it, like molten lava expelling from the mouth of a volcano.

My pleasure bursts free, tearing from the very center of my core, spraying me in heat, gushing over us with wetness. I scream from the bliss of it, from the totality of it all, my entire body covered in my own rapture.

Osrik drags his perfect cock in and out, fingers digging into the skin at my hip, and he captures my mouth, tasting my breath. Then he drives into me so hard it steals my sight, eyes squeezing shut as he groans against my lips.

His own molten lava floods into me then, spurt after spurt, until his balls empty and his head drops down against mine, and all we can do is pant and clutch each other.

When I'm finally able to talk again, I peel open my eyes and look up at this man who completely took me by surprise in every possible way. "That was…"

"Like I said. Fucking perfect," he growls again before he cradles my body into his and turns us so I'm lying on top, his cock still latched inside of me, my pussy still fluttering with the aftershocks of our pleasure.

The best pleasure I've ever felt. Not faked. Not forced. Not rushed. And certainly, not a job.

For the first time, I experienced pleasure not as a saddle. I experienced it for me…because of him.

Looking over, I take advantage of his closed eyes and watch him as he holds me with possessive adoration.

"Well?" he asks, cracking one eye open as if he could sense my gaze. "Are we a mistake, Rissa?"

The answer is easy, and I smile at him. "The best mistake I ever made."

# CHAPTER 8

## COMMANDER RYATT

B eing a new commander has its difficulties. But being a new commander when you're suddenly being invaded is just bad fucking luck.

With Slade, Lu, and Judd gone to Ranhold, and Osrik caring for Rissa, preparing our army has been assigned solely to me. It's a title I've wanted, a role I've been waiting to step into, but I'm questioning if I'm ready.

If I truly deserve it.

I'm doing everything I can to make sure our army is prepared. Now, they await orders. Mobilize or fortify.

It's one of the orders I'm going to have to give, as soon as I get a messenger hawk from Slade letting me know what the fuck is happening at Ranhold and if they've gotten Fifth's army ready.

*A message I should've gotten by now.*

That thought has been plaguing me since yesterday. I

know how fast Argo can fly. Slade should be at Ranhold. But I'm trying not to think that something is wrong. There could be a lot of reasons why I haven't heard from him yet.

I just need to be patient.

"Ho, Commander."

I turn away from watching drills, where I've been waiting for the lieutenant to finish so I can go over some more preparations with him. I see Keg walking toward me, his army leathers pristine, boots polished.

"Keg, everything alright?"

He stops next to me at the fence around the training area, his twisted black hair swinging with his movements. "We got word—shipments that were in transit arrived in the city. With this amount and the next ones on schedule, we won't have to ration anymore. City or barracks."

I let out a breath of relief. "Good. But we need to prepare for a siege as well. I hope it doesn't come to that, but just in case."

"Don't worry." Keg nods as he straightens the brown leather strap crisscrossing down his chest. "I hear those Premiers know what they're doing." He juts a thumb in the direction of the castle. "They're storing extras for that reason, in case the nearby cities need to take refuge here."

"Your parents have been working even harder than I have."

"They love this kingdom. They're not going to let anything happen to it on their watch."

"Isalee certainly wouldn't stand for it," I say wryly.

He grins. "Nope. Fae would shake in their boots if they had to face her."

"She can be formidable."

"I've never won an argument against her. Stopped trying when I was about five years old."

I smirk. "Smart."

He taps his head. "Runs in the family," he replies before offering a salute. "I'll get started on inventory so you have clear numbers."

"Thank you, Keg."

He walks off just as the soldiers start dispersing from the training yard. My lieutenant gives me a nod, letting me know he's ready for our meeting, and we both move in the direction of my office building.

As soon as we're walking side by side, he starts in. "Morale is up. Though I won't lie to you, half the soldiers don't believe the fae are invading, and the other half have become consumed with a rumor that our previous Commander Rip was a fae in disguise and that he's led the army here to take us over."

Well. That's not fucking good.

I shoot the lieutenant a look. "Where did these rumors come from?"

"I don't know, sir."

As we continue making our way through the barracks, I note the hesitation on his face. "Just say it, Lieutenant."

He's a dry man with thirty years of combat experience. Not once have I ever seen him crack his stoic expression with so much as a sneeze. He's always been solid, serious, and straightforward. Very good things to have in the higher ranks. So to see him hesitate is slightly unsettling.

"Some of the rumors also say that it's actually our king who's fae, and that's why he's left."

My movements halt and he matches my stance immediately as we turn toward one another. "King Ravinger left because he's leading the Elite to help prepare Ranhold for attack."

He nods sharply. "Of course, sir. I'm just reporting what's being said."

I swallow back more words that would only sound defensive

and nod instead. "Thank you, Lieutenant. I expect you're helping to quash those rumors when they've cropped up?"

"Yes, sir."

"Good."

We reach my building, and I walk up the steps to enter when someone rushes over, all lanky limbs and hurried feet. "Twig," I say, nodding at the boy.

He gives a hurried salute. "Permission to interrupt, sir?"

The corner of my mouth twitches. Twig does runs all day long, helping out wherever it's needed. He has a whole barracks full of soldiers who treat him like their little brother, and already, he's gotten leagues better at his self-defense training.

"Permission granted, Twig. What do you need?"

His stance relaxes slightly. "Thank you, Commander. I was told you're needed up at Brackhill Castle, sir. You've received a missive."

My heart thumps.

*Finally.*

"Thank you, Twig."

The boy salutes again and races off. I turn to the lieutenant. "Our meeting will have to be postponed for now."

"Understood, Commander."

Hopefully, the fae rumors about my brother will die out. Otherwise, it could be bad fucking timing if it catches on enough that it affects any of the men when it comes to fighting.

Just in case, I say, "If the rumors turn into grumblings, make sure all the lieutenants know to intervene. The last thing we need is for our soldiers to get this idea stuck in their heads and spread enough fearmongering that others threaten to defect. Fourth's army is better than that. Orea's safety is the priority. We are soldiers, and we fight *whoever* tries to invade or attack. Fae or Orean."

The Lieutenant gives a sharp salute. "Absolutely. No

soldier of ours would betray our own cause. We will always defend Fourth and Orea."

"Yes, we will."

With a nod, I pivot and head for Brackhill, wondering what news the message from Slade will bring. My stomach tenses and my thoughts ricochet. Will we prepare to march or prepare for siege?

Everything hinges on this.

When I get up to the castle, I waste no time entering Slade's office. Isalee, Warken, and Osrik are already here.

"When did it arrive?" I ask as I stride into the room.

"Not long. Fifteen minutes at most," Warken tells me.

Osrik closes the door behind me and leans against the wall next to the door. He looks ready to bolt and return to Rissa as soon as he can. I pass by the Premiers where they sit in the high-backed chairs facing the desk, and make my way to the window behind it. A messenger hawk awaits on a delivery perch just outside the open pane. I take the vial from its leg and unscrew the top to pull out the message. As soon as I return the empty vial, the hawk takes flight, and I yank the window closed.

Turning toward the desk to face everyone, I quickly unroll the small piece of parchment, but a frown instantly drips down my face.

This message isn't in Slade's handwriting. It's in Lu's.

My eyes scan over the hastily scrawled words, and my stomach drops. And drops. And then crashes into an obliterated broken mess of bile. "Fuck. *Fuck*!"

Normally, Isalee would rebuke me about the coarse language, but she doesn't this time, maybe sensing the severity of the situation. The corners of her lips turn down, her sharp eyes fanning over me. "What is it?"

I shake my head, warring with worry and spinning thoughts. "Slade never showed up."

Osrik jerks up from the wall. "He never fucking showed up to Ranhold?"

"No. No one knows where he is. Lu and Judd never caught up to him in the air with the other Elites. They assumed Argo had gotten him to Fifth. But he never made it. Nobody has seen him."

"Not good," Osrik mutters.

No, not good at all.

A jab of fear slices into me.

*Where the fuck is he? Did something happen to him?*

And then the rest of this message… I read Lu's words again, every sentence hooking its nails into me.

"You don't think he simply…changed his mind?" Warken asks carefully.

"No," I say with certainty. "He gave us his word. He gave *me* his word. If he didn't show up to Ranhold, there was a reason for it."

I'm not going to let my mind plummet. Not going to even consider that he was killed or captured.

"There's something else, isn't there?" Isalee presses, her attention hoed in on my face. "What is it?"

I look up at her and open my mouth, but nothing comes out at first. My heart is bemating so hard it hammers in my ears.

I finally drag the words out of me, weighed down with dread. "Ranhold is lost."

She and Warken jump to their feet. "*What*?"

"By the time our Elites arrived, the fae had already marched on the walls. They breached it within minutes. Ranhold wasn't ready." My eyes meet theirs. "It's been overtaken."

Osrik curses under his breath, his entire body gone tense.

"What about our Elites and the captains? King Thold?" Isalee questions.

"Lu said they all tried to search for survivors in the city, but it was just like Highbell. Completely overrun."

She covers her mouth as horror pools in her eyes. Warken sits back down, like this devastating news has taken away his ability to stand. No one speaks for a moment as this realization settles in. It slices through the room with bloody shock, leaving an open wound I'm not sure how we can bind.

We were supposed to have time. To be able to get our Elites there, both Thold and Slade, to prepare Fifth to fight.

Now, Ranhold is lost, and so is Slade.

"If the fae have already taken Ranhold…" Isalee begins, trailing off with a shake of her head.

"What's their plan?" Osrik asks.

"She said Judd and Digby are going with King Thold and his Elites to Fifth Kingdom's port at Breakwater. They're going to try to cut off the fae's access to the ships. Otherwise, the fae will board them and have a clear shot at getting to First, Third, and Second Kingdoms by sea. It's imperative we get to the port first and get rid of the ships so the fae can't use them."

"But the fae could still march into Fourth and then Third," Warken says.

My fists tighten, anxiety tensing down my limbs. "Lu left so she can try to head off any of the fae who branch off toward Fourth's border."

His eyes widen. "She's going by herself?"

"She's taking a few Elites with her. But it's not nearly enough. Which is why I need to leave with a small contingent immediately to meet her."

"I'm going too," Osrik states. When I open my mouth to argue, he shakes his head. "No. We're going. We're not leaving Lu alone to deal with them. These fae are fucking Orea right up the ass, and now, we've got no clue where Slade is. We need to go."

My mind starts working, looking for solutions, figuring out strategies. Everyone watches me in silence, waiting for me to speak.

I feel the threat of despondency creep in. Of hopelessness.

But I refuse to give in to that. There has to be a way we can hold them off. Has to be something we can do. And with Slade missing, it's up to me. With Sixth and Fifth taken, it's up to Fourth.

Resolve stiffens my shoulders. "Alright," I finally say, looking at the Premiers. "There's no point in mobilizing the army. With how quickly the fae are moving, we wouldn't get to our borders in time."

Dread weighs as much as a stack of bricks, but we can't be in denial. This is what's happening, this is the situation we're in, so we have to face it.

"We prepare for a siege," Warken concludes.

I tip my head. "Alert the neighboring cities and villages now. Get everyone here to Brackhill. Fill the castle, the city, the barracks, whatever is necessary. I'll alert the army and give orders to the lieutenants and the other captains. They'll answer straight to you. We'll lock Brackhill down. Make the fae come to us, let them tire. We'll use our walls and our territory to our advantage."

I look to Osrik, and the tension of what's to come ropes between us. We've been leading our soldiers and defending Fourth together for years, but we've never faced a threat like this. Never had to do it without my brother.

"Osrik and I will take only as many soldiers as we can carry in the pannier between our two timberwings. The other handful of timberwings we'll leave here, just in case they're needed for retreat."

"No," Isalee says. "Take them. Take more soldiers with you."

"But if the fae breach Brackhill—"

"Warken and I are not abandoning Fourth Kingdom," she

says fiercely, her brown eyes growing watery as her hands twist in front of her. "We don't need the beasts for retreat. Take them."

I hesitate for a moment, but the firm set of her jaw tells me it's moot. "Fine, but we'll still leave you with four, and extra panniers. Just so you can get citizens out if things turn dire."

My chest tightens. I hope to Divine it doesn't come to that. Hope that Os, Lu, and I can somehow stop the fae fuckers from getting into Fourth.

Somehow.

Turning, I open the top drawer in Slade's desk and shuffle through some pages before finding the one I need. I pass it to Osrik. "That's the schedule for the soldiers who should be at our outpost at the border. See how many are stationed at Cliffhelm right now and what their strengths are."

He comes forward and takes the paper.

"We need to leave immediately. I don't know how far behind we'll be from Lu. Dusk is in five hours. Can you make it work?"

"I got it," he says before turning and striding out of the room.

I search the next drawer down and then yank out a file before looking back to the Premiers. "I need you to send urgent missives to Second Kingdom. Warn the prince," I say. "Hopefully, Judd and King Thold can destroy the port ships before the fae get to Breakwater, but Third will need to be alerted too. I don't have any faith that Queen Kaila will actually help, but her people should be told of the incoming threat. In the meantime, we'll get down to Cliffhelm and do everything we can to keep them from breaching Fourth's border."

"And we'll prepare for the event that they do," Warken vows solemnly.

But Isalee shakes her head, ignoring her husband and looking at me. "How can you expect to stop an army that has already wiped out two kingdoms?" she asks with a shake of her head. "You're brilliant soldiers, but it's going to take more than three members of a Wrath to stop them. They don't just have thousands, they're also *fae*. Which means they have far more magic than us, and our king is nowhere to be found. They could have him for all we know."

I swallow hard. "If they have him, there will be hell to pay," I say darkly. "But we'll have to defend Orea as best we can without him."

She pulls in a tight breath, and I can practically feel the turmoil emanating from this proud woman. Hardly anything ever ruffles her, but this time, even her indomitable bearing has been shaken.

"*How*?" she presses again. "How can we stop them?"

How? A fucking miracle.

I glance down at the folder in my hand. Inside is a roster of every one of our soldiers who has magic, including a detailed report of how that magic can be used offensively and defensively. "I don't know yet," I answer her honestly, gaze flicking back up. "But I'm going to try to figure out a way. And if I can't...we'll delay them for as long as we can."

Going around the desk, I take Isalee's hand and give it a squeeze and then pat Warken on the shoulder. Out of everyone, even the other Wrath, I feel as if the Premiers and I share the same level of dedication and unflinching loyalty to this kingdom.

We have given our hearts to Fourth, so this threat is crushing.

It's one thing to defend our land against other Orean kingdoms. But a fae army isn't one we ever anticipated, and yet, we have to face it head-on. All of us. Every kingdom.

Orea, as divided as it may be, *has* to do this together.

The three of us exchange a heavy look, with worry filling up the spaces between us. We know that this might very well be the last time we see each other. After this, our kingdom—our *world*—might be overtaken. But I'm going to do everything I possibly can to try to prevent that. To come up with a plan to stop this.

I asked Slade to give Orea a chance, and now I have to figure out how to give it one too.

Looking at them both, I give a firm nod. "For Fourth."

Their answering voices are solemn but resolute. "For Fourth."

When I head back for the barracks, that vow repeats in my head over and over again. Everything I've ever done, ever strived to do, was to protect this kingdom. To defend our people. And I will do that. I will find a way, even with these odds stacked impossibly against us.

I will do it, even if it costs me my life.

For Fourth.

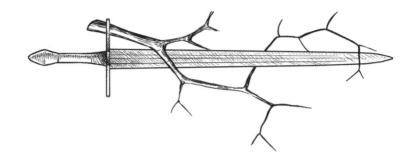

# CHAPTER 9

## OSRIK

I stride down the hallway and open the door. As soon as I walk into the room, I register the sound of shouting—*my* woman shouting. I'm already halfway across the bedroom before I recognize the other person in the room who's *also* fucking shouting.

*At* my woman.

One look at Rissa, and I see that she's standing up, hands fisted, face all blotchy with anger. I get instantly pissed.

"What the fuck is going on?" I growl at the other person.

Polly. That fucking saddle friend of hers. Except she couldn't even stay with Rissa while she was dying, so I don't consider her much of a friend.

I hate her on principle. Polly abandoned her on her deathbed, and I'll never forgive her for that.

"Nothing," Rissa snaps, but I go over to stand at her side and stare down the woman who's obviously upsetting her.

"There a problem?" I ask Polly.

She ignores me. She shoots Rissa one more glare before turning and storming out of the room, slamming the door behind her. Rissa's shoulders slump as soon as she's gone, but I can tell she's still mad.

"You gonna tell me what that was all about?" I ask.

Her bright blue eyes snap up to me. "No, because it's none of your business."

I look at her. "She piss you off?"

"Yes."

"Then it's my business."

The tension seems to drain out of her muscles, making her drip down onto the sofa as she sits down with a sigh. "I shouldn't have fought with her. She's just... She won't listen to me! She's going off with some man. She's stupid enough to believe that he's going to set her up in some grand life. She wouldn't even listen to my warnings about the fae army!"

I sit down next to her, my bulky frame making my thigh press against hers. "Lots of people don't believe in a fae army marching on Orea."

"I don't care," she retorts. "Polly should believe me."

My head tips. "Yeah, she should."

"And this *man*." She spits out the word like it's the most disgusting one in her entire vocabulary. "I cannot believe she would be so incredibly idiotic!"

"What makes you think he won't give her a *grand life*?"

Her gaze slashes to my face. "Because he's a *man*," she says again. "And because he's *already married*."

I grunt. "Oh."

She fumes in silence, so I wrack my brain to figure out how I can help. Then I have it. "You want me to go fuck him up?"

"*What*?"

I don't know why she's looking at me like that, it's a simple fucking question.

"I could fuck him up so he cuts it off with her. Wouldn't take much."

Rissa blinks at me. Then she actually seems to consider it but then quickly shakes her head. "What am I thinking? No. Absolutely not. Besides, even if you did, she would probably just find some other man and put all her trust in him too."

"You're putting your trust in a man," I point out.

She doesn't look like she appreciates me saying that. "That's different. You and I are different."

I smirk and pull her into my lap. Her breath does that thing where it goes in quick and snaps off at the end. Fucking adorable.

"Yeah, we are different, Yellow Bell." I stroke my thumb over her soft cheek while she straddles my lap. I can't get over how soft she is. My eyes drop down to her blue dress. It looks good on her. Then again, everything looks good on her.

Actually, everything looks really fucking good *off* of her too…

I clear my throat, forcing my mind to pivot from that train of thought before I get hard. "You sure you don't want me to go handle him? Last chance."

She shakes her head. "No. I'm sure. Thank you for offering though. It was…sweet. In your own barbaric, brutish, ridiculous way."

"I can threaten, hurt, or kill anyone you want. You just give me a name."

She snorts, her fingers tangling in my beard. "Thank you. I'll be sure to do that if the need arises."

My need is going to *arise* if I don't let go of her soon.

Even so, I drop my hands to her ass and squeeze and then hold her there as I stand up. She lets out a little squeal as I carry her to the bed. When I set her down on the edge, she reaches for my pants, but I step away. Fucking hate that I have to, but we're on a tight schedule.

Her face scrunches up in irritation. "What are you doing?"

"Unfortunately, Yellow Bell, we don't have time for that. We have to pack."

She sits up straighter, eyeing me. "Pack? For what?"

"We're leaving. I gotta go to a battle." I glance around the room, searching for that trunk of clothes I'd brought her, but I don't see it. Must be in the closet. When I look back at her, I realize she's gaping at me. "What?" I ask.

"You're going to a *battle*?"

Really considered more of a war, but I don't want to split hairs.

"Yeah."

She leaps to her feet. "Firstly, why are you going to a battle? And secondly, are you mad? Why would I go with you to a *battle*?"

"I'm a soldier and a captain," I say slowly. "Battles are what I do. That's why I'm going."

"Okay...and why the hell would I come?"

My brows drop down into a frown. "You think I'm leaving you behind? Fuck that. You're safer with me."

She continues to stare at me. "You're...you're serious."

"Yep."

When she scoffs, I cross my arms in front of her. "You want to be separated? Stay behind? Because if that's what you really want, then that's what we'll do."

Rissa glares at me. "I am *not* the kind of woman who will just wait around for a man who's going off to get himself killed!" she seethes.

"Okay..." I say, thoroughly fucking confused.

She storms past me, heading for her closet.

After a few seconds, I call out, "So, you *do* want to come?"

"Of course I'm coming!" she snaps, voice slightly muffled as I hear her tearing through her clothes. She mutters something else but I can't catch it.

"Alright, then. Pack warm."

Her head pops out of the doorway, blonde eyebrow arched. "*How* warm?" she demands.

"Fifth Kingdom warm."

Her lips do that thing where they get real fucking tight as she presses them together. Then she starts tearing through her closet again, muttering more shit I can't hear.

When she comes stomping out, she's got an armful of clothes that she shoves into my chest. "I need a bag."

I glance down at the huge pile and start counting all the pieces. "This is too much shit, woman."

She gives me a look so chilling it might actually make my balls shrivel. I clear my throat. "I meant, I'll make this shit fit."

"Yes, you will," she says haughtily.

In one fluid motion, I dump the clothes onto the bed and then haul her up into my arms, landing a smack on her ass. "You're being very fucking snappish."

She digs her nails into the back of my neck. Like a kitten trying to draw first blood. Fucking cute.

"I'm always snappish," she snaps.

I rub my nose against her neck and breathe her in. "It's gonna be okay," I tell her before pulling back to look her in the eye. "I'm not gonna let anything happen to you."

Rissa blinks, but she can't fool me. I see how shiny her eyes are. She's scared.

"What about you?" she demands. "What if you die? Then I won't be protected at all, and you'll be dead!"

I sit down on the bed with her, leaning up against the headboard. She eyes my boots on her mattress but doesn't say anything. Instead, she tucks her head under mine. I love how she does that. Fiery with me one second, then melting for me the next.

"I'm not planning on dying, Rissa."

"Don't be an idiot. No one plans to die."

I could argue that fact, but…better not right now.

Gripping her chin, I lift her face so she'll look at me. "I've been in a lot of fights to the death. Lots of battles. I'm not gonna die." She watches me dubiously. "But…if I do… You're a strong, capable, independent woman, right?"

Her back straightens as she sits up. "Of course I am."

"Exactly," I say, dropping my hand. "You think I'd bring just anyone along with me? There are some soldiers I wouldn't trust to handle this mission. But *you*, Yellow Bell, you can handle it. I know you won't take shit and you won't lie down and give up. You're just as much a fighter as any of my soldiers."

Her throat bobs, eyes shiny again. She takes a moment to compose herself and then clears her throat. "Well. You really should get better soldiers then."

A chuckle rolls out of me, and I kiss her on her pouty lips. "Fucking delicious," I mutter as I pull back. Then I place a kiss on her forehead before lifting her up and plopping her on the bed again as I get to my feet. "I'll get food sent up. You should bathe or primp or whatever shit you want to do. I don't know how long it'll be before you'll have the chance again. We leave in a few hours." I point at her. "Remember, dress *warm*."

She stands and points her finger right back at me. "Remember, don't *die*," she mocks. "Or I'm going to be absolutely furious with you."

Grinning, I lean in and give her another kiss. "I wouldn't fucking dare."

"See that you don't, Captain."

Then she goes on her tiptoes and kisses the hell out of me, getting my dick raging hard. She pulls away right when I'm about to say fuck it and rip off all her clothes. She shakes her ass more than usual as she walks off.

I grin at her retreating form. She thinks I'd go off and die? No fucking way.

I've never had more to live for than I do right now.

# CHAPTER 10

## SLADE

*S* *o this is where you always run off to."*

*The sound of my father's voice makes my shoulders stiffen.*
*For a second, I think about refusing to turn around, but*
*that would only piss him off, which I actively try to prevent.*
*I'm in a constant state of controlling my own reactions while*
*also attempting to regulate his so that he doesn't lash out.*

*I'm surprised my feet aren't scarred from all the times I've*
*had to walk on pins and needles around him.*

*I turn away from the table where the newly hatched*
*marewings chirp in their nest. Above us, the fully grown birds*
*are notched into their enclosures, awaiting missives to deliver.*

*My father's right—this is where I run off to when I want to*
*get away from him. Not that I'd tell him that. Now that he's found*
*my spot, I'm fuming that I will have to give it up. I like coming*

*in here, to sit with these birds. Not only are they incredible navigators and highly intelligent, but they're calming.*

*I wouldn't be surprised if my father has all the staff remove every missive marewing from our stable yard, just to spite me. He's that much of a prick.*

*If I ever show even the smallest hint of liking something or become defensive of something, he tears it apart as punishment or uses it against me. So because of that, I try not to show him that I like much of anything. Which means I just sort of...exist. Other than my mother and brother, there's nothing in my life that I like, because I can't afford to.*

*This was a stupid slip on my part. I've been coming here too often.*

*One of the marewings jumps down, her four wings fluffing out in tandem as she prods her horse-like snout against the little hatchlings before I feel her nudge the back of my arm, hoping for a scratch.*

*I don't move.*

*My father's black eyes flick down. He's quiet for a moment, and I grow tense as I wait for him to speak. "They will always have an affinity to you."*

*I frown, not understanding.*

*He walks forward, his polished boots scraping over the floor. Our missive coop is already a small building, but with him in it, the wooden walls feel like they're closing in. He stops in front of me, and I can see the other birds pop their heads out of their teardrop-shaped nests to get a look at him, a few making soft chuffs.*

*If they knew his true nature, they'd fly right out of this coop and never return.*

*Unable to stop myself, I flinch when he reaches out his hand right next to me. He notices, of course, but says nothing. Instead, I watch as he strokes a finger over the marewing's neck. She lets out a soft snickering noise, fluffing up her iridescent blue plumage.*

*"Winged creatures will feel a kinship toward you," he says as he continues to pet her. "They will sense innately that you are their authority. They will want to defer to you. Strive to please you."*

*I say nothing, but I wonder if he's mixing up the birds with how he wants me to behave with him. My nerves tighten, like string being wrapped around splintering wood. The thin strand pulls tighter, continuing to coil, just waiting for the snap.*

*He finally stops stroking the bird, and she trills before turning around to the cheeping hatchlings and settling herself over their little gray bodies to warm them. My father turns to me, and I'm forced to look him in the eyes. His are so dark it's like his character has bled through.*

*"Do you know why?"*

*"No, sir."*

*He glances down at the spikes that are poking out of my arms, and I feel myself twitch. He's always forcing me to bring them in and out, over and over again. He makes me do it while I'm training with my magic, to make sure they don't erupt uncontrollably.*

*I can't even count the number of times he's punished me for slipping and letting them rip free during a particularly difficult training session. But even if I do manage to keep them under, then he forces me to bring them out after I've already worked myself to exhaustion. If I can't, I get punished anyway.*

*I can't win. Not with him.*

*"Winged creatures will feel a kinship because of what you are. Of what we are. This," he says, moving his finger to press against the side of my spike, "is a symbol of that. We are Culls. But more than that, we are the dragon-wielders of old."*

*His eyes sweep up to glance at the light gray scales that stain my cheeks. He reaches up and tugs away the red cloth that he always wears tucked into his collar, revealing the tiny grouping of scales that litter his collarbone. They're darker than mine, but smaller, and the cluster is only about as long as his finger. I wonder if that's why he hides it. Because they aren't big or bold enough to boast.*

*In his eyes, if something isn't good enough to boast, it isn't good enough to have.*

*Which is how he treats my little brother. Ryatt's only nine years old, but because he hasn't manifested magic at a ridiculously young age like I did, our father either snubs him or sneers at him.*

*Every time I see Ryatt hold back tears, it makes me want to kill my father. But my little brother still believes in good. He is good. No matter how many times Father pushes him aside.*

*I know Ryatt despairs because of it, but I still secretly pray to the goddesses that it doesn't change. Because it's better for him to be ignored. It's safer. I don't want Father to do to Ryatt what he's done to me.*

*My father presses a thumb to my scales. "This is power, boy," he says before dropping his hand. "Every bird knows what lives in your blood. They can sense the dragon in you."*

*I don't dare roll my eyes. He's been obsessed with my scales and spikes since they first erupted. But just like his own pitiful cluster, nothing's ever come from it. That magic died a long time ago.*

*As if he's followed my train of thought, his expression darkens with anger, and I brace myself.*

*"And yet..." he goes on, his voice dropping down an octave. "After five generations of Cull blood, someone in our line finally manifests both scales and spikes, but you still cannot call forth a dragon."*

*He flicks at one of the spikes on my spine, making me flinch. I hate outwardly reacting, but my heart is pounding so hard that I can't help it.*

*"The Cull line has given you dragon-blessed blood," he seethes. "You could be king of the skies, where all winged*

*creatures would bow to you, and yet you can't even manifest an incorporeal splintered form!"*

*With every word, his voice gets louder, sharper, and my adrenaline pumps. My bones ache already as if they anticipate him breaking each and every one of them.*

*It wouldn't be the first time.*

*He lashes out, hand wrapping around the back of my neck, yanking my head to angle up toward the perched birds. "This is why you haven't risen to be a king," he spits at my face before shoving me away. "Because you are wasting time flocking with the peasants!"*

*At the snap of his finger, the shed ceiling splits, and an outcry of distress shoots from the throats of the birds. They immediately bolt, flying out of their enclosures in a panic, running into walls, a couple smacking into my head as they try to escape.*

*My father drops them one by one with his magic. Necks snapped, they land in piles, feathers bursting up, screeches filling the air.*

*The hatchlings' cries pierce my ears, and the mother starts to flap her wings, baring blunt teeth at my father in vicious protectiveness. He doesn't kill her, but breaks her wing instead, snapping it and making her cry out so horribly that panic pounds in my ears.*

*The hatchlings scream.*

*"Stop!" I shout, spinning in a circle, distress eating through my heart. He's tearing off chunks of it and tossing them onto the floor in bloody heaps.*

*My father steps up to me, halting my movement as he grips me by the collar. "You will erase this weakness of caring, do you understand me? You are a Cull—we cull the weak. Including what we find in ourselves." He removes his hand to shove me toward the table. "Rot them."*

*I blink, head whipping from the hatchlings and back*

*to him. I can't think—not with the way the mother bird is screaming in pain. Not with how loud my hate pounds through my veins. "What?"*

*"You heard me," he says darkly.*

*"I don't—"*

*"Rot them, or I break them. Bit by bit. And it will be slow."*

*I suck in a breath, his threat culminating into shards that seem to stab all over. There is nothing that oozes out more than my hate for him.*

*When I hesitate, he lifts his hand to go through with his threat, and I instantly react.*

*Rot spews out of me, lines traveling through the grains of the wooden table and engulfing their small bodies. Every single one of them drops, withering like scorched plants, shriveling up and collapsing in on themselves.*

*The mother's cries crescendo, screaming at me for what I've done, until I silence her too. Wishing I could silence the pounding of my heart. It feels like someone's taken a hammer to it, cracked it open and forced me to bleed.*

*Forced me to hurt.*

*The shed has gone completely silent. The only sound is my hard breathing as I stare down at the needless death.*

*After a second, I lift my head and look him in the eyes, letting him see the hate in mine.*

*He stares back at me with cold emptiness. "Good," he says, pointing at my gaze. "That is what it is to be a Cull."*

*My father turns and walks out then, leaving me behind in the destruction.*

*Leaving me behind in self-loathing.*

*When his footsteps fade away, I turn back, eyes blurred as I look at the seven hatchlings scattered on the table.*

*What would my mother think if she saw this? If she saw what I did?*

*Shame fills me.*

*If this is what the past Culls did in order to manifest a dragon and become king of the skies, then maybe that's why the goddesses took that ability away so many generations ago.*

*My father thinks he's so superior, thinks that cruelty is the way to power, but he's wrong. Cruelty isn't what drives me.*

*It's hate.*

*Hate for him...and love for my mother and brother.*

*If he thinks he can rid me of caring for them, of caring for anything, he has never been more wrong.*

*Because the one thing I will never allow is for me to turn into him. No matter how many times he breaks me, I won't do it.*

*Wiping a hand across my eyes, I take a breath. Then I lift a determined hand and drag my touch over the lifeless birds.*

*And I pull the rot away.*

*One by one, the hatchlings' bodies return to normal, as if time turned backward. The rot leaves them, and their little hearts start pounding wildly in their chests, throats opening to utter small cries.*

*I pick up the mother marewing, ripping off a piece of my sleeve to set and bind her wing before I pull the rot back from her too. Then I gather them all, shaking and terrified, and take them outside into the crisp air to sneak them into the woods.*

*Because my father's wrong. I'm not a Cull, and I never want to be.*

*I'm my mother's son.*

*I'm a Ravinger.*

# CHAPTER 11

## SLADE

I surge awake from the bitter cold. It's a brutal bite of an arctic air, like iced teeth tearing into my skin. It gnaws in, leaving me raw and scraped. I open my eyes, making shards of ice peel away from my lids.

After a few blinks, the world comes into focus, showing me a moonlit night and freezing clumps of clouds.

And...*also* showing me that I'm hanging stomach-down across Argo's back. My legs are dangling just in front of his right wing, getting hit with every flap, while my cricked head lolls over his other side, my face smashed into his neck.

I'm one movement away from plummeting into the air.
*Fucking hell!*

I jolt, arms flailing, hands grappling. My heart slaps up my throat when I nearly make myself fall off, but I grab a fistful of feathers and manage to stay on, nearly stabbing Argo with the spikes on my arm in the process. At my movement, he jerks around to look back and roars at me with alarmed chastisement.

Panting, I haul my leg up and over until I'm straddling him barebacked. His saddle is completely gone, but there's a single strap still attached around his middle, caught around his hindleg, with my pack hanging off it.

"What the *fuck*?" I yell at him. "Why were we flying while I was *unconscious*?"

He snaps his razor-sharp teeth and then lets out a series of hisses and clicks and squawks that don't taper off for a good minute. I think he's telling *me* off.

"*You're* mad at *me*?" I shout incredulously. "You had me flopped on your back *unconscious*!" I stress again.

I feel the vibration from his disgruntled growl travel up my legs.

"I didn't pass out on purpose," I say with a shake of my head, my pulse still racing.

He snaps at me and faces forward again, continuing to soar across the night sky.

This crazy fucking beast.

I'm covered in frost, my stubble stiff with it, and I look around, but everything is dark, and we're too high up for me to see anything other than clouds. How Argo managed to get me on his back is beyond me.

Panic suddenly hits me, and I quickly shove my hand into my pocket. What if it fell out, what if it—

Relief floods me when my fingers wrap around Auren's strip of ribbon. I can't bear to lose it.

After letting out a few more steadying breaths to calm my sprinting heart, I shake my head and straighten up. I pat Argo on the neck, because despite the rude awakening and his squawked rebuke, at least I wasn't falling to my death.

Now that I'm no longer dangling precariously, I can

think more clearly. Yet as I regain my bearings, everything that happened comes rushing back to my mind like a slap to the face.

Fuck.

I glance down where my chest is still exposed, shirt and coat gaping open where I ripped them. From the light of the moon, I see small gray scales, the same color as the ones on my cheeks, except these are rimmed in gold. They stretch from below my right pec, arcing up like a slash, each one slightly larger as they travel closer to the pure golden one over my heart—a heart that's no longer bulging. No longer hurting.

The gold gleams even in the dark. It just goes to show how thoroughly I've bonded with Auren. She's marked me.

Pure male satisfaction bursts through my chest at the sight.

Making sure my knees are notched securely against Argo's sides, I shift my sleeve. Sure enough, my rot lines are back to normal. They're thin, scattered down sparsely, no longer covering every inch of skin. But my spikes are also exposed, my ears pointed, fangs sharp, and scales littering my cheeks.

There's no denying it. Not only have I sprouted new scales on my chest, but my two forms have fused together. Rip and Rot, both on display.

Somehow, becoming pair bonded has fixed me. This isn't just me draining myself of power like at the Conflux and my body going faulty, flipping back and forth to offer me power in both forms just so I didn't fucking die. These are my fae traits actually being blended back together again the way they used to be.

I suppose it doesn't matter now that I let people see me change from one form to the next in public while I was fueled by pure retribution. Because now, I've merged anyway.

Just to make sure I can, I will the spikes along my spine

to sink back down, and they easily do, with much less force needed than before.

"Hmm," I say, moving my limbs. Nothing else seems to be different on the outside, but on the inside, I feel stronger. Whole. Fucking amazing.

And with it, I feel *her*. Feel this new pair bond thriving with Auren's light and warmth. She's healed me.

This euphoria of the bond and my melded forms is incredible. But what makes me break into a cold sweat is remembering the *other* thing that happened in that bog when the pair bond snapped into place.

The fucking *dragon*.

After years of my father trying to push my magic, it's funny that I should emit a splintered dragon now. Funny that it took being paired for it to break free.

He forced me to push my rot to the limits, to push *me* to the limits. But it wasn't just magical-control and immense power that he wanted from me. He saw the scales on my face and the spikes on my arms, and he was waiting for something else to burst out.

Only, it never did. And he never fucking forgave me for it.

For generations, every son born in my father's bloodline was able to manifest a dragon. The first Cull to do it was covered head to toe in blood-red scales that isolated him from other fae. When he manifested a fully corporeal dragon years later, he punished everyone for their snub by having his dragon wipe out the entire village.

Culls became king of the skies for centuries, until that inherited magic dwindled away. Fewer scales, fewer spikes, no dragons. I was the first to be born with both spikes and scales after five generations.

And now, I've actually manifested one. Not solid, only formed with shadow, but still. *What the fuck.*

I never actually thought it would happen, and when I was younger, I was glad. The maniacal gleam in my father's eye was enough for me to know that being punished for failing was going to be better than whatever he'd do to me if I actually managed to manifest.

I'm not quite sure how I did it or if I can control it. But… one thing at a time. I don't feel the dragon's presence right now, but I do feel Auren's, and that's more than enough.

The pair bond thrums in my chest, warming me from the inside out. It's the reassurance that I desperately needed. It's the confirmation that she's alive. A promise that, even apart, we are connected.

And she's calling to me. Like her aura did that night on the pirate ship. Leading me.

Until we're back together, our bond will carry this underlying urge. Päyurs don't do well apart. We are meant to be together. That's why we're a pair. We're no longer meant to be separated.

I instantly reach out for my raw magic just to see if…

But no. There's nothing. That well of power that allowed me to open a rip lies empty. I still can't tear open the world to get to her. I've been healed. Put back together. Yet it seems that part of my magic that allowed me to get into Orea and get Auren into Annwyn has been drained away forever.

Bitter disappointment presses into me, but I'm thankful for Auren's presence that runs beneath my skin. I may not be able to open a rip still, but I have the bridge, so my plan is the same.

Get to her.

My bond seems satisfied because I'm on the move, and I have Argo to thank for that. I stroke my hand down his neck again. "I don't know how the fuck you got me on your back, but you did good, beast," I tell him.

He flicks his head to look at me over his shoulder,

iridescent gaze glinting in the dark, and I swear, he arches his brow at me.

"Okay, yes, you did *very* good."

He trills as if satisfied, and I roll my eyes. I brush some frost off his feathers. "You obviously got us into Fifth already," I say, because it's far too cold for us to still be within Fourth's borders. I must've been out for a while.

Argo wavers suddenly, dipping down before catching himself.

"Shit," I hiss. "You're fucking exhausted."

I should've noticed it right away—the strain in his wings and the froth frozen at his mouth. I have no idea how long he's been flying me. Who knows when he last hunted for food? I've been a dead weight on his back, and now that I'm conscious, it seems like he's ready to drop right out of the sky.

"We need to land."

As if he was waiting for me to say just that, he starts descending, far less graceful than usual. The rise and fall of his wings are choppy, his breathing labored. He cuts through the clouds, but the landscape is bleak and foggy. However, his vision is far better than mine, and soon, I see the copse of trees he's aiming for.

He nearly hits the treetops, only righting himself just before his wings knock into the branches. He swoops down, body angled as he maneuvers between the trees.

"Find a spot to perch for the night," I tell him, and like always, he understands.

Just like the messenger hawks seem to be able to know what I'm saying to them. Just as the marewings once did.

*Winged creatures will feel a kinship toward you.*

The scales on my chest seem to pulse, like the dragon inside of me is proving a point. That for once, my father was partially right.

Argo flies further in, and after a couple of minutes, he

begins to circle one of the massive trees. A second later, I see what he already noticed. The base of its large trunk is cracked open like it was damaged centuries ago. Though it seems the tree lived and just kept on growing despite the wound. The dead spot on the ground has cleaved away and left a hollowed space like an eye socket. Argo swoops right in, and although it's a tight fit, he notches us inside the space.

Dismounting, I have just enough room to stand beside him inside the spot that feels like a wooden cave. He shakes out the snow and frost from his wings, sending out an icy splatter.

"Get some rest before you collapse," I tell him, scratching his chin. Argo chuffs and then lets out a jaw-cracking yawn. He spins around, knocking me down in the process. I land hard on my ass. "You did that on purpose," I grumble.

His slow blink says it all, though he's too exhausted to let out an amused rumble. He twists his body into a tight circle like he's trying to curl onto my damn lap, which he's entirely too fucking big for.

I manage to sit down, legs stretched out in front of me, just as he flops his heavy head onto my thighs. He lifts a wing to cover us both and ward off the cold. Between that, his body heat, and the tree's natural protection, I no longer feel the sharp bite of freeze.

With that, and with Auren's warmth feeding in through the bond, I fall asleep almost as quickly as Argo.

# CHAPTER 12

## SLADE

Argo's wing covering keeps out the cold and the bleak daylight. When I wake and start to shift with an uncomfortable groan, I earn a growl from him. My legs have gone numb from the weight of his head, my neck is stiff, and my stomach is aching with emptiness, but I think sleep did me some good.

It did Argo some good too, because after his initial grumpiness wears off, he wakes up like a fucking toddler ready to rampage, gripping my arm between his razor sharp teeth.

Arching a brow, I look at him. If he adds any more pressure, his fangs will pierce right through my sleeves. "I know you're hungry, but I probably taste like rot. I wouldn't risk it."

He scrapes his teeth like he's testing me, but then releases my arm. I roll my shoulder as I wipe off his slobber. "You're feeling better."

He lowers his wing and I look out from our enclosure and take in the overcast sky. Without being able to see the sun, I'm not sure what time it is. Argo stretches up, body lifting off mine, making the blood rush back into my legs that fill with pins and needles as I stand back up.

I grab the lone strap that's still hanging off Argo's body, the leather pulled and strained where it's hanging loosely from his side. I quickly unbuckle my pack and rifle through it, relief flowing through me when I realize that everything is still intact. The saddle is a loss, but I'm lucky my pack didn't get ripped off too.

I pull out my waterskin, a double portion of food rations, clean clothes, and then re-buckle the pack. "Go get yourself some breakfast," I tell him, chin jutting up.

He doesn't need to be told twice. He bounds away, snout in the snow as he attempts to scent out some prey, though I'm not sure how easy it'll be to come by.

I quickly tear into my own rations, realizing as I'm eating how fucking hungry I am. The dried and salted meal doesn't exactly hit the spot, but it's filling enough to quiet my empty gut. Although I don't relish it, I quickly strip out of my dirty clothes—filthy with dried mud from the bog.

I'm freezing my balls off by the time I've washed myself down with snow and yanked on fresh clothes. While I finish taking a piss, Argo comes up behind me and drops a dead snow hare at my feet.

I look over my shoulder at him as I lace my pants back up. "Thanks for the offer, but you go ahead."

Argo seems to lift his wings in a shrug before he starts to devour it. Washing my hands in the snow, I turn around as he swallows the rest of it down.

With a shake of my head, I fill my waterskin and then straighten back up. "You good?"

He licks his bloodied chops in obvious satisfaction.

I smirk at him just as a lick of wind starts dragging in, and I frown and turn toward it. There's something sharp in the air.

*Smoke.*

"You smell that?" I say to Argo, but he's shoving his maw into the snow, digging it up and swallowing the flakes.

Scenting the air again, there's no denying it, that is what I'm smelling. "We need to go up and see exactly where we are," I say. "We must be close to Ranhold."

Hopefully, it's not burning.

I swing up and over his back, using the strap holding my pack to wrap around my waist, somewhat securing me in place. When my hands are gripping the feathers on the back of his neck, Argo leaps up. The second he gets the air beneath him, he travels up and out of the trees.

Clouds and smoke hang low, like bushy eyebrows pulled down tight to obscure the eyes. Yet even with the clouds acting like low-hanging fruit ready to drop, there are gaps where they thin out, offering a veiled view.

"Try to get us out of this," I shout out.

Argo cuts through the clouds, flying much stronger than the night before, his energy obviously renewed. He juts up and then weaves down again when he finds a break in the air, and I blink through the haze until the landscape opens up below.

My stomach fucking drops.

*"What the fuck?"*

This isn't Ranhold. This isn't the space between Fourth and Fifth. We're past that—further than the fucking Barrens. Because below us in the icy landscape, something unmistakably gleams despite the stricken gray of the daylight.

Highbell Castle. Right there, pinned to the side of the snowy mountain.

We're not in Fifth Kingdom. We're in *Sixth*.

But that's not what has ice filling my veins. It's the fae army flooding the land below.

There are *thousands* of them.

Lu said when she was fleeing, the army that sacked Highbell kept traveling straight through, marching toward Ranhold. But that had to have been days ago now, so either they stopped just outside Highbell...or this army has been continuously flooding in with even more soldiers.

The thought grips me by the throat.

Nudging Argo with my knee, I direct him to circle, flying back in the other direction, trying to take in the full scope of their numbers and see how far they stretch.

My mind whirls, still trying to get a grip on the fact that I'm all the way in Highbell. Why wouldn't Argo have turned around and taken me back to Fourth when I passed out? Or to Ranhold to meet up with Lu and Judd? Why the hell would he take me—

It dawns on me. What I said, right before my päyur bond solidified—when I thought I was about to die.

*Just fucking get to her...*

Argo was taking me to *Auren*. To the bridge.

But by doing so, he's bypassed Ranhold completely. I have no way of truly knowing how long I was unconscious or how many days have passed. If I'm all the way in Sixth, everyone else will have definitely arrived at Ranhold by now.

Even if I flew all the way back, I'd be too late to warn them. And Argo can't travel to Fifth Kingdom and then turn around, cross into Sixth again, and fly all the way to the end of Seventh.

I'm out of time and with too much distance, so I have to choose. Orea or Auren.

And that's no choice at all.

I can't turn back.

I'm trounced with warring emotions that batter me. Fear

104

for Ranhold and Orea, a bone-deep worry about what Auren might be facing in Annwyn. If they're invading here, I can't even imagine what dangers she might be facing.

I wish I could slice through the air and instantly make a rip that would take me to her, but I can't. So I need to get to her as fast as I can without it.

*go go go go*

Swinging Argo back around, my gaze pins to the distance. Fires glow in Highbell City, but not the usual flames you see lighting up a city. This is the destructive inferno of a place razed and burnt by an invasion of war. Except most of the city is long past charred.

Now, the flames have caught onto the gigantic trees that border the city. Smoke churns from the Pitching Pines, blowing up in thick streams. I should've realized that's where we'd slept, but I was too fucking spent to make the connection.

No wonder I smelled smoke. Hundreds of trees, maybe even thousands, are already burning, the curtain of flames pulling further out to the forest.

My attention turns from the giant trees to the traveling army, whose dark stream cuts across the snow like a bleeding gash, disappearing into the distance toward Fifth Kingdom. This number of fae soldiers will devastate this world.

My jaw locks, anger making my muscles bunch as determination solidifies through me.

I can't turn back, but I *can* still help Orea.

Because I can stop this army in their fucking tracks. I will wreak wrath and wield death.

I'll unleash a fucking dragon.

# CHAPTER 13

## AUREN TURLEY

Sunlight streaks in from the window, painting the floor green like a spread of grass. Sweat drips down my temples, my fingers curling against the stone as if I can actually grip the blades of a lawn instead.

But no, the only real gripping happening is my head between clawed hands. Because she won't let go. Won't leave.

*Why won't she leave?*

I try to shove her away, this woman with the striped eyes. Una. The one who makes my head pound.

I'm tired. So tired.

"Focus, Auren!"

*"No!"*

I thrash against her, trying to break free of her grasp, trying to dig my way out.

Holes. So many *holes*. They're swallowing me. *Burying* me. But I can't feel the ground. Only this stone floor.

I don't know where I am or why I'm being punished. I don't know lie from truth or dream from wake, but I know that everything feels wrong.

Something in my head twitches, scraping against my skull. Making me shiver and flinch. I hate it.

*Hate it hate it hate it—*

"Get them out!" My scream is guttural, tearing my vocal cords, my voice coming from the depths of my stomach, my fingers curled like talons. "Get them out of my head!"

Una's face flares with angry dots upon her cheeks as her grip tightens. "There's nothing in your head! I am healing you!"

"Liar!"

With a burst of strength, I shove her away, making her slam into the wall. But even without her clutching, the things in my head crawl. Like maggots through flesh.

Rolling on the ground, I grip my head, shaking it. Panting. Writhing here just like the things in my head.

She's lying. I know she is. I *know* it.

I'm desperate. Panicked. Terrified. Unnerved.

Get them out.

Get them out.

*"GET THEM OUT!"*

My scream cracks against the walls. Someone holds me down. Or maybe more than one someone, because they're so strong.

They're trying to make me feel weak.

I'm shoved up, and the back of my skull cracks against the wall. It hurts, but the pain stuns the writhing. Makes the disturbing sensations go still.

It stops. Like it wasn't happening. Like I'm just going crazy.

*...Am I going crazy?*

I blink, my surroundings coming into focus, and I see two

men. Their appearances scrape down the hollowed-out pits of my memory.

Have I seen them before? I can't remember.

The first has eyes like granite. The other bears the loss of one.

The stony-eyed man wears a mantle lined with fur around his body and a crown upon his head. His hard face holds the carvings of anger. "Look at her!" he seethes. "Why isn't this working?"

Una shakes her head. Her face is pale. "I've been trying every day, my king. I've never encountered a mind such as hers. Her mental fortitude is the strongest I've ever come across. With the amount of magic I've used, she shouldn't just be pliable, she should be *infirm* by now. Nothing but a husk. But she fights me still."

Her words spin in front of my eyes. I try to grasp hold of them to wring out their meaning, but I'm spinning too. When she glances over at me, sliding those striped eyes over my face, I jolt forward and try to claw them out.

But there's an armored man I didn't notice. He slams me back, cracks my skull against the wall again.

Now the room spins too.

"You said I could use her," the king spits, making his accusation spray across the room.

My head boils in the sound, frothing out with a whine from my lips. When I get my vision to settle, I see the one-eyed man regarding me. I glare back at him.

I don't know who he is, but I loathe him with a fierceness that burns. The cuff at my ankle seems to grow a hundred pounds heavier, but it doesn't suffocate the flaming hate. That heat travels all the way down my back. Into my palms. Hot enough that it feels molten.

Looking down, I see a bead of moisture gathered in my hand. He notices it too, before I clench my fist and let my tired limb drop into my lap.

"More of a thorn than a flower, aren't you, pet?" he mocks.

I growl.

He regards me coolly before answering the king. "There is an alternative," he says before turning to someone through the open doorway behind them. "Bring her in."

Scuffling and footsteps sound, and an angry voice that scratches down the walls. Then suddenly, a woman is shoved into my cell, body splayed before she manages to catch herself.

She looks around wildly, eyes like a cornered animal, teeth bared to show off sharp fangs. The top of her left ear has been cut off completely, and there's dried blood caked there. I press against the wall to get away from her, and as soon as I do, her attention snaps to me.

Her body goes still, eyes widening, face losing the snarl. "Auren!"

She tries to come toward me, only to be violently kicked by the armored man who dragged her in. She goes sprawling on the ground, clutching her gut, auburn hair plastered against her sweat-slicked face, the orange tips limp and dirty. When the guard steps away, she forces herself up, coughing up a hack of pain.

Her clustered lids unfurl, eyes of swirling red and orange locking onto me. "Auren, *please…*"

The pleading in her voice and her tearstained gaze stab at me, opening invisible wounds. The longer I sit here watching her, not moving, the more misery drags down her face.

A lump clogs my throat at the hopelessness as she starts to sob. I try to speak, but my tongue is too heavy. My mind too trampled.

*Why is she crying?*

*Why do I want to cry too?*

"What's the point of this, Cull?" the king demands.

"This one has glamour magic. She used it at my estate."

"And?"

Cull—the one-eyed man—kneels down next to the crying woman and whispers something in her ear. She shakes her head frantically, but he says more and then snaps his finger.

*Pain.*

I scream, completely caught off guard from the sudden, intense break. I look down at my dangling wrist, and my ears ring, vision tunneling. I pitch forward, vomit spewing from my mouth.

Someone is yelling.

Just when I think I'll pass out, the pain suddenly vanishes. My vision returns in shards. Slicing together. I glance down at my wrist, but…it's fine.

Wasn't it broken?

But no…it's not, and there is no pain. None save for the aching in my skull, so it wasn't broken at all.

It must've just been in my head. In this dream.

*I don't know what's real. I don't know what's happening.*

Sharp bile clings to my lips, and I breathe hard as black dots pop before my blurry eyes.

"Do it now."

I didn't realize the one-eyed man was still speaking. I didn't hear. The woman's body shakes as she scoots forward, and then she gently takes my hand. I feel her tight grip pinch into my skin, feel something smooth press into my palm.

Her chin quivers. "I'm so sorry," she whispers.

I'm not sure why, but I want to tell her it's okay, even though I don't think it is.

I open my mouth, but something on her cheek flickers. Shimmers. She closes her eyes, even as tears still fall from them, and I stare, shocked, as she *changes*. Like a bucket of water being poured over her head, the change washes over her. Amber and orange hair fading, skin brightening, lips going burnished.

Right before my eyes, the woman before me disappears, and instead, I'm staring at…*me*.

I blink and blink, but the vision doesn't go away. A stem of panic nearly sprouts up, but it can't find the ground to take root. Hollow confusion and spinning distress is all I have.

But wait…maybe it's not another woman? Maybe it's a reflection of me?

I feel my face burrow into a frown.

*What's real? What's now?*

"Here's the answer, King Carrick. A perfect stand-in."

The king stares at my reflection. "Fine. Bring her."

His voice echoes and my back scrapes against the wall behind me. One blink, my reflection is there, the next, it's gone. She's gone.

*Or am I?*

I close my eyes and shake my head, rocking back and forth as I clasp my hands over my ears.

It's dark inside my head. But I can't fear the dark. I'm the light.

"I'm the light," I whisper, the words peeling past cracked lips. "I'm the light. I'm the light."

A sob chokes me.

*I have to be the light, so I can break through this dark.*

When I open my eyes again, there are no guards, no king, no striped-eyed woman. No reflection. But I jolt when I see the one-eyed man crouching in front of me.

Staring.

The room hums with unsettling silence, thickening as I watch his startlingly black eye. It's so at odds with the bright red cloth at his throat.

Looking at him makes pinpricks of heat stab through my hands. Makes my palms go slick.

I open my fingers on my left hand instinctively, and his gaze drops. We both see the beaded moisture gathered there.

The man hums. "A few drops. But you shouldn't even be able to do that in your state. Not with the dampener put on you."

I don't know what that means.

The back of my neck prickles, and I raise my hand and scratch the spot. There's a scab there. It feels hardened. Patchy. His gaze homes in on my movement, and his hand lifts. I flinch away, but his fingertip presses over the spot, the touch making me shudder. I don't like the way he's looking at me, don't like the way his expression sharpens with excitement.

"Thank you for confirming so fully," he says.

I smack his hand away.

He smirks. "I should have known you'd be strong."

His voice grates. Shreds me to pieces like frazzled thread. I drop my sight to the floor so I can see the spread of deep green instead of his black gaze.

"You're still broken though, aren't you, pet?"

My spine stiffens.

"Doesn't matter. You're the perfect bait."

Bait, like worms on a hook. The worms that you find inside the soil. Digging down, feeding off the very matter it tunnels through...

My neck cricks with an uncomfortable feeling. Something shifts in my head.

He stands, footsteps dragging across the stone floor as he leaves. My muscles unclench only after the cell door clicks shut, and I let out a shaky breath.

Now that I'm alone, I open my right hand that was still clenched shut. I glance at the small beads of runny liquid gold gathered against my palm. Notice the dark lines that run through every droplet.

But my gaze settles on the ring I'm holding—a ring too big for my fingers. There's dried blood on the top, but I scrape it off with my finger. Flakes of red peel away, and beneath it, I see an emblem of a bird. Its wing is bent and crooked.

*Broken.*

A shard of a vision abruptly slices down the center of my

skull, bleeding out through my eyes. I see this exact symbol—hundreds of different versions, laid upon a rubbled road. I see the symbols again, down a city street, on posts and shop windows.

I've seen this before. Many times.

A cold sweat breaks out over me, making my stomach roil. My head starts to pound, the memory going blurred and dark, but then I see her. The woman with the orange-tipped hair. She's smiling at me. Wearing a charm with this exact emblem dangling from her pointed ear. The top of that same ear now hacked off…

Stabbing pain punctures through my eye socket, making me cry out as the memory slips away. I pant, stomach twisting. For several moments, all I can do is breathe deeply, trying not to vomit, though there's already a puddle of it on the floor that I don't have memory of.

The confusion immediately spurs my fury. I want out of this place. I want to remember. I want to get rid of these *things in my head that writhe.*

An abrupt smack against my cell makes me jolt, and I stiffen as the slider at the bottom of the door shoves open so the guard can push a tray of food in.

I don't think, I just pounce.

The slot is only about ten inches wide, but I leap in front of it, arms squeezing through the opening. Whatever magic is embedded into the cuff at my ankle weighs on me, making me feel heavy and impeded, but I ignore its burdensome weight.

The tray clatters beneath my elbows, soup spilling and soaking my sleeves as my hands snatch at the guard's leg. He makes a noise of surprise as I grip him by the ankle and pull as hard as I can.

He's unprepared for my attack, so I knock him off balance and he goes falling back. Pebbled armor cracks against the stone floor, and a pained grunt whooshes out of him. I sacrifice my sight, shoving my head against the door to allow my arm a longer reach.

My hand grapples for the weapon at his hip as I reach as far as I can, victory surging through me when I find the pommel. My fingers wrap around it and I pull, teeth gritted as I yank it out of the hilt. Shoving backwards, I haul it toward me, getting it halfway through the gap in the door.

But the guard is up, his foot suddenly slamming down on my arm and pinning me in place. My teeth clench together in pain as he shoves all his weight down on my limb, threatening to grind my bone to dust, but I don't let go.

Spewing curses on the other side of the door, the guard moves, weight shifting, and then he snatches at the sword.

"No!" I scream, trying to pull it with all my might.

He's breathing hard, and I feel his meaty hands come down, and he bends my fingers back so violently that they nearly snap.

I cry out as the sword is dragged out of my grip, and before I can move, he lifts his foot up and slams it down on my arm so hard I see stars. When he lifts again, I snatch my limb back in. I scramble to sit up, fingers and arm throbbing, breath panting.

"You Turley bitch! I ought to come in there and beat you within an inch of your fucking life!"

I glare at the opening, staring holes into his legs. "Come in and try it, asshole!"

"I hope you fucking rot in there!" he curses before the opening at the door slams shut. I hear another insult tossed my way, and then he stomps off.

Inwardly cursing myself for not being quick enough, I grit my teeth as I flex my fingers. I was so close to having that damn weapon.

Pushing to my feet, I start to pace. Five steps is all I get from one wall to the other before I have to spin around and go the other way. Back and forth, my anger and anxiousness grow.

I feel caged. And that feeling…it makes me want to crawl through my own skin. Makes me want to rage.

The guard's words echo. *I hope you fucking rot in there.*

A burst of fury carries me across the room, and I snatch up the food tray. Everything left on it goes flying as I slam it against the door again and again and again. Every hit wrought with a furious scream.

The tray does nothing against the door of course, not even a scuff on the stone. I toss it away with disgust, looking around wildly for whatever else I can destroy, needing to get out this pressurizing ire.

Eyes locking on the crust of bread, I snatch it up, ready to crush it between my fists, to throw it against the wall, but before I can chuck it, the bread…*molds*. It grows green with fuzz and then blackens, shrinking, eating away at itself.

Shocked, I let it drop to the ground, and it falls into disintegrated pieces.

Heart pounding, I crouch down, staring at it. *What the hell?*

I look down at my open palm. Look at the black lines moving through the gold like veins of marble.

*I hope you fucking rot in there.*

Rot. This is *rot*. I'm not sure exactly how I know this, but I do.

I watch as the liquid gold and black lines soak back beneath my skin, fading away. I sit down on the floor, staring at the moldy bread, and my mind starts to spin with the sprout of an idea.

And that idea, rooted in rot, starts to *bloom*.

# CHAPTER 14

## QUEEN MALINA

They're hungry.

I know it, they know it. The wind may even know it with the way it groans, echoing the sounds of our own empty stomachs.

Enough is enough.

I walk down the crude spiral steps carved around the inside of the hollowed tree, in search of Dommik. A long time ago, huts were built into these Pitching Pines deep in the forest. It was during a time when they were still being actively harvested for their thick, sweet sap.

The pine huts are now filled with fifty-two refugees instead of workers. All of Highbell's survivors are split up amongst the half dozen hollowed-out trunks. Accommodations are not exactly luxurious, but there's enough cramped space to lay our heads down at night, thanks to the stairs that coil up the insides of the trunks, and the flooring built across.

My people are cold, even with shelter. Yet they're used to living in frigid temperatures, so they can withstand the frost. What they can't withstand is starvation.

We've been holed up here for weeks, but our supplies pilfered from the city have run out. Despite our rationing, and despite the men's efforts to hunt, there is no food left.

I press a hand to my own stomach, feeling as hollowed out as these trees.

When I reach the bottom of the giant trunk, I pass by a trio of people lying down on the bottom floorspace, their bodies huddled together in search of shared warmth. Guilt gnaws up my throat, teeth biting in to choke.

Looking away, I turn to the makeshift door, shoving up the beam that lies across it, and then pull it open just enough to slip out. As soon as I'm outside, I shut it behind me, eyes blinking as I adjust to the daylight.

The rest of the carved-out trees share the same doors cut into their sides, with dilapidated boards shoved overhead like eaves, where icicles drip down. Our steps have created paths in the snow leading from each door, but I head for the path that takes me to the small bonfire where I spot the figure wearing a cloak with the hood pulled low over his head.

Several others are gathered around him, clutching tin cups in their hands with sprigs of pine poking out. Aside from those pine needles, there's probably nothing more than boiled snow and a cube of sugar in those cups, since that's all we have left.

Dommik looks up as I approach, though someone else might not be able to notice the small shift in attention. Yet I sense when his eyes latch onto me. I always feel the weight of them as if he were gripping me.

I see him pass over a handful of snowberries to the child sitting with her mother, and the girl hungrily shoves them into her mouth. Neira is her name. Brown hair in knots, face pale, lips peeling. She's the only child that survived the attack. The same one who clutched at my skirts with an arrow stabbed through her leg. It's a miracle she survived, and now, she's starving.

My stomach squeezes.

"We need to speak," I tell Dommik as soon as I approach.

Without saying anything, he tips his head, and I follow him down the path until we're several feet away from the group.

"We need to go into the city."

He pauses at my harried tone. "Last time I checked, it was still crawling with fae."

"Well, we have to try again. We don't have any food left, Dommik," I say, wringing my hands together.

"We're still trying to hunt..."

"And mostly failing," I say with a firm shake of my head. "It's not enough to sustain everyone. We need more supplies."

"We don't even know if there's anything left. The army has been burning the whole fucking city continuously."

"Well, we can't just stay here and do nothing. They're starving to death!" My voice pitches up far higher than I intended. I steal a look over my shoulder, noting the others by the fire now looking our way.

Guilt bites down again, and when I turn back around, I shake my head, voice lowering. "I can't save them if I can't even feed them."

I hear him let out a hard breath, full of the same tension I feel. "Alright. I'll go tonight. Alone."

"But—"

"*Alone*," he growls. "If the streets are still filled with fae, then I can more easily sneak into some places that aren't burnt to a crisp and get what I can without having to worry about shadowing someone else."

I want to argue, to at least insist he bring one person

with him to help him, but I relent. He's lost weight just like everyone else, his cheeks gone gaunt. Having to shadow-leap another person may be too draining for him.

Even though he may not be able to carry as many supplies by himself, he probably has a better chance at getting something to bring back if he goes alone without risking himself too much.

"Alright."

He gives a nod, then shoves his hood back just enough for me to see his shadowed eyes, and I watch them rake over me. "Did you eat any of the berries and sugar tea today?"

I arch a brow.

He grits his teeth. "Dammit, Malina."

"I'm fine."

"You're not. And you have to stop skipping what pathetic portions we have."

"There isn't enough."

"Of course there isn't, but that's not an excuse. You need to survive too."

"Well, we won't have to worry about that, will we? Because you're going to come back with some food."

I hear a growl at the back of his throat. "I want to fucking throttle you."

"But you're too weak from hunger, so best save your strength," I say breezily before I turn around to head back to the pine huts.

I hear him come stomping up beside me, but at that same moment, I inhale, frowning at what I smell. "Dommik, we're supposed to keep our bonfire small," I quickly say, turning back. "We can't give off too much smoke, or the fae might discover us."

He lifts his nose in the air, and our gazes cut across to the bonfire. It's tiny. Yellow and low, barely giving off any warmth, let alone smoke. "That's not our bonfire you're smelling."

Confusion wafts through me for a moment. "Then what…"

Dommik slips his arm around my waist, pulling me close. My breath catches, face swinging toward his, but in the next blink, he leaps us away. The ground disappears from beneath our feet every few seconds as he transports us. Tight shadows surround us, so I don't notice how thick the smoke is until he pulls them all away once we come to a stop.

Smoke swarms, flying into my mouth, threatening to choke its way down my throat. Dommik presses his cloak against my mouth and nose, but I cough regardless, eyes burning as I stare at the inferno surrounding us.

The Pitching Pines are ablaze.

The sudden presence of its heat is in such opposition to the cold that I recoil from it. From left to right, flames are licking up the lengths of the gargantuan trees, and black clouds bubble out of them like froth, foaming up the air.

"How far away are we from the huts?" I ask with alarm, turning toward Dommik's neck.

"That's the problem—we're *not* far."

Another cough lunges up my throat just as he whisks us away. When the shadows pull back again, I glance around at the huts, then up to the sky. It's already being blocked from the insidious smoke.

Dommik was right. The fire isn't far away at all.

I could use my ice magic, but not against this much fire. Not with it so close. What if my magic ran out? I don't have very much energy as it is. Even if I *could* keep the flames away with my ice, the smoke in the air is just as dangerous. It would leak in as my magic melted and would suffocate us all.

I swallow thickly, fear dripping down my spine. "We have to evacuate." The realization punches through my stomach, leaving dents and divots, but I hear the snapping of the fire's teeth as it gnaws ever closer, and I know I'm right. "We need everyone out now!"

Dommik nods in agreement and I spin around and rush forward, shoving open the first hut door. "Fire! Grab only what you can carry!"

Voices of alarm echo back to me, but I hurry toward the next hut. I can hear Dommik doing the same, hands cupped around his mouth as he shouts out the warning.

My people start pouring out of the trees, harried and bedraggled, their faces filled with fear. I hear Dommik counting. "We're missing two!"

The group looks around, and then one of the women answers, "It's Tash and Sam. They went out to try and hunt!"

My gouged stomach crumples up in further dread, accentuated by the crying of Neira. Her wounded leg is still wrapped up, her arms clutching her mother. Another person begins to cough as the first waft of smoke drifts in.

Dommik and I share a look. Without speaking, we know what we have to do.

"I'll go search for them," he murmurs.

"I'll lead the others away from the fire."

He gives a terse nod. I can see it bothers him to separate, but he doesn't argue. Instead, he steps closer, back facing the group. "When you've found a place to stop, use your magic to mark the spot. I'll keep a lookout for the sign, and then we'll meet up with you."

"Okay."

He moves to walk away, but a terrible sense of dread overcomes me.

"Dommik—"

Body stilling, he turns back toward me.

Words fall flat in my chest, weighing down my broken organ until it feels pressed down. I don't want to separate either, but I know we have to.

"Just…be careful," I say, though that barely scratches the surface.

He watches me as if it's not only shadows he can pull in, but all my unsaid words too. My fear and worry stick to the silence, heart pounding with apprehension and unease. Yet my tongue stays still, my lips pressed together, unable to say more.

Dommik abruptly eats up the distance, grabbing my chin before pressing his mouth to mine. My heart flips as I meet his hurried kiss, tasting the emotions between us. "I know," he murmurs against my smoke-tinged lips, as if he's heard everything I didn't say. "You be careful too." I nod and then he gives me one more long look before he turns and strides away.

I let out a breath at his departure before I turn, straightening my spine with fortitude. Now, I'm left with everyone else in the group, and they're all looking to me for guidance. For protection. I can't let them down, and I can't let my fear bleed through my demeanor either, so I stand tall and keep my expression calm.

"We'll evacuate now. Make sure that none of you are carrying more than you can handle," I tell them before glancing in the direction of the smoke.

"Where will we go?"

"We'll find another safe spot in the forest," I assure them, though I think I'm also assuring *myself*.

Turning around, I start to lead them.

Hoping it's not to slaughter.

I'm meticulous about watching the progress of the flames behind us. Meticulous in ensuring we are going straight, that we aren't accidentally traveling in a circle. Yet no matter how quickly we travel, the flames seem to encroach. To close in like a curling wave coming to bat us down.

Sweat drips down my back and sticks to my clothes. The only reason the smoke hasn't overwhelmed us is because we're traveling against the wind that's started to blast through the forest, blowing with a fervor.

Yet the wind is only spreading the fire.

Someone cries out, and I jerk around to look as one of the men helps up his elderly father—Kasin. The man worked as a street sweeper his entire life, always hunched over a broom, which accounts for the curve of his back. His son followed in his footsteps. They both were born and raised in the shanties. Both lost wives during childbirth.

I've learned more about this group just from the last several days than I ever knew about the rest of my people after being their queen for decades.

Kasin wears a grimace of pain as he gets back to his feet and steps over the snow-covered rock he hadn't noticed before. He's thin, his dirty clothes hanging off of him, and his face streaked with ash. Everyone looks in much the same state, including me. We're exhausted. Dirty. And without enough food, we won't have the energy to keep up this pace for much longer.

The child's mother, Dari, leans against a tree, bony hands clutching at the girl. "We aren't getting away from it, Queen Malina. The fire is spreading closer!" she says with desperation.

Dread envelops me. I know we can't keep going like this, deeper into the forest. We're not finding the haven I'd hoped for. I thought we could move away from the flames, but it seems the entire forest is being choked out.

Going deeper in no longer seems like a viable plan. Even if we *did* find another place to stop amongst the pines, there will be no huts, and there's no telling if we'd be truly safe from the fire or if it would simply spread there too. The flames don't seem like they want to slow or stop. What if they burn the entire forest?

I look around as if a perfect solution will appear, but of course it doesn't.

I have to *make* the solution.

Turning in the other direction, I pin my sights toward Highbell instead of away from it. That's where the flames started, but I don't think it's spread the entire width quite yet. Perhaps we can veer toward the edge of the forest and get back to Highbell instead of fleeing further away.

"We need to change course," I say, holding my shoulders straight despite how sore they are.

"Toward the city?" one of the men asks incredulously. "Are you mad? That's where them fae are!"

"The forest isn't safe. We aren't staying ahead of the flames as I'd hoped. For all we know, this fire could be fueled magically and every single Pitching Pine could be ash come morning, and us with it," I say levelly.

The man quiets, and murmurs stretch between the group.

"So what are we going to do? Where will we go?"

I pause. "We will have to hide in the city."

"But the fae!" another woman calls out.

"They've been passing through for over two weeks," I point out. "They won't be expecting anyone to have survived. I will search the outskirts myself. All we need is *one* single building still intact. I'll find a place we can hide where the fae won't find us."

My promise trickles down each expression. Fifty people. It seems like a lot to try to hide, to be responsible for. And yet it's far, far too few. So many have died, and I can't let anyone else succumb, either by the hand of the fae or the flames.

"Once we're in the city, we will also search for more supplies—gather more food," I tell them, and I see a couple of them lick their lips, as if their starved bodies salivate at the very mention of eating.

"And if there isn't any food?" Dari asks. Her face stays stoic, but I see the fearful tear that drips from the corner of her eye as she clutches her daughter. "Or any safety to be found?"

She must ask. She must, because it's not her life she's thinking of—it's the life of her child.

Which is why I look her in the eye and make another promise. "If there is none to be found, then I will find another way."

I am responsible for them, just like she is responsible for her daughter. When a woman faces an impossible problem, whether she be mother or queen, she must find a solution. She must find a way.

So I will.

# CHAPTER 15

## QUEEN MALINA

Their faith in me forms a lump in my throat as we hurry toward the city. We trek through shin-high snow, the forest thickening with a blanket of heat that emanates from the encroaching flames. I keep us heading toward the trees that aren't yet consumed, in hopes that we can edge around the fire.

My people follow me, I follow the smoke, and all the while, the Pitching Pines burn. Their icicle needles crack as they fall. This forest, which has flourished for so many generations and outlived so many kings and battles and storms…is dying right in front of our eyes.

And we'll die too if we stay here. They'll die because of *me*.

We venture through the forest, everyone traveling as quickly as they're able. Yet we have the frail, the old, the young, the hurt. With all of us weak, trudging through the thick snow and cloying smoke makes us slower.

Though the threat of the biting fire keeps us moving.

The consuming flames growl with insatiable hunger as they eat through the pine trees with quickening speed, spreading faster from the wind. Ash blows with it, speckling our clothes and falling down like snow. The scent of burning pine chars my nose, and the faraway crack of falling trees sets my teeth on edge.

As we get closer to the city, the flames get closer too. No longer do we have a comfortable space between us where the trees are still untouched at the edge. Now, the heat of the flames pulses against the left side of my body, the light of the orange glow festering on my cheek. I keep part of my cloak against my mouth and nose, but the scent of smoke is overwhelming.

The fire is getting too close. Far too close.

"Keep going!"

I turn around, checking, counting—always counting to ensure I haven't left anyone behind. The mother and her daughter have fallen to the back of the group with the street sweepers, and another woman is passed out in her husband's arms. His arms shake, but he doesn't drop her.

The fire is loud, rivaling even the panic pounding in my ears. The flames are closing in, the smoke making it hard to see. My eyes burn as much as my lungs, and my people are coughing into their own face coverings, their skin getting stained by the fumes.

*CRACK!*

My head whips up to the left, just as a giant pine snaps at its base, succumbing to the chomp of the flames. Within seconds, it starts to fall, its trajectory heading right for us.

"Move!"

Everyone breaks away, running from the tree, running for their lives. A woman trips and falls, and my heart falls with her, but another man lashes out for her hand and pulls her toward him a split second before the tree lands.

It barely misses her.

The fallen pine is covered in fire, splitting our group down the middle. Right before my eyes, the top of it carries the flame to the untouched part of the forest and spreads with horrifying speed.

Now, we have flames on both sides of us, closing in. Surrounding us.

The length of the fallen tree stretches far on either side, and it's nearly too high for me to see over. Yet I catch a glimpse of the panicked faces of everyone else on the other side. They look left and right, the flames stopping them from being able to go around.

Another crack in the forest spurs me into action, and magic collects in my hands, shards of ice gathering.

I will it toward the trunk, and ice shoots out, covering it like a drape. The flames extinguish as ice melds over the bark, and my magic forms an arch. The group on the other side hurries over it, steps slipping on the slick path. Two men on my side help them all, gripping hands as everyone climbs over.

As soon as our entire group is together again, I urge them on. "Hurry!"

This time, we run as fast as possible, even where the snow is so thick it threatens to bowl us over. Smoke clogs my nose, shards of ice stick to my hands, and cold sweat dots my skin.

*What if I made the wrong choice? What if we're all going to die in this fire?*

Being a queen in a castle was *nothing* compared to leading my people through this forest. How trivial it all seems now. How wasted. I should have been here all along.

Instead, I was stuck.

Stuck in the sequestering rooms of the castle. Stuck with my nose in the air. Stuck *up*, when I should have been *standing* up—for them.

*This is what it means*, I think to myself as I urge them on. *This is what a queen should really be. A protector. A caregiver. A matriarch.*

I have to keep them going.

Dari falls, tripping over a snow pile, and Neira goes sprawling. Dari tries to stand and pick up her daughter again, but she grimaces as soon as she puts weight on her ankle. I rush over and gather the small girl from the ground. She clings to me, trembling all over, her fear taking hold of her quaking muscles.

Two men help Dari, bracing her upright, and she shoots me a grateful look before they start hauling her forward, while Neira buries her face against my neck. She's so very small, so very scared.

And the fault is my own.

My hollow stomach rebels, nausea swimming at the back of my tongue. My body is exhausted, energy waned, but behind us, beside us, all around, the fire rages. While in my arms, an innocent little girl cries against my throat.

I can't fail her. I can't fail them.

"There it is!"

My eyes fly up at the man's call, and relief sweeps through me like a rush of cool water. *Rooftops.* I can see rooftops through the pines.

We're almost to the city.

I hurry ahead, a burst of speed spurred along by hope.

*We can make it.*

Once I'm at the front of the group, I hand over the little girl to one of the men, but Dari takes her. The line of trees finally ends, and just down the slope is Highbell. My hope leaps even higher when I see that some of these outskirt buildings aren't charred through or burnt completely down.

Along this street of the shanties, homes still stand. Perhaps too poor and decrepit for the fae to worry about torching, because they already look ruined. Fortunately, they're far enough from the forest's edge that we should be safe from the flames so long as the fire doesn't jump the street.

I count everyone again, letting out a breath when all are accounted for. They're panting hard and streaked with ash and sweat, but they're here.

"Alright, I'll lead the way. Stay behind me. No talking. I'll find us a building where you'll all be safe. Then I'll go out in search of supplies."

Everyone nods, seemingly too weary to speak.

My attention focuses as I turn, gaze searching for any movement or danger. Yet the street ahead seems silent and empty. The storied homes are crooked and dilapidated, shared yards nothing but broken walls covered in snow.

Other than some charring against some of the stone, it looks far better than any of the buildings at the heart of the city, and blessedly free of fae.

I set my sights on the building that's closest to the tree line and then start leading the way down the slope. I'll get us into one of these houses, and once everyone is inside and secure, I'll search for supplies.

One positive is that with the amount of smoke already polluting the air, I don't believe it will be a risk to have a fire of our own, so my people can gather around a fireplace to warm up while I look for food.

As soon as I get them settled, I'll return to the tree line and shoot up a line of magic for Dommik to see, though I'll need to do it in a way that's not too obvious, yet enough for him to spot through the smoke.

One problem at a time.

With my plan in place, I feel more settled, more sure of myself. The snow bank opens up and swallows my feet with every step, but I ignore it as I heft my legs forward. If it weren't for the frigid magic beneath my skin, I have a feeling

I'd be frozen through, so I know my people desperately need to get out of the elements.

Someone lets out a garbled cry, and I flinch at the sound that seems to echo. When I turn around, I see two people have fallen, the bottom halves of their bodies sinking into the thick snow. Four others rush in to help pull them out.

My heart pounds, head whipping around to make sure we haven't been discovered. Yet the street stays quiet and empty.

As soon as my people are back on their feet, there's a new sense of urgency in my veins. We're too out in the open. I need to get them inside.

I wave my hand at them and hurry the rest of the way down the shallow slope. At the bottom, I stop and wait for the others, counting them once more.

When the last one has made it down, I glance up at the fire consuming the forest. Black smoke pours from hundred-foot flames, the sound of a thousand beasts consuming branches like snapping bones of dead prey. I turn around to face the street again, while the world burns at my back.

They follow me in a huddled group, and we go around the first building. There's a torn tarp and a broken cart inside the yard, though the snowbank is taller than the fence posts. The building itself is a mishmash of stonework for the bottom level and wood for the next two levels. The roof sags around the ash-stained chimney, but otherwise, it's intact.

We walk along its side and I stop everyone before I peer around the corner. There are abandoned buckets and broken crates up and down the cracked street, and puddles crusted with frost. Doors either sag against thresholds or are missing completely, while windows lie shattered and trash litters the street.

"The fae have been through here," I murmur.

Dari shifts Neira in her arms as she peeks out to look, but then she shakes her head. "No, Majesty. The shanties always look like this. Looks like the fae didn't bother to come down here at all."

Shock hits me in the chest. "This…this wasn't ransacked?"

She shakes her head again. "This is how it is out here. We live just down the way."

Shame like I've never felt before curdles my stomach, its spoiled, slimy fingers reaching up my face. I can't reply. All I'm able to do is stare at this street and feel the guilt soak in.

This is how the poor in my kingdom's capital lived. This is what they had to look forward to when they went home each night. They didn't even *own* these homes. The city's nobles rented them out, every building parceled off. Some of the streets were even owned by the crown.

How is it that I've been perched in a gilded castle, towering over these streets, without ever looking at what was truly here?

*Because I didn't want to see.*

That's the truth of it. I didn't want to see because I didn't want to care. Once you decide not to care, you can justify any amount of negligence. And that's what this is.

Negligence.

It's nailed into every dilapidated board and caught between the cracks of every broken stone. It's nudged between the shattered windows and pieces of litter and the puddles of frozen filth. I've neglected my people so thoroughly that it's no wonder they hated me.

To think, I came down from my castle in a gilded carriage with armored guards and pretended to care by passing out a few coins that cost me nothing, while they lived like this.

What an absolutely disgusting queen I was.

My stomach has soured, but I swallow down the bile in my throat.

The silence I've dropped is picked up by Dari. "Our entire street ran," she says quietly, tone rasping, sounding parched and tired. "See that two-story building there?" she continues, gesturing forward. "Bottom floor is my house. All of us on the street ran for it. Made it down a few blocks, too, but not past that. Dommik brought me my girl and told me to go to the Pines. I tried to tell the others, but not many listened. The ones who kept going got killed."

My eyes burn hotter. From my peripheral, I see Neira squirm, hear her whimper against her mother's chest. Perhaps she's recalling that day when she was injured and terrified, when she was seeing her neighbors being massacred.

Dari clears her throat, blinking like she's remembering herself. She holds her daughter tighter. "But that place just there with the tin over its eave? Been in it plenty of times when I helped watch some little ones who lived there. That building is one of the sturdiest on the street and never did leak too bad neither. We can go in there, Majesty. Won't be any dead left behind in it. They're all gone."

Her face is haunted, her tone cracking.

I stare ahead at where she's pointing. The three-story building stands directly across from us, with a rickety staircase that leads to two other doors on the upper levels, and one lonely window with its shutter hanging off. The front door is intact however, which is more than I can say for some of the other houses.

"I'll go first."

Darting my eyes left and right, I lead them across the street. Every footstep that thumps just a little too loudly makes my nerves tighten. After hiding within the cover of the trees for the past weeks, being out in the open like this makes me feel vulnerable.

"Hurry," I whisper.

We're so close. Salvation and safety just feet away. Everyone looks ready to collapse, but so very relieved.

Almost there.

My steps are hurried, clumps of snow falling off my boots with every stride like trailing breadcrumbs. I make it to the door, and my stiff fingers wrap around the metal handle. When the latch gives way and the door opens, I glance inside the dark, empty space as if it's a balm to my soul.

We made it.

"Okay," I say, turning. "Everyone in—"

"What do we have here?"

Everything in me freezes. My blood stops like it's iced over, plugging up every vein.

Jerking around, I see them file out of another shoddy building just three houses up, and my stomach plummets.

The fae have found us.

# CHAPTER 16

## QUEEN MALINA

My eyes land on one of the fae. Intense anger and shame sharpen within me like the ends of an arrow as soon as I see who it is. The charming swindler who claimed he would lead me to my heart's desire, when all he led me to was ruin.

Sir Pruinn.

His gray eyes still appear almost reflective, and his light blond hair is still shorn short to his scalp, the color making his dark brows stand out in dramatic arches. He's dressed impeccably in a bright green velvet tunic and matching cloak. I watch his gaze cast over my filthy appearance, and his lips quirk up, showing a hint of fang.

Slick ice swells from my palms.

Pruinn stops in the street before us as six other fae fan out behind him.

"Oreans," one of them sneers. "Scum ready to be scrubbed away."

"Get behind me," I tell my people, my tone firm.

Their hurried footsteps gather at my back, and Pruinn chuckles at the display. "Like chicks behind their mother hen, is that it? How quaint," he says mockingly.

I clench my teeth together as hard as I can. "What do you want?"

"I'd heard the Orean queen slipped out of her tower," he says, tilting his head in thought. "Funny. You were happy enough to stay in it when fae illusion had you thinking it was filled with music and flowers, weren't you? Once the accommodations were less than opulent, you were certainly quick to leave. Tell me, how did you escape?"

My eyes are hard as steel. "I walked out the front door."

"Hmm." His eyes flow over me, head tilting. "Our beloved king had to return to Annwyn for the time being, but he requested I bring you back to him, so I've come to find you. Quite convenient that you've shown up like this and that you aren't already dead."

Shards of fear stab into my stomach at the thought of being forced to leave with him. What if he drags me off and then Dommik never knows what happened to me?

I shake my head in defiance. "I'm not going anywhere with you," I tell him, though my voice wobbles, betraying my fright.

I know I'm outnumbered, that my people are too weak to help defend against these fae, but I won't yield and go with him. I have a responsibility to protect everyone behind me.

"I thought I'd have to spend longer tracking you down," he muses, as if I didn't speak. "Just as I thought it would take longer to force our first meeting and get you to listen to me. Once I knew you were the royal we needed, I stayed in Highbell for weeks, trying to come up with a plan to get to you. It was pure luck that you left your castle that day, wasn't it?" He lets out a prudish laugh. "It was so easy to manipulate you. Must have been ordained by the gods and goddesses."

"Your fae gods have no foothold here," I spit.

A spiteful look crosses his face, making his fae beauty fade, sharpening his features with hate instead. "Orea doesn't *deserve* anything of the fae. Not our gods, and not our magic."

"And yet you want *our* land," I snarl back.

Pruinn shrugs. "The superior species should have it. And we will, thanks to you." He tilts his head to motion toward me. "Tell me, how have you healed after willingly giving us your blood to rebuild the bridge?"

My hands curl into fists at my sides, fingertips digging into the gashes that are filled with frost.

He smiles snidely. "Thought so."

I can feel the tension in my people. Perhaps they're judging me, hating me, feeling betrayed even as they're forced to cower behind me in fear.

My heartbeat thrums wildly, but I stand my ground. I imagine this is what it's like for prey to be cornered by a predator. To know you're under threat, that your life is on the line. That one wrong move will find you clutched between deadly jaws.

"Shall I read what your greatest desire is now, Malina?" Pruinn taunts as he pulls out a scroll from his pocket. The same one that showed me a map of Seventh Kingdom. The same one I was fool enough to fall for. "Shall I see where it leads you this time?"

"I don't need your charlatan tricks to show me anything," I lob back, my body shaking with anger, more snow collecting in my hands. "My greatest desire is to undo what I've done and rid Orea of every single fae. Starting with *you*."

He looks over his shoulder at his group. "I'll take the Orean queen. Kill the rabble behind her."

My arms fling out protectively, as if to block my people from the threat. "Don't touch them!"

A fae with spiked silver hair behind Pruinn lifts his hands, and I instantly recognize the purple sparks of electricity that start to form in his hands. The hair on the back of my neck lifts, worry gathering between my tightening ribs.

This is the one who attacked the city with his lightning. Crumbled buildings, charred people alive. Left gaping pits of smoke in his wake.

But a fae to the right with a thick black beard steps forward also, jerking my attention toward him while the lightning fae seems to build up his power.

The bearded fae points his hands to the buildings beside us. Wooden boards suddenly yank from the walls as if he's gripped them with invisible fingers and suspended them in the air.

My eyes widen, everyone behind me crying out in alarm that makes me stiffen. Makes me hate how terrified they are.

I turn to Pruinn, my harshness traded for pleading. "Please," I blurt out, my head shaking back and forth, my expression pinched in panic. I can hear Neira crying and her mother trying to comfort her. Can hear whimpers and rushed prayers coming from my people. "Do not do this. They're no danger to you! Just let them go."

He tsks. "Does a master leave the roaches to crawl through his house?" he counters, nose wrinkled in disgust. "Of course they're no danger, but we do not leave pests to run rampant."

My eyes flick to the magic wielders who stare me down. Their powers are paused. Threat lying in wait.

"Sir Pruinn..." I say, trying to ingratiate myself to him, pleading once more. "*Please.*"

"Oh, Queen Malina," Pruinn singsongs with derisive pity. "We both know everyone behind you is going to be killed. But I'll offer you one thing, in respect of your royal status." He takes a step forward and holds out his hands. "Come with me now, and you won't have to watch. I'll spare you that. Your people are going to die regardless, but you won't have to see."

He thinks that's a kindness? He thinks that's a bargain I'm willing to strike?

"*No*," I snarl out. I'm done being willfully blind. I'm not going to turn away from any of it ever again. I won't leave them. "I stand with my people."

Pruinn drops his hands and lifts a shoulder. "Have it your way, Majesty."

The fae controlling the wood attacks. He sends the planks flying toward us. The cluster moves quickly, causing a spurt of wind to brush my cheek as it passes me by.

My eyes latch onto Dari's for a split second, her bony fingers gripping her daughter, her face pale with fear. Then the boards make impact.

Dari and everyone else gets thrown back and I watch with suffocating panic as she and the others hit the ground hard, the wood breaking and splintering from the force.

Neira screams as she and her mother crash onto the ground, and the sound pierces through my heart, making my adrenaline spike.

The wood pulls back again, ready to repeat the action before anyone can recover, but magic shoots from my hands, ice bursting forward with a force that rattles my chest. I watch it arc through the sky, and then it hits and envelops the planks. As soon as my ice freezes them through, the wood falls to the ground and shatters like glass.

The magical fae isn't deterred. He reaches up in the air again, his magic pulling more large boards from the dilapidated building to my right. He strips the wall until he yanks out a thick beam, making the weakened structure start to topple.

"Watch out!" I scream as I leap back, just as the building falls, half spilling out onto the road.

It nearly crashes over us.

The fae smirks from the other side of the crumble, and without reprieve, he angles the floating wood in our direction. Their ends are splintered and wickedly sharp, and he sends them flying toward us like a volley of spears.

Pure instinct has me tossing up my hands, my magic unleashing in a curved wall before me. I flinch back, eyes squeezing shut, just as the wood crashes against my ice.

My eyes spring open again, my pulse racing, seeing the fissures spread through my wall...but it holds.

I fling my hand out again, making ice attach to the roof of the building beside me, forming a spire as high as I can manage in a desperate bid for Dommik to notice—to come help.

*Please help.*

But the lightning fae steps forward.

His magic seems to be fully charged and ready now. Built up and crackling with power.

With a gritted-out cry, I force more magic from my depleting body, creating another wall that freezes up from the ground and then arcs backward to create a dome over the heads of my people.

They huddle beneath it, while some of the men have picked up pieces of metal and stone that fell from the crumbled building and are using the debris to try to block the wooden fae's continued assault.

I start to direct more ice to enclose all the way around them, but the lightning fae suddenly sends a purple bolt stabbing down from the smoke-filled clouds.

It cracks directly into the ice wall in front of me, shattering it in a blinding flash that sends me stumbling back.

Shards explode out, and I duck my head in my arms before the frozen shrapnel can slice across my exposed face. When the onslaught ends, I whip my head up again to lock gazes with the lightning fae, and he's already building up another charge of lightning, already making electricity singe the air.

He's going to decimate the icy barrier over my people too.

"Get into the house!" I cry with panicked command, because I know my ice won't be enough protection.

But the wooden fae doesn't give them the chance to run.

Before anyone can so much as reach for the door, he snaps the wooden walls directly beside us, ripping them off in thin air and making the entire structure weaken and crumble too.

My people scramble, trying to get out of the way as they panic, running as they try to escape while leaving behind my protective arc.

Before they can get more than a few running steps away, the lightning fae strikes the other end of the street right in front of them, cutting them off. Bolt after bolt, the lavender strikes crash down, splitting the road, charring the cobblestones.

"Leave them alone!" I scream before sending thin shards of ice hurtling toward the enemy. Before it can hit him, a wooden board slams into me, cracking against my chest on impact.

I land hard on my back, blinking up at the sky. The hit stuns me, breath knocked loose from my lungs and scattered around my ribs where I can't reach it.

My people's screams spur me on, forcing me to move. So I roll onto my side and push myself up, nearly teetering over again as I heave in a strangled breath.

The other fae are closing in. They're gathering around my people, with swords in hand while lightning strikes, keeping them hemmed in. The fae controlling the wood makes the planks embed into the street like a shoddy fence for livestock.

The fae are toying with us. Laughing at us.

Neira is screaming through hiccupped tears, clutching her mother, and it tatters my heart.

"Stop!" I scream, though my voice comes out in fraying pieces. My eyes land on Pruinn a few paces away.

His menace holds my gaze in place. "We're going to slaughter them. Just like we slaughtered your entire city. And since you didn't take me up on my offer, you get to watch, *Majesty*."

Lightning suddenly strikes down Kasin—the old street sweeper. The blinding light chars through his corpse. Screams rend the air.

Another fae throws a dagger and stabs Kasin's son straight through, uncaring that the man holds no weapon, has no defense. The fae controlling the wood starts spinning boards around and then slamming them down, like a paddle beating out the dirt of a rug.

Horrifying bursts of violence from every direction.

"No!" Ice magic shoots out of me as I run desperately toward them. It hits the dagger-throwing fae, knocking him down. But then I'm once again struck with a plank, this time square in the back.

I go sprawling, forehead cracking painfully against the frozen cobbles and making me see bursts of black that crawl through my vision.

I try to scramble up, but I'm held down by the board at my back. It's keeping me pinned, just like their king had done to me with the stone table. Fear scrapes down my stomach.

"Watch, Queen Malina," Pruinn taunts as he comes to a stop above me. His polished shoes are so shiny I can see my panicked reflection in them.

Lightning hits someone else then, making their entire body light up. I can see their bones glowing through their skin.

I can't tell who it is before they're nothing but a corpse left in a smoking pit.

My people scream, huddled together, pressing in, for there's nowhere to go, nowhere to escape. Another one of the fae soldiers has jumped into their pen and is taunting them with his sword. Laughing while he makes blood fly and another body drop with a slice of his blade.

144

My people are dying because of *me*. Because I made yet another wrong choice and led them into ruin. Because I allowed fae to tempt me into Seventh Kingdom, let them cut my hands and spill my blood, all while my people languished in an impoverished city within a greed-ridden kingdom.

Negligence. Willful blindness. Entitlement. Greed.

My mother would have been ashamed of me.

Fierce protectiveness cuts through me as I strain to get my hand out from under the board. I yank it past and then shove it toward my people, an arc of ice streaming out.

My magic gets cut off when Pruinn suddenly slams his boot on top of my hand. I cry out in pain, my eyes squeezing shut.

He grips the snarls of my hair and wrenches my head up. "I said, *watch*!"

My eyes snap back open, blurred with tears, and I'm forced to watch the fae start cutting down my people one at a time. Another man—Jon—by sword. Tara, who gets burnt through with lightning. Wilson's skull smashed with a board. All while the fae continue to laugh.

All while Neira screams.

This is what helpless horror is, and I'm frozen in the shock of it.

Until, suddenly, the world seems to *tremble*.

The very ground I'm pinned to darkens. At first, my heart leaps in both relief and fear that Dommik has come with his shadows.

But it's not Dommik.

"What…" Pruinn jerks away, boot leaving my hand, just as the fae controlling the wood drops dead.

My eyes widen when I see his body is now crawling with lines that snake through his skin, turning him a sickly color. Then the lightning fae drops too, one last crackling spark sputtering out as he falls.

The ground is spreading with fissuring vines of black and brown that seem to eat away at the cobblestones, disintegrating everything in its path. I shove the board off my body and jerk to my feet, head swiveling up at the darkening sky. Only, it's not darkening—it's the shadow of a timberwing flying overhead, descending toward us.

The rest of the fae soldiers drop like flies, their bodies bulging, their skin peeling, bursting like fruit that's been left too long and gorged on by maggots to spoil.

Pruinn makes a choking gasp, eyes bugging out, and I whip my head to stare at him. I watch in horrified fascination as the whites of his eyes go jaundiced, his skin wrinkling as it shrinks.

Infected veins spread up his neck to feast on his face, just as his panicked gaze meets mine. Cold retribution solidifies in my chest and ices over my panic, filling me instead with cruel satisfaction as his eyes brim with fear and confusion.

"*I'm watching,*" I hiss.

A second later, he falls dead at my feet.

I look up just as the roaring timberwing lands amongst the dead, bulging corpses of the fae. My people who are still alive cry out with joy and relief, while a shocked breath shakes out of me.

"King Rot! King Rot has saved us!"

I watch as Slade Ravinger jumps down from his beast. But this man has spikes running down his arms and back, iridescent scales along his cheeks…and pointed ears.

Pointed. Like the fae.

Fear swallows me whole when his hard green eyes land on me, because this man with his lines of famed rot, is unmistakably King Ravinger…except he's also something else. Something that chills my bones and scatters my heartbeats into useless thrums.

He has brought terrible power and terrifying wrath,

and yet…he also just saved my people. Saved them, when I could not.

So I do something I never would have ever done in the past. Something that I would have been too proud for, too selfish for. Too short-sighted for.

I, Queen Malina Colier, fall to the ground and *kneel*.

# CHAPTER 17

## SLADE

I look down at the woman at my feet.

Her body is hunched over, spine bent as her head tilts toward the ground in utter supplication. If I wasn't seeing this with my own eyes, I wouldn't have believed this woman would bow to anyone.

"Queen Malina."

She picks her head up, and icy blue eyes lift to look at me. Her face is gaunt, skin so pale her blue veins are visible at her temples and neck. Pure white hair is matted and dirty. Clothes ripped and stained with smoke.

She looks nothing like the haughty queen I expected. Especially not with the haunted look in her eyes.

My beastly thirst for revenge rears its head, just as it did throughout my stops in Orea. I want to wrap my hand around her neck and rot her through. The bloodlust is strong enough that my fangs ache in my jaw.

"I should kill you."

She trembles at my dark tone, lips cracked, frost covering her cheekbones like rouge.

"I should kill you," I repeat, "for the way you treated Auren. For the way you fucking *allowed* your husband to treat her. For doing *nothing*."

Rotted vines scourge the cobblestones at my feet. Ice slips from Malina's shaking hands, landing in small shards that break upon the road.

"Are you fae?" she asks, tone unnerved.

My brow cocks as I jut my chin to the ice magic pouring out of her. "Are *you*? Or did you just make a treacherous bargain with one?"

She glances down and fists her hands, as if only just realizing the magic she's leaking out.

"Is it true?" I demand. "Did you somehow give your blood and fix the bridge of Lemuria?"

She swallows hard, pale throat bobbing. "Yes."

Her confession cracks, though she doesn't sway. Doesn't try to defend or make excuses.

"Orea will want to kill you for that," I tell her, my voice laced with threat.

"Yes," she confesses again.

I should kill her. For all the cruelty she doled out to Auren. For what she's done to Orea itself. She allowed the fae to surge in and destroy our land.

And yet…because of that, she also forged a way for me to get to Annwyn.

Her people watch us, tense and terrified, still shaking from the attack, while others mourn the ones who lie dead on the road. Malina's eyes go from me to them, and I see her desperation. Can sense her fear.

But I also sense a warning of magic. A split second after, shadows appear to my right.

I move before he can.

The man coalesces, but I have him by the throat before the shadow power even fully pulls away.

He gasps and tries to wrench out of my grip, but he's not going anywhere. I stare at the hooded man as he tries to claw at me, but rot is already soaking into his neck.

"King Ravinger!" Malina cries with desperation. "Wait, please!"

"You think to sneak up on me?" I seethe at him.

The people scream.

"*Leave—her—alone*," the man sputters out, each word shoving past his constricted throat.

"Do you think I answer to you? Do you think you can stop me if I rot her bones and shrivel her cruel, selfish carcass?" I threaten darkly.

Rage flexes through him, dark eyes flashing with violence. His magic tries to gather but fails.

My voice drops low. "Your shadows can't hide you from me."

I'm tempted to continue on with my purge of punishment and my rite of retribution. Since this man seems important to her, I could kill him first and make her watch.

"King Ravinger, I'm *begging* you."

My head turns slowly toward her. Malina has her fingers threaded together in a plea, hands shaking even as the skin is iced over.

"No more death. *Please*. Not him. Not any of them. The only person who deserves it is me. Don't hurt him."

"Queenie—" the man chokes out.

She ignores him, her glacial eyes unblinking.

"Thank you," she whispers, surprising me. Her gaze flicks behind me to look at the Oreans. "Thank you for saving them when I couldn't. I owe you everything. Truly." Droplets of freeze seep from the corners of her desolate eyes. "I know you want to kill me, and I understand. But monarch to monarch, thank you for coming to our aid. This is all that's left of my people, and if I can die knowing they will live, then that is enough."

Her chin wobbles as I stare at her. I see the dark circles under her eyes that show up starkly against her pale skin.

"Are you truly Malina?" I taunt. "Because you look and act nothing like the haughty cold queen that everyone describes, save for that white hair."

Her icy eyes flinch and her confession whispers. "I'm not the Malina I was before."

This would be much easier if she was acting like a conceited snob. Instead, she looks broken and desperate.

I let out a growl and then roughly let go of the man, making him stagger on his feet. Malina rushes to him, and he wraps a protective arm around her, his shadows writhing around his black cloak.

He snarls at me like he wants to tear me apart.

"Try it," I dare. "And I'll change my mind about letting you both live."

Malina presses her hand to his chest and murmurs something in his ear that seems to make him stand down.

My cool gaze casts back to her face. "You're wrong, by the way."

Her white brows furrow. "Wrong?"

"These people here aren't the only survivors." I jerk my head in the direction of the castle. "Some people are being held there."

Shock pulls lines of stress around her eyes as she glances at Highbell. "*What*? Truly?"

I don't answer her. Instead, I walk back to Argo. The survivors are watching him warily, giving a wide berth.

"Wait!" Malina starts to hurry after me, and the shadow man curses beneath his breath. The shattered ice queen shoves her way in front of me, seemingly not caring about the timberwing growling at her back. "What do you mean my people are in the castle? How do you know?"

"I flew overhead. There are golden sheets flung out the windows. The word *HELP* smeared across them in white paint."

I step around her, but she does the unthinkable. Her hand lashes out, gripping my forearm, narrowly missing my spikes.

My head turns slowly, and a threatening growl rises from my throat, but she holds her ground. "Please take me to them. Help me save them." Her words are a distressed bid uttered with guttural grief.

I'm heartless enough to refuse her. To walk away. I don't owe this woman anything. She had no mercy for Auren. No mercy for her people or even Orea for that matter.

The shadows around the man flicker with fragments of coiling light, his body tensing like he's a second away from trying to fight me. But Malina's eyes go behind me. To the huddled Oreans against the broken buildings and rot-stained street. My gaze follows hers, and I see them. Mourning their dead, shivering in the cold and fear and grief, their bodies thin and weak and dirty.

"Release me," I command.

Malina wrenches back her hand, letting it drop to her side. I can see the hope dropping too. She fears me, and yet, she has the courage to beg.

A moment of tense silence passes between us until I finally break it in half. "Fine," I say, and I hear her breath catch. "I'll help your people, Queen Malina. Only because Auren would want me to."

She seems to nearly collapse in relief, her blue eyes filling. "*Thank you.*"

"Don't thank me. Thank *her*."

She nods warily, like she knows I'm still fighting back my instinct to end her.

"Can you use your magic to get the fae out of the castle? Can you get all the survivors within its walls where they can be safe?" she asks.

My gaze casts toward the mountain. To the gleaming castle teeming with fae. "I can kill the fae and get you inside."

She lets out a shaky breath, and I hear the people murmur and cry. Who knows what they've been through, what they've had to survive.

Turning, I go to Argo and mount his back, my hands gripping the reins. "I can clear out the castle, and I can even cut off their route up the mountain so no more of the fae army floods in. But *safe*?" I glance at the pillaged, burnt city. "Look around, Cold Queen. Orea isn't safe for any of you."

With a snap of the reins, Argo lifts me into the air, making Malina flinch back.

"I'll come back when it's done," I tell her, and then Argo shoots upward with a powerful push of his wings.

As we lift higher, my eyes cast to the right, outside the city, where pristine snow spreads out like a sheet. To where the fae army horde marches toward Fifth Kingdom.

I was heading for them first when I saw the sprays of magic on this broken street and happened upon a few dozen Oreans about to be massacred.

I wasn't expecting to find the bitch of a queen who somehow seems to have grown a heart.

The skies continue to pump full of smoke from the forest, mixing with the cloud coverage. My gaze scans the ground, following the direction the army is marching, the landmarks, the way the land pours into the horizon.

"There," I tell Argo with a tap of my knuckles against the side of his neck. "Get me right there."

He snaps his attention to exactly where I want to go, at the narrowest point where the army weaves around the land's snowy dune. We fly within the haze of the smoke-stained clouds, like an arrow speeding through the cover of night. All while magic builds within me. Churning. Boiling.

With piercing precision, Argo drops down through the sky toward our mark and lands with a roar and a spray of snow, right in the midst of the invading army.

Right in the middle of the marching fae.

After being stuck in this land for so long and only being around Oreans, the sight of so many pointed ears and sharp fangs is surreal.

The fae nearest me are startled for several seconds. Stopping in their tracks, they take in my appearance, obviously noting I'm fae. They hesitate, because they don't know my relation to the army or if I'm one of them.

I'm not.

The closest ones are smart enough to pull the swords from their scabbards. To feel the building threat.

One of them raises his weapon at eye level. "Who are you?"

Who am I?

I jump off Argo's back, and the second my boots touch the snow, my magic surges out.

The fae have a moment to gasp, to curse, to shout, but then I let my rot free. Let it *reign*.

And it rules with pure tyranny, showing them *exactly* who I am.

Argo and I stand at the eye of the storm while rot floods out. It pours into the ground, like spreading fractals burnt through wood. Black lines stain the snow, the reaching veins bursting beneath the soldiers' feet.

Fae start to drop.

It's a ripple effect while the erratic lines reach and

stretch and grow, poisoning all in their path. The soldiers, their clothing, their supply carts, their fucking leather boots. The brown-tinged snow and the frozen soil beneath it. It all succumbs to death. It all succumbs to *me*.

Because this is what I am.

I am hostile darkness and festering death, and with my forms now fixed, with my essence now bonded and my heart healed, my unrestrained power is stronger than ever.

For once, I don't have to hold onto control, to hold my magic back. It's like being bound with ropes and then cutting through every cord, letting the shackles fall. Letting the monster loose.

And loose it does.

Some fae try to use magic against me, try to defend themselves. Balls of fire get thrown my way. Bursts of unnatural light too. Shields. Wind. A swarm of locusts probably ready to strip the flesh from my bones. But I drop them all before they can drop me.

My rot devastates the ground, making it start to sink. Soldiers fall, looking like their corpses have been left for weeks in the sun, while the rest try to run. But there's no running from this. No running from me.

Their magic sputters out uselessly as their festering bodies split open. My rot floods further than I can see, so many bodies being swept away. Hundreds. Thousands.

Still, my power pours.

My skin feels charged, like I've brushed against a bolt of lightning, and I revel in it.

And then, I call up the dragon and wrench it free.

The splintered form of the creature pours out of my body. It takes root beside me, sprouting from the vapor that streams from my silhouette. Its smoke is thicker even than what chugs out of the forest, until it forms a shadow beast that's blacker than night.

This time, the dragon is far bigger than it was in the bog.

It coalesces beside me, standing twenty feet tall, black scaled body rippling with strength. Its spikes are hooked and deadly, stretching down its spine and legs and looking sharp enough to stab someone through. Its tail sweeps over the snow, but it does not move a single flake, just like its feet don't leave prints on the ground.

Even so, the world seems to tremble at its incorporeal presence. The fae still alive all scream out in fear when they see it.

I turn and swing up on Argo's back, and we take to the sky.

There's a perfect empty circle of untouched snow where we were standing, the rotted lines spread out from around it like the black, toxic rays of a sun. The dragon's form takes flight beside me in a wraith-like presence, black wings spreading out to their full length for the first time.

Below, I see just how far my magic has already traveled, just how many soldiers I've killed. Now, it's time to ruin their path. To stop them from their relentless pour into the rest of Orea.

Letting go of Argo's reins, I give in to my power completely. I feel it stretch like an invisible band that goes from me to the splintered manifestation as we cut across the sky. Power builds and spreads between us, swelling throughout my body, until it reaches a crescendo.

And then the dragon opens its mouth and spews out death.

Instead of fire like the tales of old, flames of rot pour from its maw, lethal vines of rotted roots expelling from its throat. It gushes into the land below, and the ground buckles.

I watch as the sweep of pure power creates a rift of rot that utterly devastates the snowy landscape. Magic pours from me, from the dragon, and the contaminated ground disintegrates, taking every nearby soldier with it.

When the dragon finally swallows down its outpour, when its maw snaps shut, the land below is ruined. Path split, gaping open, making the way across impossible. The snow is curdled at the edges, foaming with clumps and singed brown.

Thousands of soldiers lie dead.

Unless another fae comes along with enough power and skill to repair what I've ruptured, then their brutal onslaught has been cut off.

For now.

With the dragon still flying beside us, I pull on Argo's reins and head for the gilded jewel that's clasped in the snowy mountain's grip. But all I see when I look at Highbell's gleaming castle walls...is Auren.

I've given Orea a chance, and it's time to give Highbell one too. Because it's what she would want. I'm no longer on a rampage of revenge. No longer fed by only torment and reckoning.

I told her I'd be the villain for her, and I was.

Now, I need to also be the hero she would want me to be.

# CHAPTER 18

## QUEEN MALINA

Dommik's shadows pull away, revealing the last Orean at his side.

"Go right in," I tell the man reassuringly, though he sways slightly on his feet, looking discomfited from the shadow-leap. "The castle is safe and there's food in the dining room. Everyone else is there."

He bends, again and again, like a piece of paper being folded over, creases marking up his starved and filthy body as he bows. "Thank you, Your Majesty." He bends again for Dommik. "Thank you, sir."

He follows one of the other Oreans already at the threshold, and they disappear inside Highbell's castle walls. I breathe a little easier once he's inside.

They're safe. They're being fed. They're *alive*.

A miracle only made possible by the most vicious threat. King Rot.

I glance around at the aftermath of his presence. Of what *clearing out the castle* truly meant.

The castle's courtyard is grisly. My gaze falls to my feet, and I follow the lines spilled across the ground like unspooled threads lying thick within the snow. Fae soldiers are dead behind me, their bodies distended grotesquely, eyes melted, skin sloughed off.

The stench is unimaginable.

From the streets of the shanties, we watched as King Ravinger swooped over the mountain and rained down death. Everyone in Orea has always feared him, feared his magic, though I'd never seen it at work before now.

We were right to fear.

Even from my spot in the city below, I felt the danger that emanated from him as it pinched my stomach and raced my pulse. I could *feel* his power rippling, even at such a distance away.

Yet what stole my breath completely was the creature tethered to him in the air. Wisps of smoke seemed to stretch between where he flew on the timberwing, to the winged creature that soared beside him. A scaled monster that reaped death.

A *dragon*.

Terror filled me at seeing the pitch black form with spikes along its spine and a snarl at its lips. When it opened its maw, black flames were strewn out, though instead of burning anything, they rotted fae through.

I'd never seen anything like it. I never want to see it ever again.

What Ravinger is capable of is utterly fearsome. That power, that creature he had with him, his pointed ears…he's been a fae hiding in plain sight.

Yet…he's helping Orea.

I'm as grateful as I am petrified.

To think, Ravinger could've wrought such devastating havoc all this time, and yet, my late husband dared to scheme against him. Queen Kaila had called Tyndall a fraud, but he was a damn fool.

The angry, spurned woman in me wishes I could wrench Tyndall back from death's grasp just so I could show him this. So I could shove his ruined, gilded castle in his face.

King Midas may always be remembered for his golden touch, but I will always remember him for the way that touch *destroyed*. He wasn't a gift of wealth. He was a curse of unending greed.

Yet I was no better.

The people of Sixth Kingdom had a greedy king and a coldhearted queen, and because of us, our kingdom is gone.

The mountain itself looks like a septic heart pulsing with black veins. At the base, on the road leading to Seventh Kingdom, rot has created jagged gaps in the ground, cutting off the path.

Sixth Kingdom has been flooded with poison to kill off the infection of the fae.

But Ravinger was right. There are other Oreans who were trapped here. Mostly servants and guards left alive and forced to serve the fae. Our number of survivors has more than doubled.

Our death toll is too many to count.

The sound of scraping pulls my attention, and I look over to see Dommik helping one of Highbell's surviving guards. Together, they drag a bloated body to the other end of the courtyard, tossing it with the rest of the dead fae already piled there.

My assassin looks like he's ready to drop. Exhaustion drifts off him like his shadows, though right now, they're tucked away.

He used his magic to bring everyone up the mountain. He

had to make several trips, with multiple survivors each time, and I can tell it's drained him. Even so, instead of resting now, he's helping to rid Highbell from the blight of the dead.

A shadow passes over me, and my head whips up, eyes locking on the descending timberwing. Now, I have to face the one responsible for every rotted corpse.

Even though King Ravinger saved us, emptied Highbell of our enemies and liberated the survivors, I can't help but shudder when he lands. His dragon has dissipated, blown away with the wind, but chills still bubble at my skin at the memory of its presence.

His timberwing's lips part in a sneer as it sniffs the dead bodies, sharp talons scraping at the half-poisoned snow.

Swallowing hard, I force my legs forward, even as an animal instinct warns me to run the other way. The deadly king dismounts, standing before me in all his terror.

I drop my head. "Thank you, King Ravinger."

It's no wonder my voice trembles. Whose wouldn't after witnessing what he's done? What he's capable of? That wasn't mere magic. I've seen magic. I *have* magic, however new it may be.

This was another tier of power entirely.

He ignores both my indebted gratitude and the shake in my words. Instead, he surprises me by saying, "Show me her cage."

I freeze.

Cold dread gathers in my stomach, and a pulse-pounding silence stretches between us. "Her cage?"

Another snub at my words. Instead of replying, he turns on his heel and strides into the castle, and it's all too clear that he expects me to go with him.

Across the courtyard, I glance over at Dommik, because something has been made abundantly clear. King Ravinger has hate in his eyes when he looks at me, and it stems from a source I didn't expect.

The gilded pet.

*"I should kill you for the way you treated Auren. For the way you fucking allowed your husband to treat her. For doing nothing."*

And now, he wants me to show him her cage.

I owe a debt to Ravinger for saving my people, and he's come to collect. He's come to make me pay.

Turning, I head inside to lead the rotten king.

Surely, this is what it feels like to be stalked.

King Ravinger's presence behind me stifles and goads, making my entire back prickle with threat. My body is teetering on a precipice of adrenaline, not knowing whether to try to fight or flee. Though my mind knows neither of those options would work if he chooses to kill me.

The only thing I could do is fall to the floor in another bow of supplication. One doesn't run from the apex predator. One doesn't try to fight a god with mere sticks.

You bend the knee and beg for mercy.

My thighs burn as I lead the way up the many flights of stairs, my weakened body protesting the ascent just as much as my burdened mind.

Highbell is in tatters, with stolen furnishings and chipped -away gold. Even though Queen Kaila ordered the white paint to be buffed away and the castle to be put back to order, it still looks derelict. Her efforts were half-finished and no competition for the soiled spots where rotted fae were felled.

The stench in here makes my eyes water.

With my spine stiffened, we make it to the very top floor to Auren's room. The door is already open, with bleary-eyed windows feeding in a haze of light. I step aside, feeling

Ravinger's presence like a looming, deathly dark come to swallow me whole.

He steps in. Boots loud against the gilt floor. Passing by me, he stops before the cage bars. His head turns, eyes swiveling, as he takes in every single inch of the space. I look at it too, trying to see it through his eyes.

An elaborate bedroom, every inch gleaming. It would be a normal room, if not for the cage built inside of it. It stretches up from the floor, almost mocking in the beauty of its construction. Filigree bands meld around its base and top, the cage door curling with metal fretwork. The bars are thick, the space between them narrow and curving like a pretty birdcage, each one gathering together at the top like strands of hair caught in a tie.

A gilt greenhouse, trapping the golden flower that bloomed within.

As he takes it all in, Ravinger is so still that I startle when he suddenly steps inside of it. Warily, I watch as he slowly walks around the inside of the cage.

His fingers yank at the nearly sheer drapery hooked at the ceiling, letting it fall. The fabric allowed Auren to draw it down like curtains on a window. I suppose it offered some semblance of privacy against anyone who walked in the room so they couldn't see her through the bars. Though how much privacy could it truly be? Now, it seems like such a paltry offering—more of a tease than anything.

His touch trails over her glossy bed, and he pinches the fabric between his fingers. He studies her bedside table, the wine pitchers, the gilt tray with plates and cups. Then he disappears into the threshold past her bed, his footsteps receding slowly. If he walks the entire length of her barred rooms, he'll go through her closet and washroom, all the way to the library and atrium.

I stand utterly still, bones stiff, muscles tight. My

heartbeat flutters anxiously in my chest, but I've no way to calm it. I simply wait. Trembling with every tick of the clock.

When he comes back, he stops and stares at the sole window. She couldn't even have a proper look out, since the glass is iced over. Something I used to cruelly relish.

My stomach twists in a way that feels an awful lot like remorse.

Ravinger stands there for a drawn-out moment. The silence squeezes every part of my spine, like his grip is ready to grind down my bones.

Finally, he turns.

Walks toward me.

Stops.

My heart nearly falls out of my chest in trepidation. I don't dare take a breath or make any sudden movement. His looming presence bears down on me with quiet wrath. I can hear every word he's not saying as if they're striking across my face.

I don't know when something spurred between Auren and him, but it doesn't matter. To stand here with him now, to witness him seeing this barred room, it coats me in terrified shame. He looks at me, full of fuming contempt and utter blame, and the truth is right there in his eyes.

We caged the woman he loves.

My chest aches with a longing sort of grief as it recognizes such a dangerous devotion, the likes of which I have never seen. His feelings for Auren permeate the very air, making me quiver beneath its weight.

Maybe the rumors are true, that he's no Orean—no fae either—but a demon. One who burns with death and will strike me down right here and now, judging me for the part I played.

Still, he stares at me in silence, though he doesn't need to say a thing. I can feel his menace, can feel the words he spoke in the city, over and over again in his hate.

*I should kill you.*

Water beads at my eyes, and something in me, some final barrier of my cold-hearted justifications, shatters away.

My voice is just as broken. "I'm sorry."

This apology won't be enough to appease him, and we both know it, but I offer it anyway. Shame and acceptance pull down my head, neck bending, heart pounding, death imminent. My only consolation is, with his amount of power, I know my end will be swift, and I know Dommik will take care of the survivors.

Ravinger takes a step closer, and from the corner of my eye, I see the glinting black spikes along his arm. My panic rises up at the sight, because what if instead of using his magic to end me, he runs me through?

I feel his stare against my form with an abrasive drag. Even my ice is too scared to show its face, my power shriveling in his presence. Then he moves, and my eyes slam shut, my body flinching wildly.

But…his magic doesn't invade me. His spikes don't stab into my skin.

Instead, he walks away.

My eyes open at the sound of his footsteps retreating. Shocked, I watch him leave through the bedroom door, and my entire body slumps.

He didn't kill me.

*Why didn't he kill me?*

For long moments, I can't move. I'm half-expecting him to storm back through the door, deciding to end me after all. Yet he doesn't come back, and I finally snap out of it enough to leave.

My hands are shaking as I go to the door, but before I walk out, I steal a glance at the cage.

She was inside it for *years*.

No wonder she killed Tyndall—if what Kaila told me is true.

We were both trapped by King Midas, though in very different ways. Both blinded—her, by love, and me, by hate.

I think I see things now because I've finally started to look.

My body stiffens with the residual waves of shame, and I swallow hard. Thinking of her trapped in here. Thinking of how it must've been.

The favored was nothing but a prisoner.

A whisper trembles from my lips, shaking out into the cold and empty room. "I'm sorry," I say.

Though it's far too late for her to hear it.

# CHAPTER 19

## QUEEN MALINA

After walking away from Auren's cage, I shut the door behind me, leaving soft flakes of ice on the knob. I descend the stairs as if I've been encased in plaster, my movements stiff and heart brittle.

When I'm nearly at the bottom floor again, I pause to take a steadying breath. I hold the banister, looking down at the main floor below. From this vantage point, I can see the threshold of the royal dining room. Can hear the subdued chatter of the survivors inside.

At the open front doors of the castle, snow has blown in. Tracks run through it, made by the obvious drag of bodies that were pulled outside. I shudder to think just how many more bodies will be found inside these many rooms. My father must be turning over in his grave.

I hear a noise that tugs at my attention, and I glance around to find the source.

*What was that?*

I look over my shoulder at the servant's entrance cut into the wall, and see the door is slightly ajar. I walk over and pull it open, glancing inside the narrow corridor, and I hear the sound again. It's a woman's voice.

Perhaps not all the servants have been alerted that they're safe? That the fae are no longer here?

I walk down the corridor, following the sound. When I get nearer, I push open a creaky door, finding one of the servants' shared sleeping rooms. There are several beds inside, all of them built with two layers so one could sleep above the other. The window is open, no curtain in sight, and the room is empty, save for one woman lying on a bed.

She mutters something.

"Hello? Are you alright?"

I receive no clear answer, and my brow furrows as I walk further in. I stop at her bedside, and recognition comes instantly. *Mist.*

The saddle woman whom Queen Kaila brought back to Highbell. The woman who…

I swallow hard and glance down at her stomach—at what should be a pregnant belly jutting up. Instead, bloodstains steal my sight. The blood coats the layers of bedding, taking up the expanse from one side to the other.

"Mist?" I call.

My eyes fly up to her face, and her closed eyes flicker, lips uttering something nonsensical. She looks so poorly, skin tone off, black hair limp.

I glance around the room and see bloodied rags on the floor and a tipped-over bowl. Horror washes through me and I latch onto her shoulder and shake. Her skin is searing hot beneath her clothes, nearly burning my icy fingers. "Mist?"

Her brown eyes snap open and she blinks several times, though the bleariness in her gaze doesn't go away.

"Can you hear me?"

She settles her attention on me and frowns in confusion. "The cold queen's in the saddle wing? But she never comes in here…"

"Mist, you're not in the saddle wing. You're in a servant's room and you're…" My words choke off, gaze flicking again to the blood. So much blood. "I'm going to get you help."

The moment I say the last word, her eyes go from dazed to clear, and a wild desperation enters her face that's as jarring as the way she suddenly lashes out and grips my arm. "They came!" she cries, terror bulging the words and making her voice burst with it. "The fae came in—we couldn't keep them out. I hid but I started to bleed… It *hurt*…"

I swallow hard, my skin pinching where she clutches me. "What happened?"

"My baby." She starts sobbing in earnest, tears contorting her face. "I pushed and pushed. For so long. I was alone." Teardrops fall from her eyes, soaking her shirt, landing on my hand. "I tried to be quiet, but then I finally got him out…"

My throat cinches. Him. A *boy*.

Her eyes are so filled with tears it's difficult to imagine them not having this depth of misery.

"He was born with sandy hair, just like the king. So beautiful…"

Her wails are torn, ripping right through her, and I'm utterly stricken.

"I tried to wake him, but he wouldn't… He never breathed. And then the fae came and took him out. *They took him.*"

My hand covers my mouth, tears burning holes in the corners of my eyes as she starts to wail, and my heart breaks.

Devastatingly so.

When Tyndall wrote to me about impregnating his saddle, I seethed. I hated. Both him and her, and even the child who was innocent in it all. When he dared to demand that I pretend it was my heir, I wished every terrible thing on them. Wished for atrocious things because *I* am atrocious.

I wish I could take it all back.

Her sobs choke out with severed inhales, her frail body utterly spent. "I'm alone," she whispers through exhausted misery. "Queen Kaila said I would get the best care, but she's gone. I was alone the whole time, and I'm alone now."

I sit down on the bed next to her and grip her hand tight. "You are *not* alone."

A rasped cough escapes her, and she presses her other palm to her deflated middle. "It doesn't hurt anymore," she murmurs.

I'm no mender, but even I know that isn't a good sign.

"You were so very brave," I whisper.

She slumps back, fevered eyes growing heavy. "You won't leave me?" she asks.

It takes everything I have to not allow myself to sob. I shake my head firmly, squeezing her fingers once more. "No, Mist. I won't leave you. You won't be alone ever again."

Relief shudders through her, and she settles against the stained pillow, her wailing going quiet. "He was so beautiful... You'll tell the king, won't you? Midas will be so happy." She lets out another sigh. "I hope I get to hold him soon."

"You will," I whisper as a frigid tear cuts down my cheek. "Rest now."

Mist nods and her expression smooths out, and then her eyes flutter shut.

She doesn't open them again.

I exit the room with a weighed-down spirit. Mist's death, the death of her innocent child, are tragedies. I'm shaken with the fault of them, because both lines lead back directly to me.

Stopping in the corridor, my body slumps against the wall. I place my forehead against it, shoulders curled in, eyelids squeezed tight.

I always wanted to be a mother. Not just because the kingdom expected it, not just to make an heir, but to have a love that could be mine. To love a child, the way my mother had loved me. Yet the Divine gods were right to deny me my wish.

I would've failed at that too.

Ice clinks onto the floor as my frosted breath shakes out. Here in the quiet, I mourn for Mist and her baby. Mourn for everyone who died in Highbell. And just as I said in Auren's room, I whisper out a quiet apology.

"*I'm sorry.*"

All of it, every death, every fault, it cuts through me with blades, and I bleed. Bleed and bleed onto the gilded floor.

After I wipe my cheeks, exhaustion pulls at me, but I force myself to straighten. I shove my shoulders back as I walk out of the corridor and onto the main staircase. I haven't earned respite or solitude, nor do I deserve to stand here and sorrow, because none of this is about me or my feelings.

Kingdom comes first. *Orea* must come first.

My feet carry me down the staircase, and I find one of the servants. "There's—" My voice chokes off, but I clear it, forcing out the words. "A woman upstairs in the servant's chambers has died. I will need help taking care of her body."

Her eyes widen. "Of course, Your Majesty. We will see to her immediately."

Before she can walk off, I touch her arm, stilling her. "She gave birth while the fae were here. The child didn't survive, but she said the fae took him away. Can we try to find him somehow? Maybe there's someone here who might know something? So the child can be given a proper burial."

Her expression fills with sadness. "I'll speak with everyone, Queen Malina. Someone must know something."

"Thank you."

With a nod, the woman hurries away, and a weight presses on my chest.

Although I still haven't eaten, I turn for the main castle doors. Outside, the pile of fae bodies are burning, and more are still being added to the pyre. There's a group of my people gathered, watching the flames, perhaps trying to burn away their own inner agonies.

I start heading for Dommik across the way, but my gaze finds King Ravinger where he's securing a saddle atop his timberwing.

Changing course, my steps lead me to him. "Are you leaving?"

He doesn't spare me a single glance. "Soon, yes."

I wring my hands in front of me. "I know you've been gracious to my people, but I would ask more…" He snaps his attention across my face, and I feel the sting of it, though I don't back down. "Please, could you bring them with you? Allow my people sanctuary in Fourth Kingdom? I'll give you anything I can if you send timberwings to take them to your land where they can be safe."

"I'm not going to Fourth Kingdom."

"But—"

"I'm going to Seventh."

I rear back. "*Why*?"

He surprises me by actually answering. "Auren is on the other side of that bridge."

Shock pushes into me. "*Auren*? She's in… But how?"

"Doesn't matter. What matters is I'm going to find her." His fierce green gaze pins into me. "And do not be fooled, Queen Malina. There is no guarantee that even Fourth Kingdom will be safe, nor any of the others. I suggest you and your people lock your castle doors and hide inside for as long as you can. My power has given Orea a chance by buying you some time, but more fae could still come. This isn't over."

His words are a slap of cold reality. Of course we're not safe. Of course it isn't over. He made Highbell safe, but for how long will that be true? How much more blood will be on my hands?

He's right. Nowhere in Orea is safe. Not with the fae crossing in. Not with the bridge that *I* helped remake. A bridge that I'm responsible for.

"Take me with you."

The words blurt out of me, and across the courtyard, I hear Dommik's voice shouldering in. "*No.*"

King Ravinger narrows his eyes on me. "Why would I do that?"

Desperation creases into my face and pours into my tone. "Because I caused this. Because you're right—nowhere is safe. Not while that bridge is open."

"And what are you going to do in Seventh?" he challenges.

"I have magic now," I answer. "I will use it to block the bridge. To kill fae, if I have to. I'll do whatever it takes to stop them from coming in."

Around us, the courtyard has gone quiet, save for the crackling fire that's slowly gnawing its way through the bodies.

Ravinger watches me, his expression inscrutable, and though my heart pounds in my chest hard enough to hurt, I know this is right.

I can feel it in my brittle bones.

Dommik comes up to my side in a flash, gripping me by the arm and spinning me around. "Are you out of your mind?" he hisses. "You're not going back to Seventh."

"I have to."

"You fucking *don't.*"

"I do," I counter firmly. "I see that now."

"Queen Malina, you can't leave us!" one of my people cries, while murmurs break out amongst them. "We need you to protect us!"

A hard lump lodges in my throat at the looks on their faces. "This is the only way I can truly protect you," I say to her, to all of them. "So long as that bridge is open, Orea won't be safe. I need to at least try to stop them. For all our sakes."

"What will we do?" another man asks.

"You'll stay in the castle. King Ravinger used enough power that it's as fortified as it can be, and there are no fae in sight." They look at me with alarm, but I want them to understand. I'm trying to do this for them, trying to be the queen they deserve. "I must go so I can do everything in my power to stop more fae invading our land."

The dread is visible in their faces, but so is the slow acceptance of my stated truth.

I look over at Dommik, my eyes tracing over his features. "Protect them," I murmur.

His eyes flash and then he practically snarls in my face, though his words are only loud enough for me. "I'm going with you, you *ridiculous fucking fool.*"

"But—"

His hand tightens on my arm, and he pulls me closer so that I see his whole face beneath the hood. "Don't. Argue."

I press my lips together in a hard line.

"Fine. You can come with me to Seventh," King Ravinger suddenly says. "But I'm leaving in an hour, with or without you. I won't wait longer than that."

"Alright, yes, I'll hurry—"

"You'll have to find your own means of travel."

"There's one timberwing left," Dommik grinds out. "In the perch."

Relief pushes through me. I'm lucky it didn't flee when the fae arrived or get saddled up with Kaila's entourage.

Ravinger nods, his gaze narrowing on my face. "And you can try what you will with the bridge to keep the fae out, but you won't get in my way, is that clear?"

The underlying threat is sharp enough that I feel it jab against my skin.

I swallow hard. "Yes."

"Fine. One hour," he cautions before leading his timberwing away.

I share a look with Dommik and with my people, all of us shouldering this heavy silence together. Trying to bear the implications of what's to come.

Yet despite their dread, their anger, their fear, I know this is the right path.

And after a lifetime of wrongs, it's time I changed directions.

# CHAPTER 20

## AUREN TURLEY

My eyes have adjusted to the dark.

I sit tucked in the corner of the cell with my legs crossed, back braced against the walls. Above me, the green window has gone black with the night.

I've discovered it's not really a window. It's not made of glass, but something else that refuses to break. I know—I've tried. I'm sure other prisoners before me have tried too. Which makes me wonder why they put it there in the first place. Probably for false hope.

I wonder if it's made other prisoners go mad.

But that won't happen to me. I won't let it. Even with this feeling that writhes within my skull. Even with the things that wriggle through the tunnels in my mind.

I have to keep stopping myself from delving a finger into my ears to try to scoop the sensation out. I've made them raw already, scraped with my filthy nails and left to scab. I had to bite my nails down just so I'd stop scratching.

Sleep comes in tossing fits. Thinking makes my head pound. And being confined in this cell makes my eyes twitch and my teeth grind because I *hate* this feeling of being caged.

But I don't lose control. I don't waste my energy on more fits. I focus, as often and for as long as I can. Though sometimes I jerk awake, unsure of where I am or how long I've been out, confused all over again.

The three small marks gouged into the floor help me keep track of the passing time. I'm not sure it's very accurate, but I've tried to make a mark every time I get food, which, admittedly, isn't often. Apparently, traitors don't get three meals a day, and sometimes not even one. Especially not after attacking a guard and trying to steal his sword.

But while it's not a perfect system, I need those marks. I can't trust my mind, and I certainly can't trust anyone here. They say I've been in this cell for a long time, though I don't think that's true. They say I'm a traitor, but it feels like *I'm* the one who's been betrayed.

I'm going to figure this out. And I'm going to *get* out.

I focus on the hunk of fleshy yellow fruit sitting in my palm. I've been trying to rot it for hours, but the magic doesn't reappear. Hasn't at all, not since that piece of bread I molded.

My eyes flick to the floor. Right next to the leg of the bed, in a neat little pile, are the bread's blackened crumbs.

With renewed determination, I pull my attention back to the fruit, my fingers sticky and stained from its juice. "Come on…"

I stay hunched, teeth gritted, urging the magic to come up.

But nothing happens. Just like it hasn't for the past three meal trays.

It *did* though. The proof lies in those clustered pieces beneath my bed.

I needed to keep those molded bits visible so that I don't forget it really happened. Because whatever Una is doing to me is making my mind jumbled and my truths harder to see.

I know that magic was real. Just like I know there's something crawling in my head. Una can say there isn't, but there *is*.

I feel it. Feel *them*.

Like they know I'm thinking about them, the things suddenly squirm, making my neck crick and my skin shiver unpleasantly.

I want these fucking things *out*.

I curse at my hands, at my magic, at this gray cuff around my ankle.

Although I don't remember all the details with perfect clarity, I know I released power and rotted the bread. I know my hands went slick with dots of liquid gold while I was furious and lashing out.

Even though I'm not screaming and pacing, it doesn't mean I'm not angry. That anger is still there, waiting just below the surface. It's the silt beneath the sea. The sharp teeth beneath the rabid foam.

But there's something stopping it from rising up. Something more than just this cuff at my ankle. I just don't know what it is. I don't know why I was able to do it in the first place. Or why I'm here.

*Why can't I remember anything?*

Panic starts to spiral in my gut, but I can't let it. I can't be swept up, or I fear I'll drift away completely.

So I keep trying. For hours.

I lose track of time within the confines of this cell. Lose awareness of everything else but what I'm trying to do. Of the magic I'm trying to call.

*I feel it there, so why won't it come?*

The green window begins to peel back the night, and

daylight lightens the cell. It paints a lawn across my floor. Grass growing where roots can't sprout.

Gritting my teeth, I squeeze my eyes shut.

Focusing. Grounding. Gripping myself from the inside with a forceful clutch.

"I am Auren Turley," I whisper.

I know that with innate certainty, and so long as I have this truth, I can find the rest.

I *will* find the rest.

And I think the key to doing just that is piled upon the floor in decayed crumbs.

Closing my eyes, I take a deep breath and forget about being trapped. Instead, I embrace the calm tingle of morning as the sunlight breaks in. In meditative quiet, I rummage through the deepest parts of me until I uncover my festering fury.

It's ready, just waiting for me to call to it.

So I do.

I let it warm me, and as soon as I tap into it, the burn begins to spread. Surprise catches my breath, but I force myself to focus. My shoulders snap back, jaw tightening, teeth biting.

"I am Auren Turley," I say, firmer, louder this time.

It doesn't matter that there's no one but the dark to hear. I say it again. And again. I let the warming ire heat my words until they singe my lips.

Within that flaming mantra, I think of the way that rotting power felt. The way it streamed from my slick palms and infested the doughy lump.

I call to it. *Demand* it to answer.

A blackened root suddenly surges out from the shadows deep within my core. It stretches from a burst-open seed that's already begun to sprout, and I feel it sizzle and bead.

Then I sense it—the telltale presence of power.

The cuff at my ankle tries to dampen it, but my liquid gold takes the weight. Distracts it.

Allowing the rot to break free.

My eyes snap open, mouth parting in thrill. Black lines reach up from my palm like searching stems. They latch onto the pulpy fruit, and instantly, the yellow begins to darken. The sticky skin begins to collapse. Mold spreads around it, freckling it with spoil and sucking it dry.

My heart pounds with heady excitement.

*I did it.* The rot came back.

But now, the true test begins.

My pulse trills with exhilaration as I toss the fruit away. Then I pinch my fingers around one of the rotting roots sprouting from my palm. Without hesitation, I pluck it out of my skin…

And shove it into my ear.

I inwardly beg. *Please work.*

The magic wriggles for a moment, like a fish that doesn't know which way to swim. My eyes slam shut, and I screw my face up in determination as I will the magic to do my bidding.

I feel the rot slither in.

Pure grit. That's the only way I'm able to stay sitting down, to keep my focus instead of jumping up and yanking it out of my ear in a panic.

The sensation is horrible. Shiver-inducing. My fingers curl into fists as it starts to make its way deeper. As it travels further.

Chills scatter down my arms, and my entire body shudders. My neck cricks again, though I try to hold still. Even though it feels awful, I don't let myself stop, even when my anxiety doubles, triples, and I shake all over.

*Keep going…*

My back molars grind so hard my jaw aches, but the pain is a good way to distract from the sensation as the rot travels deeper.

As it breaches my brain.

I feel the things there writhe and dig, feel them leaving caverns through my mind and eating away at my memories.

And I tell the rot to *attack*.

The magic swarms, latching onto one of the worm-like creatures. As soon as that happens, a collision of magic bursts in my brain, making me see stars.

I'm thrown physically back from the crash of power against power. I fall, hitting the ground hard, though I barely feel it.

I feel everything inside so much more.

The intruder in my head screams, and the sound is like a wailing wind I think I've heard before. The screeching scrapes against the walls of my skull, making me convulse against the filthy ground.

It fights, tries to flee, but the rot seizes it anyway.

In seconds, my rooting ally constricts around the invading worm and withers it to a pulp. Instantly, memories spew up from its disintegrating corpse like they've been sprung from the satchel of a thief.

The memories fall like rain, pooling in the gaps and crevices that have been burrowed through me. As they fill, I get a scattering of memories that bury back in my depths where they belong.

I see myself being dumped in this cell. See Una pressing her bony fingers against my dazed form. See me being dragged there and the palace's courtyard filled with soldiers. It all flows in backwards.

My mind makes connections just as the scenes burst behind my eyes.

Ludogar, murdered. Emonie's ear butchered. Wick knocked unconscious. I remember their names, their faces.

What were we doing here? Why were we captured?

*Vulmin Dyrūnia.*

A flash of the symbol from the ring Emonie passed to me. Of a broken-winged bird…

Wick, Emonie, Ludogar.

Then another name whispers in my ear.

*Lyäri.*

The restored memories jolt my eyes open just as the root in my head withers away, utterly spent. I sit up from where I was sprawled on the floor. I'm panting, covered in sweat and shaking from the rush of adrenaline.

It worked. It actually *worked.*

And while I let myself celebrate this victory, I feel more of those things still writhing. Still tunneling.

How many are there? Dozens? Hundreds? Just how many memories have they eaten their way through? What else have they stolen?

The rest is still out of reach, poked through with holes. But now that I've gotten my first taste at my lost memories, I want more. I want them all.

I realize when I glance at the window that there's no soft glow of daylight left. My cell is darkening, nighttime dragging in as my stomach bottoms out.

What felt like seconds was actually *hours.*

It took me that long to destroy just *one* of those things. Who knows how long it's going to take to get rid of all of them?

I wipe at my sweaty face, trying to wipe away my anxiousness too. I try to call more rot, but it doesn't work, and I had a feeling it wouldn't. But I don't let it discourage me, because now, I know that I can do it.

One by one, for however long, I'll rid my mind of these tunneling worms.

Because I am Auren Turley.

And I'll do whatever it takes to save myself and break free.

# CHAPTER 21

## QUEEN MALINA

My arms are coiled around Dommik's waist, his cloak a pincushion of frost as it ruffles between us.

The breakneck pace we've been keeping is nearly enough to give me whiplash. There's been little time for rest.

Ever since we crossed out of Sixth, Ravinger has been like a man possessed, speaking little, focus fixed, intention clear. I didn't want to be left behind, so we had no choice but to keep up.

Dommik is furious with me, though he seethes in silence. His dark eyes dart toward the rotten king every time we stop. When we eat, we chew on food and thoughts, while I keep swallowing down my dread.

Yet we've reaped the culmination of our pace, because we're nearly to the ruins of Cauval Castle now.

This close to the edge of the world, everything's gone gray, as if the voided space between our realm and the next has spilled into our sky. The sun, wherever it is, seems to only skim the horizon, never setting and never quite arcing up either. Just trapping us in this perpetual drab dusk.

It's been said that this part of the world always did like to mutiny against both night and day. I remember old texts stating that it once took Seventh Kingdom five years to see a night sky. Then they were trapped in it for months before it finally tempered itself.

"We're dropping."

Dommik's voice blows with the wind, his head turned to look at me over his shoulder.

I nod, tightening my grip around his waist as our timberwing follows the lead of the one ahead. Ravinger starts our descent, cutting through the gray clouds until we break free and the land becomes visible once more.

Below, the landscape is a scrollwork of invasion.

Littered along the cracked and gaping ground, army tents border the entire area around the ruins of Cauval Castle. The bridge itself looks like a dammed river, with fae soldiers bunched up around the snowy entrance like it's their own personal gathering spot.

Dommik nudges our timberwing, lining up our beast with Ravinger's until we're side by side. "We should pick a spot to do some reconnaissance!" Dommik shouts over at him. "Then we'll come up with a plan!"

Ravinger glances over for the barest of seconds. "I already have a plan."

Without warning, he drops away, his timberwing nose-diving toward the ground.

"Dammit," Dommik hisses as he pulls up on the reins, making our timberwing circle the air. "What the fuck is he doing? He's going to get himself killed!"

I watch Ravinger's tense shoulders that carry the steady weight of his rage, and I shake my head. "No. He won't."

Right now, he's untouchable, fueled by more than just his ire.

He sweeps his timberwing down, veering toward the castle, and it doesn't take long for the fae to look up and notice him. Shouts ring through the frosty air, and bolts of flame are thrown at him.

Fools.

The timberwing dodges easily and lets out a roar, not even slowing its descent. Then, a second before crashing, the beast swoops up parallel to the ground, and Ravinger leaps off the back of the bird.

The very moment his boots land in the snow, power expels out of him with great force. Even from up here, I feel its scrape of deathly charge as if it runs through the air like lightning.

Black roots twist and mangle through the tents, through the soldiers, through the ground itself, exploding out in every direction. The snow browns, the tents collapse, the soldiers bloat and buckle.

So quickly. His power kills so much, so *quickly*.

More fae try to put up a fight, tossing magic in his direction. Green clouds of mist blow toward him, snow moving like waves ready to slam into him, and levitating objects are thrown his way.

None of it touches him.

He has an eerie, innate ability to sense the threats, and his magic hits them before their attempt can even come close. Rot drops them, making the soldiers succumb as their bodies decompose while they still live.

Their screams butcher the air into agonizing pieces.

"Gods…" Dommik says as we both stare at the destruction below.

It started so fast and ends so quietly.

Roots stretch out for hundreds of feet, spreading over the

RAVEN KENNEDY

already split earth and spilling down into the cracks. Bodies lie prostrate and still, crumbled like discarded branches hacked off from the trunk. Even the ruins of the castle have rot lines stretched up its crumbling gray stone with a promise of poison.

When Ravinger's timberwing lands next to him with a screech, I nudge Dommik. "Let's go."

My assassin pauses for a moment, as if he doesn't want to get close, and I don't blame him for his hesitation. When our timberwing descends to join the rotten king, we land with generous space between us.

Dommik helps me down, and then I head over to Ravinger, eyeing his back as I walk warily forward. I'm well aware that one needs to use caution when approaching a predator from behind.

"King Ravinger."

His head turns to look over his shoulder at me, and I can't suppress the gasp that passes my lips. He looks terrifying, his black veins thicker than before, stretching up his neck and pinching against his cheeks. The gray scales along his cheek shimmer with a sharp outline of gold, looking even more defined than before, and his eyes flash a deep green, almost iridescent.

He looks utterly fae, and utterly menacing.

Eyeing his sharp spikes, I clear my throat and look around, the stench of the bodies already permeating the air. "Everyone is dead?"

"Everyone here. But more will come," he says, jerking his head in the direction of the bridge.

My gaze follows his line of sight, skipping over the grisly scene that leads to the fog-cloaked bridge. "I'll make sure they don't."

"Do what you will to blockade it," he says, and I see a hint of his fangs as he speaks. "But don't get in my way when I'm using it."

I swallow hard at the viciousness. "I won't get in your way."

Who really could?

He turns and walks over to his timberwing and starts running his hand down its feathered neck. The intimidating beast tucks his head toward him. Ravinger murmurs something to it, and the bird blinks and listens, as if it actually understands. It rumbles in response, showing its teeth for a moment before huffing. Ravinger gives it another stroke and then unbuckles its saddle, letting it drop to the ground.

Dommik and I exchange a look.

Then, Ravinger turns back to us. "Argo is staying behind. He'll be going back to Fourth."

I eye the bird warily.

The king turns and starts walking toward the bridge, and I follow, with Dommik by my side.

We track over clotted snow, passing by twisted, horrific corpses that make acid rise in my throat and threaten to spill. I sway on my feet, nearly stumbling, but Dommik grips my arm.

"Don't look."

It's a hard command to follow, for the dead lie everywhere. Yet I lift my gaze and keep it on the bridge instead, not allowing my eyes to drop to the ground again. I blindly trust Dommik as he maneuvers us over every obstacle, whether it be a fallen fae or split earth. It's so unnervingly quiet here, even the wind seems to be sucked toward the haze ahead.

My body shakes as we approach it.

We near the edge of the world, where snow and ice give way to a void of nothing. Where the land simply stops against thick sheets of mist.

And then my eyes fall onto the bridge of Lemuria. A path of gray dirt suspended in the air, with nothing below or above to support it. At its mouth, two intricately carved white pillars act as its threshold, with a stretch of splintered rope that extends from each one.

We come to a stop in front of it. The bridge's length disappears into the fog that drapes over it like an eerie shroud. A colorless tongue spat out of a murky gullet. It chews me up, making me burn with bile.

The unhealed slices along my palms where I willingly gave the fae my blood start to sting. Throb. Shards of ice collecting along the gashes like sharp-edged scabs.

Is it the proximity to the bridge that makes them ache so, or is it only in my head? In my own guilt?

As if he can sense my distress, Dommik comes up and slips his gloved hand into mine. The supple leather sticks to my frosty grip, and he curls his fingers around my stiff ones until they finally stop shaking enough that I can grip him back.

A few paces in front of us, Ravinger stands and stares down the length of the bridge in silence. His black-clad form is all leather and spikes, onyx veins against pale skin.

Even without a crown, he looks like a king, for he stands proud and powerful. He looks into the endless eye of the unknown path, and he does not glance away from it.

He does not waver.

If it were me facing that bridge, knowing I needed to walk it, I don't think I'd have the courage to cross it. I don't think I could face myself in that fog.

Dommik and I are silent spectators, anticipation as thick as the snow beneath our feet as we watch him. Then he moves, taking a step toward the bridge.

His timberwing suddenly lands in a spray of snow with a keening cry.

Ravinger turns around and faces him, his expression stern. "No, beast. You have to stay."

It lets out a low snarl.

The king goes forward, but instead of disciplining it, he

strokes its neck, saying something. The bird's snarl lessens, eyes blinking. Ravinger sets his forehead against the beast's, and the move is so...soft. So unlike anything I've seen from this man before, that it actually shocks me more than the countless corpses at our backs.

To see this side of him is almost unnerving. It feels as if we shouldn't be watching this private moment between them.

He murmurs something under his breath again, and the timberwing whines.

The king steps away, expression going firm and tone now full of command. "Go, Argo." The beast rumbles, but Ravinger shakes his head. "You can't come with me. Go back to Fourth. That's an order."

It growls savagely, and my grip on Dommik's hand tightens enough to hurt.

"Go!" he orders, making Dommik and me both flinch at the crack of sound.

The timberwing opens his maw and roars.

I stagger back, but Ravinger stands firm, not moving an inch even with those sharp teeth only inches from his face. Then, with one last growl, the timberwing turns and shoots up into the sky, heading in the direction of Sixth Kingdom.

It's only because my eyes quickly dart back to Ravinger that I catch it—the muscle in his jaw jumping, the tic as he grinds his teeth.

That's regret he's chewing on.

It makes me understand immediately. The snap of command wasn't impatience or even anger at his mount not following orders. It was the only way he could get his loyal beast to go. For while Orea is far from safe...crossing the bridge into a fae realm is infinitely more dangerous.

This time, when Ravinger turns toward the bridge and starts walking, there is no interruption. He goes past the pillars, entering onto that endless gray path. It feels like an ethereal, otherworldly sight to see him walk down it.

My eyes burn from lack of blinking, but still, I watch, unwilling to miss a single second.

He goes steadily, his lone, dark visage entering the fray of the fog. He walks the path alone, and he does not stop.

He does not waver.

King Ravinger walks down the bridge...

And is swallowed by the vaporous void.

# CHAPTER 22

## SLADE

The bridge to nowhere was aptly named. There is no *place* to be seen in this thick fog. No location that could ever be tracked on this narrow stretch of dirt.

Before it was connected to Annwyn and our realms were tied together, this bridge was probably never-ending. Perhaps the first Oreans who ever walked upon it are still in the nowhere, walking.

But despite the way it looks, I can tell the bridge is connected. I can scent it. It's faint, bogged down by the wet brume, but the unmistakable, unforgettable smell of Annwyn is hinted in the air.

My steps are muffled as I stride forward, my pace steady, my determination rigid. The prints of thousands of other boots are crushed into the dirt, evidence of just how many soldiers have crossed through.

For Orea's sake, I hope no more come. If they do, Queen Malina will have to deal with them.

As I walk down the bridge, my magic starts to feel muted. My sleeves are rolled partially up, spikes exposed. Though my black veins are receding little by little, and my skin itches uncomfortably, like something is scraping against me.

I don't dare try to force my power up, just in case. But the feeling of my power being stifled is unnerving.

I ignore it.

I'm not surprised that the bridge does strange things, but I know better than to try to fight it.

Hopefully, Argo will follow my command and go back to Fourth, because I don't want him anywhere near this twisting fog. The bridge is no place for a timberwing. There's no telling what could happen in this voided air should he try to fly through it.

Centuries ago, when Seventh Kingdom tried, the beasts never returned. I'm not willing to risk Argo. And even though the bridge is reconnected now, there's also no telling what I'm going to find on the other side.

So although he was anxious and furious, not wanting to part ways, it's too dangerous for him to come with me. And I promised a very special little girl that I would keep him safe and send him home, so that's what I did.

This journey must be made by me, and me alone.

There are whispers in the fog, but I know better than to stop and listen to them. I know better than to linger.

I keep my mind focused on Auren instead. Thinking of her with every breath I take. My hand delves into my pocket every so often to feel her piece of ribbon, and with every step, our pair bond thrums.

*go go go go*

I'm coming.

I keep going until there isn't just a hint of Annwyn in

the air anymore. Instead, it nearly chokes me. Its scent is nostalgic. Bringing up memories I mostly tried to forget, and yet, I suck it down with gratification in its familiarity.

I'm not sure how much time has passed by the time I finally reach the end of the bridge.

Slowly, the fog lifts away, like fingers gripping the corner of a curtain and pulling it back. My heart pounds as the last of the haze dissipates, and I brace myself for what's to come.

Then, I step off the bridge and into Annwyn.

A place I never thought I'd return to.

My body responds, recognizing the land. Something prickles my fae senses and pumps through my body. I look down, seeing my blackened veins return, spreading down to my wrists, my power no longer feeling like it's being held back.

I take in a breath, and my lungs feel fuller. Like this is the air the fae are supposed to breathe. My gaze disperses, taking everything in, noting the light purple sky. But that's where the beauty stops, because the land I stand in is…

Dead.

That's the only way it can be described. I thought the dirt bridge was drab, but this is different. The ground here looks leeched. Like all the color has been drained and the land has bled out, leaving it nothing but a pale, lifeless corpse.

Clumps of grass are withered and white, the soil equally colorless and parched. There are hills and mountains and a city clustered in the valley near a wide-mouthed riverbed. It should be a land of beauty.

It's not.

Because that mountain, those hills, the city, even the river, it's all dead. Ashen and unnatural. Not a single tree or blade of grass grows. Even the river has run dry. As if it was all scorched and then never recovered. Never came back to life.

Even from here, I can see the city looks empty, the buildings decrepit. There's nobody in the streets, no sign of movement or life. Beneath the sweet scent of Annwyn's air, there's a lifelessness that reverberates up from the ground and hangs down from the clumped, pallid clouds that are stilted in the sky.

This is a different sort of death than my own power, but something just as fatal has taken root here. And by the looks of it, the infection is spreading.

Miles away in the distance, I can see the expected vibrant fields and green forests and impressive mountains. But this disease of the land is encroaching on that lush, colorful beauty. And the death stems from here, right at the entrance of the bridge.

Seventh Kingdom was destroyed when the bridge was first broken. It wiped out the entire kingdom and every living thing that resided there. But it looks like that destruction landed on both sides, because Annwyn seems to have suffered the separation too, with this crawling, growing death.

A death that feels angry. Feels *hungry*.

Maybe this is why the fae have repaired the bridge and invaded Orea. I never heard about the land dying. It doesn't seem like it's happened recently, either. I can sense how far the death reaches, and something tells me it's been happening for a long time.

My expression hardens. It appears my father broke far more than just the path from Annwyn to Orea. Not that I'm surprised. He enjoys breaking things.

Things *and* people.

Pulling my grim gaze from the dead city, I try to determine which way to go. Then, something in the distance catches my eye. A column of rising smoke.

"So there is life amidst the death," I murmur.

Different paths branch off, though they're nothing more

than simple trails in the ash for me to follow. Taking the one that leads toward the direction of the smoke, I start walking.

The smoke is my guide. I follow it without stopping, and as I get closer, I see its source.

A bonfire in the middle of an army base camp.

There are only a few dozen fae gathered here. Maybe the rest were all sent across the bridge to wreak their havoc.

I'll be wreaking havoc of my own.

The soldiers are eating and drinking around their fire, while others haul supplies from carts to the buildings.

The ashy soil has stuck to my boots from the walk over, littering me with the land's dead grime. But the base camp has obviously been subject to its assault for much longer, because the roughshod buildings are completely covered in it.

Thick layers of the dust coat the wooden buildings, the splay of tents, the supply carts, and the soldiers themselves. The large fire burning at the center of the camp seems to burn duller too, as if it has also gotten clogged up with the loam.

One good thing about it? The ground keeps my steps muffled, choking out the sound as I near. None of the gathered fae around their fire notice me until I stop just beside the wooden building and spook them with my voice.

"I'm looking for someone."

The soldiers snap their heads in my direction, some of them startling so badly they spill their bowls of muck.

"Who are you?" one of them asks, confusion on his face.

I send a rift of rot toward him. A single reaching root that stabs through the ground and then splinters up his body. He jolts, stunned, while black poisoned veins erupt through him.

In a blink, he collapses on the ground, skin browning with rot, and the soldiers around him jerk up in surprise.

"What the fuck?"

One of them aims magic at me. Some sort of blip of light. I don't know what it does. Doesn't matter either, because I kill him before his magic can reach me.

Some of them hurry to grab weapons strewn around haphazardly. "Don't do it," I say in warning, but they move to attack anyway, and I'm about to shove out more magic when something unexpected happens.

Behind the gathered soldiers, a new group suddenly appears. Swiftly and silently, they start to charge.

Though, not at me.

The soldiers are caught completely unaware as the group attacks them.

With a battle cry, the new group pounces, the element of surprise allowing them to cut the soldiers down before half of them even realize what's happening. I watch the slaughter, head cocked as they clash.

The attackers aren't in the same attire as the soldiers. Each of them is dressed in civilian clothing, yet they move with practiced uniformity and obvious combat training.

Swords clash, axes hack, while blood and shouts stream out. Magic bursts from one of the attackers' hands in a cluster of something that resembles teeth. The sharp projectiles hit the marks of the soldiers, digging into eyes, jabbing through jugulars, while around them, their comrades fight savagely.

Within seconds, the skirmish is over, every soldier dead on the ground.

I look around. "I have to admit, I'm impressed."

The group snaps their attention toward me, and I shake my head at the male who starts to move forward, his sword dripping blood. "I wouldn't," I warn.

He has a thick red beard and bushy brows, with a scar at the side of his neck. His assessing gaze flicks over me before moving to the body I rotted. "You're no Stone Sword."

"No, I'm not."

The group gathers closer, only a handful of them, yet what they lack in numbers, they made up for in pure brutality. The fae with the magic hangs his arms loose at his sides, though I can see another one of those clusters gathering in his palm. He takes a step toward me, fingers twitching.

"You try to aim those little teeth at me and I'll rot yours from your mouth and then crush your jaw with my fist."

He goes still, glaring at me with eerie yellow eyes.

The first fae raises his hand, as if telling the others to hold. "Why did you kill one of the Stone Swords?" he asks. Perhaps he's the leader of this little contingent, though there's nothing on his clothes to mark him as such.

"Because they didn't give me the information I asked for."

He exchanges a look with the others. "And what information is that?"

"I'm looking for someone."

"Here?" he says in surprise, motioning around the anemic scenery. "This place is cursed. No one comes here. Except the Stone Swords, but that's a recent development," he says, kicking at the corpse of one of the soldiers.

I arch a brow. "And who are you?"

The group seems to tense all at once, sharing silent exchanges. The leader steps forward, hand still gripping his sword. I watch him and the rest like a hawk, ready to kill in a single blink.

But instead of attacking, he lifts his hand. "This is who we are," he says as he knocks a fist at his own chest. "Do you wear the symbol?"

My gaze drops down to the pin fastened against his tunic. It's no bigger than the pad of my thumb. The circle of metal has a bird in the center, one wing clearly broken.

"We wear the sigil of the Vulmin Dyrūnia."

I frown at the words. They sound familiar. I think I've heard them many years ago.

"The—" My mind snaps with long-forgotten knowledge of the ancient fae language. A language I haven't studied since I was a boy. It creaks in my head like entering a dusty room whose door hasn't been shoved open in decades. Struggling to break open the rusted locks, I shake my head. "Vul—light?" I question.

"Vul*min* Dyrūnia," he repeats, stressing the suffix of the word. "*Dawn*. It means dawn's bird."

Something shifts in my chest. Makes me pause.

"And what exactly is that?"

"We are the resistance to the tyranny of the Carricks."

Now I remember. I heard my father mention them before, but they were spoken of like vagabonds. Petty criminals.

"So the Vulmin oppose the invasion that's happening in Orea?"

He looks around his group, some of them whispering tensely, and he rubs a hand down his beard. "So it's true?" he asks. "Carrick mobilized the army, but we didn't know… The bridge?"

"Rebuilt."

He swallows hard. I see another go pale.

"And what are you doing here? You say you're no Stone Sword, and yet, you seem to know quite a lot." His hand tightens on his sword. "How do you know this?"

"Because I came from Orea."

This time, some of them gasp, but his brows fall into a frown, eyes skimming over my spiked arms and pointed ears. "You're no Orean."

"I didn't say I was. Now, either help me find out what I want to know, or move aside. I can promise you, attacking me won't end well for your group."

He pauses, as if weighing his options. I see his eyes drift

over to the soldier I rotted through. "Who are you looking for?" he asks.

"Her name is Auren."

The change that overtakes them all is so tangible, so solid, that I wouldn't be surprised if I could reach out and grab it. They rear back, and instant recognition flares in their expressions. It makes every muscle in my body tense.

They know her.

"The Lyäri Ulvêre?" he asks, his tone sharp, eyes narrowed.

My mind trips over more of that old fae dialect. I try to pick out the roots of their meaning. *Lya*…was it…shine? Gleaming? No. Wait. It's—

*Gold.*

"You know her. How?" I demand, my tension mounting.

"All Vulmin knew of her before, and soon, every fae in Annwyn will," he tells me. "She was our golden girl gone who was found…only to be lost to us again."

My stomach twists and my spikes pulse. "What the fuck does that mean?" I seethe out.

When he doesn't immediately answer, rot thrusts up from the ground and starts crawling over everyone else in his group. He whirls, watching them struggle as poisoned death invades their bodies like constricting vines, only these wrap beneath their skin.

In a flash, I'm before him, wrenching him by the collar and forcing him to look at me. "Tell me right fucking now or I will kill you all."

"She is lost to us," he chokes out, scrabbling at my one-handed grip. "King Carrick has her."

My lungs constrict. "Why the fuck would the fae king want her?"

He looks at me like I'm mad. "Why would you ask that?" he spits out, jerking in panic as some of his people start to fall onto the dirt, choking on the rot that begins to fester their organs.

"Tell me!"

His fearful eyes swing back. "The Carricks hate them! They tried to kill her entire line. But she survived somehow. Auren Turley is the last-birthed heir, and she's come back to us to finally unite Annwyn and end the Carricks' reign."

I drop him, and my power jerks back from the group. They cough and sputter, but my ears are drowned out with the clicks of connections that snap into place.

*Turley.*

I know that name.

My magical and combat training took precedence once my power manifested, but my father still ensured my schooling continued as was appropriate for the son of a noble.

I remember briefly learning about the Turleys. For a handful of centuries or so, they ruled Annwyn. As my tutor taught it, they ruled until abdication, when the favored Carricks took over. The Carricks had political connections and they were stronger and better liked by the people.

My great-grandfather became a rich man when he backed the first Carrick's rule. My father became a famous one when King Tyminnor Carrick called for him to aid in breaking the bridge.

"I thought all the Turleys died a long time ago," I finally say.

"That's just what they wanted everyone to think. To forget them. But when that still didn't work, when the Vulmin still followed them...the Carricks slaughtered them during an attack. We thought their line was ended for good when the golden girl disappeared. Most people believed she was dead. But she came back. They say she fell through the sky."

*Fell through my rip.*

My emotions battle inside my chest, my heart pumping

wildly. Auren is here. I knew it instinctually, but to hear it confirmed fills me with fierce hope.

"But the king has her?" I ask, my excitement cut through with the sharp edges of worry.

He nods. "That's what we heard."

My rot pulses with my spiking panic. If King Carrick has her, and the Carricks hate the Turleys...

"Where does your allegiance lie?" he asks pointedly.

"With her," I answer. "My allegiance lies with *her*."

Everyone from the group has gotten back to their feet, though they don't dare move. The fae with the teeth magic keeps the cluster clutched in his fist, but his hand trembles. "Our allegiance is with her too," he tells me, his voice raspy but full of challenge.

"Then I'll let you live," I reply.

Tension and wariness builds between them. "Who is Auren Turley to you?" the leader asks.

Who is she?

She's fucking everything.

"We are a päyur. So stop fucking wasting my time and tell me where she is," I grit out.

Another ripple of shock goes through the group. "You are fate bonded?" he breathes.

My jaw locks. "*Where*?"

He obviously senses my growing impatience, and he's smart enough not to test the limits. "The capital kingdom. It's not far. Two days' walk. One if you're quick."

"Then I suggest you be quick."

His bushy brows lift and he looks around as if at a loss. "We can't take you. We need to see where the Stone Swords have gone."

"There's nothing to see on the other side of that bridge. I killed them. So you're taking me." There's no room for argument.

He blanches. "Who *are* you?"

"Slade Ravinger."

"Slade…" His eyes dart to the side, as if he's reaching into the corners of his mind, trying to pull out a recollection. "I've heard of a Slade…"

The yellow eyes of the magical fae go wide, and the clump of teeth in his palm falls at his feet. "Wait…Slade *Cull*. You're The Breaker's son? You're…The *Rot*?"

I haven't heard anyone call me that in a very long time.

When I don't contradict his statement, the leader's face goes pale. Everyone in the group seems to lose their breath.

My reply is stabbing, stark and quiet. "*Ravinger*. Not Cull."

I see him visibly swallow.

"Auren Turley is paired with *you*?"

"Yes," I reply, knowing exactly what they're all thinking. How can the fates have bonded her to someone like me?

But there's something they don't understand yet, though I have a feeling they will soon.

There is *nothing* I won't do for her.

Auren is life. I am death. *That* is why the goddesses paired us together.

She is the gleaming power of light, and she needed her antithesis to stand at her side. Because she's the golden sun of warmth and growth, while I am decay and darkness, with a magic that comes from the deepest core of the earth.

There is no growth without rot. There is no sun without the dark sky. And there is no me without her.

But even if we were never paired, it wouldn't matter. Because I would have made her mine, whether the goddesses deemed it or not.

And I'm going to find her.

So I turn and start to walk. "Let's go."

# CHAPTER 23

## AUREN TURLEY

I jerk awake at the sound of footsteps in the corridor, and I go instantly alert. Shooting a quick glance over, I see it's daytime. I slept hard after shoving that rot into my ear and destroying one of those tunneling worms. The effort it took was staggering.

My teeth grind together as a fresh wave of anger etches in. But this anger energizes me. Fuels me. My head might be aching, but I'm furious enough that I can shove that away and ignore it. They've meddled with my mind, taken my memories, and locked me in this dungeon.

Anger is just the tip of the iceberg for the emotions I feel.

I push out of the bed and get to my feet, my expression hardening as I stand against the wall. I hear a guard speaking to someone, and then a key is shoved into the lock. My muscles tense in preparation as the cell door swings open, and Una walks in.

The guard slams the door shut behind her, and she glances at the bed. All I see is her chessboard brown hair set off against her scalp until she swings around. Blue-striped eyes lock onto me, and her thin lips turn down into a frown.

Probably because for once, she's not finding me lying on the pallet bed, drenched in sweat and confusion, weakened and hollowed out. Instead, I'm standing with my hands fisted at my sides and my spine so stiff it feels like I could snap at any moment.

The door clicks shut behind her, and my wrath locks into place.

"*You*."

She pauses, her gaze running over me with assessment.

"Your magic is stealing my memories." My tone is rigid with rage, fingers itching to reach forward and claw out her eyes. "These things in my head, they're from *you*."

"I don't know what you're talking about," she replies, and it's the wrong thing to say.

I brace my stance. "Take them out," I demand.

Una's eyes narrow, the stripes in them thinning. "You're confused," she says with a patronizing tone. "Sit down on the bed so I can work on healing you."

I tip my head back and laugh coldly. "You're the one who's confused if you think I actually believe you're healing me." My gaze bears down on her. "Take. Them. Out."

I'm not going to tell her again.

She should stumble back from the harshness of my words, but instead, she digs in her heels. A tense moment passes, both of us staying completely still. Like animals sizing each other up, determining who will attack first.

She stupidly decides she's going to be the one to do it.

My vision flashes with the reddened haze of rage.

I don't care that I'm still spent after using the rot. I don't care that the ankle cuff is weighing down my magic. I don't even care that parts of my mind feel like they've been scooped out with a spoon.

All I care about is making her pay for what she's done to me. For trying to strip me down and hollow me out. For digging up every memory and leaving me a barren void of holes to lose myself in.

Because she failed.

Even if I know nothing else, I know who I am.

My name is Auren Turley, and I am stronger than *her*.

Instead of flinching back, I pounce, my strength overpowering her own. I shove her hard against the door, making her head smack against the stone.

She tries to scream, but I slap my hand against her lips and knee her in the gut at the same time. Air punches out of her mouth against my slick palm, but she doesn't try to push me away.

Instead, she reaches up and clamps her hands over my ears. Pinches her fingers in, like she's ready to shove in more of those gluttonous grubs to feast on my mind.

How *dare* she.

She doesn't have a chance to fill me with her magic. My fury reaches a fever pitch. We lock eyes, and within those blue bars, I break free.

That rot that I managed to utilize, the source that grows from the hatched seed in my chest, instead of rushing up to rot *her*, it does something else.

It reaches out and rouses a gleaming beast curled in my center.

Animalistic malice rises as the creature cracks open its eye, awakening with a roar that rattles my ribs.

I stagger back from the force of it, and Una rips free from my hold as blinding light suddenly surges through the room.

Through *me*.

I don't have time for confusion or panic. Don't have time to wonder what's happening.

My back arcs with sudden pain, like a blade dragging down and splitting skin. Then my shirt tears open, that light breaking through behind me into dozens of rays that stream like ribboned sunlight.

Una's eyes go fearfully wide, and I look over my shoulder, following her gaze. Long, satiny strands drenched in liquid gold with veins of black move around me, their lengths twisting and lifting.

I can feel them.

Stemmed from my spine and tugging at my skin in a comforting familiarity that makes tears spring to my eyes as they move. There's a moment where I pause and wonder what they are, but then one word pours from the ledge of my tongue at the cusp of a memory.

*Ribbons.*

*They're my ribbons.*

My elation is even brighter than the glow that surrounds them. I look down at the gold that drips from their lengths onto the floor. Like the flexing of fingers and extending of arms, I'm able to control the drenched strands at my back with ease, and I sigh in relief at the feel of it. At the heady strength that emanates from every strand.

In her shock, Una stands frozen, back plastered against the wall, shaking all over. "What *are* you?" she asks.

My gaze stabs into her. "Really fucking pissed."

She parts her lips to cry out, but my ribbons are faster. They come around and snatch her up, tying around her like a puppet sewed to strings. Each one wraps around her limbs and winds around her neck before gagging her gaping mouth.

Una fights and screams around them, expression pleading and terrified, but we're well past that now. Caught in my tangle, she has nowhere to go. The creature inside of me roars with the demand for retribution.

My ribbons go sharp, tightening and tensing…

And then the veined strands snap her like a twig.

Una's body goes slack, and the ribbons let go, making her drop to the floor in a heap. Breathing hard, I wait for several seconds, wondering…hoping…

But none of my other memories come rushing back.

*Dammit.*

Part of me expected her death to kill off her magic, but it didn't. Apparently, her magic doesn't end with her. Frustration boils through me and I stare at her lifeless body with hate.

Fine.

I roll my shoulders back and flex my ribbons. I'll just have to rot the memory worms myself. I'll destroy them one by one until I rid the infestation and get back everything she tried to take away.

I can do it. I *will* do it. No matter how long it takes.

Glancing over my shoulder, I study the rippling, winding ribbons, and the sight of them makes my anger dissipate. The strands curl around my outstretched hands, ready to grab hold.

I can't stop the smile tipping my lips as I slide my fingers through their silky lengths and over the dribbling gold that smears down their edges. I tug at them, counting every one, reveling in the feel of them.

They're another part of me that I've gotten back on my own. First, the flashes of memories with the rot, and now this.

My truths are growing, and I repeat them now, from last to first, letting them cloister within this cell and stick to my skull.

Ribbons.

Emonie, Wick, Ludogar.

Vulmin.

*Lyäri.*

Rot power.

Gold power.

A light in the dark.

My name is Auren Turley.

Now that I have these truths, these certainties, I'm famished for more. It's an aching hunger that gnaws through my gut, pushing for the need to be fed.

But what's even more insistent is my desire to get the hell out of this cell.

My eyes snap down to the shackle around my ankle—this thing that somehow dampens my magic. If I'm going to get out of here, I need this gone. And I saw what my ribbons did to Una. They're *strong*.

I send a group of them down to the cuff, and they slip beneath the polished gray surface. My ribbons wrap around it, again and again, going taut in four different directions. Then, they *pull*.

The cuff snaps open with a crack, releasing a puff of gray dust in its wake. The pieces fall to the floor, spilling out dirt, and I instantly feel its absence.

I rub at the raw spot on my skin with a sigh of relief. The burdensome weight that draped over me like a heavy, sodden blanket is now blessedly gone. Just like the itchiness that kept crawling over my skin.

Excitement and victory thrum through me, making my heart beat faster. Straightening back up, I lift my hands and then call to my magic.

It answers instantly. Easily.

Gold drifts up, puddling into my palms in such a familiar way. With a smile, I turn my hands over and let the liquid metal start to pool upon the floor. It comes out steadily, like someone's turned on the tap of a tub to fill it with a rush.

Soon, there's enough that it floods the room, and the black veins of rot run through its gleaming surface. I'm able to make it easily drag Una's body away from the door with a flick of my wrist. Then I rip off my filthy and torn shirt that's barely hanging on, and liquid gold starts to slither up my torso.

It forms in layers over my body, molding like a chest plate of golden armor that's marbled with black roots. It spreads down my arms like gauntlets next, ending in feather-tipped shapes above my wrists. I glance down at my handiwork, feeling the armor connect at my back, leaving spots for my ribbons to feed through, and I'm filled with pride.

The easy control of this magic, the way it flows out of me, it's like a dam knocked away from the river. To be so powerful is *invigorating*. The gold feels as familiar as the ribbons do, and because of that, I feel stronger than ever.

Because this is *me*.

I call more rot, making it sprout up from my fingertips, ready to see if I can rot straight through the door, but suddenly, I hear footsteps again. It must be the guard, coming to let Una back out.

*Perfect.*

The slosh of gold on the floor gathers in front of me, and I wait, breath paused, eyes unblinking.

The beast within me is ready to hunt for more prey.

When the cell door opens, the guard freezes. His eyes go so wide I'm surprised they don't just pop right out of his sockets and roll around on the floor.

"You lock yourself in here while I walk away, and I won't kill you," I say, giving him a chance.

He doesn't take it.

A warning call tears from his throat. His cry cuts off as my magic moves up to his lips and clogs his throat, choking off the sound. He falls into the room, hands tearing at his mouth, fingers plunging into the glutinous metal. But no matter how hard he tries, he's unable to clear his airway.

"You should've taken me up on my offer," I tell him as my ribbons grip him by the ankles and pull him out of the doorway.

I step over his soon-to-be corpse but then pause when I spot the Vulmin ring that Emonie gave me. My ribbon snatches it off the floor, and I pluck it up and shove it into my pants pocket while the guard lets out one last choke.

Then I exit the cell with my ribbons twisting at my back and my gold trailing behind me like a gleaming beast slithering along the floor.

But the true beast about to tear through this place is *me*.

# CHAPTER 24

## AUREN TURLEY

The dungeon's corridor is made up of a half wall of thick gray stone. Gripping the top like a balcony railing, I look over and down, taking in the multiple levels that seem to sink below at least four stories.

*Just how many people does this king keep imprisoned?*

Sparse echoes and muffled shouting come from somewhere in this labyrinth, and there are blocks of light that filter in through large open grates at the ceiling.

Even with that fresh air filtering in, the smell in here… well, it's not great. I guess that's to be expected. I probably don't smell great either.

"Hey!"

I snap my attention over to another guard hurrying toward me. "What are you—"

My ribbons surge forward and wrap around his body before slamming him into the wall. I hear a woman scream in alarm behind the thick stone door of the next cell over.

My stomach seizes, eyes pinning to the guard. "Who's the prisoner in that cell? Is it Emonie?" I demand, anxiousness tearing into my chest.

He sputters, and I let a few of the ribbons loosen from his neck so he can answer. "Fuck. You," he spits.

I let out a growl of frustration, and my ribbons toss him into my cell with Una and the other dead guard. Then my gold grabs the bottom of the door like curled knuckles, and shuts it firmly in place, locking him in.

Breathing hard, I look around, trying to come up with a plan. The size of this dungeon is overwhelming, but I can't waste any time. I need to look for Emonie and Wick. If I can find them, I can ask them questions, and maybe more of my memories will untwist.

I need to check the cells.

Hurrying over, I stand in front of the door where I heard the muffled scream. But there's a whole row of doors beyond too, and even more in the levels below. I need to be quick and quiet.

My gaze flashes down to where the gold sloshes at my feet, and an idea catches fire. Instantly, I direct some of my magic to narrow into a thin strip, and then let it sink into the lock of the door. As soon as the keyhole is plugged, the liquid metal hardens into the key.

*Please work...*

The key turns and the lock disengages. Excitement swells through me, and a smile bursts on my face as I shove the cell door open—

But it's not Emonie inside.

The female fae is hunched in the corner, her face pale, clothes mere rags. She looks at me with fear.

"I won't hurt you," I tell her. "You're free to go."

She's too scared to move with me standing here, so I head for the next door, my gathered gold streaming behind me. I stop and look down the line at the cells, and then I send my magic flowing all the way down the corridor. Once it reaches the end, the gold breaks off into several small cords, each one delving into the locks and snicking open the doors one after the other.

I stride forward, the golden armor over my torso and arms moving with me like a second—although far stronger—skin. I push the door open, searching for Emonie and Wick, but I find a skeleton inside instead, skin and sinew long gone.

At the next, there's an old fae lying on his bed who looks at me with awe. "You're free," I tell him before hurrying on.

The next cell is empty, and the one after that too, but the following one holds a male with dark hair, and my heart leaps at the sight. Until he turns to fully face me and I see it's not Wick.

This male has a different shaped face, and there's a thick barb that's been stabbed through his tongue. It hangs from his mouth, leaving him wordless. The female I find in the adjacent enclosure takes one look at the open door, leaps past me, and sprints away.

I don't know why any of these prisoners are in here, whether it's rightfully earned or not, but I don't care. I'm not leaving until I check every room.

Rumbled footsteps come running, and I tense as more guards appear around the corner, probably tipped off by some of the escaping prisoners. I glance up, sizing them up, my magic readying. All six of them lift their weapons and charge toward me, their steps echoing throughout the dungeon.

"Where are Emonie and Wick?" I call.

The one at the front shouts back, "Arrest her!"

My lips pull into a sneer and my ribbons tense. "Go ahead and try."

Their steps falter when I start sprinting toward them instead of running away. I see their expressions flash with concern just as I release my gold on them like a pack of wild dogs.

The guards might as well be holding their dicks instead of swords for all the good it does them. My gold races ahead and tackles their group to the ground, feasting on them with molten retribution.

As soon as they hit the floor, the gold solidifies, hardening their bodies beneath the shell. Their screams are muffled under the thick layer, bones knocking against the hollow trap.

Looking around, I see I've cleared this entire section of cells, but I'm not leaving yet. I might not know exactly who Emonie and Wick are or who they are *to me*, but I know that we were arrested together. And I know that Emonie gave me that Vulmin ring, trying to help me remember.

I have to find them.

So I work meticulously. Thoroughly. As quickly as I can.

The inmates crawl out from their dark spaces like rats flooded from their holes. Some look like they're near death, others like they've only just been tossed in. Most take one look at me and my coiling ribbons and run the other way toward freedom.

But none of them are the two people I saw in my memory.

I pull at my tangled hair in frustration. *Where are they?*

A sinister thought enters my head, telling me they could be dead already, that I could be searching for them for nothing. I bat the thought away. I refuse to believe that until I see it with my own eyes.

But my frustration continues to build with every cell I open. Luckily, I get to take it out on the next two groups of guards that I run into. After they refuse to tell me any information, I leave them as gold lumps upon the floor.

When I open the very last cell on the very bottom level and find another woman who isn't Emonie, I lean against the wall, panting hard, sweat dripping down my temples.

*They're not here.*

I slam my hand against the wall in frustration, teeth gritted and eyes burning.

"Lady Auren?"

I jerk upright at the call, looking at the woman as she gets up from where she was crouched in her cell. She has a mark on her cheek, like someone took a whip and lashed it across her face.

I study her, hoping recognition will flare, but it doesn't. Tears fill her eyes as she rushes over to me, her bare feet scraping against the floor that's now littered with flecks of gold.

"Lady Auren," she pants again, reaching forward to grip my hand. "You saved us!"

My eyes flick up to her ears that are blunt and rounded like mine. My brow furrows, thoughts tripping over the divots in my mind. The information I seek is *just* out of reach.

Even though I don't recognize her, she recognizes me, and it makes a fragment of relief fit into me. It might be strange, but her knowing me makes me feel more real. To her, I'm someone. I just have to figure out exactly who without making myself vulnerable.

The look on my face must show something concerning, because she pauses and peers at me, her hands dropping mine. "Are you alright?"

"How do you know me?" I ask carefully, my tone guarded.

She blinks. "You…you came to save us. At the manor. Remember? I first saw you in the village."

My thoughts stall, her words not bringing up any connections. "Do you know who Wick and Emonie are?" I ask, changing tactics.

Her face screws up in thought, and she shoves away limp, oily clumps of hair. "Are they the ones who came with you?"

"I...think so?"

She shakes her head. "You three weren't brought down to these levels with us."

"Us?"

"More of us Oreans, yes. They didn't kill us all," she tells me, tongue darting out to her cracking lip as it quivers. "Though I think that's only because they wanted to use us against you."

Oreans.

I feel my brows draw together in a frown. That word is just at the edge of a memory...

The woman's eyes drift over my shoulder, and then she suddenly runs past me. "You're okay!"

I watch as she hugs another man, and then five others reunite with wet eyes. I'm guessing these are the Oreans she mentioned. Each of them is marked with their own evidence of abuse, and each of them has blunt ears.

My mind continues to delve, trying to grasp hold of something tangible, but the memories slip past my fingers.

"Lady Auren, where is the king?" one of the men asks.

I turn to him and shake my head, remembering the crowned man with the cold eyes. "I don't know, but he better hope he's nowhere nearby," I say, vengeance coating my words like the gold that coats the ground.

The man frowns.

My fingers press against my throbbing temple, a grimace slipping past before I can stop it. My mind might be muddled, but my body is speaking to me crystal clear—I'm run down and my strength is waning.

"Time to go," I say once I drop my hand. "Anyone know the way out?"

A male fae with pointed ears lifts his hand. "I do."

With a nod, he starts leading the way. We head down the long corridor and up the slatted stairs to the higher levels. My legs burn from exertion, and the rest of the inmates struggle too, but escaping imprisonment is quite the motivator.

Once we reach the top, we walk down a tunnel, coming out from a cave that's right beside a thundering waterfall. The water gushes down off the cliff we're inside of, kicking out spray as it falls far below us, and hits the awaiting river with churning mist.

We walk along a narrow path, the stone slick beneath my bare feet. We wind up and away from the cave, and then we reach sunlight and grass and fresh air. I take a deep breath, reveling in the freedom, my ribbons basking in it as much as I am.

The prisoners who've slunk out with me all stop and stare, eyeing everything warily while I look around. There aren't any guards lying in wait, no soldiers here to try to shove us back into the dungeon. Instead, trees stand sentinel, proving just how arrogant the king really is. How much he's underestimated me.

The forest is quiet, blue sap bleeding from the trees' white-trimmed bark. Their green leaves hang heavy, like unrolled balls of wool bunched up along the branches.

Through these timber troops, I can see we're on a tall, flat circle of land. The rest of the landscape sits in a sunken valley, with a river fed from this very waterfall. But my eyes drift to the grand palace straight ahead, standing right at the center of this plateau, with a mountain at its back and the valley below.

The palace is ethereal. Smooth white stone like quartz bolts upward in graceful arching lines. The top of the turrets bloom with geodes, and the sloping rooftops glitter with a spray of crystals that sparkle in the sunlight. Hundreds of stained glass windows decorate the lengths of every wall, like the building is adorned with elaborate pieces of jewelry in every color.

"Never thought I'd see Glassworth Palace," the woman

with the whip mark murmurs. "Now I want to get as far away from it as I can."

I know what she means. It might be beautiful to look at, but there's a danger that lurks beneath the allure. An elegant mask over a monstrous face.

Spinning in a circle, mind spinning with me, I know that I need to get these people safely away from here. I need to get somewhere we can rest and wait, where I can use more rot magic to exterminate the infestation in my head.

"I know who you are."

The sentence startles me, making my heart skip a beat. Turning, I take in a stooped fae male. He has an iron collar around his neck and rotted teeth lining his gums. "You're a Turley, aren't you? That's why you're gold. You're that dead golden girl the Vulmin always told stories about." He looks me over, glassy eyes bulbous inside his thin face. "Didn't think you were *actually* gold."

That word again—Vulmin. That's what Emonie and Wick are. I think that might be what I am.

"And the Vulmin are…"

His brows lift in surprise and he looks around at some of the others. "The rebellion, of course. Never was a part of it myself… For all the good it did me," he adds bitterly before spitting at the ground that leads back toward the dungeon. "Still got locked up for ten years, didn't I? This monarchy will arrest anyone who even thinks of looking at the king sideways."

"I need to get you all away from here," I say, looking around again.

"We need to get off the plateau," a different male fae says, lips hidden behind a beard that's twisted in thick, matted knots. He points with his pinky, for he has no other fingers on his hand. The nubs left behind all look like they've been hacked off long ago, the skin uneven and stretched. "This way."

The other Oreans look at me in question.

I glance back at the palace. The urge for me to find Emonie and Wick is riding me hard, but I can't storm the place. I don't even know if that's where they are. All that's clear right now in my memories are their names and faces, and the king who imprisoned us. I need to find somewhere I can get my bearings, find out more information, and formulate a plan.

"Lead the way."

The prisoner starts limping ahead, while I take up the rear. I keep my senses peeled for any guards, and keep looking over my shoulder at the palace. It feels like its stained glass windows are watching me.

We walk for about five minutes past the waterfall before coming to another spot on the perpendicular cliff. A path has been molded into its side like a raised scar against skin, leading all the way to the bottom where the valley sits.

Some of the inmates shoot me worried looks, and I have to admit, the steep, narrow path does look daunting. But unless we want to go toward the palace, this seems like the only way to go.

I give them a comforting smile while I swallow down my own unease, and then we start to make our way down. There's only a splintered wooden rail that's more rickety than secure, so I keep my hands at my sides and stay with the inmates who have a harder time walking, just in case one of them slips.

We're somewhat exposed here against the cliffside, but I can't help but appreciate the view. There's a large, beautiful city down there in the valley, amongst the tall trees that must be at least a hundred feet high. Their deep green leaves offset the lavender sky, and their branches and trunks twist like plaited hair.

Orbs of light glitter from the trees, casting a glow below of purples, blues, and yellows that must look beautiful at night. The white stone buildings themselves have swooping architecture and intricate designs with arches and steeples, glass atriums and draping eaves.

From here, I can see glimpses of covered stone roads and half-moon bridges that arc over crystalline canals fed from the waterfall. The river branches off into different directions, feeding both forest and city.

"What is that place called?" I ask.

"Lydia," a fae female answers. It's the first sound I've heard her make. "Annwyn's capital city." She says nothing more, though she eyes it with distrust.

When we get to the bottom, I think everyone breathes out a sigh of relief. The road isn't far from the river that churns out from the falls, and down here, beneath the canopy of the branches, the air is brisk and fresh. We go beneath the thick trees to get out of the open. By the angle of the sun in the sky, I think it's nearly midday.

Everyone is antsy to keep going. The question is, which way?

"That road'll take you right to the city, but you're mad if you go anywhere near there," the male fae says before pointing at the collar that rings his neck. "Stone Swords are everywhere in the city, and they'll take one look at you all and toss you right back in a cell. I'm heading *away* from Lydia, and you all should too if you have half a brain."

He glances at the Oreans. "And cover those ears of yours. Oreans aren't welcome in this part of the kingdom." He turns and hurries away, heading deeper into the trees. Most of the other prisoners do the same, swiftly disappearing from sight.

"He's right," the Orean woman tells me. "We should go."

A distant swell of cheering comes from somewhere in the city then, making me stop and turn. I try to look through the thick trees, but I can't see any of the buildings from here.

Another burst of noise rises from Lydia, and I frown,

feeling something in my gut wedging its way in. I understand that everyone else wants to move in the opposite direction as fast as they can, but...I can't seem to force my feet away. Something is telling me not to.

"Lady Auren? Are we going?"

Without my memories, I don't have a lot to go on, so I can't ignore my intuition. Something is screaming at me to go toward the city instead, and I have to pay attention to that.

I turn back toward the woman and glance at the other Oreans. "You all stay hidden here," I say. "I'm going to check the city."

Her eyes widen. "But it's dangerous."

"It's okay," I tell her with a smile. "I'm dangerous too."

# CHAPTER 25

## COMMANDER RYATT

At the top of Cliffhelm's defensive wall, I stand here at Fourth's outpost with all of my soldiers as we overlook the icy land of Fifth Kingdom below.

Far off to the right, I can barely spot the familiar shadows making up the serrated mountains of Deadwell. Those lone peaks in the distance seem just as bare and inhospitable as ever.

Except this time, they really *are* inhospitable. No one's left in Drollard Village. The rip's closed and everyone's been ripped away right along with it.

But straight ahead, the landscape is far bleaker.

Ribbons of darkness cut through the snowy ground like an open gash sliced through fair skin. The fae army travels forward like a spreading infection, ready to make the land bleed. Ready to make *everyone* bleed.

There are thousands of them. My pulse hasn't stopped racing since they first appeared on the horizon.

I don't know what's happened at Breakwater Port on Fifth's shore. But with these numbers, it seems that Judd and King Thold were successful in cutting them off and not allowing access to any Orean ships.

But that means that the entire fae army might be heading here, toward Fourth's border instead.

Considering how much distance they've already traveled, they're moving fast. But it makes sense. This is a complete invasion. We were expecting them to behave as Oreans would and secure their newly won kingdoms. But it's clear that's not what they're here for.

The last thing the fae are going to do is slow down and fortify, since that would only give us more time to fight back and defend our world. They don't care about holding Highbell and Ranhold. They want total control over *all* Orean land. They want to eradicate us.

And we're here to try to stop that from happening.

This outpost's sole purpose is to guard the border separating Fifth from Fourth. It's a bulky fortress built on a sheer cliff, with a protective wall of slanted stone that stands up against the wind. Thick guard towers are on either side of the outer wall, and there's a threat of sharp spikes spread along the base. Every inch is made from the black stone from our mines and always covered in a layer of frost.

Lu and Osrik stand on the wall on either side of me, all of us in our fighting leathers and full armor. Black metal encases our bodies, with strips of brown leather crossed over our chest plates and Fourth's sigil engraved right in the center.

To my right, Lu rests her hand on the hilt of her sword, fingers wrapped around the twisted wood. Even out here, Osrik has his arms bare, with only straps of leather wrapped around his biceps.

I don't know how the bastard doesn't get frostbite. At least I convinced him to wear a damn helmet this time.

Although, I think that might actually be because Rissa glared at him when he started to refuse it. When he put it on, she nodded victoriously and then breezed back inside the barracks.

I think she's good for him.

Roland, one of the soldiers I brought with me, lets out a low whistle. "They look like a cursed river. Like sludge seeping this way."

My gaze follows the parade of marching fae. They *do* look like a curse flooding in. Thousands of them are filing toward us, and the twenty-two of us on this wall are all that stands between them and the border we're trying to defend.

Every one of us knows that our odds are impossible. That in all likelihood, this is a suicide mission.

For most of my adult life, I've wanted to be an army commander. Wanted the chance to step out of my brother's shoes and lead these soldiers by myself, *as* myself.

Now, I'm standing here doing just that, and this responsibility is the heaviest thing I'll ever have to carry. Because this isn't just a matter of life and death—with war, that's always the case.

What's at stake here is our entire *world*.

Which is why I've poured everything I'm capable of, everything I've learned, into planning the strategies of this single battle. Because in many ways, the fate of Orea will be decided *right here*. In the empty land straddling the line between Fourth and Fifth.

Despite the enormity of the task we face, these soldiers choose to stand here with me. Lu and Osrik choose to stand here with me, giving me their trust.

And that means more to me than they'll ever know.

With a pang, I think of my mother. Wishing I could've seen her and that I could go into this fight knowing that she's alright. Wishing I could know what the hell happened to Slade.

Fucking *praying* that I can make it out of this and find them both.

The chilled silence drags on as we watch the fae seep in, and I hear the scrape of my soldiers' boots against the stony ground. Hear the creak of their leathers cinch every time they shift. All while the icy air chaps our faces and spits frost at our feet.

Finally, one of the soldiers to my left, Gideon, breaks the grim silence. He has magic in his veins that makes him unbelievably quick despite how bulky he looks. His form often blurs when he moves. "You know what I hate the most about battles?" he says.

The soldier next to him, Varg, picks at his teeth with a hare bone. He's got a superstition about that damn sliver. If he's not picking at his teeth with it, he's got it clamped between his lips. He says he's never lost a battle while it was in his mouth. But that could have something to do with his own power, which is the fact that his own bones are unbreakable. So while he's well into his fifties, he's a damn formidable fighter.

"Gettin' your shitty face all scarred up?" Varg muses around his toothpick.

Gideon glowers at him. "Fuck off, I'm still prettier than you. And no, it's the food. Battle food is either the dry shit we carry in our fuckin' pockets all day or this charred shit we gotta catch ourselves that's barely got any fat on it and tastes like smoke. Just once, it would be nice to camp next to a fuckin' tavern."

A few of the soldiers chuckle.

"Or a saddle house!" someone else calls, and that earns even more laughs. Lu and I exchange an amused look.

"Well, what I hate about battles is having to dig our own shit hole," Varg jokes.

"Or having to piss in the snow and watch your dick shrink from the cold," another soldier says.

"Hate to break it to you, but your cock is always that small!"

More and more of them toss out replies and chuckles.

"Nah, the worst is this heavy ass armor."

"The helmets we gotta wear."

"Fucking marching. I hate marching."

"How 'bout you, Tyde? What do you hate the most about battles?"

Tyde has his gaze pinned straight ahead, the only soldier whose serious expression hasn't cracked.

For a long moment, he doesn't answer, until finally he says, "The wait."

His words and quiet tone sober everyone in an instant.

"You rush to make plans and defensive strategies. Rush to prep and pack and travel. Rush to arrive at the place where you're going to take your stand. But when all that rush is over, all that's left is *the wait*," he says, still looking ahead at the enemy army. "The wait is like a night that won't end. You keep waiting for the sun to crest, but it doesn't. So you gotta keep watching the horizon, because you know it's coming, you know it's inevitable, but the anticipation chews up your nerves and spits them back out. You don't know when the wait is going to turn into something else. But it will. And that something else is really just death. It's death that we're waiting for. We just don't know if it's ours or theirs." He pauses. "That's why the wait is the worst."

Silence stumbles between everyone. A clumsy presence that elbows its way in. It grows bigger, taking up all the empty space and infiltrating our thoughts.

"Changed my mind," Varg finally says, breaking past it. "I think the worst part of the battle is the fucking conversation."

Laughter snaps out, ease and humor returning to the soldiers. I don't blame them one bit for embracing it. Both this joking distraction or Tyde's sobering words. Everyone faces battles differently. Everyone has their own way to cope.

If they *didn't* find that way to cope, none of them would still be standing here. Because the army that marches toward us is unfathomable. There are so many that they don't even seem real. Just some fae trickery to scare us away.

But they *are* real. And all we can do is stand here and watch death approach. Because Tyde is right. That's what marches toward us.

Above us, the clouds begin to cough out chunks of snow in fits of hacking thunder. Below us, the fae get closer.

"Tyde?" I call.

The serious soldier is still staring straight ahead, frost gathered at his blond lashes. He's ready to give me his report immediately. "Stone armor like river rocks. Swords seem to be made of some sort of stone too, maybe granite, though I wouldn't imagine they'll shatter as easily, so don't count on that."

His magic is sight. He can focus his teal-eyed view, the distance yanking in until he can see something as if it were right in front of him. A very useful power for spying or cataloging an incoming army.

"No weak point at the neck," he goes on. "They have mesh from helmet to throat, and they've got stone gauntlets on their forearms. Under the arms are open, but it will be difficult to make that strike unless they're lifting up their sword or shield. Their legs are the most vulnerable," Tyde says, head cocked as he considers. "Though not the knees—those are plated with stone. The flesh of the thigh is open, their gloves and boots are simple leather. Helmets protect their skull and ears, but eyes and mouths are open for archers."

Everyone takes in Tyde's assessment with rapt attention, cataloging everything he said. It could be a matter of life or death.

"Anything else?" I ask.

"Some are wearing different insignia badges, though I don't know what they depict, but they're only worn by a few of them."

"Could be rank," Lu offers.

I nod. "Could be."

When we see the front lines of the enemy start to round the bend of a shallow dune of snow, I feel everyone tense.

"They're passing the crevice now," I say, though they can all see it for themselves. My heart gets stuck in my fucking throat as I watch.

I've calculated this. I've run through the scenarios a thousand times. We need the first battalion of fae to cross that part of the land, just like they're doing right now. Then, I need them to shift slightly.

It's time to draw them slightly away from Cliffhelm.

I look down the line of the wall. The tension has heightened, and although everyone made the voluntary choice to be here, I wonder if a part of them wishes they could run.

I wouldn't blame them.

There is no room for error. Every single one of us knows that.

"I know we are facing an inconceivable mission," I say, taking in each grim face. "But victories can still be earned even when the odds are stacked against us. The truth is, we aren't here for ourselves. We're not even here solely for Fourth. We're here for *Orea*. Because this is *our* home. *Our* land. And we won't sit by and let the fae take it." Their heads nod, backs straightening. "So we will stand our ground until we can no longer stand."

Determination fills in the cracks of their rupturing edges, replacing it with the purpose for our perseverance.

"We stand our ground," Lu repeats, her tone firm.

They all say it back in response, a few of them slamming a fist against their armor-clad chests. "We stand our ground!"

"Archers, ready yourselves at Captain Osrik's order," I command, and thirteen of the soldiers nod, their bows already strapped to their backs along with their long-distance arrows.

Turning, I give Osrik a nod. "You got it?"

He gives me a menacing grin and cracks his knuckles as he glances over at the iron catapult built into the wall. He's the only bastard strong enough to man it by himself. "I got it. Fae will be flattened thinner than fucking flapjacks when I'm done with them."

I let out a dry laugh fueled more by nervousness than humor. Then I pat him on the shoulder. "Good luck, Captain."

He tips his head. "Commander." Then his eyes move to Lu. "Captain, give 'em hell."

"I don't give anything else," she says.

I look between them both, hoping this isn't the last time we're together. That we all make it out of this alive.

"Riders, with me," I announce, and then Lu and I start making our way down the slick steps, passing by the guard tower, with six soldiers accompanying us.

At the bottom of the wall, we pass the armory and head for the stables. Four timberwings are already saddled and ready, and we quickly mount—one rider and one archer per beast.

I situate myself on Kitt's saddle, and Tyde buckles himself behind me so we're back-to-back. As soon as everyone is ready, we leave the stables and launch into the sky. We take advantage of the low cloud coverage, quickly disappearing inside them, getting drenched in the icy mist.

We've traveled the distance of this flight four times during our practice runs, so despite not being able to see, I know exactly when to signal Kitt and the others to drop.

We tear through the frigid fog, and I spot the cluster of trees ahead. Not real trees. Nothing grows out here. These were forged with iron and spikes, built when Slade took the crown.

They're meant to deter—or at the very least split apart—an enemy army from this narrow junction so that they're forced to veer straight for Cliffhelm's base.

But today, we want them veering here instead.

I'm the first to land in the middle of the iron forest, the trees ten feet tall, and big enough to disguise our presence. I wait for the others to land, and one by one, we track the army's progress.

"How long?" Varg asks from where he sits on the saddle, back-to-back with Gideon.

Tyde hesitates, probably judging the distance between us and how quickly they've moving. "Ten minutes."

Turning, I lock gazes with Finley where he sits on top of his timberwing, and Maston who's buckled to his back with an arrow in his hand and his red beard coated in frost.

From the roster of magicked soldiers in our army, I specifically handpicked these two for this mission. Finley's black hair is braided down his back. Maston's cheeks are bright red from the windchill. But both of them have the same determined look in their eyes.

Right now, these two unassuming-looking soldiers are the most important people in this entire kingdom. Probably in this entire fucking world.

*Everything* depends on them.

"Ready?"

"Just like the practice run, Commander," Maston says with a grin.

Finley rolls his shoulders back and looks at the others. "Yep. We'll be back in no time."

My chest feels like I've got every stone brick in Cliffhelm weighing on me, but I don't let it show as I give them the order. "Just like the practice run," I repeat with a nod. "Go."

They both give firm salutes. "For Orea," they say.

Then, Finley yanks at the reins, and the timberwing lifts

them into the air. They disappear into the dense clouds as snow continues to flake down.

At Lu's back, Roland messes with the buckles around his waist. A bead of sweat drips off Gideon's temple. Varg flicks the hare bone between his teeth. Behind me, Tyde holds perfectly still.

I start to count the seconds.

Five minutes. If all goes the way it should, Finley and Maston should be able to land on the other side of the slope. Then they can make their way on foot, getting right where they need to be.

Hopefully, without being spotted.

Because if the fae see them, if they're shot down before they can get into position...

"Don't," Lu mutters on her timberwing beside me. I look over and meet her gaze. "They'll do it."

They *have* to.

If they can't, we don't have a fucking chance.

# CHAPTER 26

## COMMANDER RYATT

The anxiety between the six of us is palpable, like a thick presence that closes in around us. Because just like Isalee asked me, how can so few possibly stand against so many?

The truthful answer is, we can't.

Not numbers against numbers. Not sword against sword.

But we *do* have the upper hand with one single thing: We know this land. *I* know this land.

The fae have no idea how many times I've come to Cliffhelm pretending to be Rip as I ran training sessions. No idea how many times I've flown across this very border and gone straight to Deadwell to visit my mother and the other villagers.

I know everything there is to know about this strip of land between Fourth and Fifth. And while it may look like a vast, empty stretch of snow and ice, it hides a sinister secret.

I keep counting down the time in my head—two minutes already passed. Lu and I share a look. I know she's as tense as I am, but she's as stoic as ever. She always ensures her strength bleeds into the soldiers she leads. It's one of the reasons she's such a good captain.

"Gideon, send Captain Osrik the signal."

The bulky soldier grabs hold of a thick, twisted iron branch beside him. This tree is the tallest out of all of them, and a couple of days ago, we attached a strip of metal and glass at the top. Even in the dreary daylight, it's enough to cast a reflection for Osrik to see at the wall.

Gideon makes the iron shake back and forth, and even from the ground, I can see the reflection that the metal and glass casts off. After a few more seconds, he stops, just as there's the slightest tremble that travels through the ground.

An inhale sucks in, and my eyes fly to Lu's.

*The plan is working.*

My adrenaline spikes just as a wicked grin spreads over Lu's face. Every single one of us tightens like a coil. Ready to spring.

Now, it's time to reveal ourselves and hope like hell we can draw the fae toward us.

"Roland?" I call, looking over at the brawny soldier with deep gray eyes.

"On it, Commander."

He unbuckles from the saddle and jumps off, landing in the snow shin-deep. Then he leans over, reaches for his shadow on the ground, and yanks it up. Like it's a physical entity instead of just blocked light.

We all watch as he shakes it out like a fucking blanket and then starts ripping it apart and tossing it into the air.

Varg picks at his teeth, watching the shadow fragments as they stretch and flatten. When Roland stops tearing it into

238

pieces, they build and ripple, until he's made a good five dozen shadow figures that resemble his own silhouette. When he moves, they move.

"That's really fuckin' creepy, mate," Gideon tells him.

Roland smirks and looks over at me. "I think that'll do it."

"Alright," I say. "Then let's lure a fucking army."

Still on our timberwings, we leave the confines of the clustered iron and cross out of the tree line. Roland stays on the ground, moving his pitch-black shadow silhouettes, filling in the gaps, making it seem like there are way more of us than there actually are. His magic wouldn't work up close, but far away, it'll do the trick.

The instant we leave the cover of the trees, the fae spot us, their shouts clashing into the air. I can feel their gazes yanking away from Cliffhelm, brought here instead, to the line of twisting iron.

"Come to us, you fuckers," I mutter atop Kitt. She paws at the snow, talons scraping through the slush.

If this is going to work the way I've calculated it, we need their trajectory to shift toward us slightly.

Cutting my gaze toward Cliffhelm, I see Osrik has notched Fourth's flag into the wall, the black fabric snapping in the wind. It signals that the catapult is loaded and ready, but other than that, the wall looks empty while he and the others lie in wait.

I pull my blade from my sheath and lift it high into the air.

Then I let out a battle cry as loud as I can.

Everyone else joins in with me. Gideon knocks his fist against an iron tree, making that noise split the air too, and our timberwings open their mouths and roar.

We sound fierce. We sound threatening. We sound and look like we're more than six fucking Oreans and a trio of timberwings standing here.

And the fae...take the bait.

Their battle drums suddenly sound, and their front lines pivot.

Victory and adrenaline surge through my chest, and our shouts become even louder in answer. Their drums are caustic and unsettling, trying to gorge themselves with dissonant teeth, but we answer back.

*"We stand our ground!"*
*"We stand our ground!"*
*"We stand our ground!"*

Our own battle cry and the roars of our beasts make fresh bloodlust pump through our veins. The fae start to race toward us, as if they can't wait to crush us beneath their might.

Their front lines are so close now we can hear their shouts. See their faces. Feel the stomping of their running steps over an already reverberating ground. Their swords are raised, legs sprinting. They don't even bother with their magic. They want to cut us down by blood and blade.

*Good.*

They're getting louder, louder, louder.

Closer, closer, closer—

"Hold!" I order, watching them breach the distance, tracking the ground behind them… *"Hold…"*

Then, their army is right where I want them.

It's time.

I look over, voice raising. "Roland!" I shout.

Instantly, he jumps back onto Lu's timberwing and buckles himself in, his shadowed forms evaporating. As soon as he's secured to the saddle, I see the shift of snowy ground in the distance, and my heart gallops.

It's the sign of the second phase. Meaning Finley and Maston are doing exactly what we need them to do.

Elation fills me, pumping through my veins with a burst of energy.

I give the order. "Riders, lift! Archers, loose!"

Our timberwings launch into the air without hesitation, and as soon as we gain altitude above the iron trees, arrows shoot from our archers' bows.

Kitt aims straight for the rumbling clouds above us, making snow pelt my face. Behind me, I feel Tyde against my back, shooting off his arrows with wicked speed. The rest of our group is doing the same thing.

What can three timberwings do against an entire army?

Nothing.

Except make them look *up*.

So that with our distraction, they don't see how the snow has shifted. How the snowy dune they passed has flattened out. They've become so focused on us they don't notice how the top layer of snow has started to melt away.

Or that beneath it, the ground is actually riddled with lines.

Because while the fae may have the numbers, we have the land, and they have no way of knowing what I know.

I've spent a lot of time out here at this border...but so has my brother. Hundreds of trips over the years to this *very* spot.

To this piece of empty, frozen land where he's poured out all of his pent-up power.

He'd loose his deathly magic right here, partly to deter people from traveling near Deadwell, partly to protect our border, and partly just because he had to expel his magic.

Which means the rot he's dumped into the earth has accumulated. Decades' worth of rot amassed within Fifth's frozen soil.

The frigid cold and empty landscape has always helped hide it. And for the most part, the freeze has contained it.

Until now.

The fae can march upon us, but this is *our* ground. And our ground is *exactly* what Finley and Maston will exploit.

Both of them have very unique powers—it's why I

picked them. Finley works in our armory as a blacksmith for a reason. His touch can melt metal straight through.

Or…heat an entire area of snow and ice that's solidified my brother's rot.

And Maston? He can cause the earth to shake with a single stomp of his foot.

The plan was simple. Wait for the fae to pass a certain point, and get Finley and Maston to that slope of snow. Because there, they'd have the cover to land at that dune, where one of the largest clusters of rotted veins lies in wait.

Right there, where Finley's magic could melt through the icy ground just enough to free the trapped poison beneath. And then, Maston could tremble the earth to aggravate it.

To set it *free*.

Because just like we practiced with the smallest strings of poison near Deadwell, you can rid the freeze and shake the rot loose.

Which is exactly what happens right now.

I flinch at the sound, my hands tightening on the reins. It's like a stampede. Like thousands of timberwings blaring out an ear-splitting growl.

Then, the ground cracks.

Beneath the melting snow, the land suddenly splits open right beneath the middle of the rushing army. Instantly, hundreds of them fall in. Screams competing with the rumbling noises of the ground.

The melted snow reveals the thick brown and black veins running through it, and now that the land has cracked, it starts a chain reaction. Like yanking up the roots of a tree, it spreads, rupturing and gaping, filling the air with its deafening break.

From the sky, I pull Kitt around to watch as the snow shatters, splitting apart the panicking army, fracturing open and swallowing them whole.

My stomach leaps with a thrill. It's working. My plan is actually fucking *working*.

I can't help but grin as triumph pumps through my chest. Behind me, even Tyde lets out a cheer, breaking his usual quiet. "It's working, Commander!"

Somewhere, I hear Gideon answer with another whoop and Lu laughing, the sound traveling through the frost.

We have a chance now, and I'm not going to waste it. The front lines of the army are rushing toward the iron trees, so we focus our timberwings on following them. Tyde looses more arrows, his sight magic helping him make killing shots.

The ground at the middle continues to rupture, the snow giving way. It starts collapsing in on itself, further and further out. The stinking soil of slush caving in, pulling down hundreds of fae in its wake.

They try to flee, but their running steps get swallowed. Their hands scrabble at the disintegrating edges, but they drop into the festering depths anyway.

And the ground isn't done splitting.

The stench of rot is now exposed to the air and lets off its putrid smell of death as it spreads more destruction.

"Out!" Tyde shouts, alerting me that he's out of his arrows and he needs to grab the extras kept in the side saddlebag.

I level Kitt out so he can shift safely and fill his supplies, and I take note of Lu flying ferociously. She's letting her timberwing glide low to the ground, snatching up running fae before knocking them into their fellow soldiers or tossing them into the crevices.

Gideon and Varg are flying in circles, focusing their arrows on a group trying to run in the direction of Cliffhelm. But a thundering crash makes me jerk, and I whip around to see that Osrik has launched the catapult. The hunk of stone smashes into the ground, striking the fae retreating on the other side of the rift. Within seconds, Osrik is reloading and letting loose again.

I turn, searching the sky for Finley and Maston's timberwing, but I can't see them. They should be well off the ground by now, picking off fae with us. They should've been back up on their timberwing the split second the ground started to give way.

Worry slams into me, my shoulders tightening as I keep looking through the spitting snowfall, counting the timberwings dipping in the air.

I still don't see them.

"Fuck," I say into the wind as snow drops down thicker, coating Kitt's feathers.

Gripping her reins, I pull her around and lower, searching the slope where the worst of the rot disintegrated the ground. My breath freezes and I feel the blood drain from my face when I see that the entire dune where they would've been is just...gone. There's more than a three-hundred-foot gouge where that spot used to be.

I aim Kitt in that direction anyway, determined to find them, even though my gut is telling me they were already swallowed up. That they never even made it to the back of their timberwing again.

That there's nothing left to rescue.

"Fuck," I grit out again, dread and anger tightening my throat.

Kitt takes us closer, but a volley of arrows suddenly comes through the air in a downpour. We try to dodge, but one strikes Tyde right in the arm. Blood sprays out of him as he cries out in pain, his back slamming against mine as he jerks in the saddle.

"I've been hit, Commander!"

My nerves triple, the tension in my body bunching my arms and making my pulse drum. Another arrow nearly slices through Kitt, her chest only saved by the thick chained armor worn at her breast. Tyde flinches from her jerky movement, and his bow and arrows fall from his grip.

"Hold on!" I call over my shoulder to him.

Sparing a quick look down, I spot the group of fae shooting at us. They're on our side of the split, a dozen of them aiming arrows at our timberwings. Roland and Gideon manage to strike two of them, but we're outnumbered.

When I start to redirect Kitt, my gaze catches on black chest plates and helmets. Black—not the drab color of the fae's rocky armor.

*Maston and Finley?*

I try to see, but the snow is falling down faster, and I'm too far away. "Tyde! My left flank!"

Tyde strains to get a look in that direction, and my heart beats wildly.

"It's them. Stranded. Their timberwing's down. They're under fire and vulnerable." He gives the report through grunted gasps, and I know his arm must be hurting like a son of a bitch.

But I can't leave them out there.

Setting my sights on the dots of black armor, I direct Kitt their way, and she flies as fast as she can. As we get closer, my men become clearer, and I see what Tyde already did. Their timberwing, dead on the sliver of broken land beside them. They're surrounded by cracks that are far too big to cross. They're sitting ducks, using their dead bird as cover, but the fae attacking them are relentless with arrows.

We race through the slapping snow, my attention pinned in place, but my stomach drops when I see one of the men go down with an arrow at his neck.

Maston.

"No!"

Finley tries to get to him, but he gets struck down too,

making a furious roar tear from my throat. "Come on!" I yell to Kitt.

Suddenly, a ball of green light lobs toward us in a crackling streak. The blaze nearly slams into Kitt's neck, and she screeches, pulling up short, wings flapping wildly.

Tyde grunts in pain as he gets jostled again. There's another heave of light that nearly hits me, but Kitt drops at just the right time with a roar.

My timberwing then looks down at the ground, narrows her iridescent eyes, and *dives*.

"Kitt, no!"

I try to make her pull up, but she ignores my directions completely. She's locked in on her prey, too pissed to listen to me.

Another ball of green shoots at us, but she jerks to the side, avoiding it without stopping. Below us, the magical fae starts to throw another fistful, but when he realizes she's almost upon him, he shouts and tries to dive out of the way.

It doesn't work.

Mouth opening full of razor-sharp teeth, she swoops down, maw clamping shut over the fae's head and cutting off his scream. Kitt lifts in an arc, shaking the fae like a rag toy and decapitating him in the process. She tosses the rest of him away and flies back upward, circling, while the fae below us scatter.

Except for one archer that points his arrow right at her.

It happens slowly—like time is squeezed in a fist. I watch the arrow aim for her. I jerk on her reins, trying to move her, but her prey drive has overwhelmed her. She's listening to that instead of me.

She doesn't budge, doesn't move, even as I pull with all my might, the reins slicing into my palms. A bellow of warning tears from my mouth for her to turn back, but it's too late.

*I'm* too late.

The arrow hits with a sickening gush that makes my stomach drop, piercing right through her eye.

I shout out, my own voice clashing with Kitt's screech that abruptly cuts off. Her entire body goes slack as we begin to plummet, the ground rushing up at us while Tyde and I can do nothing but hold on.

"Brace!" I warn him, and then a second later, we hit.

We land hard, in a spray of snow and the cracking bones of my timberwing that also cracks something in me.

The fist around time lets go. Everything is so much faster and louder on the ground. The screams, the cracking earth, the catapults launching.

We're on a strip of narrow snow with gaping chasms on either side of us, and when I whip my head over, I see fae running at us, swords drawn.

"Tyde!"

Unbuckling myself as fast as possible, I tear myself free of the saddle and rip the sword from my scabbard as I leap off Kitt's back. Three fae soldiers are upon me in an instant, and I barely have time to meet the first's blade.

Raging grief over the death of my timberwing fuels my movements, and everything else empties from my thoughts except my need to kill.

Years of training and combat take over.

I block the fae soldier's sword attack, letting stone clang against metal. Another one of them tries to come at me from the left, but I drag my blade down enough to shove the first aside, and then kick him in the knee as hard as I fucking can.

He goes sprawling back, and I press in, swinging my sword at his neck and slicing through his throat before he's even able to get his feet steady. Spinning, I meet the other fae's sword again, circling him, pressing my advantage and blocking his strikes, remembering every single vulnerable part in their armor.

When he lifts his arms higher to block another one of my attacks, I yank the dagger from my waist and stab him in the exposed part of his underarm.

The second he falters, I grip my sword with both hands again and pierce him through his armor, at a weak spot right between two stones. He falls to the ground, and I pull my dagger out of him and turn, looking for the third fae. Fear flashes through me when I see he's moving toward Tyde.

Tyde, who still hasn't managed to unbuckle from the saddle, one arm useless with the arrow stabbed through it, holding his sword sloppily in the other.

With my hands flexing around my sword and dagger, I leap forward just as the fae manages to knock the weapon from Tyde's grip. With a cry, I hack into the fae's neck, teeth gritted, eyes full of fury.

Blood spews from the wound and splatters onto his helmet. He whirls around to look at me, but it's too late. I've landed the killing blow. His eyes go wide just before he falls to the ground, his blood staining the snow.

Slamming my sword and dagger back into their scabbards, I tug at the buckles and get Tyde off the saddle. He nearly tumbles down as soon as I release him, but I shove my shoulder under his good arm to prop him up. Then I notice the bloody wound at his side.

*Fuck.*

I whirl us around, realizing that just like Finley and Maston, I'm surrounded by gaps too wide to jump across with Tyde. Dread drenches my guts. The cracks on all sides of us are widening, the ground groaning and shaking, and my poor timberwing lies in a dead, broken heap while snow dumps down.

We're trapped.

"Leave. Me," Tyde coughs out, his body barely able to stay upright even with me propping him up.

"Fourth soldiers don't abandon each other," I snarl out, hating myself for not being able to get to Maston and Finley in time.

I lost them. I'm not going to lose Tyde too.

The ground trembles beneath me, nearly sending me crashing into Kitt. I look down in alarm, my hands shaking.

This piece of land could give way any second.

I underestimated how much rot would spread and break, and I never accounted for any of us being on the ground, because I knew that was a guaranteed way to fucking die.

A chunk of ground just ten feet away from us falls away, and panic freezes my limbs.

We're fucking stuck. I can't get Tyde across these gaps, and every time I turn around in another direction, the crevices widen, threatening to drop away completely.

Cold sweat breaks over my skin, my ribs freezing in place.

Suddenly, I hear a voice shout down. "Hey, fucker, you miss me?"

I'm stunned for a second, and then my head snaps up. I blink up in shock, brain trying to catch up to the fact that somehow, fucking *Judd* is on the back of his timberwing and grinning down at me.

His beast lands in front of us, and I waste no time rushing forward, dragging Tyde with me. I shove him onto the timberwing's back, my muscles straining with his weight. He's unconscious now, slumped over and bleeding way too fucking much.

"What the hell are you doing here?" I ask as I start fumbling with the straps, trying to get Tyde buckled in as fast as I can.

Judd tsks. "What, you thought you could just go and have a battle without me?" he replies with a scoff. "Fucking rude. You know how much I like battles. They're my favorite hobby, Commander."

Shaking my head in a daze of relief, I secure Tyde before I leap up, keeping my back to Judd so I can make sure Tyde doesn't slip out of the straps.

When I'm on, Judd takes us into the air, and then I see them. Dozens of timberwings.

"What…"

In the distance, on the other side of the rift where the rest of the fae army was feeding in from Fifth Kingdom, I can now see white ships gliding over the snow.

*Red Raid ships.*

"What the hell are the snow pirates doing here?"

"Oh that? Called in a favor," Judd shouts back at me with a grin in his voice. "Thought we could use the help."

"And the timberwings? Are those King Thold and his Elites?"

The beasts are everywhere, attacking the fae in fatal swoops and roaring mouths.

"Nope," Judd calls.

The answer comes in a thousand screams that suddenly rip through the air. The noise pierces my eardrums, making the fae below either stop to slam their hands over their ears or run in terror.

Then I see her on her timbering, flanked by her guards. Her black hair is littered with snow, and her body is clad in silver armor.

Queen Kaila.

She came to help. She *actually came.*

The magical sounds cut off, only to start blasting all around in different directions at different times, confusing the fae even more, making their horses bolt.

Ecstatic relief charges through me because…we're winning. We're fucking *winning.*

A groan from Tyde makes me check on him, and I know we need to get his wounds bound so that he stops losing blood. "We need to get him to Cliffhelm!" I shout.

Judd must hear me, because he yanks his timberwing around, and I brace Tyde and myself for the turn. But then Judd spits out a curse. When I wrench around in the saddle to look and see why, my stomach drops.

The fissuring ground has spread all the way to our outpost. Rifts lengthening, reaching further into Fourth's border.

*Shit.*

My plan to stop the fae by cracking the earth didn't just work—it's working too fucking well. I thought I'd measured things out, thought I'd had us plan accordingly. I calculated where to focus Finley and Maston's magic so that it was far enough away from Cliffhelm that it wouldn't spread there.

I was wrong.

With a ferocious crack of cliff and stone, Cliffhelm begins to fall. The guard towers give way beneath the crumbling snow, and the protective wall snaps in half as the ground snaps with it.

"Os and our men are still up there!" I yell.

A few of Kaila's soldiers try to swoop their timberwings down to get them, but it's too late. The ground rumbles and shatters with thundering chaos, and I have no choice but to look on with horror as Cliffhelm's wall collapses completely.

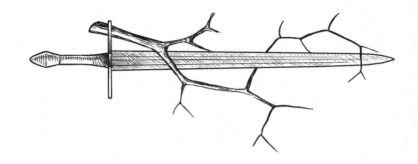

# CHAPTER 27

## OSRIK

I load chunks of stone into the catapult and let the pieces fly, making sure I obliterate as many bodies as fucking possible.

At first, the guard tower to my right was practically bursting full of pieces of debris. Small enough for me to load into the catapult, big enough to be heavy as shit.

When we got the signal from Ryatt and readied the trigger, I waited inside the guard tower, attention fixed on the sky for our timberwings.

The rest of the men stayed crouched down along the wall, making Cliffhelm appear empty. We needed to draw the fae's eyes to the threat at the iron forest so that the big veins of rot could hopefully bleed them out.

And it worked. This crazy ass plan of Ryatt's fucking worked.

The second we saw the rot tearing open the frozen

ground, my men started launching arrows at whatever fae got within range. There was a group of them who tried to split off and race for Cliffhelm when the ground started to give way, but we were ready and easily picked them off.

And I keep launching the catapult. Arms burning, muscles straining, sweat dripping down my skin just as much as the shitty snow. It's not just the stones that are heavy, the whole fucking catapult is. It's meant to be a three-person load, but we can't spare two more men. So I do it myself. Launching, then re-aiming the arm and setting the trigger again with gritted teeth before loading another piece and launching into another group of fae.

I enjoy that part.

I *don't* fucking enjoy when someone comes in and threatens us. I won't stand for it, no matter how bad the odds are.

Before I shoot off the catapult again, movement catches my eye far in the distance. White wood on white snow, pulled by creatures with flaming feet.

That's a sight I didn't fucking expect.

Fire claws are pulling Red Raid ships, and they're cutting off the fae who are running back toward Fifth Kingdom. I watch nearly a dozen of the ships slide right through their contingents, and the flames from the fire claws spread through the army, seeming to burn them where they stand.

Down the wall, the soldiers I have with me let out cheers and whoops of victory. Then, timberwings—*not* ours—start dropping down from the clouds and roar. I stare in surprise, watching as one of them takes a shit mid-flight, and I see the splatter from here as it lands on some of the fae.

Fucking amazing.

The men laugh as I yank off my helmet to wipe the sweat off my brow, and I can't help but smirk too. I don't know how all this help just swooped in, but what could've been a suicide mission just turned around to become a fucking victory.

With the ground splitting and now the added defense, we're winning.

Everything changed so fucking fast. Not a half hour ago, things looked bleak as shit.

"They're getting their asses handed to them!" one of the men shouts.

Then one of the men beside me calls out, "Captain!"

Jerking my attention, I look where he's pointing below the wall. I follow his line of sight and realize what he's seeing. There's a rift, and it's stretching fast, heading straight for us.

"*Shit.*" My helmet drops to the ground with a clang.

We knew there was a risk of the splits making it to Cliffhelm, but Ryatt tried to plan it so that wouldn't happen. Tried to hone our soldiers' magic so it was far enough away. But clearly, now that Slade's rot has been unleashed, it doesn't want to be *leashed* again.

I feel all the blood drain from my face when I realize that the crack isn't going to stop spreading. And it's not a small fissure, either, it's big.

Then the wall starts to shake.

I lift my head, bellowing as loud as I can. "*Get off the fucking wall!*"

My roaring order makes the men scramble from their stations and start racing for the stairs. I yell at them to move their asses, counting each of them, attention snapping from them to the rift heading toward our cliff.

There are three men left when it reaches the base. The ground jostles so hard I nearly get tossed right over the side. The men almost topple too, but they catch themselves while struggling to keep running for the stairs.

Then the wall fucking *snaps*.

One of our soldiers isn't fast enough. He goes careening off the split, and the rest of the wall starts to give way.

"*Run!*" I roar.

The other two haul ass, but the wall is sinking, and it drags another soldier with it, his scream soon cut off. The last man nearly falls too, but I leap forward, fist closing around his arm. I yank him up and haul him toward the stairs with a forceful shove. Then I jump down the stairs behind him just as they start crumbling beneath my fucking boots.

Debris shoots through the air, and right as I slam to the ground on the balls of my feet, there's another loud crack, and the guard tower starts tipping like a falling tree.

It's going to flatten us.

The soldier I yanked with me stumbles, but I grip his arm again and keep him upright. "Go!"

The ground shakes so much it feels like the whole cliff could give way any second, and that thought fills me with fear colder than this fucking snow.

*Rissa.*

I race past the armory, barking out orders for the men to keep running, to push harder, to go faster.

"Don't stop!" I thunder as the ground thunders back, and I can hear more of the cliff toppling behind us.

Then shadows appear, and I look up to see timberwings overhead. They start swooping down, the soldiers on the saddles trying to grab for my men and yank them up. When there's another crash, I look over my shoulder and see the armory starting to fall too.

All of Cliffhelm is going to turn to rubble. I need to get to Rissa *now*.

One timberwing comes down in front of me, but I ignore the soldier on its saddle and keep running for the barracks. When I reach the door, I practically rip it off the hinges as I call her name, looking around frantically.

But she's not here.

She's not fucking here.

A terrified bellow rips from my throat. "*Rissa!*"

Where is she? *Where the fuck is she?*

Fear slams through my chest so hard I can't think. What if she was next to the wall when it was falling? What if she already got fucking crushed? I turn and start to run, heading back the way I came, but the ground is splitting, opening up—

"Osrik!"

I snap my head around, and there she is, racing toward me from the stables. Her yellow hair whips around her pale, terrified face as we run for each other.

She's too close to danger.

I hear another crack of ground, and a man screams. Rissa leaps for me. My hands shoot out and I catch her, and then I turn and run as fast as I can, just as the stables beside us start crumbling.

Her body jostles with my pounding steps, but I try to outrun the rot that's tearing through the earth. Because I'm not going to let it tear through *her*.

No fucking way.

Around us, snow splinters, and crevices start to sink in with corroded soil and a stench so foul it turns my stomach. My pounding steps take us to the end of Cliffhelm's outer fence, and I leap over the stacked bricks. When my feet land on the other side, I keep going, tearing ahead, my heart pounding and blood pumping so loudly I can't hear anything else. I'll keep running all the way back to Brackhill if I have to. I'll keep her safe.

*I have to keep her safe.*

But her voice suddenly pierces through my panicked brain. "Osrik!" She pinches me on the side of the neck hard enough to yank my attention, to realize I've run a really fucking long way. "The shaking stopped!"

I skid to a halt in the snow, breath panting heavily. Turning, I look around to see the rest of our soldiers have already stopped, everyone facing the way we came. Above us, timberwings circle.

We all wait, watching, but the splits don't spread, and the ground stays still and quiet.

Rissa's right. It stopped.

Thank. Fuck.

"You can put me down now," she says after a few more minutes, her voice shaky. Her body shaky too.

"Absolutely fucking not."

She doesn't argue, and her hands still clutch the back of my neck. I'm pumped through with so much adrenaline, fucking reeling with the aftermath as I note who's still here.

Who's still alive.

As more minutes pass, timberwings start landing beside us, and we all stare at the crumbled remains of Cliffhelm and the split-apart landscape below that's littered with bodies from the battleground.

"We're alright," Rissa murmurs to me, her body finally easing off from the shaking.

But all I can think of is how I couldn't find her.

When she squirms again, I finally relent and set her down. Then I glare at her. "Stay in the barracks. That's what I told you," I snarl. "I told you ten times to *stay in the fucking barracks!*"

Her eyes narrow and she fists her hands on her hips and looks down her nose at me. I don't know how she manages it with me towering over her, but she does. "Don't you speak to me like that. I am not a child, nor am I one of your soldiers you can order around."

"No," I say, taking a step forward. "You are my woman, and if I'm going to keep you safe, *during a fucking battle*, then you have to listen to me!"

She's got a scarf wrapped around her neck, and she's bundled up in a thick leather and fur coat, but it looks like her temper is keeping her plenty warm with the way her cheeks flare red. "I *did* stay in the barracks," she retorts. "Until the ground started shaking. Then what did you expect me to do?"

"Stay. In. The. Barracks!"

She scoffs.

*Scoffs*.

I've had men three times her size cower when I yelled like this, but not her. And deep in my gut, I know I'm crazed with anger right now because if she'd gotten hurt or killed, I would have lost my mind.

So I try to take a deep breath to calm my shit down. "I told you our plan, Rissa. I explained that you might feel some shaking."

"*Some* shaking?" she spouts off. "This wasn't some shaking, Osrik! It sounded like the entire earth was cracking open!"

"That's because it fucking was!"

"Well, excuse me, *Sir Army Captain*, that I decided to not simply stand around and let the building collapse on me," she says snappishly. "I went outside so I could see what was going on."

I pinch my nose between my thumb and finger, like I can squeeze some reasoning into her pretty fucking head. When I take a breath and drop my hand, I look her in the eye. "You could have *died*. I went to the barracks to find you, and you weren't there. I thought you were stuck in a pile of rubble and buried ten feet in the ground somewhere."

Her blue eyes flash. "I saw the wall and the guard towers start to fall. The ground was shaking so hard I couldn't even stand straight. But I wanted to see where you were. I needed to make sure you were okay too, you giant oaf!" she yells, her fiery tone lashing at me with accusation.

The retort I was about to spout dies on my tongue. We stare at each other, both of us breathing hard, still exhaling out our panic.

After a second, a sigh leaks out of me, poked through with the holes in my chest from where the fear clawed into me.

"When I came down here and couldn't find you…" My own admission grates out between us. "It scared me to fucking death."

She pushes out a sigh of her own, her anger loosening. "I'm sorry for scaring you."

"Are you going to start listening to me?"

"Yes. Sometimes. When it seems like the right thing to do. And if it suits me."

I grind my teeth. "At least you're fucking honest." I pull her to my chest. My pulse is still fucking pounding, but holding her helps. Reassures me that she's okay.

"Soldiers died?" she asks quietly.

I pause at rubbing her back. "Yeah."

"Is it difficult for you?"

I see a flash of the soldiers' faces as they fell into the breaking wall. Hear the sounds of them screaming…

"Every fucking time," I admit with acid burning my gut.

Rissa looks up at my face, her voice softening. "I really am sorry that I wasn't in the barracks. That I made you panic."

"I'm sorry that I yelled." I curl my hand around the back of her head and pull her in so I can lean down and kiss her. "You can't scare me like that again."

She hums. "Well, then you know the solution for next time, don't you?"

"What?"

"Simple. We don't separate. You should've had me with you on the wall," she says breezily.

I blink at her. She must be joking.

When she continues to look at me, I shake my head. "Yellow Bell. I'm not bringing you up on a *fucking fortress wall* to throw *catapults* into a *fae army*."

She leans away with a frown. "And why not?"

Fucking hell. This woman.

I shake my head in frustration. "You don't go onto the actual battlegrounds. I'm not arguing with you about this."

"There's nothing to argue," she argues. "We stay together. We don't want to worry about each other, so that's what's going to work best for us."

I mutter under my breath about this difficult, frustrating, beautiful fucking woman of mine. Who absolutely will *not* be going on the battle lines.

For fuck's sake.

"Anyway, I'm not hurt, so that right there should prove something," she says before dragging her blue eyes over me. "You, however, are an absolute *mess*."

Glancing down, I only see a few minor scrapes and slices on my bare arms. "I'm good."

"You're not *good*. You're covered in dirt and sweat and blood."

"It's really very normal for him, love," Judd says, sidling up beside us.

"Don't call her *love*," I growl.

"Yeah, don't call me *love*," she snips, giving him a look of disgust that instantly makes me feel even better than *good*.

Judd grins. "Wow. You two are made for each other."

"Of course we are," we both say in our own irritated tones.

Then we share a look, and now that my adrenaline is calming and telling me she's okay, all this rushing blood and hormones want to do something else.

Judd clears his throat, looking between us. "Uh, right. Before this takes a turn...I just wanted to warn you that Queen Kaila and her brother Manu are here."

My head snaps over to him. "*What*?"

He points at me. "But you can't kill him. Slade gave them a pardon, remember?"

"You see Slade here?" I retort with an angry growl. "It's

261

their fault Rissa almost died. So I'll kill them if she fucking wants me to."

I look down at her expectantly. I told her to give me a name, so I wait for her to part those pretty lips and say it so I can fucking *end* them—

She shrugs. "All is forgiven."

I have to do a double take. "Ex-fucking-scuse me?"

Rissa gives me a scathing look. "We're in the middle of a war, *Captain*. Stop threatening people on my behalf, because we don't have time for that. The queen is obviously here to help. Even I know we have to be politically sensitive about these things. Correct?" she asks, and Judd nods in confirmation. "There. See?"

"No, I don't fucking see," I bite out. "I want to kill them for what they did to you."

She rolls her eyes. It makes me hard as a rock because that's what this infuriating woman does to me.

"Well, too bad. You can't," she says.

I'm going to have to talk to her about letting me kill people for her. Later.

After I fuck her in whatever building still stands.

Someone cries out, pulling our attention away. We look over just as one of Queen Kaila's guards dumps an injured fae soldier off the back of his timberwing. He screams from the impact, trying to roll upright in the snow.

The three of us exchange a look before we make our way over. Ryatt steps closer and looms over the fae and says something I don't catch.

The fae shakes his head. "You think this will stop us?"

"I think we *did* stop you," Ryatt tells him.

The fae's laugh is raspy. "This won't stop the fae from taking Orea. The Stone King has been planning this for *years*. He'll make sure this world is ours, and your species is too weak to stop him. This isn't a victory. It's just a setback."

"Look at where you are, and look at where I am," Ryatt snarls. "Oreans aren't weak. Our land was rid of you once, and we'll make sure we rid you again like the infestation you are."

The fae laughs again, but this time, blood bubbles up from his throat. He chokes on it, and then his eyes bug and he tips over onto the ground, his sputtered breath cutting off as he dies.

Rissa presses herself against me, and I put my arm around her protectively.

Everyone stares at the dead fae, and his words repeat in my ears. *This won't stop the fae from taking Orea.*

Queen Kaila walks over, breaking the silence as she looks at her men. "We're leaving. Ready yourselves."

Ryatt snaps his attention toward her. "Leaving?"

"Yes," she says, already striding for her timberwing. "You heard what he said. The fae aren't going to stop. I fulfilled my part of the bargain with your king. Now I'm going back to my kingdom where I can defend my land and ready for the next onslaught."

"We've just had a victory here," Ryatt argues. "We need to press our advantage."

Queen Kaila arches an imposing brow at him. "I helped at Breakwater Port, and at my brother's insistence, I helped here as well. But I don't see *your* king anywhere, Commander," she says with a pointed look. "I fulfilled my promise."

Before she can step away again, Manu comes forward and mutters in her ear. She gives him a sharp glance, but then the two of them start whispering heatedly back and forth.

I glare at Manu, my hands tightening into fists, my teeth grinding. He looks a lot better now than he did in the dungeons.

I should've knocked his teeth in.

"Stop it," Rissa hisses with a jab of her elbow to my side.

I look down at her, and she arches her brows at me in challenge.

Yep. Fucking hard again.

"Fine," I grumble.

When Kaila and Manu turn and walk back over, Kaila's face has hardened. "My brother and advisor has suggested a different course of action," she clips out, clearly unhappy with it, though her eyes move to Ryatt. "Third Kingdom will aid Orea."

The relief in Ryatt is obvious as his shoulders loosen. "Thank you, Queen Kaila," he says with a tip of his head.

"Don't thank me," she says harshly, brown eyes darting to her brother. "Thank Manu." Her guards gather around her as she tosses her black braid over her shoulder, her silver chest plate covered with frost. "Now let's discuss a plan, Commander, and we'll see if we truly can save Orea."

"We can," Ryatt says nobly, and I have to hand it to him, he sounds like a hero through and through.

And right now, Orea really needs a fucking hero.

# CHAPTER 28

## SLADE

The dead land ends.

After miles, it finally gives way to an earth that still lives. The border between the two is like the jagged edge of a scab. One step, it's the ashy, unnatural silt, and the next, it's lush grass and centuries-old trees. Birds fly overhead, insects flock to low-hanging fruits, and the air no longer carries an edge of death.

We passed two cities on our way. No doubt they flourished at one time, but they're nothing but empty ruins now. At one point, fae tried to build a wall in front of the encroaching decay, and I could sense echoes of magic also used to try to stop the spread.

But it didn't work. The dead lands just kept reaching.

I haven't let myself stop to rest or to slow down. Travel has been grueling, but my bond beckons. I know she's here and I'm getting closer, so there's no time to waste.

The Vulmin leading the way give me a wide berth. They

continue to watch me warily, and they're wise to do so. But finally, my destination comes into view.

The sprawling, beautiful land of Lydia.

It was once just one of the many kingdoms of Annwyn. Each territory had its own ruler, culture, protections. But then everything changed, and the separate lands were ingested into the belly of one beast, bowing to a single monarch and falling under a united rule.

Across this stretch of green valley, I see Glassworth Palace where the monarch lays claim. It sits on a flat expanse of land, and a waterfall cascades off its sharp edge like syrup dripping off a plate.

The palace used to be made solely of stone that was riddled with stained glass windows to earn its name. Those stained glass walls and domed ceilings are still there, but it now has crystal spires and gemstones growing out of it. Its vibrancy spits in the face of the bereft land we just left, standing arrogant and vivid, when everything just miles away is a colorless corpse.

Even with being built up high on the plateau that overlooks the city, the palace doesn't have much of a defensive wall. There's only a short parapet at the front with a wide open gate that seems to be more for looks than safeguarding. It seems arrogant in its lack of defense, although Glassworth was built in a time of peace and beauty.

It's a lack that I have every intention of exploiting.

"Lord Rot."

The male who's been leading the group of Vulmin comes up to my side. They call him Hare, though I think it's a nickname because his two front teeth slightly resemble that of a rabbit. "What's the plan?"

I give him a fleeting look. "This *is* the plan."

There's a disbelieving pause before he sputters, "What— you can't mean to simply…walk up to the palace gates?"

"That's precisely what I mean to do."

"They'll kill you on the spot!"

"I'm sure they'll try."

They said their king has Auren. So I'll walk right up to those gates and start rotting everything in my path until I find her.

Hare's eyes widen with wariness. It seems my absence from Annwyn has watered down the knowledge of my power. Otherwise, he wouldn't look so scared for me.

The city where I once lived used to fear *me*, and with good reason.

"We need to go with you," Hare says.

"We can't go with him!" someone else hisses behind us. "They'll kill us! We need to go into the city and get in contact with the others."

"We can't just leave the Lyäri's bonded!" someone else argues.

I feel their eyes on me, and curiosity has me stopping on the road. Their clothes are covered in dust from the deadlands, their faces weary, their packs heavy. Though their tight-lipped regard has given me little to nothing to go on for their intentions.

But I know they hate the king, hate the war, and they have some sort of loyalty to Auren because of her family name. That's been more than enough for me to trust them to lead me.

Plus, if they did anything, I'd just fucking kill them.

But judging by the way they talk about Auren, it's obvious she's more than just a notable figure for Turley loyalists. They speak of her with reverence, though they've admitted that they haven't actually met her.

"If you feel a sense of responsibility to stay with me on Auren's behalf, I can assure you, I don't need anyone risking their lives for me."

"But you're alone, walking straight up to the palace,"

Hare argues. "If you think King Carrick has sent all his forces to Orea, you're wrong. I know for a fact he still has plenty of protection here."

"There wouldn't be enough forces in the entire realm for him to stop me."

Hare blinks. They all look at me as if the way I speak is rooted in nothing but arrogance. It's not.

It's fact.

"Come with me or don't, the choice is yours. But do so at your own risk."

"We should go to the city," another male says—the one who possesses power to attack with teeth. He wears a string of them around his neck. They call him Fang.

My strides cut past a shallow hillside, and just up ahead, the dirt road splits off. If I continue straight, I'll reach the cliffside where a fae-built slope leads to the top of the plateau where the palace awaits.

But noise snares my attention, tugging my gaze to the right. To where the forked road splits off, leading to the city. A tall lavender archway is there to mark Lydia's entrance.

And the path is teeming with fae waiting to pass through.

"Celebrating a holiday?" I ask, though I have a feeling that's not the case.

Hare and the others stop, everyone's eyes now on the city's entrance. "No," Hare says, shaking his head. "There's no holiday. I don't know what this is…"

"Looks like fae from the neighboring villages are swarming in," Fang adds, glancing around at the groups along the road traveling toward Lydia. Some are coming from the direction of the forest, others past the other side of the plateau.

"We should go see what's going on," another says.

"There could be trouble. You know Carrick has been more violent than ever," Fang says, looking to Hare. "The rise of the movement has shaken him. He could be pressing his thumb down on the capital. Could have found some of us…"

They all hesitate. Hare looks to me.

"Go," I tell them with a jerk of my chin. With them in the city, I won't have to worry about any of them dying for following me.

"We could split up…"

The reluctance in their faces is actually quite profound. That they're even considering splitting up so that some of them can stay with me. Their sense of loyalty on Auren's behalf is shocking.

But with the fae flooding into the city, it might be the perfect time for me to walk right up to the palace gates, since the king might be distracted.

My power thrums with impatience, but I fist my hands and hold it back. "Go to the city, ensure your people are safe, and—"

Something in the distance makes me stop, and my eyes suddenly widen. My words slice off as my breath grips tight.

Then my fucking heart clenches in my chest, because there, in the city, something appears in the air.

Like a flare in the swallowed dark. A soft golden light illuminates from the city's depths, its rays breaking through the high treetops like sunlight.

I stagger back.

Because there, Auren's aura shines from the city's core.

Leading me to her.

My bond doesn't just sing inside my chest now—it *peals*. Thunders. Releases with a clamor that even the stars can hear. The song it plays is the perfect rhythm of her beating heart. Just like the beacon that first led me to her in the Barrens, she calls again to me now.

I nearly fall to my knees in relief and elation.

"*Auren.*"

I say it like a breath. Her name yanked from the deepest parts of me. My jaw aches and my eyes burn, and I'm flooded with every emotion I've felt since we were ripped from one another.

My steps turn sharply toward the city road.

"What are you doing?" Hare asks, he and the other Vulmin hurrying to keep up. "I thought you were going to the palace?"

"Not anymore."

"Why?"

"Because Auren isn't in Glassworth," I say, not bothering to slow down.

Fang comes up on my other side, twisting his ball of teeth at his neck. "How do you know?" he asks. "How do you know where she is?"

I glance at him.

How do I know?

Because I'd know that light anywhere, whether in the depths of darkness or in a sea of stars. Her brightness, her *soul*, sings a song I'd follow anywhere.

I know because she's my other half, and her aura is leading me back to her.

I know because she's mine.

But to him, I answer simply.

"I just do."

# CHAPTER 29

## AUREN TURLEY

To enter the city of Lydia, you have to pass under an arch made of translucent rock that matches the color of the lavender sky. It stands at least thirty feet high between two twisting trees, and there's a road of pewter gray bricks that leads you in.

Right now, that road is busy with fae flowing past. I have a feeling that all these people entering the city have to do with the commotion I heard.

A few city guards stand beside the arch, their gazes skimming the crowd as they wave people through. I stay behind the tree line, chewing on my bottom lip as I watch. There's a dirt road that curves from the forest to my right, which is full of fae passing by to go into the city. Some are on horseback, while others are on foot.

I eye every group. If I'm going to get past the city entrance, I need to be able to blend in.

I glance down at the golden chest plate I made for myself. I'm slightly regretting that decision right about now. It's going to make me stick out like a sore thumb even more than I already do, but…I look at the way it stretches around my waist, encasing my torso perfectly in elaborate rivulets of melded metal. Not only does it make me feel stronger, it's pretty too.

Bright side.

My brow instantly furrows, a lost memory clinking against a hollow space in my head.

*Bright side…*

I can hear myself saying that at another place. Another time. It feels so familiar.

But the strained recollection is pulled away when my gaze snags on a fae riding alone atop his horse, petting at the animal's long blue braided mane. Right there on one of the saddlebags is a gray cloak draped over the top of it.

I dart forward. With the trees growing so dense and close to the road, it's surprisingly easy. Staying behind a thick rope of leaves that dangle in front of me, I wait, and then right as he passes by, one of my ribbons plucks the cloak from its spot.

As soon as I slip it over me, my nose wrinkles at the unfamiliar scent. I don't like smelling this male. It doesn't reek or anything like that, but for some reason, it bothers me. But it's better than getting spotted by the city guards before I can even get through the arch.

Making sure to secure the clasp at the neck, I fix the draping fabric, tucking it around my front. I glance down at the ribbons curling around the forest floor, their lengths fluttering through the grass and wildflowers. Even though I'm loath to tuck them away, I have to, so I wrap them around my waist and then give them a reassuring pat through my cloak.

Taking a fortifying breath, I pull up the hood and then

dart out past the net of trees and onto the road behind a group of walking fae. I match their pace, keeping my face tilted down, but not too much that I draw attention.

The road bends around, and I allow myself a quick glance up at the arch as I pass beneath it. Then, I'm swallowed up by the shade of the trees, bare feet tracking over the smooth bricks of the city's road.

Lydia is a tangle of braided trees that drift far up into the sky, and beautiful buildings that somehow look both quaint and dazzling. They're made up of smooth stones, sparkling glass, steeples and arched doorways.

Some of the buildings are even woven into the thick trees themselves, blending with the nature that seems to hold magic in the air. It feels both ancient and exciting to be on these streets. I can practically feel centuries' worth of other fae walking along this very same path. Maybe someone else who was once just as awed as I am now.

The crowd today seems to move with one mind though, not taking in the sights. Instead of looking up at the high branches draping down with pods of lights that dangle prettily from the vines, they're all surging ahead with excitement. So I follow the herd, and the cheering and applause that I'd heard before lifts into the air again.

When the throng is clogged to a stop, I break off, slipping down a tight space between two buildings. I have to go sideways as I squeeze my way through, but then I get out to the next street over.

It's busier here. There are people above, standing on rooftops and even hanging from the branches of the loping trees. Even the canal I can see from beneath an arched bridge is full of boats.

More cheers rise.

Something urges me on, so despite the street being crammed, I start making my way through, winding past bodies, using every available space. When there isn't any, I simply *make* space and shove my way past.

Finally, just past a large flowing fountain, the street opens up to a half circle of descending steps. Instead of normal stairs, each step is about as wide as I am tall. A few areas even hold closed-up carts and fastened barrels, as if this space is used for an open-air market. Though right now, it serves a different purpose.

At the bottom of the wide circular stone arena, there's an outdoor theater set up. The wooden platform rests on the sunken ground, with fabric hanging at the back of the stage that has landscapes painted on it. Behind that is an enclosed area, maybe to keep props and performers.

People applaud just as two performers come out from behind the painted drapery. An ample-chested fae female with a bright pink dress inundated with frills comes hurrying out. Right on her heels is a male with green hair whose vest is open, showing off his tanned torso. Both of them have exaggerated rouge and lip stain, with dark liner along their eyes. The female's cleavage gleams with gold shimmer to draw the eye.

Frilly Dress whirls around the prop table, pretending to fuss and straighten plates. "Come, it's time for our dinner meeting!"

"Dinner meeting?" the male asks curiously as he sits.

Their voices easily carry over the crowd, either from the acoustics or magic.

Another performer comes bustling out on the stage then—a male with black and gray dots in his hair like a spotted fish. He must be a popular actor, because the crowd cheers wildly as soon as he enters.

"Welcome, welcome! Please, sit!" the frilly female tells him.

"What's all this about, my sweet?" Green Hair says to her.

"Can't you see? He's a Vermin!" the female exclaims excitedly as she sits down.

The spotted-hair male clears his throat. "*Vulmin,*"

he corrects, and then he points at a big wooden emblem hanging around his neck. It's the symbol of the bird with the broken wing.

A frown digs between my brows.

She waves. "Same thing."

Laughter sounds off throughout the audience, the word *vermin* repeated.

"He's going to make me a queen!" she goes on excitedly, clapping her hands as she bounces in her seat. She looks perilously close to having her breasts spill out of her low-cut dress—probably the point.

Green Hair frowns. "What are you on about?"

"Well, I'm a Turley, aren't I?" she says with a huff. "The Vermin say my family should be the ones ruling Annwyn!"

My stomach drops. Shock and confusion whirl through me.

*Why are they talking about the Turleys?*

He scrunches up his face. "You're a Turley?" he asks dubiously, then pauses, tapping his chin in thought. "Is that why your tits are gold?"

Crude snickering bursts around me, making me flinch at the people I'm pressed against in the crowd. My pulse stretches, wrapping around my muscles and making them go tense.

"That's right," Frills nods excitedly, turning to the fake Vulmin as she runs her hand along her cleavage. "Do you want to see?"

Her question spurs the amusement of the spectators even more. One male next to me shouts at her to give them a flash.

Anger, embarrassment, confusion, it all writhes through my nerves, coiling me tight. But then I remember something.

Cruel, sharp words that sliced through me.

*Don't give them a martyr. Give them a mockery.*

My vision nearly tunnels with the words. With the satirical and taunting laughter that seems to be closing in around me.

Green Hair leaps up from his chair and comes around to the actress. "No, he does *not* want to see." He lifts Frills up from the chair. "Wait a moment, didn't you have an uncle who took golden shits?"

People in the crowd snicker. My cheeks begin to burn, hands shaking beneath my cloak.

"No!" Frills says indignantly, crossing her arms in front of her to prop up her breasts even more. Then pauses. "It was his piss. Though it was hard to tell."

Another round of laughter bursts from the city square, while anger boils up my throat and singes the back of my tongue.

"Anyway, it doesn't matter. I'm a Turley, so I can be queen! I can have fabulous balls and take everyone's money and make them all bow to me!" she exclaims ecstatically.

*Is this the truth? Is this a real story about my family?*

But no. That doesn't feel right. This feels exactly like what that voice suggested. A mockery.

A mockery of the Turleys. A mockery of *me*.

Someone dashes out from behind the curtains and onto the stage. It's a female who has her lips painted a gaudy, yellowed gold, the color exaggerated to make her lips seem much bigger than they really are. "If anyone should be queen, it should be me!" she shouts as she comes up to Frills. "I'm more golden than you!"

Frills rolls her eyes. "Please, those lips are good for nothing!"

"That's not what your husband said last night!" the actress petulantly snaps before she spins and bends over, hiking up her skirts. "And *your* lips can kiss my a—"

Frills screeches and acts like she's going to pounce on her, but Green Hair holds her back.

"Ladies, ladies," the Vulmin performer shouts, easing between them. "Please, you can *both* live in the palace!"

276

They both straighten up, eyes snagging on him with hunger. "We can?" they ask in unison.

"Of course," he says smoothly. "You deserve it!"

"Because we're Turleys," Frills says with a nod.

"Exactly!" the Vulmin performer purrs. "All of Annwyn needs to be under the boot of the Vermin…" He shakes his head and pretends to slap himself. The crowd eats it up, offering him jeering titters. "What am I saying? I meant the Turleys! Annwyn is meant to be ruled by the *Turleys*. And anyone who disagrees needs to die."

The crowd boos and hisses on cue.

"Yes!" Frills exclaims delightedly. "Kill everyone who doesn't want to be ruled by us."

The one with the painted lips clasps her hands and beams. "We're going to be royals!"

Interrupting their celebration, a voice suddenly booms from behind the stage. "The only thing you're going to be is under arrest for committing treason against the good and benevolent King Carrick!"

Two actors dressed as guards come on the stage, wooden swords painted to look like marble. "We won't let you evil, selfish Turley traitors ruin Annwyn!"

People cheer.

This is ridiculous, dumbed-down, and openly vulgarized propaganda. And yet, the crowd is eating it up.

But as I glance around at everyone on the steps, seeing their smiles, hearing their laughter and their jeers, I realize that I'm wrong.

Not *everyone* is eating it up.

There are those in the crowd that I spot. Males standing stock-still, tension in their jaws as they watch. Females without even so much as a smirk on their faces. A fae just five people to the left of me grinds his teeth and looks at someone else in the crowd. I follow his line of sight to another male and realize with a jolt that there's a pin of the broken-winged bird emblem at the fold of his cloak. The same one from the ring that's currently in my pocket.

The stage snatches my attention when the female actresses screech and run around the table in a comical display of trying to evade the guards. Frills bounces around so much that most of her glittery breasts are working to free themselves from her top.

"Don't take me. It was him!" She shoves the fake Vulmin toward the guards. "It's the Vermin's fault!"

"*Vulmin*!" he snaps just before the guard comes forward and slaps a shackle on his wrist. He starts to pretend to struggle, face growing indignant. "You'll pay for this! The Vulmin should rule Annwyn!"

Frills gasps. "Hey! You said the Turleys were supposed to!"

Before he can answer, the Vulmin is dragged off the stage, while she and Green Hair stomp after him, disappearing behind the curtain with a shout. "Down with the Vermin!"

Then it's just the yellow-lipped female and the other guard left. She puts on a sweet smile and bats her eyelashes at him. "How about instead of arresting me, I use my lips to make *you* feel golden, good sir?"

Shouts of *Turley whore* and *traitor* burst from the spectators, making rot and gold smear against my fisted palms.

"Nice try, Turley scum," the guard says, "but I'm loyal to the rightful ruler, King Carrick!"

King Carrick—that crowned fae with the hard, cruel eyes. The one who threatened me. Locked me in that cell. Made Una use her magic on my mind.

My anger twists and knots, and my blood steams beneath my skin, making veined gold puddle at my feet.

I wish I remembered everything. Wish I could know the nuances I've lost. But I don't need all my memories to know that this whole spectacle is pure vilification. Of the Vulmin, of my family, and of me.

Rotting just one of those memory worms drained me and took hours, but I'm going to uncover every single thing King Carrick stole from me, and I'm going to make him pay.

I'm glad I'm covered beneath this cloak where no one can see my face, because my anger burns straight through my eyes.

The actress makes an exaggerated pout with her painted lips as she's dragged away. Then the performers come back out to take a collective bow to the cheers and applause of the spectators while my magic continues to pool.

While I continue to seethe.

Once the performers leave, a hush descends in the arena. Behind the stage, where the half circle of steps are split apart, there's another street directly across from me. I see a line of soldiers marching on it, heading this way. They file in with synchronized footsteps and then stomp up the arena's wide steps to my left, forcing people to clear the way.

A male wearing a furred mantle and a stone crown on his head walks in the middle of them.

King Carrick.

He ascends the arena, and once he's at the top step to look down upon the stage below, he turns.

With a flick of his hand, the stone wall behind him shifts and forms into a throne. He takes a seat as his guards take position behind him. The quieted crowd begins to murmur, and I can feel their excitement mounting.

My fiery, hateful gaze stays latched on his face and my ribbons tighten around me. More gold bubbles up to gather at my feet, thickening beneath my bare soles. Clotting with fury.

"Lydians!" a fae calls as he walks out onto the stage with his arms outstretched in a flourish. He's dressed in bright purple, his sleeves puffed and hat feathered.

"We know these rumblings of the Vulmin fanatics have caused trouble in our beautiful land for too long!" he says as he strides from one end of the stage to the other. "They have disrupted our way of life, and they have sullied Annwyn with their cowardly actions and their sabotaging insurgency."

Maybe I'm imagining it, but I feel tension sprouting in the air.

"But the Vermin's mutinies have shown their true colors, because our king has exposed their lies!" His voice carries, every performed word calculatingly convincing. "People of Lydia, we have the truth with us here today. The Vulmin aren't as strong as they would have you believe."

He pauses dramatically, and the crowd seems to collectively lean in, waiting on his next words, while others seem to go still, that tension in the air coming from the same ones who didn't laugh at the play.

"Everyone is turning on them…including their own so-called Dawn's Bird."

Movement cuts through the soldiers lining the street behind the stage, and then I see a figure being led forward by guards.

Murmurs erupt through the crowd.

My breath stops. My eyes widen.

Because the next figure that stands upon the stage…is *me*.

# CHAPTER 30

## AUREN TURLEY

My breath plugs in my chest like the stopper on a vial. I watch the gold figure stand there, and seeing her makes a jolting, harrowing flash of a memory erupt.

I see Emonie in the cell. How her face dripped away like wax, melting into my own appearance with gold skin, gold hair, gold eyes.

Right before she passed me the ring that's stuffed in my pocket.

*Wick's* ring.

"Here she is," the fae announces with a sweep of his hand. "Their very own Lyäri Ulvêre. Except, she was never the golden one gone. She has been here with us all along!" he says with a grin. "She is no rebel. She does not lead them or stand by them. She has been here with the king! And to prove it once and for all, she is here to bow before the Stone

King and show everyone in Annwyn that this mockery of a rebellion is *over*. All hail King Carrick!"

The crowd titters back, a frenetic excitement filling the air.

Emonie gleams in the sunlight, dressed in a provocative gold dress. It cuts down into a V, past her breasts and below her navel, the skirt splitting up both sides of her thighs. The crowd leers at her with incomprehensible shouts.

It makes me feel vulnerable. As if everyone's eyes are on *me*. Leering at *me*. The rot through my puddling gold pulses as if sensing my emotions.

Around Emonie's wrists and ankles are stone bands, and though they seem to be mere jewelry, I can't help but think that she's wearing them for a more sinister reason. Can't help but wonder if they're shackles instead.

My gaze darts to the so-called Stone King. He watches her with victory cleaving through his expression, and anger heats my face.

"Here is this Lyäri that the Vulmin have claimed. The one they say leads you. She does not! She is no rightful heir. Auren Turley will bow to the true king with you all here to witness!"

With her chin up, eyes straight ahead at King Carrick, Emonie does exactly as he said. The crowd shouts wildly as she bends one knee, and then the other, until her legs are curled beneath her. Then she lowers even further, until her arms are outstretched, palms and forehead kissing the ground.

More magic spurts from my palms, landing in aggressive splatters at my feet.

The volume of the spectators is so loud it thrashes my ears. I glance around, skipping over those who cheer, instead focusing on the ones who don't celebrate.

I take in the ones who look on with visible anger. Or confusion. Or misery that they can't seem to hide. One female fae has tears slipping down her cheeks. The sunlight glares on a single button sewn into her shirtsleeve, and I notice the broken-winged bird sigil melded right into it.

Seeing that button sends me another flash of memory.

People surrounding me, crying, smiling, celebrating and believing—believing in a movement that was bigger than myself.

But then I hear those cruel words again, except this time, I *see* it too. See King Carrick glaring down at me. Hear that other voice speak.

*Don't give them a martyr. Give them a mockery.*

That other person's face slowly comes into focus. One eye, strong jaw, a sneering mouth. In my mind's eye, I stare at him as if he's standing in front of me, the vision taking over everything.

*I hear screaming. Feel power rippling. My hands pour out gold, and the ground quakes with massive roots of rot. There's a woman standing beside the male, and I feel such suffering fear from her that it cripples me. Steals away my breath.*

The vision is abruptly yanked away, like a rope tugged out of my hands. I lose my grip on the flashback, nearly losing my footing where I stand too. Beneath my armor, my ribbons ripple, my spine slicking with gold.

I just barely catch the end of the announcer's words. "… with her aid. Because of Auren Turley's loyalty to the crown, we have these traitors to present before you. She has led the rebels to their penance!"

The Vulmin in the crowd—because that must be who they are—they look tormented. The rest of the audience roars with a fervor.

My own fervor is an inward intensity that's ready to boil over.

I watch as soldiers drag people out from behind the stage. People who are gagged and bound. They're forced to stand in a line behind Emonie, and she sits up from her prostrate position, eyes widening when she sees them. She says something, but I'm too far away to hear. Too focused on the fae male just beside her.

It's *Wick*.

I remember his name, his face, a flash. It's enough to fill me with dread for him and Emonie both.

"Good fae of Lydia, you will stand witness! These Vulmin traitors will be whipped and hanged for their crimes against the crown!"

Frenzied cheers blare in my ears, while my fury takes flight.

They absolutely will *not*.

"Listen to me!" Wick shouts, his voice cutting through the arena. "The Vulmin aren't traitors! We believe in treating our fellow fae and Oreans with respect! We believe in a leadership that doesn't drain us dry with taxes and punish us for differing views! We can do better than this! We can demand an Annwyn of peace! A land that doesn't rule by greed and cruelty! We can do *better*!"

His voice is loud and holds the unmistakable edge of both determination and desperation. But most of the people just continue to shout and curse, fists raised in the air, calling for blood. The sound crescendos just as I let my ribbons unwind, falling loose and free from beneath my cloak.

A hooded fae walks on the stage with a long, spiked whip in his grip.

More gold collects in my hands like lumps of clay, and I roll them between my palms. Then I reach forward with my ribbons and shove apart the spectators around me like curtains.

I step forward and glare at the stage below while fae stagger beside me, questions and gasps forming on their lips, gold splashing beneath their feet.

I barely pay them any mind.

The whip wielder steps up to Emonie, and my entire body tenses as he hands her the weapon. She's standing now, but Wick is kneeling beside her, held down by a soldier. The rest of the Vulmin are all kneeling too, soldiers in a row behind them. I recognize the same cuff I wore on my ankle is also on Wick's, the gray band suppressing whatever magic he has.

Emonie, however, wears the stone shackles, and when she hesitates, I see her arm jerk forward, fingers fumbling before she takes hold of the whip. Her entire body is tight and stiff, but I instantly know—the Stone King is using his magic. The cuffs around her wrists are forcing her jerky movements.

Anger locks in my jaw, and the bulge of veined gold continues to gather in my hand.

*Give them a mockery.*

*Use her.*

*Make it a spectacle.*

Snippets of memories flutter behind my eyes, and I've had enough.

"Let this be a lesson to anyone who thinks they can go against the king! Watch this *Lyäri* do his bidding and end this false rebellion once and for all!" He turns to Emonie. "Begin!" he shouts at her, and I see her arm lift despite the stricken look on her face.

"*Enough!*"

My voice rings out through the arena as I shove back my hood and reveal my face. Emonie spots me instantly, her wet eyes widening as she looks up. Exclamations erupt in the air as gold pours from my hands and drips down my ribbons, encasing my legs in armor and covering my feet in gilded boots.

"My name is Auren Turley, and *I* am the true Lyäri Ulvêre," I call out, my voice lashing against the steps, echoing through the entire arena and snatching every single person's attention. But my eyes find the king's. "I am not gone, and I *do not bow*."

My cloak rips off with a shove of my ribbons, and gold shoots forward, the liquid metal clotted with veins of black. I race down the steps of the arena toward Emonie and Wick, and people scream as my gold streams with me, but I'm not here to hurt innocents.

I'm here for the guilty.

They tried to erase me, but they didn't succeed. They tried to say who I was, but I'm going to show them.

Guards surround the king and clunkily move him away at the other end of the viewing arena. At the stage below, Vulmin prisoners struggle against their bindings and try to get away.

Cords of gold split off and circle the soldiers like caught livestock. Every single one of them gets cinched inside my molten rope and yanked away from the Vulmin.

I make it to Emonie and Wick seconds after my gold does. My magic already cutting through the Vulmin's bindings.

"Get their weapons!" Wick shouts at the others as they stagger to their feet, and we all jump off the stage.

"Attack!" I hear the king roar from behind his circle of guards that are leading him back down the steps.

The stone beneath our feet cracks violently and starts to lift from his magic. Before the chunk can toss us on our asses, my gold solidifies the foundation we're standing on.

I whip around to face the king, and his expression is incensed. "You *Turley filth*, I should have slit your throat!"

Rage seeps out from my molten expression. "Yes. You should have."

"Kill her!" he barks out as more soldiers stream toward us.

I lunge a wave of gold toward him, but before it can hit, he pulls stone from the stair in front of him. It lashes up into a barrier, making my liquid metal splash against it. Behind me, the Vulmin are fighting against the soldiers, and the spectators are screaming and running.

But some people from the crowd are rushing *in*, taking up arms. Not against the Vulmin, but *helping*.

Someone from a rooftop shouts, "We rise with the dawn!"

Answering calls pepper the air, and I'm stunned as fae leap from rooftops and appear through the trees. They sprint down the steps, rushing down into the square to help the other Vulmin and join the fight.

Dozens of them. More than I can count.

And it's suddenly clear. *This* is why they tried to make the Vulmin a laughing stock. Because if there are this many ready to risk their identities and their lives in the capital city, then how many more are there throughout all of Annwyn?

There's fighting in the square and on the steps, the clash of soldiers and Vulmin ringing out all around me. It's a crescendo of violence in the ruthless song of battle, and the beast inside of me sings.

Another contingent of soldiers rushes in to defend the king, trying to cut me off from him. I hold my hand out and gold pours down, forming a sword just as the first soldier lifts a weapon and swings it at me. My metal hardens in an instant to meet the attack, and our blades clash.

The soldier's sword shatters on impact, and shards go flying off. I raise my weapon and slam it into his neck, slicing right through with the sharpened edge.

More soldiers rush at me, so I call to my saturated ribbons. With a dozen on each side, they bend before me like layered ribs, and then fling back with amazing strength. It sends four soldiers flying.

The others coming in to attack me don't get as close. I've pooled gold at my feet, and I waste no time using it. It rises, like a tidal wave against a beach. The soldiers freeze, staring up at its swell before they try to turn and run back. With a mighty force, the swell crashes down over them, knocking them off their feet, their armored bodies swept away.

A crackling in the air warns me of magic a split second before a flame nearly hits me. Gold brackets around my palm, elongating into a shield. I raise it just in time for the magic stream of hot fire to slam against it.

I'm not sure how my gold will hold up against the flames, but already, the scent of hot metal soaks the air. Before the fire can melt through, I call on the lines of rot instead, and they latches onto the soldier, choking him out with veins of black and sputtering out his flames as he perishes.

Vicious victory spreads through my expression.

There's a shout, and I look up to see King Carrick sneering at me. He has Emonie by her hair, and her face is a mixture of fury and fear that makes me pause. "You attack, and she's dead!"

My reply is a growl. "I think you've threatened me enough, Stone King."

But then, there's a rumble, like a quaking earth.

Everyone seems to still, attention jerked toward the city. Down the packed streets, people start to scream.

The sound makes my stomach dip right down to my toes.

Something is coming. Something big. Powerful. I can feel the magic in the air like it's brushing against my skin.

The king looks positively gleeful. "The Breaker comes," he says with a threatening twist of his lips.

My insides wring, mind trying to soak up the inherent fear and discover its meaning.

*Who's The Breaker?*

The pitted-out points in my head echo, reverberating with a single flash.

My bones breaking. Arm, ribs. Inescapable pain.

Then the cold, heartless face of the fae who voiced those ugly words. *"Give them a mockery."*

With fingers curling into fists, I look at the king, and he's waiting for my reaction, hoping I'll be afraid.

I'm not.

They've already tried to break me, but instead, I broke *free*.

Another fae lobs magic at me, and my ribbon extends, smacking the magic away in a spray of sparks that rain down. Someone else—a soldier to my right—slaps his hands together, and a cloud of magic bursts between his palms. It coalesces like smoke, maybe dense with poison based on the greenish tinge. My magic can't fight against air, so I melt down my shield and slam the thick cord forward.

It hits him and the soldiers nearby, knocking them off their feet before covering them with thick, syrupy strings that net around them and hold them down.

Then I go for the king.

Using the gold puddled at my feet, I send strips forward, thin enough that they dodge Emonie and wrap around Carrick's throat. But he retaliates before I can finish cinching. The stone beneath my feet cracks apart as it juts up and tries to dislodge me. I go falling backward on the tipping stonework, but my ribbons lash out, catching me before my skull can crack against the ground.

Leaping to my feet with frustration, I cast magic toward the king, but he tosses up a stone barrier again in front of him and Emonie.

My magic slams into it, clanging wildly, the metal denting.

Sweat drips down my temples, and I stagger, my body reminding me of how drained I already was. Worry spreads down my spine, but determination fills in the cracks.

I can't let him defeat me. I *won't*.

With another forceful shove, I push against him, but he pushes back. It's a battle of wills and magic, and I know he thinks his stone is stronger, that he's unbeatable. But I grit my teeth and narrow my eyes in determination.

Gold bends, but stone *breaks*.

Hand shaking, I push it forward, making more magic careen forward. It forms into a thick spear that hits his barrier right in the middle. The rock shatters from the impact, spewing chunks and dust into the air as it crumbles.

Victory and adrenaline race through me, and I rush toward him. The king's eyes widen. I see the panic that twitches across his face. See the moment where he realizes he *can* lose.

Then Carrick lets out a shout. "Brennur!"

That name makes a terrible feeling scoop into my brain. *Brennur*...

My eyes shift. With my focus on the king, I failed to notice the old fae with the squared beard and clay-colored eyes behind him. Failed to notice the ring of grass growing up through the stone.

That terrible feeling grows.

"No!" Emonie shouts.

Panic booms in my ears, and I sprint toward them, legs pumping, ribbons outstretched, gold sloshing toward them as I push myself faster and faster—

I'm too late.

Right before me, their two forms are sucked away. Emonie and I lock eyes the instant before she disappears. I skid to a stop right in front of the grass, and I watch it wilt and wither. One blink it's there...

Gone the next.

With a growl, I spin, shoving magic at the older fae. Gold ropes wrap around him, pinning him in place, making him drop his cane with a clatter.

"What did you do?" I snarl, my pulse raging.

His eyes widen but his mouth stays shut.

"Where did they go?" I demand as I grip my sword, the gold shining with the glare of my fury.

He refuses to answer.

"Auren!"

I look over my shoulder at Wick's call just as he skids to a stop at my side. When he sees Brennur, his entire face creases with betrayal. "You! You *traitor*!"

On instinct, my ribbons block Wick before he can swing his sword at the fae. Then with the hilt of my sword, I land a fierce blow against Brennur's temple. He crumples to the ground, unconscious.

My ribbons drop away. "I need him alive," I tell Wick.

"I—" Wick's words are hacked off with a blunt sound that thrashes the air. The entire city seems to tremble.

Wick and I look at each other, and then we both turn and race toward the city. Toward the sound. Toward the screams.

Because the king warned us. The Breaker is coming.

But he won't break *me*.

# CHAPTER 31

## SLADE

The Vulmin follow me as I sprint toward the city. They try to stay hot on my heels, but once I have that aura locked in my sights, distance becomes an opponent I have to defeat.

Then, it's the crowd. People everywhere, plugging up the street. The more people I have to maneuver past, the more my irritation rises.

Luckily, Hare catches up and yanks on my arm with a solution. "This way, Lord Rot."

He shoves sideways past the flow of the crowd, heading toward the canals, and then jumps right off the ledge of the street. There isn't a splash, so I follow. Unlike him, I don't have to push anyone away as I cut across. Even with so many fae, none of them touch me, leaving at least a few inches of space. Maybe because of some instinct telling them to stay away.

Smart instincts.

When I make it to the edge of the walkway, I spot the ledge below right next to the water. I jump up and over, landing easily. As soon as I do, Hare waves me over from a narrow gondola, a paddle already in his grip. I step from the ledge into the skinny vessel, and the water sloshes with my weight.

The canals are dammed up with other boats, but I quickly realize how Hare got his name, and it has nothing to do with his teeth. He seems to know where every tunnel in the city exists, and he's just as fast on the water as any rabbit on foot.

He maneuvers us deftly, passing by clusters of other boats and beneath bridges, going down narrow passages squeezed between covered roads and trees. He takes us off the beaten path, finding every nook and cranny our skinny boat can fit through, going down each channel like a rabbit racing away from a fox.

Then he takes us into an underground tunnel, the air dark and musty, but the water empty of other boats.

"Are we actually getting somewhere?" I ask.

I don't like being down in these covered waterways. There's barely enough space to stand, and the air is clogged with dripping moisture that clings to the stone. I want to be back out in the air, able to see the golden aura I desperately need to keep in my sights.

"Yes. Nearly there, my lord."

Seconds later, we come out the other side of the dark, ducking under the low-hanging tunnel exit.

"Here," he says before the front of our needle-point boat knocks into the ledge of a bricked road.

The noise of the city seems to have amplified now. Hare's alternate routes must have gotten us closer to…whatever it is that everyone's swarming toward. As I step off the boat and onto a narrow alleyway, I walk between two buildings and look up once I pass them, realizing with a jolt that I'm closer to Auren. Much closer.

Her aura glosses the air with light, slicking it with shine. But there's also something that hasn't ever been in her aura before. Black vaporous tendrils that snake through her golden glow. They drift through it, like vines down a stream, floating in its surface.

Seeing her aura and mine roiling together like this is a fucking gift. One that knocks the air right out of me. An ebb and flow of light and dark that saturates the sky and sears into my brain.

My chest tightens with anticipation.

*I'm coming, Auren. I'm fucking coming.*

Hare squeezes next to me, eyeing the busy street ahead. There are people surrounding us, packing us in. "We'll try to cut across. It's just that way." He points. "I know someone who lives a few blocks down who has a rooftop view of the city square. If we can get past all these people and get there, we can—"

He doesn't get to finish his sentence.

People suddenly scream. The sound doesn't come from the square, but from the other direction. The fae in front of us jerk around to look, and I can see some further down the street trying to get away, which makes the packed-in crowd push even closer against the fringes.

Hare and I get jostled back, shoved into the alley again. I yank my spikes beneath my skin as a frown takes over my face. I lean forward to look around the corner of the building so I can figure out what the fuck is happening.

A second later, I see Stone Swords marching. They're shoving people out of the way, with no care for who gets hurt.

Anger pulses down my veins.

One of them wields magic when the packed crowd doesn't move quick enough. A torrent of wind magic gusts out like a cyclone. It whips down the bricked street with a powerful vortex, churning with dirt and branches torn from the trees. I can even see ripped clothing spiraling through its mass.

Fae hurry to get out of the way, hands covering their eyes and mouths squeezed shut, while dirt and debris start to batter everyone's bodies. I jerk my head back as a spray of dust stings my eyes.

"There must be trouble in the square!" Hare says, half hollering in my ear so he can be heard over the gusts. "Looks like someone signaled for reinforcements!"

I blink to clear my eyes and look ahead again. There are a good fifty soldiers from what I can tell, all of them with their marbled shields lifted, blocking them from neck to knee. The crowd is forced aside, allowing the contingent of Stone Swords a clear path as they travel toward the square.

But suddenly, someone from the crowd rushes out. A young male—not even past his teen years—with a round face and a flop of cherry red hair. "Carrick-following traitors!" he shouts as he steps in the middle of the street, directly in their way.

Then he turns his head and *spits*.

Except instead of just a simple glob of saliva left on the street, streams of white spew from his mouth. The substance sticks to the building on his right and starts to stretch, like underwater tentacles reaching for prey.

People in the crowd gasp and move away.

In a blink, he turns to the left and spits again, sticking another clump to the other building with a wet smack. The two globs grasp for each other in frothing strings that remind me of the left-behinds of spittlebugs, their clots of bubbly refuse sticking to grass and twigs.

The boy's strange magic lengthens and drops down, until the entire width of the street is blocked with his foaming webs of saliva that act as a barrier against the oncoming soldiers.

Hare and I get knocked back against the brick wall as a group of fae race down the alley to get away from the scene, putting distance between themselves and this show-down on the street.

A holler tears down from the rooftops. "*Baz*!" I look up to see an older fae screaming at the boy. There's fear in his face as he reaches toward him as if he can yank him up from the street. "*No*!"

Worry starts to twist my insides, and I push myself away from the wall. I have to physically pry open spaces for me to move forward in the crowd.

"Lord Rot?" Hare calls behind me, but I ignore him.

When I shove my way past a few more fae, I spot the boy again, just as the magical cyclone slams into his sticky barrier.

The spinning air magic rips it from the walls, clearing the path with ease. But then it suddenly heads right for the boy.

*Shit.*

I hurry forward again, but the twister slams into his body, picking him up like he weighs nothing. I see his shocked, terrified face just before his body is sucked further into the spin. Then the tornado pivots, sending him flying out with incredible force.

I watch in shock as his body crashes against a building with a sickening hit that seems to stun the entire street. He falls, landing in a broken heap and covered in dust, his bones bent and eyes unseeing.

*What the fuck?*

The male on the rooftop lets out a bloodcurdling wail that flays my insides.

"You didn't have to kill him!" someone else screams from the street, a male with a deep blue robe and bare feet. "He didn't hurt anyone!"

"He was obstructing the crown's justice," the cyclone soldier yells. "Now move aside or face the same fate!"

The soldiers start to step toward the robed fae with threat, just as fresh screams rip from the city square. Coming from the same direction where Auren's aura blooms.

A surge of anxiety rushes through me, making the spikes beneath my spine pulse.

I need to deal with these fucking soldiers and get to Auren *now*.

I shove aside more people, tossing them behind me, and finally manage to wrench forward. Dark intent fills my whole body as I make it to the front of the pack, and the cyclone fae swivels his attention toward me. Our eyes lock.

He's fucking done, but he doesn't know it yet.

My magic pulses through the ground and grips him so that when he starts to say something to me, he finds he can't. His eyes widen as his tongue starts to rot inside his mouth. "Not so tough when you're up against someone your own size, are you?" I snarl into the dying wind. "You had no right to kill him."

The power of the cyclone goes petering out as the fae's tongue turns black, shriveling inside his jaw. I look behind him to all the other gaping soldiers, just as the male who was on the rooftop races out onto the street and collapses over the boy's dead body. His wails soak my ears.

Rot spreads out from my feet, slithering like snakes, and the bricks start to buckle with decay as it reaches the Stone Swords.

I'm going to break them just like they broke that boy.

Their screams of panic start catching on right as the black veins along the ground reach their clustered feet. The soldiers begin to topple, bones decaying within the confines of their moldering skin.

And then I let my dragon tear free.

Like billowing smoke and streaking shadows, it swarms out of my skin, collecting, building, feeding off my emotions.

When it lands hard at my side, its chest gleams with gilded scales, and its body is completely *solid*.

For the first time, I've just manifested a fully physical dragon.

Not vaporous, not intangible. A solidified menace that now stands even taller and more monstrous than it was when its splintered form streaked over the skies of Sixth Kingdom.

It stretches taller than the steepled buildings along the street, its spiked body and coiled tail barely fitting. Then it opens its mouth, showing off its wicked sharp teeth, and breathes fire of black rot, taking out what's left of the soldiers.

Panic decimates the street.

The gathered crowd bolts. Abandoning their tightly packed positions from where they were trying to get closer to the square, they now turn and flee. The grieving fae whose body is draped over the boy shakes in fear, tears caught in every crevice of his face. "Don't destroy him, please!" he cries as he clutches at the body.

I shake my head. "You have nothing to fear from us."

Then I turn and start walking, and people scatter as fast as they can while the dragon stomps behind me, every step shaking the street.

Hare appears at my side out of nowhere. "A *dragon*?" he shouts, shock dripping off his face like drool as he stares at the creature. "You can manifest a dragon? I thought that magic died out in your family generations ago!"

"It did."

He clamps his mouth shut after that, staying behind as I make my way down the street. The weight of the dragon snaps the stone as it walks, tail whipping, eyes flashing.

People run past us screaming, but my attention is locked on the blinding aura ahead. Anxiety rises up like acid at the back of my throat, because my bond isn't singing, it isn't even blaring. It's fucking hammering against my chest, demanding with ferocity.

*GO GO GO GO GO GO*

As soon as the last of the people flee in the face of my dragon, leaving the way clear, I start to *sprint*. My heart pounds hard in my chest as that aura glows up from the ground like a fallen star, streaked with darkness that flares like a pulse.

I'm getting closer, *closer*, so fucking close after weeks and weeks of pure darkness, pure agony.

And then, I reach the end of the street, and I see a golden figure running toward me. My heart breaks open.

*Auren.*

# CHAPTER 32

## SLADE

She's a vision.

Auren gleams in the sunlight, dressed head to toe in armor that melds against her body. She's so fucking beautiful, so fucking strong.

And *here.* After all this time, after walking from one world to the next, she's finally here, right in front of me.

The sight of her takes my breath away.

I edge around a fountain, see her eyes widen at the looming dragon behind me, her steps slowing.

"It's okay," I reassure her, my eyes delving into hers, my throat closing from joy and emotion. "I—"

Liquid gold suddenly slams into my chest.

It's so unexpected that it staggers me. I manage to stay on my feet, but just barely. She stops, leaving distance between us, just as that gold partially solidifies to slide down my torso and wrap around me like ropes. It binds my arms behind my back and hardens around my boots.

I look down at the gold holding me in place and then back at her with a smirk. "If you wanted to tie me up, then may I suggest we do so in private?"

It doesn't escape me that her gold is riddled with roots of rot—*my* rot.

Pure male satisfaction surges through me.

Her expression is unreadable. "You're not The Breaker. Who are you?"

I blink, thoughts cutting off as I replay her words. "What?"

"You heard me," she says, jutting her chin up, legs braced, a gleaming sword held in her palm. It's the most fearless, sexiest sight I've ever seen in my life. But in all my anticipation, in view of her gleaming perfection, I failed to see that there's something missing. Right there in her eyes.

My stomach plummets.

"Auren?"

I try to move forward even though I'm cemented in place, but she flinches back.

Flinches. Back.

"How do you know my name?"

She might as well have shoved her sword through my heart. I can't breathe as her words soak in, as I realize the unfamiliarity in her wary gaze.

*What the fuck is happening?*

Panic pulses through my head, and I feel real, cold fear that ices over my heart.

"What is this? What happened?" I demand. "Auren. It's *me*."

But there's nothing. She looks at me like she's never seen me before, and my heart fucking shatters. I can hear every fragment fall.

Her eyes dart to look at the beast behind me, and I see her notice the tendrils of rot that have bloomed over the bricks from our feet.

My mouth is parted in shock, heartbreak pinching my chest as I desperately try to figure out what's going on. Then a male carrying a sword comes running up from the sloped area below. He has long black hair tossed over to the left side, and he's splattered with both bruises on his face and blood on his shirt.

He sees the dragon and comes to a jolting halt, his face paling. "What…"

"Yeah, I didn't expect to find a dragon," Auren mutters to him.

"No?" I say. "Well, I *did* expect to find a goldfinch."

Her golden eyes flare.

Something there, something *almost* there.

Hope surges in my chest.

Obviously, something happened to her memories, but she's still there. She's still mine. The proof of that is right there in her aura.

"What did you say?" she whispers, and her voice sounds so fucking fragile beneath all that armor that it hurts to breathe.

"Goldfinch," I say softly.

Her gold bindings loosen around me ever so slightly, and it makes my shattered heart lift. Try to piece back together.

Determination steels my bones.

I don't know why the fuck she doesn't remember me, or what's happened while we've been separated. But physical distance couldn't keep us apart, and a mental one won't either.

"Who *are* you?" she asks again, but her voice seems unsure now. Wavering.

The male looks between us, but wisely stays quiet and still.

"You know who I am, Auren," I tell her gently.

She starts to shake her head, and her gaze flicks up to the dragon again. "Eyes on me," I murmur.

Her gaze pins and sharpens. I can see the flare of defiance, but behind that is her uncertain vulnerability.

"You can see it, can't you?" I ask her. "You can see my aura?"

Her breath hitches. I want to wrap that breath around me and pull it into my chest. Feed her air right into my lungs. I need her with a ferocity that extends beyond anything else.

We aren't going to finally find each other only for her to be stolen away from me. I won't let that happen.

She won't let that happen either.

I watch her eyes scrape against my outline, no doubt eyeing the aura that must be flaring around my body the way hers does for me. Our energies always called to one another, even before our päyur bond solidified. Even before we ever met.

Behind me, the dragon dissipates. I don't have to see it, I feel it disintegrating into the air like smoke on the empty street.

"Come here."

Her lips part and her chest starts rising and falling rapidly, as if she's not sure if she should attack again or run in the other direction. She's not afraid of me though. Wary and confused, yes. But there's a part of her that knows I'd never hurt her. Even if she doesn't remember, she knows that.

So I wait. I have faith. Because the only thing I believe in, is her.

She takes a step. One small step. Then she stops, like she's surprised she did it.

"Auren…" the other male says, but she ignores him, which is a really good thing for him.

"Are you going to tell me who you are?" she says.

"You're not asking the right question," I reply.

I watch as she takes another step forward, almost subconsciously, like she can't help but be drawn toward me. If it weren't for the gold holding me in place, I wouldn't have been able to stop myself either.

They say old spirits are drawn to the dawn. That they can't help but haunt the light. That's what I feel like. Without her, I'm caught in endless darkness.

Her throat bobs, and then her voice comes out softly. Tentatively. "Who are you...to me?"

A smile of pure pride tips my lips, and I swallow down a lump of emotion. "Very good. Now come to me, baby, and I'll show you."

There must be a force in the realms unknown, a goddess-sent gift that pulls us toward one another. Because even though she seems lost in the dark too, she comes.

She comes toward me willingly.

Our auras reach for each other, dark and light tendrils stretching...

When she's right in front of me, I call to the rot within her magic, making it tug the gold away from my arms. Her eyes widen as she sees the golden ropes fall away. "How—"

Then our auras meet. Join. *Collide.*

Our bond shatters the air.

Shadow and light blinds, shoving away everything else, until all that exists is her. We stare at each other, caught in this cocoon of our own atmosphere while the world trembles with our bond and everything else disappears.

Together. We're finally fucking *together.*

She sucks in a breath, like she's been holding it for too long. Like she's been lacking air since we were ripped apart.

Then, her face changes in an instant, and gone is the shock, the wariness, the uncertainty. In its place is something utterly life-changing.

Her beautiful eyes fill, and her gilded lips part.

"*Slade.*"

Our auras might've shattered the sky, but her saying my name shatters *me.*

And it seems to shatter her too. I can see every line that

cracks through her eyes, every thought that breaks across her face.

"I remember…" she whispers upon a trembled breath. "Great Divine…I *remember*."

Her expression looks haunted yet awed, a thousand words caught there, and I want to release every single one.

My eyes burn, my chest feeling ready to explode, but I reach forward and clasp her beautiful face. Drag my thumb over her soft cheek to catch the first tear that falls.

"You found me," she whispers, lip trembling.

The relief and heartbreaking joy is so intense I have to shove it aside before I can answer. "I'll always find you, Goldfinch."

*Always*.

A devastating smile breaks out across her face, watery eyes spilling over and flooding right into me. Then she leaps into my arms and I catch her.

I hold her so tightly against me in a way that threatens the Fates if they ever fucking dare to separate us again.

"Slade…Slade…Slade…"

She says it over and over again. Just my name. Repeated a thousand different times, in a thousand different ways.

I press my face into her hair, breathing her in, squeezing my wet eyes against the golden strands. Her legs are wrapped around my waist, arms holding me tight, and I clasp her to me so there's no space between us. Never again.

"Slade…"

"I'm here, Auren."

I'm *finally* here. Right where I belong.

With her.

# CHAPTER 33

## SLADE

As I hold her tight, Auren clutches me just as fiercely, and everything in me finally settles. The rage, the terror, the unrelenting pain of being separated from her.

Then my attention is pulled when I feel something else wrapping around us, something soft yet strong, and I turn my head to look.

And there they are.

Golden tendrils flowing from her back like rays of sunlight.

My entire body stills with shock, and I blink, expecting the incredible sight to disappear, but it doesn't.

"Auren…" I choke out. "Your *ribbons*."

A sob snaps off from her lips, left in pieces against my neck. "They're back," she tells me, but it sounds like she's telling herself too. Reassuring herself that her ribbons really are there. That she has them again.

"Let me see you."

She leans back in my arms just enough so we're face to face. Eye to eye. Breath to breath.

She hiccups, cheeks glistening as she stares at me like she's in as much awe as I am. "How?" I ask, just as the tendrils come up around us, stroking me, curling around my shoulders, slipping around my arms. They wind around us, like they're tying Auren and me together.

"I don't know," she answers, and I can see the joy in her gilded irises—can see the utter relief. And then she cripples me. "They're back, and so are you. I'm whole again."

*I'm whole again.*

I yank her forward and slam my lips against hers. She meets my kiss like she's been looking for me for a lifetime, and maybe she has.

Maybe I have too.

We've lived a thousand little lifetimes, dying a little bit every second we were apart.

"I missed you with my entire soul," she says, swiping her lips across my jaw.

I know exactly what she means.

"My heart didn't work without you," I tell her.

She smiles and looks into my eyes. "We're quite the pair, you and I."

It feels like I said those words so long ago, and hearing her repeat them now makes my chest tighten. "You figured it out?"

She shakes her head. "Not until it happened."

Being wholly fixated on her, I didn't notice what our auras were doing until her ribbons start reaching out to dance in the shadowed light. Our auras have surrounded us completely and are growing denser.

"What's happening?" she asks quietly.

"It's us."

Our bonded auras start feeding in, both golden glow and basking darkness. It soaks through us. *Into* us.

The magic that pulses with it is incomprehensible. Unfathomable. It feels as if I'm touching a star and standing in the middle of a parted sea.

Then a sudden need to be buried inside of her snares me, stealing my fucking breath and setting my veins on fire. The bond flooding in demands no separation. I can feel her even more intensely than I did before.

We're not two anymore. We're one pair, and that magic is *consuming*. The päyur bond surges, heating me from the inside out, flooding me with an intense urgency that's demanding to be sated.

Auren clutches me with serrated breath, her ribbons fluttering around with anxiousness. Then the flare of our auras dims, drifting away, and the ground settles, but she's still trembling. I look down at her, and now, I'm trembling too. Brimming with ravenous *need*.

She stares at me, no longer crying, her cheeks flushed and her lips parted, and I can see the need in her too—right there in her dilated eyes.

"Slade…I…"

Her words choke off like she's dying of thirst, but I know her scorched throat has nothing to do with water and everything to do with the bond magic demanding that we quench a different kind of thirst.

"It's okay, Goldfinch. I know."

Her arms tighten around my neck, and she buries her face there. I can feel her core pressing up against my front. Her body is always warm, but right now, she's blazing.

Now that we seem to have fused, her aura has gone back to a faint shimmer around her skin, no longer blotting out the rest of the world.

The street is still blessedly empty, save for the shell-shocked male who stands beside the fountain. "Auren?"

As soon as he says her name, a snarl rips out of me, and

RAVEN KENNEDY

my teeth flash at him with unbidden fury. I want to tear him apart. I want to gut him from groin to grin and spill out his lifeblood for daring to speak her name.

I take a threatening step forward, but Auren's grip tenses around me, and she leans back. "Slade."

Only her voice could yank my attention so thoroughly. My breath pants through gritted teeth, and I'm fucking hard as a rock, enraged at the nearness of this strange male so close to her.

A small part of me knows I'm acting insane, but there is no room for logical, rational thought. There's nothing but a base, animalistic need that's ignited every nerve, demanding me to claim her, to protect her. To satiate her every need.

"Slade," she murmurs again, and one ribbon comes up, tapping against my cheek like a finger. "Eyes on me, baby."

My gaze snaps to hers and she nods with a smile. "Take us somewhere safe. Somewhere we can be alone," she says against my lips, fingers digging in where she clutches me. "*Please*."

Her plea undoes me, and my hands grip her ass as I turn around, looking every which way. I'm so out of my mind I can't even fathom a thought as to where to go. All I know is she needs me.

I'm a split second away from taking her right here, bent over the city's fountain. But my bonded deserves so much fucking more than that.

"This way," the male says.

I bare my teeth at him, my canines so sharp they nearly slice through my lips.

"Shh," Auren soothes, even as she starts to rock against me. I have to bite back a groan as she presses fevered lips against the pulse at my neck. "Let him show us where to go. I need you."

My head swings toward the male. "*Where.*" I demand.

He turns and quickly starts leading us away. I put one foot in front of the other. It's all I can do.

310

Auren's hips move as I hold her against me, seeking a satisfaction she can't yet reach. And she won't—not until I'm inside her. Not until I'm pumping her full and the pair bond is fully sated.

I never personally knew anyone who was a päyur, but I heard crass stories of the newly bonded and how they'd shut themselves into a room for days at a time.

The male keeps a good distance ahead, squeezing us down an alleyway and then to a narrow building on the next street over. My head swivels around, but everyone ran from the dragon.

Thank fuck. I don't think I could handle anyone else being near Auren right now. I'm barely holding it together as it is.

Instead of going to the front door, the male goes around the back of the steepled building, its sides smoothed with decorative arches around every window and vines growing down from the roof. He stops at the building's back and kneels down, shoving aside the vines that have draped over the ground to reveal a cellar entrance.

"*Slade...*"

It kills me to hear the desperation in her voice.

I grip Auren harder, one hand at her ass, the other holding the back of her head so that her face can be pressed against the skin at my neck. I'm hoping my scent can soothe her at least somewhat. Her scent surrounding me is one of the only things keeping me fucking sane right now.

But then her hot, wet tongue darts out, tasting my skin, and I nearly explode in my pants.

"Hurry. The fuck. Up," I say to him through my teeth.

The cellar doors squeak open, and the male quickly hands me a key. "It locks from the inside," he tells me. "Go down the stairs, and you'll come to a private underground waterway. There's always at least a boat or two there to use. Take one and row downstream until you see the house with the green bulbs.

It's a Vulmin safe house. No one will be there, and I'll ensure no one will disturb you. It's secure."

Auren stops licking me to turn her face, her cheeks blotched with heat and probably a bit of embarrassment too. "Thanks, Wick."

It feels like every muscle in my body fucking bulges.

"Goldfinch?" I grit out.

She tips her head up at me, her eyes lidded, my blood surging.

"I'm hanging on by a *fraying thread*. I really need you to not say another male's name right now."

Her eyes widen. "Oh," she breathes.

"Yeah. *Oh*."

"I'm going," the male—Wick—says as he starts backing away, hands held up in front of him like he's warding off a rabid animal. "When you two are…done, go to the building with the blue roof in the city. We'll be waiting there."

"Wait!" Auren suddenly blurts. "Oreans. Just outside the city. I got them out of the dungeons. They'll need your help."

Wick nods. "Don't worry. I'll take care of them."

I barely hear him, already stepping down into the cellar. As soon as I clear the stairs, I reach one arm up and slam the doors closed and then engage the lock. Slipping the key into my pocket, I turn, letting my sight adjust to the darkness of the tunnel while my bond burns with my need to take her.

Have to get somewhere safe first. Have to take care of her.

My feet crossed two realms to get to her, and now, my hands itch to cross over every inch of her skin. With the way she's shaking and rocking against me, I know we're running out of time.

The bond is demanding that we pair. In *every* way.

# CHAPTER 34

## SLADE

Inside the space, the walls are damp, the air humid, and just ahead, there's a waterway. The ornate grates along the arched stone ceiling feed in some light, but mostly, it comes from the blue glow emanating from the glass orbs strung along the wall. Some sort of magicked light that flickers like stars.

Hunching down slightly, I carry Auren toward the canal, while her ribbons stroke over my arms and shoulders. I find two boats already bobbing in the black water, tied to a post with rope. I choose the widest one, the wood a sleek gray with carvings around the lip.

Carefully, I set Auren onto the cushioned bench at the middle before I climb in behind her, my movements stiff. The bond is shoving at me with incessant hands, except these hands are trying to push away all rational thought and tip me over into pure feral lust.

Instead of *go go go* like the bond was thrumming before, now it's screaming at me to bury myself inside of her. To take her until we are joined in *every way*. To fuck her hard and fast and hear her moaning with pleasure.

I struggle to hold on, to keep my thoughts coherent. I need to get her somewhere safe before I can surrender. Before I can succumb to the bond's hunger and become nothing more than a feral fae ready to slake lust and yank every inch of pleasure from my pair's body.

Gritting my teeth, I quickly untie the rope and kick us away from the wall. The boat sloshes as I sit on the bench at the back, and my eyes lock on hers.

Auren faces me, stock still, her fingers and ribbons both curled around the bench with a tight grip like she's trying to hold herself back as much as I am. She's wound up, her entire body as tense as mine.

My feral need rages.

*Take her. Fuck her. Claim her.*

My spikes throb, but I keep them shoved beneath my skin, even as my eyes drag over the pulse at Auren's neck that beats wildly.

My bond pushes. Pounds. My cock hard and lust flooded.

She watches me with a hungry flare in her eyes as I take hold of the paddles hooked into the oarlocks on either side. But as soon as I drag the oars back to cast us away, she launches into my arms.

An *oof* escapes me as she lands in my lap, chest to chest, her thighs straddling, core pressing against my groin. The boat rocks, splashes of water sloshing in, but I barely notice.

Wicked ecstasy lashes into me, and my fingers tighten around her. I want to tear off her clothes, to spread my hands over her bare skin and bury myself inside her wet heat.

*Fuck...*

"I can't wait," she hisses as her fingers come up to my

314

leather jerkin. In hurried movements, she starts to undo the ties down my collar as she rocks against me. "You're here, and the bond…and…*I can't wait*," she says again.

My dick goes harder than steel.

Need to get us to that house. Get us alone. But it's *really* damn hard to focus when she's rocking herself against me like this. When her scent is surrounding me.

The oars are forgotten as I let go, our boat drifting down toward the darkened tunnel.

I can't deny her.

"Tell me what you need and I'll give it to you," I say, but even I can hear the rough growl in my voice that's scraped with animalistic hunger.

The gold armor over her pants and the boots on her feet start to melt away, gilding the bottom of the boat and evening out the weight to keep it from tipping. She keeps the chest plate on, but the gauntlets on her arms drip away too.

She keeps fumbling with my ties, so I help her, loosening the straps enough until her frantic hands can delve beneath my shirt, her fingers splaying over my bare skin.

The contact feels like bolts of lightning. She sighs, though her touch jolts me.

"I need to feel you right now." She starts peppering my jaw and neck with kisses. "I need you to fill me. I feel like I might die without it," she admits with tears in her eyes, pure desperation glassing them. "Please don't stop me. *I can't wait*," she says again.

"Then you don't have to wait. Not another second," I tell her. "Lift up."

Auren's eyes flare at my words, and she braces her feet on the bench so she can lift herself. As soon as she does, I yank her pants down and then rip them off completely.

My eyes flare at the sight of her, and then I drag her back down to my lap. Grip her bare ass in my hands. She's so fucking soft. So warm.

I start to move her hips in a steady rhythm against me, and my eyes nearly roll back. She braces her hands on my shoulders, moaning with every movement.

"Not enough. Need more," she says breathlessly.

*Yes. More. Need more.*

I lean forward and nip at her lush lips. "You need me to fill you right here in this boat, baby?" I grind out.

Her chest stutters. *"Yes. Please."*

The desperation of her low voice, the potency of her heat, it makes my mouth water. Makes the bond keep shoving.

My fingers squeeze into her skin. "You don't need to beg, but the words sound so fucking sweet."

I can tell my reply pleases her by the way her golden eyes ignite, flashing even in the dark underground.

"That male had better have told the truth about this being a private tunnel," I say. "Because I'll rot out the eyes of anyone who looks at you."

Her pulse jumps. Maybe with an edge of fear, but I think that's *thrill* in her flushed face. She likes how utterly protective I am of her, and that thought makes me savage with need.

"Undo my pants," I growl.

Auren's fingers instantly drop to the ties. She yanks them away, hand slipping inside to pull out my cock, making me almost come right here and now.

Her eyes stare, her little pink tongue coming out to lick her lips.

My body jerks with intense pleasure as she squeezes me, sending through bolts that singe. *"Fuck."*

The bond is burning through my veins now, tunneling my vision and demanding more. Her aura is erratic, reaching and twisting, while her heartbeat races in her chest and her arousal lifts into the air.

She smells so. Fucking. Good.

"Put me inside you," I gasp. "I need to feel you, Auren."

GOLDFINCH

"*Yes…*"

I lift her hips up so she can position me right at her entrance. My muscles are bunched, spikes threatening to force back out as desperation flows through my veins. My cock is already dripping. Our eyes lock.

Then I slam her down onto me.

Her head flings back, a cry tearing from her throat that bounces down the tunnel.

I see stars as soon as I'm buried inside of her.

It's bliss. Pure. Fucking. Bliss.

She shudders. Lip caught between her teeth, biting down. Her nails dig into my shoulders. "Perfect. You're thick and hard and *perfect*," she purrs.

"You're already stretching around me. You feel that?"

Her entire body trembles as she nods, and I lift her up before slamming her back down. Again. *Again.*

I lift her and keep her there. "Lower yourself," I demand gutturally. "I want to see it. I want to see your perfect cunt swallowing my cock. Inch by inch."

A throaty whimper escapes her parted mouth as she starts to do just that. We both look down, watching my length disappear into her body while she squeezes me. Floods me with her wetness that's already glistening down her thighs.

She slams down the last inch, and I'm buried all the way inside of her again. We share a moan, and the bond flares, like a million little fires sparking throughout every crevice, filling us with desire and heat.

"Look at your perfect pussy," I say, my voice low. Bitten with lust. "We were made for each other, weren't we, baby?"

Auren nods, the dazed look in her eyes driving me wild. Making my muscles strain and shake.

I grip her hips and then jut mine up. Hard.

She chokes out a moan of surprise. "So *deep…*"

"I'm going to get fucking *deeper*," I growl as I drag my

teeth over her pulse. "I'm going to be so deep inside of you, through the bond, through your body, through your *soul*, that we will never have any separation ever again." My snarled promise is met with her pussy tightening around me, her nails digging into the skin at my neck.

My fang teases over her delicious vein, and I inhale her decadent, needy scent. Then I thrust my hips up again, and she shudders, our groans breaking out as our boat continues to drift.

She starts rocking over me, back undulating, hips moving like an erotic dance while her ribbons twist around and grip my back. A part of me can't believe I have her here in my arms. That this bliss is meant for me.

But she *is* here. I can feel her and scent her and touch her, and she's all fucking mine.

"Give me your mouth," I demand. Because I want to swallow her down. To taste her moans and feed her mine.

Our lips fuse together instantly. Tongues lapping. Teeth and taste and groans slipping from her throat to mine. Our kiss is frenzied. Feral. All that exists is her panting breaths and the demand for more.

I drag her body up and down on my cock. Hard. Steady. Never relenting.

"You feel…so…*good*." Her confession travels down the narrow confines of the tunneled waterway, dripping with the humid air. Just like she's dripping all over me, her liquid heat soaking my dick, my balls, permeating my senses.

My fingers dig into her waist as I drag her up and down again, making her clutch me, dragging another moan from her lips. I delve my hand through her hair and through her soft, undulating ribbons. Then she arches back, taking control of our movements as she starts to fuck me. My teeth clench at the feel of her exquisite body as she takes my cock and demands more.

"You perfect creature," I purr as I nip the skin at her neck and lick.

Auren makes a desperate noise and starts slamming down over me so hard the movement starts to sway the boat. The water laps at the sides, threatening to spill in, while thrill spills through *me*. "That's it. Fuck me harder, Auren."

Her moan echoes down the tunnel, coiling in every crevice of the smoothed bricks and catching inside the brackets of my very bones.

I capture the sound in a hungry kiss. "I'm going to keep your sounds forever, Goldfinch. Every. Single. One." I punctuate each word with a thrust, helping her as her thighs begin to shake, her body straining as she races for her peak.

"Come on my cock, baby. Squeeze me with this perfect cunt of yours."

She dives for my mouth. Tongue lashing, drinking me down. I'd let her drain me dry if she wanted to.

Then she slams down so hard over me I black out for a second.

Her entire body jerks, pussy clamping around me as she comes. I feel her drenching me, slick dripping out of her with her release. My eyes roll to the back of my head as she cries out, the blissful sound soaking into me and making me nearly come too.

She falls against me just as the front of the boat slams into a wall.

Dazed, I look up, and see a green orb light hanging over the door of a building that has access to the underground canal.

Thank fuck we're here.

"Hold on," I tell her.

But before I can stand and pull out of her to secure the boat, Auren's nails dig into my arms, her ribbons snap around my back, and she glares at me with fierce possession. "No. Stay inside of me," she growls at me.

*Growls.*

Filthiest, sexiest thing I've ever heard.

Gold lashes out of her palm, and she sends it streaming to the wall that acts as both a dock and the separation from building to water. The gold forms into links of a chain, looping around the hook at the boat's end and securing it to the hitch on the post.

"Let's go," she orders, and her firm tone, the way she makes it very clear she has no intention of letting my cock out of her, makes me even harder.

I grin in the dark. "At your command."

# CHAPTER 35

## SLADE

With my hands covering her ass, I stand and step us out of the boat. This entrance is nothing but a narrow stop in the canals. Just enough space for the belly of this building to open up within this underground tunnel.

Auren groans against my ear as I move, jostling my still-hard cock within her sheath, and I grit my teeth, stopping myself from thrusting into her.

Focus. I have to fucking *focus*.

I get us to the door in front of the building and reach for the handle. I tug on it, but it doesn't budge. "There's—"

She starts rocking on me again, using her wrapped legs to fuck herself over me, her moans delirious and heady. "*Yes…*"

My vision starts to blacken, like my body is deciding to sacrifice my sight for my cock. I don't blame it one bit. There's not enough rushing blood to go around.

With desperation, I try the handle again, but can't get it to turn. So I lift my foot and kick in the door. Auren doesn't even seem to notice.

I need a soft surface to lay her down so I can fuck her hard. For hours. Days. Forever.

My balls are so tight, so full, and my head is throbbing with the need to explode inside of her. I'm barely holding on. Only able to do so because my need to take care of her outweighs my need to keep fucking her.

"Hurry," she says as I step past the door and into the building. I reach back to shove the door shut. "Gold," I grit out.

She doesn't need me to explain. Her hand lifts, and gold splatters against the wood, sealing the broken door in place.

I climb up the staircase in front of us, taking the steps three at a time. Auren's moans deepen as my movements make my dick shift inside of her, but when I feel her pussy squeeze over me, I stumble against the wall.

Lust takes over. My hips punch forward as I start to piston into her, making her squeal and writhe before I remember myself.

"*Shit...*" I curse before forcing myself to move, to keep going. I pull her away from the wall, finding that we're in a narrow corridor. I latch my focus onto the open door and the bed I can see just past it.

I'm there within five steps, kicking the bedroom door shut behind me. It slams so hard that the wooden rafters along the ceiling creak. With a quick glance around, I make sure that the room is safe. Window is boarded. Bedding is clean. There are no other doors in here and definitely no people—luckily for them.

I set Auren on the bed gently, but as soon as I do, she starts tearing at my clothes. "Off," she demands. "I want everything off."

My mouth hitches up at the corner. "Demanding thing, aren't you?" I kick off my boots and let my trousers drop.

Auren reaches up and rips my shirt right down the middle, shocking us both.

"Hmm," I say, glancing down. "*Very* demanding."

She looks at me with defiance. "I'm not sorry."

I chuckle before dragging my cock out of her. She whines. "I wouldn't want you to be," I say, and then I shove back in hard, pinning her in place as I roll my hips and grind in deep. She flings back on the bed, her moan drowning out the sound of the headboard smacking into the plaster.

Leaning down, I smooth my hand over the golden chest plate that's still melded to her torso. "Drop your gold. I want to see all of you."

She blinks open her eyes, glancing down like she forgot it was even there. Then, the armor starts to ripple, the metal melting down, and she bares herself to me. My eyes devour her. My heart feasts.

I trace the curve of her waist, the underside of her breast, and over the line of her collarbone before smoothing up her lips. "You are the most Divine being to have ever walked the earth," I whisper.

A pretty blush darkens her cheeks. Her ribbons curl toward me, stroking against my chest, dipping to my groin, and then sliding even further *down...*

I smirk. "Little flirts."

Auren's breath hitches. Her ribbons come up to wrap around my back, slipping between the spikes on my arms and the ones that have punched down my spine. I don't even know when they came out. Don't remember it happening. But it's no wonder she's making me lose control. Not with her scent so heady. Not with this hunger throbbing between us.

"Now. Right now, Slade."

She's demanding, desperate. Divine. So perfectly fucking divine.

I pull out. Push in. Out. In.

Dragging my cock through her slick heat is complete bliss. Her ribbons pull against my spikes to tug me down, pressing us together so we're chest to chest.

Heart to heart.

I brace a knee against the bed and pick up her hips to tilt her body like I'm serving myself a gilded platter of perfection. Then I start fucking her in earnest. My thrusts hit her deep, making noise rip from her throat. I lean down, tongue lapping over her breasts, flicking over her nipples. Sucking, tasting, nibbling the skin. Canines aching.

The bond demanding.

I reach between us and stroke her needy clit. The bundle of nerves is engorged and throbbing. The second I start to move my fingers over it, Auren shakes and moans.

"Come for me, baby. I need to feel you."

She does.

Body undulating, she lets out her release with an arc of her spine and a clamour from her throat, and I groan.

"Your pussy is squeezing me so…fucking…tightly…"

My fingers don't relent. My cock doesn't either. I keep fucking her. Fucking *into* her. Wanting to bury myself so deeply there's no separation possible.

"Keep going," I command. "Keep coming. Keep squeezing my cock. You're not done yet."

I thrust harder and faster, not letting up, and she gives everything to me. Her body ripples around my length, demanding my own release as her pussy clamps down, soaking me, milking me.

I explode.

Cum pumps into her like scalding lava as my entire body ignites with pleasure. A pleasure that isn't even of this world. Pleasure that surpasses just the physical.

The päyur power fuels the fire, and I'm still fucking her, still rock hard, even as I finish coming in her.

"More," I growl, but it doesn't even sound like me. It sounds like a fae beast in a rut.

Auren writhes on my cock. "More," she agrees as desperate tears slide down her face. "More more more more—I need more. Don't leave me."

"Never," I snarl, the bond pulsing through every inch of me. It isn't fulfilled yet. If anything, it's more intense than ever. More demanding than before.

I flip her over with a growl. Words becoming difficult to say. I feel like a fucking animal. I think it might be the same for her, because she turns around and claws at me when my dick slides out of her for a second.

My hand lands against her ass, making the flesh quiver. Her knees slide beneath her, back arching, hands braced, and she looks at me over her shoulder, wordlessly asking.

But I pause, noticing something at the back of her neck. I push aside her hair, and my breath sucks in at the small golden scale that gleams right there upon her skin.

A scale from *me*. From our bond. The same color as my own that sits over my heart.

Satisfaction imbeds into me, leaving behind every impression of her. Making my desire flare at the sight of her body showing its bond with mine.

"You. Are. Perfect."

Lining up, I grip her hips and then slam my own forward, entering her with a powerful punch. Her fingers grip the blankets and she holds on as I start fucking her from behind with a ruthlessness that cracks the wall and shakes the rafters. All while Auren moans for more, her pussy soaking me, slick running down her glistening thighs.

I spank her other ass cheek, eyes flaring as I watch the skin ripple with the sting, relishing in the way it makes her cunt clamp around me.

I shove my arm spikes down beneath my skin and then

wind my hands beneath her arms, yanking her up until her back is against my chest. I cup her breasts in my hands, rolling her nipples, squeezing both handfuls.

Gorgeous. So fucking gorgeous.

One hand goes to her clit, pressing, stroking with demand. "*Come.*" My order is guttural—it's all I can manage to say. I'm being taken over more and more. Driven by pure lust.

Her pussy squeezes me, her ribbons flailing. A cry of pleasure splits the air. She makes my body come with her, *again*, gushing even more of my seed into her body.

By the time I'm done with her, she's going to be so full of my cum, she'll be soaked for days.

The thought makes my balls fill right back up.

Auren flips over and this time, I growl when my cock leaves the confines of her perfect pussy. I reach for her, but with a lightning-fast deftness, she leaps away, landing on her feet next to the bed. When I move to stalk toward her, she bares her teeth at me with a snarl, halting me in place.

I stop and tilt my head.

She starts to look around with jerky movements, while making sure she keeps me in her sights. Our shared moisture drips down her thighs, and the sight makes my cock jump. Unbidden, I start to move toward her, mouth watering, wanting to lick her pretty dripping pussy. But she stops me again with another growl.

I halt, muscles tense, my fae nature wanting to bend her over and mount her, to make her scream with more pleasure.

"What's wrong, baby?" I manage to scrape out.

"Not…right." Her words are clumpy and breathless, like her tongue is too laden with lust to even speak.

I look at her with question, not understanding.

"Not right!" she repeats, more agitated this time. "Scents…not yours. Not mine."

Blinking, I tip my chin and breathe in, picking up what

I'd ignored before—all the scents of other fae who have been in this room. Her sense of smell must be more attuned, more sensitive at the moment.

But now that she's pointed it out, I can't get it out of my nose, and it starts aggravating me too. I don't want our space to have any other scents besides hers and mine.

Auren looks around the bedroom with narrowed eyes, and then her gold starts to gather at her palms. I watch as she walks around, gilding everything in sight. Covering the stone floor. Letting gold soak up the walls. Reaching to the rafters and covering the shutters. Every thread on the bed and blankets and pillows, it all saturates through with gleaming gold.

Her movements are fast with an edge of franticness. But even still, her precision is astounding as she goes methodically through the room, leaving no item or inch untouched.

Only once the entire room is gilded does she let out a relieved breath. The tension in her body relaxes somewhat. Because now, the room smells like her. Like me. Like her molten magic.

I look around the space in appreciation. The sight of her gold and the thin veins of my rot marbled through it makes satisfaction purr through me. I like seeing the proof of how intertwined we are. And with the way she keeps glancing down at the gold scale upon my chest makes me wonder if she thinks the same.

"All of this for us," I say with appreciation, my voice gravelly. "Finished?"

I step forward, testing her reaction. This time, she doesn't growl or bare her teeth. She just waits.

I take that as a good sign.

When I come forward another step, the corner of her mouth twitches with mirth. Yet when I nearly reach her, she leaps on top of the bed away from me at the last second.

I turn to face her. "Naughty thing," I grind out with a tsk.

Her nipples pebble with an excited shudder.

"There's no escape," I promise her, my heated gaze dragging down her glistening body. "I'm going to do *filthy* things to you."

A whine crawls up her throat. "Tell me."

Her urging me on only drives me fucking wild. It plays with the fire of our lusts, driving up our burning need. I move closer to the bed, barely keeping myself from pouncing.

"Going to fuck your pussy so many times you'll be aching and wet with unending slick. Going to lick you. Mount you. Take you against a wall. Make you sit on my face until you see stars. I'll take you from behind. In my arms. Bent over, arced back. Screaming. Soundless. I'm going to take you so many times that you'll fall asleep, but I'll still be buried inside of you."

Auren is the one to pounce. Ribbons lashing out, they grip my arms, and I find myself suddenly yanked forward and flipped onto the bed. The spikes on my back punch through the feather mattress, but I barely notice because she's sitting on my face. Her delicious pussy given right to me like an offering, her sexy ass right there for me to bite.

And I do. Can't fucking help it.

My hands grip her luscious cheeks, and then I drag her the rest of the way to my waiting tongue. I gorge myself on her pussy. Flat tongue dragging up her dripping slit, delving in, tasting the sweetest fucking nectar. Tasting her and me combined.

She cries out, body shaking, and when I latch onto her clit, she collapses forward. At first I think she's fallen, but—

*Fuck.*

Her tongue comes down over my cock with the same ferocity as my own as I eat her pussy. My eyes nearly cross, it feels so fucking good. She laps at me, saliva coating me with every lick. Then her mouth opens wide and she sinks that hot, wet mouth over me, and I nearly come up off the bed. She swallows me, hands massaging my swollen balls.

Reaching down, I take her by the throat. Wanting—needing—to feel the way it contracts as she swallows me down. With my hold on her, I thrust up, fucking her mouth, and she gags and moans, spittle dribbling.

So fucking filthy.

She holds on, nails digging into my thighs as I attack her clit with my mouth. Sucking her down like she's sucking me. There is nothing else but this. Nothing else but pleasure and us, together.

Paired.

Auren's mouth bobs frantically, and when she swallows me again, I burst.

Jets of cum spew from my dick. Like it's pulling all the way up from my guts. So much of it that it starts to spill out of her mouth.

"*Swallow.*"

The feral part of me wants all of it inside of her. Every drop.

With my fingers still around her throat, she complies greedily, happily, humming even as she gags and chokes. "Fucking perfect, so fucking perfect."

Unable to wait, needing her own cum to flood my mouth, I let go of her throat to start devouring her anew. Tongue stabbing into her cunt, fingers playing her clit like a damned instrument, hitting every note, listening to every moan like music to my ears.

Her juices flood me just as her voice floods the room in a beautiful cry of release.

I keep sucking her, keep licking, mouth going from sheath to clit, drawing out every last wave of her pleasure as she cries out my name.

Part of me thinks she'll be spent, expecting her to collapse against me, but no. She's not done. Not even close.

Her ribbons loop around the backs of her thighs, and then the ends reach upward and wrap around the upper panel of the four poster bed. The golden lengths lift her up completely, like silken strips of a swing, and her nude, sweat-slicked body is on display.

And at the perfect height for me to fuck her as I stand.

I jerk up from the bed, feathers flying as my spikes tear free from the mattress. Chest heaving, I stand in front of her, cock pulsing, throbbing, already dripping more precum. My body is on fire, driven by pure lust, bond not yet sated.

Auren sits upon her silken strips, swaying gently, a smile on her stunning face. The ribbons slowly widen her thighs, opening herself to me like a sinful gift.

"All mine," I growl out.

She nods, eyes flashing with hunger. "Yours."

The sight of her like this, her giving herself to me, it brings me to my knees. Literally.

Kneeling upon the floor, I grip her calves, pressing a kiss there. My hands come up to dig into the delicate arches of her foot, making her let out a surprised groan as I work the bend. I move onto the next with meticulous care, all while she stares down at me in awe.

Then my touch moves up to her calves. Her thighs. Massaging every muscle. Feeling every inch of her soft skin. I press my mouth to her pussy. Kiss. Suck her swollen bud. Lave at her with adoration and make noises squeeze from her throat.

Straightening back up to my full height, I rub her hips, squeeze her ass. Knead her back and work the knots at her shoulders. Her eyes have fallen closed, her breath slowing, taking off the edge of her frantic demand. Now relaxed, her muscles are no longer tense, her body loose and pliant.

When I reach her neck, I pull her forward, her beautiful gaze fluttering open. "My gorgeous Goldfinch," I murmur. "Now, I'm going to make love to you."

She trembles.

I kiss her with a slow decadence that tells her all the things I cannot yet say.

That I raged.

That I grieved.

That I lost myself without her.

Through this kiss, I tell her every heartbreaking second that we lived apart was a moment I didn't truly exist. That the depth of my love for her stretches further than this mortal body could ever contain.

A tear falls from the corner of her eye, but I kiss it away. Then I slowly, lovingly grip her waist and feed my cock into her waiting body. She accepts me like a bloom waiting for the bee. Opening, accepting, surrounding me with her sweetness.

She is ambrosia. And for a male who was never anything but rot and hate, Auren has become my salvation. My purpose.

My other half.

I move inside her, and her ribbons help rock her even deeper onto my shaft. Our tongues taste, lapping at one another as if we both wish we could drink each other down.

Swallow whole.

"Never again," I swear fiercely against her lips. "Never ever will we be separated again."

Her head shakes, hand gripping my neck and squeezing tight. "Never."

The vow soaks into our bond and makes her aura flare. We rock together, the ribbons both letting her body swing with me and keeping her in place enough for my thrusts to bury deep. They stretch and lift, lower and twist. Pivoting her in the perfect angle that makes her start to lose control.

When she tears her mouth away so she can pant out quickening breaths, I take advantage by licking down her pulse. My fangs fucking ache with mouthwatering need that I can't contain anymore.

My canines sink down, plunging into the curve of her neck so I can lap at the small beads of gold.

She comes instantly.

Crying out, I feel her pussy clamp and ripple as I suck down her blood. The metallic warmth drips down my throat and fills me with gratification. Her head lifts as my hips keep snapping in, and she opens her mouth and latches onto the crook of my shoulder.

"Take it, baby. Take what you need."

*Take everything.*

Even though her teeth are blunt, Auren bites down. Pricks of a sharp, fleeting pain burst from the spot, but then she starts licking, tasting, drinking in my blood to finish fulfilling our bond, and pleasure rips through me.

I fuck her harder with each swallow, with each drag of her darting tongue.

When her lips pull away, her hands come up to clamp around my face, holding me between her palms. "You're mine now."

My heart squeezes at the fierceness in her words. "I was always yours, Goldfinch."

Even when she didn't know it.

We come with a kiss. With blood still swirling between our tongues. Seated deep inside of her, my cock bursts within her heated depths, while her own release coats me.

Her aura pulses, and her throat drags out a guttural groan of my name. I whisper hers right back. Again and again. Filling the room with the sound of her.

As soon as her body lets out the last ripple of her pleasure, her ribbons unwrap, letting her drop into my waiting arms. I hold her, clutching her to me, laying the both of us down as our breaths try to slow. Our heartbeats still pounding in rhythm.

I make sure my spikes are all tucked beneath my skin so I don't hurt her, and then situate her until her body lies on top of mine. With her leg hitched up around my waist, foot stroking my calves, arm draped over my middle, and head resting right over my heart.

Perfect.

"Is the pair bond magic always this…intense?" she asks, her fingers coming down to stroke around my still-hard dick.

Her wicked touch makes me bite my lip as I try real fucking hard not to jerk up into her palm. "I don't know, but I have a feeling we won't be leaving this room for a while."

I feel her cheeks pulling up into a smile. "Good."

Chuckling, I stroke her golden hair, then my touch grazes down her back, over every single ribbon. Goose bumps spread across her skin as I stroke through them, letting my fingers tangle with their lengths. Some of them come up to twist around my cheeks like a loving caress.

"I love you, Slade," Auren whispers as tears fill her eyes.

My heart swells, and I hold her jaw as I kiss away her tears. Then I tilt her face so I can look into the eyes of perfection.

"Oh, Goldfinch. My love for you consumes every part of my soul. It's in every word, every movement. With each morning that dawns and every night that falls. You are completely mine, and I am yours, and that is all I ever need in this life and all the others." I kiss her forehead, tears burning in my eyes. "I love you, Auren."

She falls asleep with a smile on her face and her ribbons curled around my body. I hold her, letting her rest, until she awakens with more ravaging need, and the bond pushes us again.

And again.

And again.

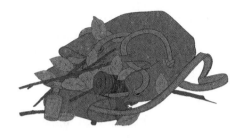

# CHAPTER 36

### EMONIE

Normally, I love going in a fairy ring. It's pure magic, traveling straight through a vein of Annwyn, like drinking fresh water from the source. You can sense the magic and the connection with the land, and it makes you feel powerful and alive.

But as I get sucked through it with the Stone King, I'm not invigorated and I don't feel powerful. Just terrified and reeling.

I watched Auren run toward me with fear and anger, but she couldn't get to me in time. The world crumpled away, and the king kept hold of me.

It feels like we've been stuck in this ring for ages and it still doesn't want to let go. Like the vein we're traveling in is pinched. Suffocating. Trying to keep us in its fist.

My stomach roils, my head pressurizing, and all the while, Carrick's grip is clamped down painfully on my arm, refusing to let go. I fight, trying to get out, but the logical part of me knows it's impossible. You can't stop it once you're in it. The only way through is out the other side.

Finally, after who knows how long, we come to the end. My body topples over as we abruptly land. The king's off-centering hold makes me lose my footing. My knees slam to the ground, though he still keeps my arm wrenched in his grip.

I gasp through the pain, and then immediately I notice the packed and parched ground we've settled on.

*Where are we?*

I expected to travel back to the palace where he'd throw me toward some guards and lock me up in the dungeons again.

But this isn't anywhere near Glassworth. We aren't even in Lydia anymore.

With shallow breaths, I take in the sight of a desolate earth that stretches further than I can see. Everything is gray and lifeless, and the ground itself feels *wrong*. It doesn't feel like the rest of Annwyn.

It's drained. Maybe that's what was wrong with the fairy ring. The land here isn't powerful, isn't alive with magical connection. There's just…*nothing.*

"This is the deadlands," I say out loud to myself, my eyes gone wide as fear soaks into me, weighing me down.

My eyes instantly swing around to find the infamous Orean bridge. I've never actually been this far out to the end of Annwyn. Never saw the broken bridge or the ruined lands around it. Most of us consider it cursed, since the land is dead and fae near here started being born without magic.

And I'm here *in* it—with my knees shoved into the gray dust.

I shudder.

The king suddenly hauls me up to my feet, nearly pulling my arm right out of its socket. Hissing in pain, I try to yank out of his grip, but his hold is unrelenting.

Just like my guilt.

My mind spools, pulling in everything that just happened.

They made me use my glamour to look like Auren. Made me practice and prance around. And then they brought me up there to that stage after that mockery of a performance.

Made me *bow*.

I swallow the bile that comes rushing up the back of my throat. What I did up there on the stage—it feels like a betrayal.

My eyes fill with tears.

What if everyone thinks I'm a traitor? For helping the crown make a mockery out of not just Auren, but all the Turleys, and the Vulmin cause too?

*What if Auren hates me for what I did? Or Wick? What will the other Vulmin think?*

My parents died for this cause, and I just helped *mock* it.

A tear falls.

I just didn't want them to keep hurting Auren. She's been my first real friend. I hated watching Lord Cull break her bones while the king broke her mind.

They were threatening the Oreans too. I tried to call them on their bluff—but I lost. Watched one woman get tortured and killed because of it. I couldn't bear to let anyone else die because of my refusal.

Maybe I should've fought harder. Or figured out a way to trick them.

But then they described my sister's house in Lydia. Talked about her family, like they'd already been watching them. They threatened to hurt her and make me watch, and I couldn't bear it. They found my breaking point.

So, I bowed.

My eyes lift, locking onto the king, and I feel my face knot up with hate. He doesn't even spare me a glance.

As soon as I'm steady on my feet, he lets go of my arm

and shoves me forward out of the fairy ring. I look over my shoulder at it, watching it already start to wither, knowing that traitor Brennur closed it up and blocked the way we came.

I'm stuck here.

Desperate unease makes my shoulders stiffen, and exhaustion suddenly pulls at me from all these weighing emotions and my magical use over the past few days.

I don't know how Auren was able to show up, but thank the goddesses that she did. Because I just made everything worse.

When another tear drips down my face, the glamour starts dripping down too. It melts away, Auren's coloring and features draining until my own appearance returns again.

I take in a shaky breath, looking down at my wrists and ankles still trapped in stone shackles, at the golden dress hanging more loosely on my body. Out of sight, there's another half-circle of stone clamped around my back, the ends stopping just at my ribs. Another shackle to keep me compliant.

"Go," the king commands with another shove.

Instead of listening, I dig in my slippered feet and glare at him. His unmalleable eyes narrow, and then he uses his magic to yank at my shackles to pull me forward.

He walks in front of me, not at all worried that I'm at his back, because he knows I can't do anything.

Being shackled by his stone makes me furious. I stare daggers at his back as he drags me along, while his feet kick up ashy silt, giving me a face-full of dust.

My steps wobble, sweat starting to gather at my neck and forehead while the stone shackles keep tugging me forward.

As we walk, I soon see that there is some life in these deadlands after all. Or maybe it can be argued that it's just more death—because ahead are a bunch of soldiers who look like they're readying for battle.

This is an *army camp*.

There are Stone Swords everywhere. Some must've just arrived, because they're still offloading supplies and marching in.

I'm *really* outnumbered here.

My thickening fear and my threaded guilt are going to be just two more shackles that weigh me down. If I let them, these emotions will get me killed.

I have to be strong.

No more crying. No more panicking. I'm surrounded by enemies, but I'm a damn *Vulmi*, and I need to prove it. To prove which side I'm on.

I've been spying and working for this cause since before I can remember, and although I've let the Vulmin down today, I'm not going to let that happen again. I just need to face this like another mission. I've been in countless predicaments over the years. This is just another one that I have to find my way out of, that's all.

I can handle it. It's fine. Completely *fine*.

Licking my lips, I force out a bolstering breath, while also forcing my emotions to crumple away. I'm not Auren anymore, I'm not even Emonie.

I'm a Vulmi.

As I let my demeanor solidify, I take in whatever information I can from the sights. The army camp looks hastily built. King Carrick must have had it constructed to send his soldiers down the bridge.

He kept his plans close to the chest. We knew he was preparing for something big, but we never heard about this.

As we get closer, a few soldiers start to notice our approach, and they quickly rush around. Then a male of higher rank—a Badge—comes striding out to meet the king. "Your Majesty, we were not expecting you."

"Have all the soldiers arrived?"

"Yes, my king. The final ones just now."

Carrick nods, looking out at the bursting camp. "Good. I need a contingent back at Lydia at once."

The soldier looks taken aback. "Back at Lydia?"

"There's been an insurgence, I want it taken care of immediately."

That news makes the Badge stiffen. "I will gather troops right away. We'll do an immediate sweep of the city."

"No," Carrick says. "Burn it."

Everyone pauses. Several of the soldiers exchange glances.

"Sire?"

"I want the golden Turley female killed, and I want every single Vulmin taken out with her. Exterminate the pests. Burn the whole city to the ground."

"But, my king, the people—"

Whatever look King Carrick gives the male instantly shuts him up.

"The vermin have been breeding within the walls of our very own capital. Do you think that's acceptable, soldier?" he asks with growing fury.

"No, Sire."

"It is Lydia's fault for not weeding out this vermin threat. Purge the city with flames. Let it be a lesson to the rest of Annwyn," Carrick seethes. "I'll make a new capital."

"You'll make a whole bunch of new enemies—that's what you'll make," I call out.

The king stops and slowly turns. I think he might have forgotten I was here.

He remembers now.

When I see the look of terrifying anger on his face, my stomach does a flip. I wish I could stuff those words right back into my mouth, but there they are, undercooked in the brain and spewed out still raw.

I lock my shoulders back, keeping my head up. Carrick

doesn't like that. Doesn't like things that he considers beneath him to look him in the eye.

When he faces me, I notice that the rest of the soldiers in the camp have all gone quiet. Every one of them watching. He wants to make a spectacle of me. Probably because Auren made a spectacle out of *him*.

That thought makes me smile a little.

The second he sees the corners of my mouth twitch, he takes me down to the ground. The stone bands pin my arms against the ashy dirt, the clamp around my spine crippling me into a bow.

Just like he made me bow on the stage in front of the entire city. Except this time, I'm wearing my own appearance and there are no Vulmin or Auren. I'm on my own.

I turn my head so I'm not face-first in the silt.

"She can be the first in the pyre. Take her back to Lydia tomorrow. Whipped and bared for all to see."

Anger stretches through every inch of my insides. It only worsens the ache in my legs with how uncomfortably I'm folded over on top of them.

"It will be done, Sire," I hear the Badge tell him.

It will definitely *not* be done, but I won't argue with him about it. I just need to get away. Simple.

I shove past my knotting nerves.

"I'll be going with the Lydia contingent to see the Turley female killed," Carrick says. "We will postpone the charge of the second wave until Annwyn is brought to heel. In the meantime—"

The king's words are cut off at a sudden disturbance ahead. There's shouting and running, enough of a distraction that the king's hold on my cuffs releases.

I sit up, watching as the king and the soldiers with him start striding over to see what's happening. I'm hauled to my feet by another soldier, his hand locked on my forearm as he begins to pull me forward.

We cross the dusty yard of the camp, coming to a spot where rows of soldiers have stopped to circle around. The king goes right up to the front of the crowd, but I'm yanked to a stop at the back, which is disappointing, because my curiosity is piqued. I want to know what's going on too.

My guard shoves me down to the ground, and it sends a spike of pain to my poor knees. I shoot the soldier a glare over my shoulder but swallow down my curse. When I turn back around, all I see are the legs of the soldiers in front of me, but actually…

I squat further down, lean a bit to the right, and—there. I'd like to give the guard a sneering look of victory since I can see better down here anyway, but I can't. I'm too busy staring at the soldier on the ground.

He looks…awful. Something is terribly wrong with him. The veins on his face are black, and his mouth looks sunken in. I'm not sure he has all his teeth. The camp has gone deathly quiet as they watch him. He's so covered in the silty dust of the ground it looks like he might've crawled his way here.

There are a couple of soldiers next to him propping him up, and his eyes, when they roll up to look at the king, look shrunken. Chills travel down my back, and I can't help but wince at the sight of him.

"What happened?" the king demands.

I strain to listen, pushing my head nearly between the legs of the soldier in front of me, but I can't hear the fae's reply. I see his recessed mouth move, though, and the soldier holding him up tips his head to listen and then repeats his words. "He says he was on the other side, Sire. Says they were attacked. Everyone killed. He crawled back across the bridge to warn us."

"Attacked?" the king says in disbelief. "An Orean army attacked us, and he's the only one who survived?"

The soldier shakes his head, mouth moving again. The

other male's eyes widen at what he hears, and then he looks back up at the king to repeat it. "He says not an army. Just one male."

"*One* male took out hundreds of troops?"

The veined fae nods. When he opens his mouth this time, something seems wrong. His eyes go wide, knobby fingers scrabbling for the soldier. Before he can say anything else, he lets out a terrible sound, like tearing paper, except, I think it might be coming from inside his chest.

Then he falls back, unmoving, unblinking, sunken face pointed up at the sky.

I shudder, cringing away.

"Burn him," the king orders, not even three seconds after the poor male died. "He might have something catching."

I'm not a Carrick expert or anything, but him demanding to burn so many people in such a short amount of time seems quite excessive.

Which is good. Not the burning people part, but the excessive part. Because it tells me one thing.

He's scared.

You'd never be able to tell under his stony exterior—*ha*. But males like him don't like weaknesses. Don't like to feel like they've suffered a loss. And Auren showing up and destroying his public spectacle has gotten under his skin. The fact that he fled instead of staying to fight also tells me that he didn't think he was going to win against her.

Now, he's got problems on *both* sides of the bridge.

I'm thrilled.

A smile spreads across my face as my guard yanks me back up again while the rest of the soldiers start to disperse. I'm dragged toward a prisoner cart. There's a Stone Sword leaning against the wheel, talking to two others.

"Jailer," my guard says before tossing me in the direction of the fae who looks over. I slam into him. "Lock her up. The king wants her taken to Lydia. She's to be burned in the city. Made an example of."

The jailer nods, wrenching me by the arm as he starts hauling me toward the end of the cart. He takes a key from his belt and unlocks it. I try to yank my arm away, but he has a solid grip.

Reaching up, I pull at his hair and claw at his face, but he only wrenches open the cart door and shoves me inside. I land in a painful sprawl, unable to get up before he closes it and locks me inside.

He and the others walk away, but I spin around and search the cart. It would be nice if I could find a sword laying around to stab someone with, but there's not even a splinter sticking up.

I grind my teeth with frustration and curl my hands around the metal bars to look around. At least the cart isn't hitched to any horses yet. It's also empty, so I have the place to myself. When I spot Carrick again, I move to the end of the cart to see him better.

He looks furious.

"Where are Fassa and Friano?"

"Here, my king!"

A couple of males hurry over from across the camp. Both have long black hair and identical faces. They're the only ones around not in Stone Sword uniforms.

"Get in here now!" the king shouts before he storms into one of the buildings.

The twins and a few of the higher ranking Badges follow him in, the door slamming shut behind them.

I let out a tense breath and sit back, my attention shifting to the soldier who just died. A couple of other Stone Swords have wrapped him in sheets. They lift him up and start to carry him away.

Both males are doing their very best not to touch the

body, even wrapped up. I can't help but feel sorry for the poor dead fae. He crawled all the way here to warn them, and this is the thanks he gets.

Though, if he *is* truly contagious like the king mentioned, maybe Carrick will die a horrible, veiny death in his sleep tonight. I cross my fingers in my lap. May the goddesses bless us all.

My sore body slumps, and I crawl to the back of the cart and lean against the wall with a sigh. I pull at my dress, making sure I'm covered up as much as I can be in this swathe of golden fabric. Though I can't get comfortable or take in a nice deep breath—not with this stone around my middle. But I rest my eyes anyway, because I'm exhausted.

I fall asleep still crossing my fingers.

# CHAPTER 37

## AUREN TURLEY

T*hump.*
*Two thousand nine hundred and ninety-seven*
*Thump.*
*Two thousand nine hundred and ninety-eight*
*Thump.*
*Two thousand nine hundred and ninety-nine*

I've been counting every single one of Slade's heartbeats since I woke up. Hand splayed right over his pure golden scale, eyes watching the rise and fall of his breaths. Ribbons itching to trace over his muscled pecs and abs.

I'm content to watch him breathe. To feel his warmth. To marvel at the changes on his body. To simply let myself revel in the fact that he's here and that we're together again. That his empowering presence made our pair bond flare, destroying all the other worms writhing in my head.

They're gone. Finally, satisfyingly, *gone.*

Our connection did that. Destroyed the barrier that dared try to block him from me. Because our bond is so much stronger than anything else. Than distance and time, than magic and threat.

So I count his heartbeats, and I savor.

*Thump.*

*Three thousand*

Instead of hearing the next one, I'm startled when he speaks. "You're awake." His voice is low and sexy, weighed down from sleep.

"I didn't want to wake you," I murmur. "You needed your rest."

His hands come down to grip both of my arms, and then he drags me right up so we're face-to-face, my entire length on top of him like the icing on a layered cake.

"You did have me quite exhausted," he says with a playful smirk. "You were *insatiable*."

I flick him on the nose. "That was the bond."

His chuckle warms my entire self, inside and out. "Oh no, don't go blaming all of it on the bond. Some of that was all you."

He's right.

My finger traces over the subtle scales on his cheek that are now edged in gold, and the black lines I can see through his stubble. "I like seeing you like this," I say. "Rot and Rip together."

"You made me whole," he says. "Fixed how I'd been ripped apart."

I was ripped apart too. But his presence, his aura stretching out to meet mine, it burned through every thief in my head. And my ribbons seemed to come even more alive as I looked at this spiked, scaled, terrifying male, and yet, I wasn't afraid. Because I knew innately, he'd never hurt me.

"You fixed me too," I tell him.

I can't help but touch and stare at all these changes in him.

I can't get enough of him at all. Which is why even when my body aches deliciously, the space between my legs starts to tingle again as my hands rove, still seeking connection.

"You knew," I say, eyes flicking up to his face. "You knew we were a päyur the moment we met."

His head tips. There is no denial. "Yes."

"Why didn't you tell me?"

His hands stroke gently up my arms. "You weren't ready for that. You didn't deserve to have such pressure put on you. You deserved a choice."

I take in his words, my brow furrowing. "But we're fated."

"Yes, but fate shouldn't be a noose. Bonds shouldn't be a shackle. You needed your freedom. You needed to have the opportunity to stand on your own two feet and decide."

I hum in thought, considering his words, and I know there's logic in what he's saying. If the spiked and frightening Commander Rip had told me right away that I was supposed to be his, I would have fought against it. Rejected it.

He's right. I wasn't ready.

"Why didn't the bond start to connect until we were apart?" I ask.

His shoulder lifts. "I don't know for sure. But päyur bonds don't always complete. There is a choice in it, if the fated chooses to stay apart. Our bond must've been growing stronger over time."

Now, I can sense the bond steadily, like a solid foundation to prop up my soul, reassuring me that I will forever be grounded. It feels like him. Protective. Safe. Fierce. And through it, like a string connected from his heart to mine, I can also sense his love for me. His utter devotion that fills my chest with flutters.

"Part of me wishes we were still consumed with the bond magic," I admit quietly. "That we could just...stay here. Together. Without anything else. No troubles or worries or threats. Just you and me."

After a pause, he tilts my face and kisses me tenderly on my forehead. Each closed eyelid, my cheeks, and then a gentle one left upon my lips. When he pulls away, I can see in his green eyes that the fire has calmed for him too, and in its wake, the rushing waters of reality.

I don't want to get swept away in it. But I know we have to.

"Just you and me." His thumb strokes against my jaw, and I can see his expression warring with the same wish I have. "One day soon, Goldfinch, we will have that. I promise you," he murmurs.

I smile sadly. "But not today."

"No, not today."

With a nod, I give him one more kiss, and then we both get up from the bed. We find a washroom down the corridor, and then we bathe together, all tender caresses and quiet gestures while we speak such difficult words.

And we have so many things to say.

At my urging, he fills me in on what happened in Orea first. Then, it's my turn, and I tell him everything. Every single thing that happened, from the second I jumped into the rip, to the moment he found me on that street. He listens with rapt attention, taking in every word, asking a question here or there, but mostly, just letting me get it all out.

It's cathartic, in a way. Like opening a festering wound. Letting the confined infection drain away, making me face the pain and admit the aches.

I let it all out while he washes me gently, fingers delving through my hair, soaping up every single ribbon and stroking over my skin. As if his touch is trying to ease the harder parts I have to say.

But I can tell those parts hurt him too. I can feel his guilt. His fury. His regret for not being with me.

"It's not your fault," I say to him as the bathwater cools around us and the soap bubbles dissipate.

He doesn't reply, though. Probably because he doesn't agree.

When I get to the end, I have to tell him the worst parts. About his father. His mother. The king. My memories...

His body shakes, but it's not from the cold water. He turns me around, gripping my face in his hands, eyes locking onto mine. "I am so fucking sorry," he tells me, emotion thick in his throat. A tear slips down from my eye, but his thumb catches it. "And I am so entirely in awe of you. So incredibly proud."

I shake my head, ready to tell him all the ways I failed, but his fingers still my lips. "No, Auren. You were so fucking strong. Don't refute that."

"Your mother..."

"We'll find her," he says, and there's no doubt in his tone.

"I know we will." There's no doubt in mine either.

With all the words drained away, we finally let the water drain too. Then we both get out and dry off. We go through the motions slowly as we try to reconcile our current reality, now that we know everything.

But this time, we don't have to carry these burdens or make decisions alone. Slade looks at me across the washroom as he towels off his wet hair, and he nods. Bolstering me. Silently reassuring me that whatever we face next, we'll face it together.

We find extra clothes in an armoire right next to the tub and start getting dressed. Slade finds a gray shirt that gapes open at the collar, and thick black pants. They're tight, but he manages. I grab plum trousers that fit pretty well, but the only tunic I find is white and incredibly thin. So thin that it shows my nipples.

Slade eyes me. "Maybe we should trade shirts. As much as I love the sight of you in that one, it will make me have to kill a lot of people if they dare to look your way."

Snorting, I shake my head at him. The shirt is also too loose, gaping to reveal my cleavage. So I fix it all by forming another golden chest plate. Except this one I make to only meld over my bust, belly, and back. I create the perfect openings for every single ribbon too, while leaving my arms and shoulders bare for my shirt to fit snugly beneath.

"There, that's better," I say happily, plucking at the sleeves and straightening the collar of the shirt. I pull on some worn brown boots next. They pinch my toes a bit, but they'll do.

I smile as I watch Slade struggle to lace up the front of his too-small pants. I have to say though, his ass looks *amazing* in them. "Want me to gild you a pair of trousers?" I tease.

He flashes me a grin. "Would you make it fit even tighter than what I have on now?"

"It's a possibility." I shrug as my ribbons finish combing through my hair.

He straightens up and presses a kiss to my lips. "Next time."

The conversation is playful, but the promise isn't, because I know he's talking about so many more next times.

All the next times we desperately want to have. All of our *one days* where we won't have to rush. Won't have to face insurmountable problems. Days where we can simply lie in each other's arms and…live.

But in order to make sure we get that, we have to face these worries and threats. We have to face these hard realities so that we can finally be free.

And then, we will get our one days, our next times, our happy.

*One day.*

# CHAPTER 38

## AUREN TURLEY

Before Slade and I leave the house, he stops to grab his old pants, and I see him take something out of the pocket. I arch a brow, but when I see what it is, my heart skips a beat.

"A piece of my ribbon?" I ask breathlessly.

He nods, coming forward to show me. It's worn and frayed slightly, the golden color not as bright and glossy as the ones on my back. My eyes fill with tears. "This is the piece…"

The piece that Midas had cruelly tied around my wrist once he cut the rest from my back. The piece I saved and looked at, while believing I'd never have them again.

"You kept it all this time?"

Slade nods and slips the piece back into his pocket. "I keep every part of you you've ever given to me," he murmurs. "Your heart, your soul, your mind, your bond, your body…and your ribbon."

Tears spring to my eyes and I tuck myself against him. All my ribbons curl around to wrap us up, like they want to squeeze him in a hug. "Thank you," I whisper. "For keeping all the parts of me safe."

He kisses the top of my head. "Always," he promises.

And Slade never goes back on a promise.

Together, he and I leave the safe house, returning to the darkened underground waterway. We're quiet, watching each other from either side of the boat as Slade pulls on the oars, bringing us back to the entrance.

Every second, at least one of my ribbons is always stretched out, stroking over some part of him or wrapping around his limbs. He gives me a knowing smile, and I smile back, wondering how in the realms I got so lucky to have him.

He offers me his hand once we tie the boat to the post, and we make our way up the short steps of the cellar door. We pause, and Slade's head cocks, both of us listening. But there are no sounds on the street.

We share a glance before Slade uses the key to unlock the cellar door. He opens it and looks around and then motions me forward, both of us climbing out into the daylight. When we're out in the open again at the back of the building, we wait and listen, eyes peeled.

"I don't hear anything," I murmur.

"No," he agrees. "The city is quiet."

"Too quiet," I say with unease.

Nodding, he looks over at me. I can already see rot lines starting to writhe on his forearms where he's partially rolled up his sleeves, and his spikes are on display. "Be prepared for an attack."

I turn my palms, showing him I already have gold clamped in my hand.

"Good girl," he says with a smile. "Let's go."

The two of us round the corner of the building and walk

down the narrow path at its side. Before we can reach the street though, somebody suddenly jolts up from the building's front stoop.

Slade has the blond-haired male by the throat and against the door before I can even blink.

I spin around, looking for more people attacking, but all I see is another male across the street, holding his hands up. "Lyäri!" he calls. "We are not your enemy!"

I spot the broken-winged bird symbol pinned to his bright green lapel.

"Wait," I tell Slade. "They're Vulmin. Let him go."

Without hesitation, Slade releases him.

The blond male wheezes, looking between the two of us. He rubs a hand down his wayward hair, eyes slightly glassy, like we interrupted a nap. "I didn't mean to startle you," he says. "We were just told to keep watch for you."

"Why?" Slade asks.

"Wick wanted to make sure no one disturbed you. Said we were to wait right here and then help escort you to our gathering place so you didn't have trouble finding it."

The other Vulmin crosses the street and stands before us. "Lyäri," he says, bowing at the waist. "Lord Rot. We can take you there now, if you're ready?"

Slade and I exchange a look, and then I motion for them to lead. We start making our way down the empty street, my senses on high alert.

"Lord Rot?" I murmur with an arched brow.

I hear Slade snort under his breath.

The buildings we pass by are dripping with plant life and molded with meticulous architecture of smoothed stone. There are pretty domes, ornate steeples, and perfect symmetry. Each doorway and eave seems to be a piece of art.

I'd love to be able to walk along the arched bridges and explore the covered walkways. Would love to climb up the molded stairs I see notched along the braided trunks and twisting branches, up to the taller buildings above where the floating lights brim among the leaves. It's beautiful, but right now, it's also eerie with emptiness.

"Where is everyone?" I ask.

The blond turns, walking backwards as he answers. "Because of you two, the soldiers fled as soon as the king disappeared. Then the Vulmin were able to take over the city. We've locked it down."

"What about the citizens?"

"Most of them are lying low. We closed this street while you two...occupied it," he says, clearing this throat. The male beside him cuffs him on the back of the head, and he turns around again to face forward, right after sending me a sheepish look.

A blush threatens to heat my cheeks.

"How many days have passed?" I ask.

"Two."

Slade gives me a smirking look that makes my cheeks burn even hotter.

I clear my throat. "So none of the Stone Swords have attempted to storm the city?"

"Not yet," the other male answers as he slows to walk at my side. "Between the magic from the two of you, and the manifested dragon, we think they're trying to formulate a plan."

"And the king?" Slade puts in. "Has he returned?"

"We don't know. Haven't heard a thing. My guess is he's up in Glassworth, and he'll make a plan to take the two of you out."

Slade chuckles darkly. "He can certainly fucking try."

"Manifesting a dragon has made you quite confident," I tease quietly.

He shoots me a smirk.

The blond whirls, lanky limbs carrying him backward

once more as he grins. "So it's true? Did you actually manifest a dragon?" he asks with excitement.

"Yes."

He whistles sharply before a wide grin spreads across his lips. "Amazing! I mean, I saw the road. The bricks are all smashed up where it stepped, and there are scrape marks along the buildings from its tail. But still...a real *dragon*. Right here in Lydia! Everyone is terrified!"

He sounds ecstatic, and I can tell Slade is amused by his enthusiasm. The creature was huge and threatening. I'm not surprised it made everyone run.

"And, Lyäri, the way you made the Stone King flee! Everyone is talking about it. About how you showed up and tossed back your cloak, with golden armor covering you. The arena is covered in spots of gold! Everyone keeps going to look at it," he says excitedly.

"Including you," the other Vulmin says with a roll of his eyes. "He's been four times already, Lady Auren."

I can't help but smile, though I feel uncomfortable with the praise.

The blond puts his head down as a blush creeps up his cheeks. "This way."

We're led onto an arched bridge that stretches over a canal. Slade reaches down and clasps my hand, giving it a squeeze. "He's right. What you did was amazing. You should be fucking proud."

I'm not used to overt compliments like this. I don't quite know what to do with it, so I just nod.

"And this," Slade says quietly, as his hand drifts up to the back of my neck. I feel him rub against the skin there. "I haven't told you yet how much I fucking love this."

My brow furrows and I lift my hand. My fingers brush up against something smooth, something that feels different. "What is that?"

He blinks, and then his lips curve. "You didn't know?"

I shake my head, still trying to feel around it.

"You turned my scales golden," he says, hand moving to tap his own cheek. "And you grew one of your own."

My eyes widen. "This…is a scale?"

"Yep," he says, pride practically flooding through the word.

The spot is directly centered at the back of my neck, a curved diamond shape that feels smoother and a bit harder than the rest of my skin.

"First my gold sprouted roots of rot, and now I have a scale," I say, my hand dropping. "You've staked quite the claim on me, Ravinger."

His grin is sinful and makes my inner beast purr while my pulse heats. Then he leans in and talks close to my ear, his words fanning me with his hot breath. "And I can't even begin to tell you how *absolutely feral* it makes me to see it."

My stomach jumps.

Then we reach the end of the bridge, and I have to clear my throat and look away, or else I might be in danger of trying to drag him right back to our underground safe house.

He chuckles and grips my hand again. Wicked male.

I've cooled by the time we round a corner and make it onto the connecting street. This one, unlike the other, actually has people on it. Some are in groups, talking to each other in hurried whispers. There are several children playing, one of them blowing light into the air while the others try to chase the colors.

When everyone notices us though, the street goes still and quiet. I feel their eyes on us, and my tension sparks.

Then, the people suddenly start to cheer. Hands clapping, faces breaking out into smiles. I take in a surprised breath.

"Lyäri! It's the Lyäri!"

Their voices catch down the street too, coming from more and more throats, and the crowd comes over, walking with us like it's a celebration. They reach out to touch me, grinning, calling my name, and I smile at them with friendly acknowledgement, not knowing quite what to say. I'm glad for the steadiness of Slade's hand holding mine.

Finally, the Vulmin lead us to a building. It has pillars at its front and a dome over its doorway, but the roof stands out the most. Among the other gray stone rooftops, this one is the familiar bright blue in the exact shade as Saira Turley's field of flowers.

Just before we reach the front door, it swings open and Wick stands there, his brown eyes guarded. The rest of the Vulmin still call after me, but I walk up the stoop's steps with Slade. I turn and wave at them before entering the building, and once we're inside, Wick closes the door.

There are sacks full of flour and sugar stacked against the walls, and different powders in glass canisters along the shelves. The whole place smells like wheat and cinnamon and something else I can't quite place.

Wick looks over at the two males who brought us. "Thank you for escorting them."

With quick nods to him and us, they take their leave, walking back outside and shutting the door behind them. Then it's just the three of us.

Wick turns and motions us deeper into the building. "We'll go upstairs so we can talk."

Slade doesn't move. "Before we go anywhere with you, explain why I can scent blood."

*That's* the hint of what I was smelling. I look from him to Wick, waiting for his answer.

"There are a few prisoners in the cellar below," Wick replies.

We don't say anything, and when Slade continues to stand here and stare at him, Wick shifts on his feet. "I wouldn't put Auren at risk."

"No, *I* wouldn't put Auren at risk," Slade states evenly, his tone blunt and low. His protectiveness reared its head when I first explained everything that happened, and it's baring its teeth now. "You are a rebel leader whose cause has outweighed all else and whose choices have indeed put her at risk. Multiple times."

Wick's brown gaze flicks to me, and I can see hints of guilt there. "The Vulmin cause is indeed my driving force. But I have also done my best to protect her."

"Which is why you're still breathing."

Slade says it so matter-of-factly that, somehow, it makes the statement all the more of a threat. The tension between the two of them mounts as I look between them. Slade's shoulders are stiff, his eyes hard, and Wick looks like he's expecting Slade to lash out at him any second.

"Alright," I say, breaking the silence. "I have questions that I want the answers to, so lead the way."

Wick glances at me, losing some of his tension, before he gives a stiff nod and turns. Slade and I look at each other, and I squeeze his hand in reassurance. Then we follow Wick as he takes us across the room, to a doorway that leads to a set of winding stairs.

I notice his bare wrist as we start to climb. "You got that magical cuff off?" I ask. "The one that dampens magic?"

He looks over his shoulder at me with a nod. "Yeah. One of the other Vulmin was able to."

"Good. What is it anyway?"

"I don't know. We're going to try to do some tests on it to figure it out. But for now, I found another use for it."

I eye him curiously, but he doesn't divulge further. We reach the top of the stairs, which brings us to a big loft-style room that looks over an open space below. I can see a dozen Vulmin down there, around what seems to be an area for packing different herbs and spices.

"This has been a Vulmin building for years," Wick

explains as we grip the railing to look below. "No one in the city has ever caught us, because the spices and herb repository has always been legitimate. But we've held many meetings here and housed extra Vulmin, and even smuggled Oreans out, having them pretend to be workers taking shipments outside the capital."

The fact that Oreans had to be smuggled out in the first place makes me furious.

Instead of leading us down the open stairwell that would take us to the drying and packing area below, Wick takes us to the left of the landing, where a set of doors are. He opens up the first and leads us inside to a small but clean office and sitting room.

There's a table and chairs littered around, with incredibly detailed maps hung up on every inch of wall space. The sole window in this room is round and slightly bigger than my head. It domes out from the wall, which I suspect offers better angles for viewing the street below.

"Please, sit," Wick says, and he waits for Slade and me to take a seat before he does too.

For a moment, he looks at me, as if he doesn't know where to begin. "You're alright?"

My head tips. "I'm alright."

"And you remember?"

I glance over at Slade before answering. "Yes."

Wick lets out a breath, and I take the chance to really study him. His sleek black hair is flopped over to one side like always, exposing the shaved sides while the long ends brush down to his shoulder. I can see splotches of bruises along his jaw and beneath each of his eyes, and I wonder if he holds even more marks under his clothes.

"I'm so sorry. About Ludogar," I say thickly. The flash of memory of the blue-haired fae dying in the palace's courtyard haunts me. The way his body jolted. The way his blood poured out.

Wick flinches, and I know the loss is still incredibly fresh and painful. He trusted Ludo above all others. "Thank you," he murmurs, his throat bobbing. "He was a good Vulmin and an even better friend. He will be greatly missed."

"Too many have died," I reply. "But what you said—on the stage. About there being a better way. You meant that?"

His strong jaw locks in and he nods. "I did. The Vulmin want to get rid of the tyranny, but we don't want to be tyrants in return. We want peace. We want to stop spilling fae and Orean blood."

Relief fills my chest. "Good."

We study each other in silence for a long moment until he finally lets out a tight sigh. "Go ahead, Auren. Ask."

I look at him evenly, though tension aches along my shoulders. "You bled gold," I say evenly.

"I did."

My ribbons twist nervously upon the floor. "Who *are* you?"

Wick shifts in his seat, but he doesn't look away as he answers. "My full name is Wickum Almon Turley."

The breath catches in my chest, and his words roll through my mind.

Even though I knew it, saw the truth when he blocked the strike meant for me, and I watched the slice in his arm bleed gold, hearing him say it out loud feels like a punch to the gut.

"We're related," I say.

He nods. "We're second cousins, strictly speaking. We share the same great-grandmother. Your mother and my father were cousins. But you're the more direct line from Saira Turley," he explains. "Think of it this way: you're the capital, I'm the outskirts."

"But why did you keep it from me? Why not tell me right away? You knew—" I cut off my words as soon as I feel my throat closing up. I can't help the emotions twisting my throat and strangling my vocal cords, but I hate sounding so vulnerable.

GOLDFINCH

Beside me, Slade tenses, but he gently puts his hand on my thigh, giving me a comforting squeeze. A ribbon comes up and strokes over his fingers.

Wick runs his hand through his hair in another surprising show of his own emotion. Except maybe it's not so surprising—not after what the two of us have gone through. We fought for our lives. We watched his friend and right hand be murdered right in front of him. We saw each other get captured, Oreans executed, Emonie dragged away. He and other Vulmin were nearly whipped and killed in a public display.

And now we're here, after all of that, sitting across from each other and trying to find our footing after our lives have been shaken.

"It wasn't just you. Very few Vulmin knew that I carried the Turley name. Only those I trusted most."

Realization dawns. "Ludogar knew."

He nods, the muscles in his jaw tensing. "But I didn't want anyone to know, especially you. Not yet."

"*Why?*"

He shakes his head and then slumps so that his next words are spoken down to the table, his gaze locked on the knots in the wood. "I didn't want to tell you, didn't want to tell anyone… because I'm a traitor who doesn't deserve to carry the Turley name."

A frown slices down my expression while dread slices down my stomach. "What do you mean?"

He looks up at me then, dark eyes the color of soil after being drenched in rain. There's a heaviness in them, as if they're saturated through with a weighty truth he hasn't been able to unbury.

But he does now.

His answer topples out, unearthing the buried burden in one fatal scoop.

"That night in Bryol, when you were taken with the other

363

children, I was there," he admits, and my pulse pounds in my ears so hard it sounds like drums. "I was there, Auren, and I *let* them take you."

# CHAPTER 39

## AUREN TURLEY

I shake my head, trying to roll around the information so it will settle and make sense. Slade is rigid with fury, his eyes narrowed and jaw muscles jumping.

But Wick looks at me with dueling expressions. One side guilt, and the other side resolved, like that part of him already knows the outcome of this talk.

"You were there that night? When Bryol was attacked?" I ask. Though he already admitted it, I can't believe my ears.

"I was. My family had come to visit yours. Our two households were the last of the Turley family, but my parents and I lived in a place called Dramor. Without a fairy ring, it was a three-week journey for us to get to Bryol. The last time I'd visited, I didn't even remember. You were just a baby, and I was a toddler."

My heart pounds. "Keep going."

Wick flattens his hands on the table like he's bracing himself. "I was jealous of you."

I rear back in surprise, and my ribbons skitter against the floor. That's not what I was expecting.

"My parents doted on you. *Everyone* did. Everyone called you *little sun*. The entire city was smitten." His mouth pulls into a tightened, shameful grimace. "You probably don't remember, but I locked you in a closet once. You cried until your father found you. My own father lectured me for hours about it—about the importance of family. Of loyalty, kindness. And you…I thought you were going to hate me, but you just smiled and asked if I wanted to play. You forgave me, forgetting it before I even got done being lectured."

I shake my head, feeling bewildered. "I don't remember any of this."

"You were barely five years old," he says. "I was nearly eight by then. And horribly jealous."

"You were just a child."

"No excuse," he says bitterly. "Especially when that jealousy led to such horror."

My pulse quickens, anxiety filling my stomach with stones.

"When our parents realized that the city was under attack, they had a feeling it was timed that way because we were there visiting. After all, we'd traveled for three weeks across Annwyn. There was plenty of time for the monarchy's spies to inform them we were heading for Bryol. Our parents hadn't considered the risk of all of us being together in one place. But that night, they realized their mistake. Soldiers came with blades and magic to destroy the city so that it could look like an insurgent attack instead of an execution of a bloodline."

My throat gets tight, and I slip my hand through Slade's, needing his touch. His grip tightens around mine, keeping me steady while my world spins.

"I had snuck out of bed to grab food from the kitchen, and I heard them talking. Heard the commotion from the Vulmin at the front door. Our parents soon figured out what was happening and why the city was under attack. They wanted to protect us, so they used a few Vulmin guards to sneak out all the children on our street. They were going to hide us outside the city walls until it was safe. But our parents...they were going to turn themselves in. Exchanging their capture with a cease of hostilities. To spare the lives of everyone else who lived in Bryol."

My eyes go wide. It feels like a fist just grabbed hold of my heart and burst it open.

"Of course, they lied to our parents. Accepted the exchange but then killed them in cold blood. Then they still destroyed the city and nearly everyone in it."

"What about us?" I ask tightly, feeling my eyes swarm with tears.

"Our Vulmin guards never got us out of the city. They were attacked by a group, I don't know who. But while the fighting was happening, everyone was distracted, and I... snuck away. Without you."

He says those words like one would swing an ax. One blow after the other. Hitting in deep. Ready to make something topple.

In this case, it's me.

"You were scared," I offer, though the words feel numb. "You were just acting on impulse."

Wick shakes his head, and his expression turns angry. "Don't do that," he grinds out. "Don't give excuses for my behavior." He looks me dead in the eye, and a tear escapes down my cheek. "I was standing right next to you, Auren. I could've just taken your hand and run. I could've gotten us both away. But I didn't. I looked at you, and I just...*went*." His voice rasps. "I *left* you."

More tears well up in my eyes. And they burn. Right down to my chest.

*I left you.*

I squeeze Slade's hand hard. He grips me firmly in return. He's the only person who hasn't ever left me. Who's always been here, holding me together through it all.

When Wick sees the agony in my face, his shoulders slump, head bowing from the weight of his shame. "I left you and then tried to find our parents, but I saw them get murdered. Then I ran. I tried to go back and find you, but you were gone. And I knew…"

He chokes with thickened emotion.

I'm spinning, with a ground that won't still. I'm remembering what the ruins of Bryol looked like when he took me there. Filling in the gaps with his words.

"I made it out of the city somehow," he says. "Walked all the way to a nearby village. My father always told me to look for the Vulmin symbol because I could trust them. I found a fae wearing the pin there, and he took me in. But I never told him or anyone else my real name. Never told them I was a Turley. All they knew was that I was an orphan from the Bryol attack. I didn't want them to know anything else. I was ashamed of what I'd done, and I knew that my parents would have been ashamed of me too. That I'd failed them. Failed you."

A tear tracks down his russet cheek, and he digs the heels of his hands into his eyes like he can shove it back in. Shove away the guilt and regret.

It's difficult to imagine what would have happened if I'd been able to sneak away with Wick. Difficult to come to terms with how different my life could have been.

I wipe at my eyes and take a shaky breath. "So that's why you didn't tell me. When we first met in Geisel."

He nods. "Sometimes, feelings build up and become our foundation. Shame and guilt aren't like pages in a book. I couldn't simply turn it over and move past it. This regret…I'll carry it for the rest of my life."

I try to imagine what he looked like as a little boy. Try to jar my thoughts to remember.

But…I *did* remember something.

When I was falling through the rip, I heard a little boy's voice calling my name. Somehow, with intense certainty, I know that it was him. That it was Wick calling my name. That was us when we were happy and playful, laughing together and untouched by tragedy.

My shoulders tremble.

"When I heard about you in Geisel, I didn't believe it. And then when I saw you…" He trails off with a shake of his head. "I wanted to keep you at a distance. A part of me blamed you—and I know how damn ridiculous that sounds, but it's the truth. I blamed you for my own hate. My own shame that I'd carried around for my entire life. When you showed up, I wouldn't allow myself to think of you as family—as that little girl I abandoned. I only wanted to see you as a good thing for the Vulmin, because that's all my life had become. I've dedicated my entire life to the Vulmin cause. Maybe in some vain effort to redeem myself and avenge our parents."

Now that he's started to get the words out, they're rushing out of him. The floodgate has opened, and he's letting the truth surge. Causing damage in its wake, but no longer holding back.

"Admitting you were anything else to me would've forced me to relive my mistakes all over again, and I didn't want to do that," he admits. "Didn't want to look you in the eye and tell you what I'd done. Because the truth is, I don't deserve to carry the Turley name. Don't deserve to tell you I'm your family. Not after abandoning you. Hell, if most Vulmin knew what I'd done, they'd never have followed me in the first place. And this cause…it's the only thing that's kept me going. When I stopped being a Turley, becoming a Vulmin was all I had."

It's hard to hear.

Every confession from his mouth is another stone tossed at me, landing in my gut. My thoughts and reactions war with one another, and I know it's going to take time for me to pick it all apart. To digest every piece.

He looks at me with wet eyes and rattling desperation. "I'm sorry, Auren. I'm *so*—sorry."

I take in a shaky breath, and the two of us stare at each other. All the words that poured out now trying to find where to settle.

Devastation has ripped up my roots and left me scattered. There's no denying that.

But I reach across the table to Wick's hand, startling him when I grip his fingers. He looks up at me and flinches, like he's waiting for me to deliver a blow.

"You were a child who made a mistake," I say slowly, and I cut him off before he can interrupt. "Sometimes, our mistakes are so big that when they land, the consequences stretch out farther than you ever could've imagined."

He swallows hard, watching me like he's hanging on my every word.

"What's done is done," I tell him. "What happened that night was a tragedy for us both. We lost our parents. Our homes. Our safety. Our identities…" Grief threatens to strike my tongue, but I push on. "But the two of us have reunited now. I think we owe it to our parents and ourselves to be each other's family. Because you *are* a Turley. The proof is right there in your veins. And I think we've lost enough. We don't need to add each other to the list."

His jaw muscle jumps, like he's trying to lock down his emotions, though his eyes shine with moisture.

I give him a sad smile for the boy he was, for the terrible regret and shame he's carried that's so obviously affected him. I could yell and scream. I could choose hate. But it's like Wick said in the city square.

We can do better.

I give his hand a squeeze. "You don't just have the Vulmin, Wick. You have me too now."

He looks utterly ransacked. Like he's kept all his emotions and secrets hidden away, and now that they've been dumped out, he's unsure what to do with all the pieces.

For a moment, he just stares at me as if he expects me to change my mind and tell him I hate him and want nothing to do with him.

When I don't, he clears his throat, shaking his head. "You're still the same. Just like when you were a little girl. Forgiving me. Smiling when I deserve to be shunned. No wonder they all called you *little sun*. You have the warmest heart I've ever known, Auren."

This time, he squeezes my hand back before we let go.

I blow out a big breath and look between him and Slade. "I think that's enough rehashing the past for today," I say, trying to keep the shake out of my smile. "Now let's move on to Vulmin business."

He seems relieved at the topic change, and honestly, so am I. Everything I said to him was genuine. I'm not going to punish his eight-year-old self for a mistake that was made over twenty years ago. It's obvious he's punished himself over that choice plenty. But I also need time to take everything in on my own, and we'll both have to learn what it means to be family.

So for now, we'll focus on being Vulmin.

Wick starts telling us about everything that's happened in Lydia since Slade and I reunited, catching us up on all the details.

"Keeping our control of the capital is vital," he says. "But it's tenuous. The royal guard could storm the city any moment and retake control. I have Vulmin on the move, all the ones trained in combat and willing to fight, but it'll be a couple more days before the first influx arrives."

"But the invasion on Orea has to have greatly depleted Carrick's army," Slade says.

"Exactly. He's stacked the odds by sending most of his forces into another realm. This is the perfect time for us to strike. He's the weakest he's ever been. But if we want to end the Carrick tyranny once and for all, we have to end the king."

"But we still don't know where he escaped to?" Slade asks.

Wick shakes his head.

"Right." I get to my feet, my chair scraping against the floor. "You have him prisoner, I assume?"

Wick knows exactly who I'm talking about, and he nods. "I do. He's down with the Stone Swords we have captured. But he hasn't talked."

"Who?" Slade asks as he also gets to his feet.

I lock eyes with him as I answer. "The fae who betrayed us," I say, but inside, I whisper.

The fae who betrayed *me*.

# CHAPTER 40

## AUREN TURLEY

What I've quickly learned about Lydia is that this city is very fond of tunnels. Both water and walking ones. Wick leads us into the cellar of the blue-roofed building, and inside of it is a hidden tunnel. The walkway is dark and damp, the stone crevices speckled with fluorescent moss, and lit up with the familiar blue bulbs of flameless light.

The tunnel is nothing more than a short corridor, and then Wick, Slade, and I are crossing through a stone threshold and looking through a glass door. On the other side is the space that the Vulmin are using as a prison.

The room is large and long. There are no cells or bars in sight, but it does have wide benches nailed to the walls and hooks attached to the floor. Those hooks could pass as something innocent, like a way to secure stacks of supplies. Yet right now, they're used to connect to the shackles worn around the prisoners' ankles.

The scent of blood is far stronger here, and through the glass, I can see that it's coming from one of the Stone Swords. He has a vicious slice against his neck that's wrapped but still appears to be bleeding.

Wick notices my line of sight. "Tried to end himself with his own sword. We intervened before he could."

Aside from that self-inflicted wound, neither him nor the other soldier have any other injuries. I glance at Wick in question, and he seems to pick up on my thoughts, because he shakes his head. "Vulmin have had to be ruthless, it's true. But like I said in the square. We fae also have to be better. And since we have taken the city, that starts now, even with our prisoners."

Something like pride wells up in my chest.

"Well, that explains why your prisoners won't talk," Slade drawls. When I shoot him a look, he shrugs. "I'm not saying it's not noble. It is. But when people are put to pain, their tongues loosen."

"But then we'd only be perpetuating the very same things we hope to erase from Annwyn," Wick argues. "The Vulmin have always had a plan. We grow, we fight, we kill if we must, but then once we take control, we implement a new way. A better way. If Annwyn has any hope of ushering in true peace, it has to start with our opponents, or it isn't really peace. Isn't really change. We can't pick and choose between friend and enemy."

"You also can't *confuse* friend for enemy."

"And we won't," Wick replies firmly. "But we have to make Annwyn realize that fae against fae is no way of life. We need to become united. We can't do that by killing and hating half the population."

Slade doesn't reply, though it's obvious he doesn't necessarily agree with Wick's ideology. But coming from someone who was recently in a dungeon and having seen others who endured beatings and torture, I have to say, Wick's plan for a peaceful Annwyn is a welcome one.

"Speaking of being imprisoned…are the Oreans okay? The ones I got out from the dungeons?" I ask.

"They're all here, staying in the city and being taken care of."

I exchange a look with Slade. "We should speak to them. See if they have any information about your mother."

He nods, and although he keeps the rest of his expression unreadable, I can see the flash of worry in his eyes.

I look back through the glass, past the sleeping Stone Swords, and my gaze lands on the figure at the other end of the room. He's lying on a bench facing the bricked wall. From here, I can see his shoulder-length hair, brown but streaked with gray.

Brennur.

"Ready?" Wick asks me.

I nod, and the three of us walk into the dim room. It's drafty, thanks to the vents in the ceiling that look more like gutters, sending wisps of wind inside. Four Vulmin sit around the table right next to the door. One of them is reading, and the other three are playing some sort of dice game while the lanterns in front of them flicker.

When they see us, they immediately jump to their feet.

"We'd like the room," Wick tells them.

The males hurry out, shutting the door behind them.

"Bring him over here," I say.

With a nod, Wick heads across the room, slipping a key from his pocket. I sit down at the vacated table, and Slade leans against the wall by the door with his arms crossed in front of him.

Wick unlocks the chain from the hook, and then goes over and nudges the sleeping fae with the toe of his boot. "Get up."

Brennur jolts awake.

I watch him try to gain his wits as he sloughs off sleep, but Wick is already tugging on the chain connected to his ankle. He's halfway across the room before he actually spots me, clay-colored eyes appearing more reddish from how bloodshot they are.

"Have a seat," Wick orders before pushing him into the chair across the table from me.

Brennur steals a look over his shoulder at Slade, clearly not comfortable having him at his back.

"Don't look at me. Look at her." The chill in Slade's voice is so frigid I nearly shiver.

Brennur audibly gulps and turns around to face me. His beard used to be neatly cut and perfectly straight at the end. Now, it's far messier, as is his hair.

The hate I feel for him is unfathomable. My stomach turns just from looking at him. My ribbons tighten, their edges sharpening, and it's tempting to simply let them lash forward and slice his throat. But I'm here for answers.

I've waited this long. I can wait a little longer.

Brennur's gaze shifts around, and the way he holds himself reminds me of a darting rodent. One that's looking for a hole to skitter through or a scrap to steal. His fingers fidget with the magical cuff around his wrist that's blocking his magic.

So *that's* the other use Wick mentioned. He put his cuff on Brennur.

"Are you ready to talk?" I ask.

The male shrugs as if he's unbothered. "That depends."

"Let's start with why you betrayed us and took us to Glassworth Palace."

"A fae has to do what a fae has to do to stay alive," he explains, as if he's talking about something as easy as disagreeing about the weather instead of sending dozens of people to their death.

"When exactly did you jump sides?" Wick asks him.

When Brennur hesitates, I hum in thought, flicking my gaze to Wick. "He didn't jump sides. He never actually chose one."

I have to admit, he carried himself very well. The cane, the altruistic behavior, the graying hair and deferring tone—it was all a fantastic disguise for the rat that was hiding beneath.

"You think you're better than me?" Brennur grits out. "I see an opportunity and I take it. That's all."

"So you're not loyal to anybody except yourself," Wick surmises.

"That's right. And everyone else would be smart to be the same way."

Visible anger radiates out of Wick's eyes. "How many Oreans and fae were killed because of you? How many of our missions were compromised?"

"It was either that or slip the noose over my own head. I'm not dying for anybody," he says defiantly. "And you still got use of my magic. I helped you too."

"While you were feeding the king information every step of the way!" Wick growls out, slamming his fist against the table. It startles the other Stone Sword who was sleeping, but the bloodied one doesn't so much as flinch.

Brennur looks on without a lick of remorse. "I didn't tell him everything. I was smart about it. I knew you'd pick up on it if too many missions were compromised."

"So you tricked us both."

He shrugs. "Like I said, I'm not dying for anybody."

"That mission in Kuvell last year. When forty Vulmin were found in that safe house and ambushed. That was you?"

Brennur stays silent, which is answer enough.

Wick's glare is chilling. "I trusted you to bring countless fae and Oreans to safe harbor, to sneak us into dangerous territory for our cause, and all the while you were nothing but a selfish fucking traitor."

"I bow to whoever I need to so I can keep my head," Brennur replies. "King, rebel leader, noble, doesn't matter. Roles and politics change all the time. I'm nearly a hundred and eighty years old. You think I'd still be alive if I'd been something as stupid as *loyal*? Bah!" He waves his hand, the chain around his ankle clinking with his movements. "Loyalty is a good way to get yourself killed."

"Funny," Wick grinds out, "considering *disloyalty* is going to be the thing that actually ends you."

# CHAPTER 41

## AUREN TURLEY

Despite Wick's threat, Brennur doesn't look affected whatsoever.

"You won't kill me," he replies evenly. "You think someone hasn't threatened that before? I know my worth. My magic is rare—very rare. I'm one of the only fae who can still control ring magic. I'm far too valuable."

His words echo in my ears and make my teeth snap together as if I could gnash him between them.

"Are you?" Wick challenges. "Because you still refuse to tell us where that fairy ring took the king."

Brennur looks between us. "I'll tell you. For a price."

"How about your life?" Wick growls.

He rolls his eyes. "As I said, you won't kill me. So it will take more than that."

Instantly, I open my palm and let chunks of gold fall onto the table, startling him. They land with metallic clinks, each and every one tracked by his seedy eyes.

"Alright, what's your price?" I question lightly. "Gold? Enough wealth that you can become a king in your own right? Enough riches to own all of Annwyn?" I clasp my hand around one of the larger gold nuggets and hold it out to him.

He reaches forward and takes it from my grasp, turning it around in the lantern light, and eyeing every black vein. I let more gold nuggets form, some tipping off the table and falling onto the ground. Then I push the pile toward him like he's just won the winning hand in a card game.

"There," I say as his greedy eyes take it in. "Now, where did your fairy ring take the king?"

Brennur strokes his beard as he regards me for a long, silent moment. He's not going to answer. He knows gold does him no good if he's stuck in this room. But that's fine.

I have other questions for him.

I glance down at the wrinkled leather vest he's wearing. Open at the front, a muddy brown color.

"Do you tan your own leather?"

Brennur frowns in confusion at my change in subject. "What?"

I jerk my chin. "Your vest. You were wearing one before too. I'm just wondering if you tan your leather yourself."

"Yes, I tan my own leather," he answers with a scoffed impatience. "What of it?"

My fingers twist around a nugget of gold as I spin it on the table. "You use oak bark, is that right?"

The question is simple. My intent behind it is not.

And even though I keep my face expressionless, my tone easy, I'm coiled so tight I could spring at any moment because I recall what happened when he took me through the fairy ring, just before Una stole my memories.

I remember...*remembering.*

Brennur hasn't caught onto the rage that's simmering

beneath my skin, because he looks impatiently to Wick. "What is this about?"

I lean forward slowly, and I can feel the flame from the lantern casting off against my face as I draw his gaze back to me. "It's the scent. The taste," I say, my tone gone dark. "It leaves an impression when someone shoves a piece of polishing cloth into your mouth to shut you up as you're being kidnapped. That oak bark was very distinct, and you *still reek of it.*"

His eyes widen. Only a fraction, only for a second.

But it's enough.

"It *was* you." My voice is low. Even.

Full of terrible rage.

"You were the one to kidnap me from Bryol and take me into Orea. It didn't matter that the bridge of Lemuria had been destroyed for hundreds of years. Because you...you can make a fairy ring capable of transporting between *realms*."

His face stays absolutely still, but I hear it. The quickening of his heartbeat. Behind him, Slade seems to swell with chilling fury.

"Tell me. Whose side were you on when you took me?"

"I don't know what you're talking about," he spits.

I ignore him as my head cocks in thought. "That's what I can't quite work out. Why take me to Orea? If you were working for the king, then surely he would've wanted me either as his prisoner or executed with my parents. But if you were working with the rebels...you could've given me to them. I must've been far more valuable in Annwyn. So why Orea? Who were you working for?"

Silence spreads, but this time, the balance has tipped.

Slade takes a step forward.

Just one step. A colossal threat.

"*Answer her,*" he says, his voice cold and terrifying.

From the edge of my vision, his spikes seem to lengthen.

Anger pushes through him, filling the room and making it snap against my skin as his gaze stays locked onto the back of Brennur's head.

Brennur stiffens, but he shakes his head. "You should be thanking me."

"*Thanking* you?" I say incredulously. "For kidnapping me and taking me to Orea?"

"Yes," he snarls. "The king wanted the entire family wiped out. You would've been captured and killed right alongside your parents if I hadn't done what I did. I practically saved you."

"*Practically saved me*?" I lash out, studying the red tinge of his suddenly skittish gaze. "I think we both know that if you had any good intentions rooted in what you did, you'd have taken me to the Vulmin. But you didn't, did you?"

He stays silent.

"The other children with me that night. What happened to them?"

He looks at me blankly, but there's an undercurrent of apprehension. His thin lips flatten even more as he presses them together, silently showing that he has no intention of answering me.

Magic tingles at my fingertips, demanding to be let out, and I give in. Power grips me, and all the gold piled up on the table in front of him liquifies in an instant.

Before he can even jolt back, the molten metal encapsulates his hands and arms, pinning his limbs to the table. It hardens over them like a shell, trapping them in place.

He struggles, and I watch his face grow blotchy, teeth gritted as he tries to get out from within its grip.

"Uncomfortable, isn't it?" I ask. "To be helpless. At the mercy of someone else who wishes you harm."

"You can't kill me!" he screeches in panic.

My brows lift. "Who said anything about killing? I'm not

killing you, Brennur. I'm not even injuring you. But for every lie you tell or every question you choose to ignore, more of that gold will spread. If you refuse to tell me everything I want to know, you'll be stuck inside a gilded statue. Alive. Breathing. Unable to move."

Fury and fear seem to war within him, making his jaw jump, his arms straining.

"But…" I go on. "For every truth, I'll drag the gold away. Simple as that." I glance up at Slade. "Humane, even."

"Very," he agrees with dark menace. "I would've just started rotting him alive."

"See?" I say, turning back to Brennur. "*Much* more humane. Now, let's get back to it. What happened to the other children that night?"

When he doesn't answer immediately, more gold ripples and pours up his arms. It hardens past his elbows, reaching up to his shoulders. "Wait!" he cries as his body jerks awkwardly, half sitting on the chair, half yanked from it. "You think the soldiers who get sent in for a mission like Bryol have the best character?" he shouts. "The ones sent were chosen because they're the most vicious during a raid, and they don't do so out of duty. They *enjoy* it. Pillaging, killing, kidnapping… they know how to get more coin from it. Raids are lucrative if you're brutal enough."

I pull back a few inches of gold. "Keep going."

Panting, he tries to catch his anxious breath, though I can see he's slightly relieved that I've stayed true to my word. "They offered me half if I helped smuggle a group of kids out. They were going to sell them to someone up the coast. I don't know who. But then we realized we had *you*."

My stomach twists.

"Couldn't risk selling you. You're too recognizable. Anyone in Annwyn could figure out who you were."

"And the king?"

"Wanted you dead, of course," he answers. "The whole family."

I drag away the magic another inch, even as I start to shake with mounting rage.

"That would have been a problem for you and your group," I muse as the pieces come together. "And selling the rest of the children wasn't enough. You still wanted to make coin off me, but you knew you couldn't do it in Annwyn."

He nods. "I had contacts in Orea."

My gaze hardens. "Of course you did."

His lips stiffen before he lets out a cough, hacking at a scrape in his throat. "I had to make a living. Once the bridge was destroyed, smuggling things in using the fairy ring brought in a lot of coin. Buyers in Orea would pay well for fae goods, and vice versa."

Fury fires my heated words. "Not just goods. People. *Children.*"

But he shakes his head. "No, I hadn't ever dealt with flesh traders before *or* after you," he says, as if that absolves him of his guilt. "You were the only one I ever took to Orea."

"How magnanimous," I say flatly.

"Connecting a ring within Annwyn is one thing. Connecting it to an entirely different realm takes far more power. That magic left me crippled for days. I used it sparingly." He tips his head to gesture at his arms, and I grudgingly pull away more gold. It's below his elbows now, but his released skin is discolored from where the metal pinched.

"I saved your life," he repeats again. "Once the soldiers realized they weren't going to be able to get anything for you, they were ready to just kill you like the king wanted. So I told them I'd end you. They took off with the other kids, and I made a ring and smuggled you into Orea instead."

My voice seethes. "You didn't take me there to save me. You took me there to *sell* me."

"Better sold than dead."

I laugh coldly, thinking of my childhood in Derfort Harbor. Thinking of what I endured. For him to say that, with his tone so horribly benign, makes me want him to suffer.

Behind him, Slade ripples with rage.

"So you sold me to Orean flesh traders," I say evenly. "Then what?"

"The king was quietly informed that you and your family were dead just like he wanted," he says with a shrug. "So when it was rumored that you'd returned…he was looking to point fingers."

The gold slips down to the middle of his forearms.

"But that finger didn't land on you?"

"Of course not," Brennur replies, actually having the audacity to look offended. "I made sure nothing could come back on me."

Every single one of his confessions makes impact. His words rupture me from within, sending shards flying, dust spraying.

Kidnapped for coin. I was taken away from everything I knew. Ripped from safety. Abused, used, destroyed. All for *coin*.

How cheap it makes me feel. How utterly devastating that someone decided what my life was worth.

Beside me, Wick looks distraught.

Slade looks *murderous*.

Keeping my composure, I give a sharp nod and then pull away my gold until it's only capturing his hands, still fusing them to the wooden table. "What part of Annwyn did your fairy ring bring the king and Emonie?"

He chews on his answer for a moment, but then he decides to finally answer. "Near the bridge."

I can feel Wick tense, but I lean in. "Near the bridge—but *which side*?" Brennur's eyes flash, and I hum in affirmation.

"That's why you're so valuable to the king, isn't it? Because he knows now that you can open a ring in Orea. You've been using your magic to transport him directly there so that he could figure out a way to rebuild the bridge and invade."

He tips his head, arrogance bleeding into his expression. "Like I said, far too valuable to kill."

"How did they manage to fix the bridge?"

"I don't know."

I arch a brow.

"Truly, I don't," he says with frustration and a sneer. "I've told you everything. Take away your shiny little threat now. I've done my part."

Slade audibly growls, but I give him the tiniest shake of my head, and the sound cuts off.

With a sweep of my hand, the rest of the gold puddles, slithering back toward me and drifting up my arms where it hardens like spiraling arm bands.

"Now." Brennur coughs again before he straightens up and smooths down his vest. "You will release me, we will negotiate a price, and only then will I take you to the spot where I transported the king and that female impersonator. We're done here."

Nodding, I slide my chair back and get to my feet. "We are done."

Brennur starts to get up too, only to realize he can't.

Body stiffening, he looks down. The golden nuggets that had fallen to the floor are gone. His gaze shoots back up to me when he realizes, but it's too late. They've already melted down and fused to the bottom of his shoes, though there isn't a single blackened vein to be seen.

"What is the meaning of this?" he asks, trying and failing again to move his feet.

"Oh, that? That gold melted down right around the

time you told us how you'd decided to help flesh traders sell children."

He looks around the room with confusion, like he's trying to figure out what's going on. His demeanor grows more agitated, and he starts to cough again, but this time he can't quite get it cleared.

"That'll be the rot soaking into your throat," I tell him calmly, and he blanches at me.

"*What?*" he shouts, eyes bugging out, the blood draining from his face. "You can't!" His voice has gone raspy and jagged, barely able to chafe out.

"Hmm, seems I can."

Forgetting he can't move, he tries to lunge for me, but Slade is a step ahead of him. All it takes is one hand slamming down onto his shoulder, and he holds Brennur in place in his chair.

Slade's eyes don't even drop down to him. They stay on me. Ready to support me in whatever way I choose for this to play out.

"Unfortunately for you, Brennur, you've made a very large error."

He glares at me as I sense the rot settling into his lungs, tainting his labored breaths. It becomes harder for him to draw his inhales. His heart slugs out poison through the rest of his veins, making him shake violently as he has another coughing fit.

"You thought you were worth more to me alive than you are dead," I say as the rot in his throat thickens, decaying the windpipe with his next scraping inhale. "You're *not.*"

His body jerks and he collapses against the table, wheezing with a failing ability to breathe as the rot attacks his every organ, focusing on his heart.

He doesn't need it. He certainly never showed he had one.

I pass him on my way to the door and tip my hand, letting

a gold coin land right in front of his mottled face. "Your payment."

Then I walk away, leaving him to rot.

Because that is *exactly* what he did to me.

# CHAPTER 42

## QUEEN MALINA

It's been several days, and yet smoke from the fae corpses still pollutes the air. The scent of burned bodies is foul enough as it is, but the scent of *rotted* burned bodies? Absolutely atrocious.

I look out at the land beyond. It was already an ugly, broken place, but now, the snow is coagulated with clots of Ravinger's rot. I trudge out of the ruins of Cauval Castle, where rot lines crawl up its outer walls like dead vines. My hand presses against the borrowed scarf that's wrapped around my nose and mouth to help me breathe past the stench.

Dommik pilfered from the bodies of the fae to get us more supplies before he started working his way through burning them. He presses flame to each prostrate form, ridding the land of their rotted corpses. We have plenty of food for the time being—but my appetite has soured with the smell.

I've instead been keeping busy with fortifying the bridge.

Yet so far, no other fae have tried to come across. The bridge of Lemuria remains clear, and Seventh Kingdom empty.

Except for the dead, of course.

Today, I'm in a thick woolen dress and fleece leggings, with a furred collar at my throat and cuffs at my wrists. Dommik tells me it's much more practical for me to wear trousers, but I feel more myself in my dresses. Even if they are more difficult to manage when I walk through the thick snow.

When I reach the end of the path and stop in front of the bridge, I eye my fortifications critically. It's certainly better than what I managed at Highbell.

Unlike the attack on my city, I've had more time here.

I've also had the opportunity to continuously improve and add to them. Because I know that this is only a reprieve. More fae will come, it's just a matter of time. So I have to be ready.

The pillars that stand on either side of the bridge have been extended with ice, reaching twenty feet high. But that's as close as the bridge will allow my magic to work. I quickly learned that no matter what I do, my ice power can't touch the bridge itself.

I don't know if it repels all magic or if it perhaps has something to do specifically with mine. After all, we were both reborn at the same time, and with my blood.

To be perfectly honest, a part of me is relieved my ice power doesn't work on the bridge itself. I walked on it for a few steps after King Ravinger had disappeared down its foggy depths. Yet after only a few paces down the drab, unnatural dirt, I started to get a sense of utter wrongness. As if I didn't belong there and it wanted me off.

I didn't dare test it.

I turned right back around, safe on Seventh's snowy soil, and then I got to work. My barrier now blocks the entrance, from the pillars of the bridge to the very first inch of Seventh's land. I've created several layers, arcing them from left to right. This way, if the fae break through one part, it won't destroy the entire thing in one fell swoop like what happened in Highbell. It will give me more time to refortify, and give Dommik more time to assassinate. After all, the bridge is only so wide. It cannot fit more than two or three fae across at a time.

I've made the ground slick and slippery, and right now, I have six layers of defenses erected. Each one differs slightly, some with sharp icicles like spikes that jut out, some riddled with shards, while others are simply thick slabs.

I'm hoping that each layer is dense enough to sustain against either physical or magical force by the fae. Yet as I eye the rounded layer I worked on yesterday, I frown at the cracks that have formed from the weight. I must have made this one too tall. The structure is weakened because of it.

I need to fix it.

Drawing back the fur-lined hood from my face, I call up my icy magic. I don't have enough power to completely tear the barrier down and start again, because this took me all day. So instead, I try to mend the cracks, pressing my palms against each one, hoping to fill the little crevices.

I lose track of time as I travel from one end to the other, not even noticing that it's nearly dusk when I feel a hand on my shoulder that makes me jump in fright.

"It's me, Queenie," Dommik murmurs as I whirl around with a sharpened icicle raised in my fist. When he sees it, his brows lift. "Nicely done." He presses his gloved finger to its tip, and then clicks his tongue when it doesn't pierce through to his skin. "If you're going to try and stab me with ice, make sure it's sharp enough to do the job."

My eyes narrow as I toss away the icicle and yank down the scarf from my face. "It's not my *job* to kill anyone. Unlike you, assassin."

His mouth twitches. "At least your tongue is plenty sharp."

I pin him with a stare.

Unmoved, Dommik's gaze travels to the block wall I've been working on. "You're out here again?"

I turn and let my attention trace along the filled-in fissures. "It was cracking. I needed to fix it."

"You've been working on this every waking minute."

Irritation passes through me, because of course I have. "That is the entire point of us being here."

"But so far, no fae have come."

My frustration puffs up. "But they *will*, Dommik."

"We don't know that for sure," he says with a shrug. "Don't worry."

Scoffing, I turn away from him. "Why is it that some men seem to shake their heads and say *don't worry*? As if it is a woman's affliction?"

"Because you're borrowing trouble."

My eyes flare. "I'm not *borrowing* anything. Trouble is coming, and we have to try to prepare for any outcome."

"And one of the outcomes could be that Ravinger killed the threat on the other side," Dommik offers.

"You are being foolish," I say as I stare through the ice. Even now, with everything quiet and clear, I can sense an impending bleakness. Like the shocked inhale of someone waking from a nightmare only to realize it wasn't a dream.

"Why?" he counters roughly. "We obviously know what he's capable of. It's not out of the realm of possibility."

"The fae realm being attached to ours is what should be out of the realm of possibility," I retort. "It's unnatural."

Dommik steps up beside me, and his shadows twist in thin strips at his feet. "I heard that this bridge was always here. Even before Orea was formed."

"Perhaps," I say, feeling the vitriol leave my tone. "That's what the lore says. Yet it wasn't attached to any other world. The bridge to nowhere led to *nowhere.* For centuries. Until a girl from Seventh Kingdom crossed it, and then the fae used their magic to bind us. Or so they say."

He's quiet for a moment and his eyes meet mine, dark irises with flecks of light. "Unless…"

I note the snow and ash caught on his cape. "Unless what?"

He looks toward the layers of ice as if he can see the bridge beyond. "Unless it *was* attached to something. To somewhere. Just…a different realm than Annwyn."

"Impossible," I say with a shake of my head.

He glances at me, dark brow cocked. "Why is it impossible?"

I wave my hand around. "Because Seventh Kingdom was obsessed with this bridge. They sent countless people down it. No one ever came back."

"Maybe they didn't want to. Or maybe it was a one-way trip."

"Guesses and conjecture," I tell him impatiently. "What is the point?"

He shrugs. "Maybe there is no point. I'm just saying that maybe our bridge to nowhere was lying. Maybe it led somewhere all along—a different realm where all those Oreans went and never came back."

"Well, we're dealing with *this* realm," I say peevishly as I rub at my temples and close my eyes, trying to ease the headache coming on. "Who knows when it's going to try to infect us with another onslaught?"

Dommik clasps my hand, making my eyes snap back open as he tugs it down and runs his thumb over mine. "You're using too much magic," he mutters. "You need to take a break. Have you eaten anything today?"

"Yes."

"Liar."

"Well, it's positively putrid. Who has an appetite breathing this in all day?" I gesture behind us to the land with streams of smoke rising from several dozen bodies.

Dommik curses. "You should have said something."

"Said what exactly? The stench must be bothering you too."

"I've been around a lot of corpses. Burned a lot of them."

"But not *rotten*, burning corpses," I point out.

He hums, neither confirming nor denying. Then he starts to tug me away from the wall. "Come on."

I resist, trying to yank my hand from his. "There are a few more cracks—"

"Leave them. You need to eat."

With a sigh, I relent and let him lead me through the snow, because I *am* weakened. I'm tired and feeling empty. Yet instead of heading toward the front of the ruined castle, he veers us to the right, toward the back. "Why are we going this way?"

"Just going for a walk, Queenie."

"A walk?"

He looks over with a smirk. "Yes. A walk. I thought you'd be familiar. Isn't that what you royal ladies do in your spare time? Take a promenade around your different palatial rooms or through your gardens?"

"I loathe walking."

Dommik laughs. "Sure you do."

"I thought you were going to make me eat?"

"I am. Now stop needling me and just walk."

An irritated sigh escapes me, but I stop trying to pull from his grip. "Fine."

Together, we walk behind the ruins of the castle. I haven't been back this way, so I eye the crumbled structure, the gaping walls and the missing roofs. My tutors had paintings of this castle, of what it supposedly looked like before it was destroyed. It was once quite beautiful. Now, it looks like a husk. A skeleton with all the guts and life scooped out.

Dommik and I walk in silence as we pass it by, and after several minutes, we're still walking. Still silent. Though the tension starts to leave me the further I get from the bridge. The further I get from Cauval.

I feel myself physically decompress, all my squeezed muscles and rigid bones finally going loose. I let out a sigh, and Dommik's thumb grazes over my hand.

Above us, the gray-hued sky darkens, not quite night, not quite day, but stuck somewhere in between. I eye the edge of the world at our right, wondering how many people have tipped over into the void.

Dommik notices me stealing glances, so he starts tugging me toward it. I instantly snap my grip, trying to pull him away. "What do you think you're doing?"

"Come on."

My mouth pinches.

"Trust me, Queenie."

I hesitate, but then for some strange reason, I let him pull me toward it. We go right up to the end, and then Dommik actually sits down.

*Sits.* At the edge of the world.

"Get up!" I hiss in fear.

He laughs and then pats the snow beside him. "Sit with me."

I feel my eyes nearly bug out of my sockets. "Are you out of your mind?"

"Scared of heights?" he teases, looking up at me.

"Of course not."

He continues to stare, while I bristle, his face utterly calm but thoroughly challenging. "It's okay. If you can't do it…"

I press my lips together tightly. Yet because my ornery streak refuses to back down from Dommik's provocation, I carefully sidle forward and settle onto the snow beside him. He reaches over and uncurls my legs, making them untangle until my feet dangle over the edge of the world.

I nearly hyperventilate.

*Nearly.* I don't, of course, because I am still a queen.

"There," Dommik says with a grin. "How do you feel?"

"Like I want to stab you," I grind out, scared stiff.

Instead of teasing me, he shakes his head calmly. "No, Queenie. Look. Take it in."

He points ahead at the nothing. The vaporous ether of fog in front of us that seems to never end. Then at the dark void below us that holds our world cradled in its bottomless grasp.

I breathe in a shuddering breath and stare at it, doing as he said and trying to simply take it in.

After a few minutes, the fear of falling actually loosens its hold around me. Then, I realize that sitting here and facing the edge of the world is actually quite…liberating.

"That's it…" Dommik encourages as he takes my hand. "How do you feel now?"

"I feel…small," I admit. "Only, in a good way."

Because this makes our problems feel smaller too.

We are only two specks sitting at the fringe of a world. A world that has seen so many other people. And something about that makes me feel like this threat we face is small enough that perhaps we just might overcome it.

So I let out a breath, and I smile out at the void, because now, it doesn't seem so dismal after all.

Perhaps it just takes sitting at the edge of your world to find a little bit of hope.

# CHAPTER 43

## QUEEN MALINA

We sit here at Orea's edge for a while. Watching the fog and feeling the biting air while we savor the silence together.

Then, Dommik gets up and carefully helps me back to my feet. When we start walking again, he continues on instead of heading back the way we came toward the ruins.

I dart a questioning look his way, but he says nothing.

After a couple more minutes, just as it begins to start snowing, I spot something in the distance. I squint, trying to figure out what it could be. "What is that?"

"Well, I'm not positive, since I'm not as versed in history as you, but I believe...this used to be Seventh Kingdom's capital city. Or what's left of it."

My eyes widen as I take in the sight. Dommik is right. There's a road. Or I think it may have been a road a very long time ago. Now, it's only patches of flat stone upon the snow, still bricked together in some places. The only reason we can even see it is because the wind seems to have dislodged a snow drift, leaving the patchwork of the ancient street exposed.

Judging by the distance from the castle, I'd say this could be considered the outskirts of Cauval City. And there, just beside the remnants of the quilted bricks, is a single building, that somehow managed to keep existing after all this time.

"I didn't think anything was still standing."

"Me either," Dommik replies.

Together, we make our way toward it. There isn't any roof, but three walls stand, one of them arced with the space where a window used to be. We skirt around to the inside of the walls and see the snow gathered in tall piles at each corner.

"There must have been a lot of it that collapsed," I murmur as I trail my hand down the rough stone.

"I don't think so," Dommik tells me as he looks it over. "I think this was it."

Surprised, I glance around the space. "It's so small."

"I grew up in a house about this size."

I pause at that. Dommik rarely talks about himself, so it's hard for me to imagine his life. Admittedly, I've never been very good at putting myself in other people's shoes. "You did?"

He smirks my way. "We don't all live in castles, Queenie."

"I know that, it's just…" I stop at the hole where the window used to be.

Dommik comes up beside me. "It's jarring to see the view from someone else's life?"

"Yes." I nod before my gaze falls down to the corner of the window space. There are little grooves sliced into it. Perhaps they were caused by time. Or perhaps many, many years ago, someone dragged down these marks into the stone with purposeful scrapes.

It's strange to think of someone else once living here, of having a full life, while I now stand in their echoes.

Lifting my hand, I bring my magic up, creating a thin sheet of ice within the window cut-out until it looks just like a pane of glass.

Dommik raps his knuckle against it lightly. "Very nice."

Then I turn, both hands pressing against the stone, and I make more ice spread up. Slowly fixing the parts of the home that have crumbled and fallen away. I encase us, even making an arcing ceiling above that closes out the flakes of snow, though I leave a small doorway open for us to slip out of.

Dommik glances around, and now that the walls are all closed up, it makes the space seem even smaller than before. Yet there's a feeling about this place—it's calming. There's something about it that makes me wish to stay a bit longer.

Just then, my stomach growls loudly. I place a hand on my middle as mortified warmth spreads across my cheeks.

Dommik grins over at me. "That must be the dinner bell."

I scowl at him as he reaches up and undoes the clasp of his cape. "What are you doing?"

Instead of answering, he shakes it out and turns it over, and then lays it upon the snow. "Sit."

Keeping still, I watch as he then takes a satchel from his belt and starts pulling out food and placing it on the cloak. He unwraps a piece of bread, cheeses, meats, strange fruits I've never seen before, and even a teardrop-shaped bottle that appears to be a deep red wine.

Dommik sits down on one corner of the cloak and then gestures to the other side, waiting. I hesitate for a moment longer and then sit down across from him, tucking my legs beneath me. The snow we sit on is surprisingly soft and pillowed, like it drifted in to help cushion our bodies. And since Dommik's cloak is lined with leather, it's not soaking through.

I glance down, watching Dommik as he starts to tear off pieces of everything with meticulous neatness. Bread first, then a bit of cheese and a slice of salted meat, all stacked on top of each other. He hands it to me first, and I take it, realizing that I can actually smell the food instead of gruesome death.

"The stench. It's not spread over this way."

He only nods, and I realize that's why he brought us out here. As soon as he knew the smell was bothering me, he got me away from it.

Something softens in my chest as I watch him break off the same bits of food until he has his own stack. Then he raises it to me, waiting. Only when I lift it to my lips does he mimic the movement, both of us watching each other as we start to eat.

Surprisingly, the flavor of the food is delicious, the meat rich and the cheese perfectly creamy. Even the bread isn't a hardened chunk of stale wheat. This is actually still tender, as if it was freshly baked.

"Say what you will about the fae, but their food is fucking good," Dommik says around a mouthful.

Amusement fills me, because he's right. I realize now, away from the burning corpses, that I'm too famished to be prideful about not wanting to eat their food. Plus, it really is delicious.

The two of us have another stack, and then he peels open the purple and red fruits, revealing squishy pods inside that burst with sweet flavor. We finish those off too, licking the syrup from our fingers. Then Dommik yanks out the cork of the bottle with his teeth and takes a swig. I watch his throat bob as he drinks, face warming when he catches me staring.

He only smirks and passes it over, and I lift it slightly, giving it a sip.

"Not like that, Queenie," he chastises. "Give it a good swig. Like you mean it. Like you're out here at the edge of the world and you can say, 'Fuck it. I'm going to gulp down this fairy wine and hope it warms me up or gets me drunk—or both.'"

My lips curl, but then I do just that, lifting the bottle high up, letting the liquid start pouring down. I take a big swallow, then another before I pass it back to him with a cough that makes him grin.

"How did that feel?" he asks.

The airy heat dissipates from my throat enough for me to answer. "Surprisingly, rather good."

"Good."

We pass the bottle back and forth a few more times, until I'm relaxed and languid, feeling the warmth of the wine settle in my stomach.

I lean back against the wall of the house and shake my head. "I used to be bored with life," I admit as I look around the frosty walls. "Now I wish that all this danger and uncertainty would go away. To feel bored again would be a gift."

"Life has a way of teaching us things."

I nod at that as I glance up at the ice ceiling, watching snow land upon it like icing sugar. Dommik cleans up the food and then sits next to me, putting his arm behind my back and letting me tuck into his side. My heart squeezes in my chest.

"What has life taught you?" I ask, lifting my head to study his handsome face. The strong cut of his jaw, the patches of light skin around his mouth and nose, his black beard trimmed against his chin, and his hair gathered at his nape. I itch to trail my hand over his features and turn his face so I can look at his dark eyes and count the light flecks in them.

He lets out a huffing laugh. "Where do I even start?" he says. "I've learned a lot of things. But I believe it just taught me one of the most valuable lessons of all."

"Which is?"

"That one kill can actually lead to life," he answers, looking down at me with a weightiness to his words and a significance to his gaze. When he lifts his hand to grip my neck and drag a thumb along my jaw, I can't quite breathe, because

I'm hanging on each low word he speaks and every inch of his touch. "And that something that seems so cold can actually be the warmest thing you'll ever feel."

I swallow hard and lean in closer, as if seeking more of him.

"What has life taught you, Malina?" he asks, and my chest constricts at the sound of him rumbling my name.

"Painful things and hard lessons," I answer honestly. "Everything I didn't want but desperately needed."

"You're a different woman than you were in that gilded castle."

"I certainly hope so." My answer is quiet, because inside, it holds a fear. One that rolls right off my loosened tongue. "But I'm afraid that it's not true."

Dommik frowns down at me. "Why would you think that?"

"What if I only think I've become a better person?" I ask shakily. "What if I find myself months, years from now, sitting in some lavish room in some pretty life, and as soon as I have that back, *I* also go back? Back to behaving and thinking the same way as before. Perhaps I'm still a nasty, bitter woman with a cold heart, and all of this is only because of fear and desperation."

He's quiet for a moment, his hand moving up to grip a part of my hair and rub the white strands together. "There could've been a chance for that, sure. That once the danger is gone, you'd revert to the way you were before. But I know you won't. I know you've truly changed from how you were before—do you know how?"

"How?"

"Because you chose to leave…and then stay, and leave, and then stay again."

I frown at him in confusion, and he starts counting on his fingers. "Leave: you begged me to help get you out of Seventh so you could warn your people. Stay: you chose to stay in Highbell even when it was under attack, even when it seemed like all was lost. Leave: you chose to leave Highbell again, once it was secure and your people were safe inside the castle, so you could come here…" He holds up a fourth finger. "And stay, because you're *here*. Choosing to remain at the bridge, doing everything you can to protect this world even under great threat to yourself."

My heart pounds with his words, and he drops his hand to press it over the organ, as if he can feel its pulse. "Your heart has changed. Bit by bit. The Cold Queen isn't so cold anymore."

His words leave me trembling, but then I let out a confession that feels like it's been scraped raw from my depths. "I don't *want* to be cold anymore, Dommik."

His eyes soften. "I know."

He shocks me by gently shifting me, arms picking me up and then settling me down until I'm lying on my back while he braces himself over me.

My breath catches. "What are you doing?"

"I'm kissing you properly, Queenie. The way you should've been kissed and adored before shitty men came into your life and took you for granted. Took you for *their* advantage. Took and took until you felt like you had to be cold to protect that shattered warmth."

Tears spring to my eyes and flake off against my cheeks.

"May I have permission to kiss you, Malina?"

His formal question makes my chest squeeze. "Yes," I say quietly.

Dommik lowers his lips to mine, and my eyes flutter closed with the gentleness of his kiss. We've had stolen moments. A quick thrill. Bodies netting together in a frenzied pull of lust.

This is different.

There is no war hammering down around us. No impending death right around the corner. For the first time, we have *time*.

So we take it. Every single second.

He slowly strips me of my clothing, while I do the same for him. We get the chance to look at each other, to stroke and feel and explore. He drifts his lips down my body, and I drag my fingers over his.

I let myself feel every contour, every muscle, tracing every lightened patch across his dark skin. He seems to cherish every inch of my body, while I marvel at every dip and cleft of his.

I'm bared to him with far more than just my body, though. I feel as if he's bared my heart after I've kept it tucked away for so long.

Dommik caresses my breasts and strokes my hip, his mouth leaving chills in the wake of the path he takes along my neck. "Will you give yourself to me, Malina?"

Such a question.

One I've never been asked before. One I never even thought I was allowed to answer. If there was ever anyone I would willingly give myself to like this, it's Dommik, for he's the only one who has ever truly understood me.

The bad parts and the good.

"Yes," I whisper, feeling my chin wobble.

He carefully picks up my leg and drapes it over his hip, and then slowly, he enters me. I gasp at the intrusion from his body to mine, from his heat that seems to melt me from within.

My body stretches for him, and he starts to move in slow, decadent strokes, all while filling my ears with praise. "Do you feel us?" he asks as he kisses my lips, tilting me up to drag along a fissure of pleasure deep inside of me.

My answer is breathless and honest and driving with desire. "I feel us."

This joining is so different from our tryst back in Highbell. Soft snow peppers the ceiling. A low hum of the arctic wind fills the background. We're protected in this ancient house of ice and rock, everything else falling away so that I feel the two of us completely. Feel us inside and out.

It's not only time that Dommik and I have, but a gentleness too. A tender intimacy I've never experienced with anyone. Certainly not with Tyndall, who only took my body and then left me to wither. Not Jeo, who I was determined to use solely for pleasure. Dommik kisses me, makes love to me, with a tenderness that I once longed for yet never received.

A tenderness that both bleeds my heart and fills it all at once.

"No more doubting yourself, Malina," he says against my ear as he thrusts up deep, seating himself completely, rolling his hips in a way that nearly makes my eyes roll back. "You are beautiful. Strong. And so fucking warm." His hands grip my face, forcing me to look him in the eyes, while his shadows dance around us. "You are *good*, Malina. And I'm proud of the woman you are."

My body releases with pleasure and tears. An exultation laced with grief. I'm left amazed at how words can be woven together in such a way that they cause healing on wounds I'd long since ignored.

I clutch Dommik as he releases himself inside of me, pressing kisses to his shoulder and neck while his breath slows back to normal.

We lie together like this, tucked beneath scattered clothes and cloaks, wrapped up in Dommik's magic, and we sleep with skin and touch and warmth.

At this moment, nobody could accuse me of being cold.

Least of all, my heart.

# CHAPTER 44

## RISSA

S creams can be heard in the distance. Clangs and cracks. Timberwings roaring. Then there's a deafening crash, and the room I'm in shakes.

I'm barely able to stop myself from slamming my hands over my ears.

My pacing steps come to a halt on the carpeted floor of this cold, dark house we're hiding in. "What's happening?" I ask the soldier. Cran is his name. Osrik chose him to be my guard as I wait in this estate house, while the battle rages outside in Ranhold.

Cran straightens up away from the window and looks over at me. His black hair and armor blend in with the shadows. "I can't be sure, Lady Rissa. I believe that sound may have been the castle's walls, but I don't have a clear line of sight."

I clench my molars together with irritation—irritation and fear. I start to pace again, ignoring the bloodstains on the floor.

I don't want to know what happened to the previous owners of this house, but I can draw enough conclusions. It's the same thing that's happened to the rest of this ruined and empty street.

Death.

Everywhere they go, it appears the fae are very thorough. If I had still been in Ranhold Castle when they'd come…I'd be dead too.

I shiver with the thought, and then another crash sounds in the distance, like an entire building has toppled, and I'm ready to jump right out of my skin.

"Enough!" I hiss out before I stalk toward the front door. I can't stay here. I *can't.*

"Lady Rissa, what are you doing?" Cran calls with alarm.

"Manu got the better house to watch the battle from," I say over my shoulder. "We're going there. Right now."

When I reach for the doorknob, Cran's hand lands on my arm. "My lady, we can't go out there!"

I turn to him, arching a brow. "You were just staring out the window. Are there any nefarious fae out on the street?"

"Well…no, but—"

"Great, so we won't have any trouble walking up the block to the estate where Manu is," I say before dropping my eyes to where he's still gripping me. "And I can assure you, Captain Osrik will not be pleased if I tell him you wouldn't unhand me."

His grip releases like his palm has been seared with fire.

"Let's go."

Cran curses as I yank open the door. I peer out, but the shadowed street is just as empty as it was when I was dumped here several hours ago. I step down from the stoop and onto the frosty cobbles while Cran sticks himself to my side, sword in hand and head swiveling.

The view out here screams of a hasty retreat. There are abandoned carriages, barrels and chests overturned, food and clothing left behind in piles, and body-shaped clumps of snow that I avert my attention from.

"Which one is it?" I whisper to Cran. Despite the bravado I'm putting on, my heart is pounding in my chest. Any one of these clustered houses could be hiding a fae. Every shadowed alley we pass could reveal an enemy about to jump out at us and attack.

But I couldn't stand being in that other house a second longer. I need to know what's happening. I need to know if Osrik is okay.

Our steps seem far too loud, even with the sounds of the fierce battle coming from the direction of the castle. I can see its stone walls looming ahead, the top of the turrets visible even from the bottom of this hill.

Cran and I crest it, steps hurrying up the slope, and then he points. "Queen Kaila's brother is there, Lady Rissa."

My eyes narrow on the white-painted estate. The iron gate lies knocked off its hinges, and I believe that oblong shape in the snow is a frozen corpse, but this place has a far better vantage point, which is probably why Manu chose it.

"Why does his house have a tower?" I say to Cran, gesturing upward. "We didn't have a tower."

He gives me a sidelong look and then walks ahead of me. "Let me announce us…so we don't get stabbed." He mutters that last part, but I choose to ignore it.

We walk past the bent gates, and I wait in the yard while Cran hurries up to the door. He opens it, calling softly, and I hear an answering voice. They go back and forth for a moment, and I hear something like, "Why?" Then, "I don't know, but I can't just say no!"

I leave them to it, craning to look in the direction of the battle, but even here, the rows of houses along the road make it impossible to see. My hands twist in front of me, fingers twitching over my thick fur coat.

"Lady Rissa?" Cran calls.

I quickly turn and go into the estate. My gaze sweeps through the dark house, and I hear the guards shut the door behind me as I make my way through the entry. "Where's Manu?"

"Up in the tower room, Lady Rissa," the Third Kingdom soldier answers. "This way."

"Of course he is," I mutter.

I follow him up a set of spiral stairs, my own guard hot on my heels. "Lady Rissa," Cran says quietly, "Captain Osrik will not like you being in the same room as Manu…"

"Then Captain Osrik should've put me in a house with a tower so I could adequately see what the hell is going on."

He doesn't have a reply to that.

"Besides, are you going to let Manu hurt me?"

"Of course not, my lady."

"Then everything is fine. We're just here for the view."

Manu's guard reaches the top floor, and I hear him speaking just as I enter the room. I spot Manu instantly. He looks from the guard to me, black brows lifting in surprise. "Lady Rissa?"

"You have the better house," I explain curtly as I look around.

We're in a solar tower room, with a few chairs gathered around a dark fireplace. Against one of the walls, there's glass littered around an overturned bookshelf and broken bar cart. But there are no dead bodies and it's not burnt down, which is more than I can say for most of the other houses in the city.

I can feel all three men staring at me as I head for the window where Manu is standing. I stop in front of it and look out. "Much better," I say, because now, I have a full view of the castle and its walls.

And the battle raging in front of it.

We're still quite a distance away, but I can see people

in the snow in front of the protective walls. I can tell the difference of who is who just by the colors. Fourth Kingdom is easy to spot in their black armor that shows up starkly against the snow, while the fae are blobs of gray.

There are far more gray blobs. We're very clearly outnumbered.

I wring my hands again as worry starts peeling at me, leaving my heart in strips. I strain to see. To find him in the fray.

*Where is he?*

Manu is careful not to stand too close to me. Despite how cold it is here, he has the window open to see better, and ice has gathered along the windowpane. The only light we have comes from the patchy dawn that's trying to sew itself into the sky. A deplorable hour, if you ask me. But now, I'm desperate for the muted light.

Osrik tried to explain the main points of their plans, but I have no mind for battles or strategies. All I heard was violence. All I could imagine was him running straight into danger.

If he gets himself killed, I will *kill* him.

Then there's another loud sound, and this time, I see it: timberwings dropping chunks of stone onto the fae who stand on Ranhold's wall. In response, the fae are shooting some sort of magic into the sky that streaks across like dripping yolk.

It lands against one of the timberwings, and the winged beast screeches in pain as it starts to plummet. I flinch when it crashes to the ground in a spray of snow and doesn't move again.

Alarm blares through my ears and I turn away from the window and start to pace. *What if that was Osrik on that bird?*

I'm going to be sick.

This room isn't overly large, especially not with three men in it, but I walk the entire length of it from wall to wall like I can walk off some of this worry.

The ground shakes again with a distant rumble, and I think I hear another building crashing down.

I go still. "Manu, what's happening?"

I don't know anything about battles other than I've never wanted to be near one. Which just proves how vastly different my life has become.

If Osrik had tried to send me away from him, I would've released my temper in a way he hasn't even seen yet—and he's seen quite a bit.

Not that I *want* to be near an active battle, but I'd rather choose this than be separated from him. *That* would be more dangerous. It would eat away at me, bite by bite. It would chew up my thoughts, consume every emotion. I'd dissolve into a puddle of anxiety that I wouldn't be able to digest.

I don't have the sort of strength it takes to wait.

Though I have to admit…being in the barracks during the battle at Cliffhelm and being here, listening and seeing it…it's horrible.

And yet, I can't *not* be here.

There is no good scenario. Either way, I do end up waiting. Either from afar or up close. At least up close, I can get back to Osrik faster. Whether it's to throw my arms around him and feel that he's okay…

Or be here where he dies.

Furious fear makes a tear drip from my eye at the thought.

I *hate* armies and battles and war. Just one glance out this window, and you can see the devastation of it. Most of the city has been burned, everyone who lived here gone.

I don't know anything about fighting, but I know that no matter how many times I pace the room, this battle is going to end, one way or another, so I need to know what's happening.

"Manu," I say again sharply.

His gaze is fixed out the window. "So far, everything has been going to plan. We're drawing the fae out from the castle's walls, and our side has advanced past their first line of defense on the ground."

I stare at him as he speaks, studying him. His long black hair is tied back neatly, the shape of his face perfectly offsetting deep brown eyes. I told Osrik all was forgiven, but that isn't true. I only said it so that he wouldn't go and commit murder and then be punished for it. I won't let Manu Ioana *or* his queen sister ruin any more of our time or our lives. Especially not when I've barely escaped with mine.

Manu turns his head, catching me looking. "You're glaring at me again."

"Am I?" I ask, though I know he's right. I can feel the edges of my gaze hanging off the corners of my face. It's quite sharp.

"I'm not going to hurt you," he says.

"Again," I say curtly. "Hurt me *again*."

He winces slightly and turns to fully face me. "I have already said it multiple times, but I say it again, Lady Rissa. I apologize for the harm that fell upon you because of me and my actions. You've no idea how much I wish that hadn't happened to you."

I don't even attempt to suppress the roll of my eyes. "This repeated conversation is boring me."

The corner of his lips twitches in the smallest movement. "You know, I believe in a different life, under different circumstances, we could have been friends."

"Doubtful. I loathe most people."

He cocks his head. "You seem to be very friendly with the captain."

"Osrik doesn't count."

"No?" he says lightly. "What about Lady Auren?"

My eyes narrow. "Oh, you mean the Lady Auren that you knocked out and kidnapped? That Lady Auren?" I say waspishly, my lips curling up when I see him wince again. "Yes, actually. She doesn't count either. I don't loathe her."

"No need for me to ask which category I'm in, I presume?"

"You presume correctly," I reply. "You're firmly in the loathe pile."

"I deserve that." He starts to say something else, but the sound of screaming suddenly bolts through the air and strikes my eardrums.

My heart lurches up my throat, and I rush over to the window and look out again. "What's happening now?"

"It's alright." Manu's voice is calm, which infuriates me. I flinch when I hear another massive boom. "This is part of the first phase, remember?"

"No, I don't remember," I snap as I grip the wooden windowsill. The horrible screaming echoing through the air makes me want to run. "Osrik told me a lot of things, but I'm not a soldier!"

Manu doesn't speak harshly back to me. Instead, he only nods and then points his finger. "That's my sister's magic. She's confusing the fae."

I look out with a tight chest and darting eyes, noting several timberwings circling the air. Manu points at Ranhold Castle, his fingertip skimming over its ruined wall that's fallen and charred, like perhaps fae magic burnt right through it. Then my gaze drags down to the ground below where people are fighting.

"We've drawn them all out. The fae are fully engaged, and my sister's magic is confusing them. See?"

I don't know exactly what I'm supposed to be seeing, because I'm overwhelmed with all those gray blobs. "There's so many of them," I say, fear tightening my throat. I shouldn't have looked.

*Why did I look?*

"They're going to overwhelm us…" I say shakily, scared and angry all at once.

"We planned for this," Manu says gently. "Watch."

Stuck to the view, I do just that. Watch as the fighting rages on.

"This was a stupid idea," I hiss at him. "For us to come here. There are too many of them. We don't have the advantage here that we had at Cliffhelm—and even *that* was planned on a damn prayer. We don't have a rotten ground to work with here. I don't know how they thought this was a good idea…"

Fae are slaying Orean soldiers down there. I just *know* it. What if it's *my* Orean soldier? What if Osrik is hurt, or dying?

My stomach roils.

"We might not have a rotten ground, but Fourth's army is the fiercest for a reason, and it's not only because of King Rot. They're known for being master strategists."

"I don't care," I snarl. "We're going to lose. Everyone is going to die. Look at all of them!"

Manu carefully places his hand on mine where my nails are digging into the sill. I didn't realize I was shaking until right now, but his touch makes me freeze in place.

"You aren't going to die," he says quietly, and I finally slash my gaze from the battle to his face. He's looking at me with soft sympathy. A shared humanity, which is so very different from how he looked at me in the gardens of Brackhill right before I was stabbed by the very people he let in.

"I promise you this, Lady Rissa. If we should lose today, I will personally do everything in my power to get you out. You will *not* die."

I believe what he says—his tone is too vehement for me not to. And while I am afraid for myself, I'm mostly terrified for Osrik. I can't bear to go down to that battlefield and see him in a puddle of blood, all hacked up.

Tears burn my eyes.

"Aren't you frightened for your sister?" I whisper.

Manu nods. "Yes. But I believe we are going to make it out of this."

"Why?"

He lifts a shoulder. "Sometimes, you have to live on faith."

Through the open window, snow starts to blow in alongside another crash of stone. The screaming has stopped, but now, it sounds like a thousand voices are yelling at once. If it's this loud here, I can't even imagine how blaring it is right in the thick of it.

A blinding light tosses into the sky toward a group of circling timberwings. I hear Manu suck in a breath, his face going pale as the birds start to screech.

Trails of smoke follow as four of them fall through the air.

"Who is it?" I desperately ask. "Who got hit?"

"I—I don't know," he says, shaken for the first time. "It looked like Third's colors, but I'm not sure…"

It could be his sister, or he could be wrong and it could've been Osrik.

The back of my throat burns with bile, and this time, I squeeze his hand.

"Live on faith," I grit out. "Right?"

He glances over at me, his expression grim, but he squeezes my hand back. The two of us, him full of regret, me with hate, now joined together with fear.

"Yes, Lady Rissa. We must keep faith."

But how do you do that when it feels so futile?

# CHAPTER 45

## RISSA

My breath rattles in my chest like someone is shaking it in a bottle. Manu and I watch out the window as the fae start to overwhelm our soldiers. Even I can tell we're losing.

We squeeze each other's hands hard, worry gripping us both.

But then, a terrible roaring rends the air, and it's not from the timberwings or Kaila's magic. We flinch, gazes lurching to find the source.

"What's that?" I ask, pointing toward the curve of the sloping hill.

Manu's eyes flash, something like relief crawling down his face. "That's phase two."

"Phase two...what was phase two?"

But he doesn't have to say, because the movement along the snow forms into actual shapes I can decipher. Ships of white wood being pulled by a line of fire claws whose paws spark with flames.

"The Red Raids have arrived."

There are five ships that I can see, and they stream down the slope with amazing speed, the fiery felines pulling them in an outright sprint.

One of the ships gets rocked by a hit of magic that strikes its hull. A spray of violet light bursts from it, making the animals scream. The vessel flings and tips, dark plum smoke blasting out of it and rising into the air.

"Oh, no…"

I have no love lost for the snow pirates, but they're fighting *with* Orea. We need their numbers. But as heartless as it may seem, I'll gladly see them sacrifice themselves if it means Osrik and the others live.

The other four ships skid to a stop. The ramps toss open, and pirates stream out, pouring into the fray. Their animals are loosed too. The fire claws start racing toward the fae and tackling them, the large beasts roaring with bloodthirst and predatory hunger.

But more fae come out to meet them.

With the morning light, it's easier to see as fae flood into the battle from the innards of Ranhold Castle.

"There are more of them…"

*Great Divine, how are there more of them?*

"That must be their last line of defense," Manu replies, though his voice is shaken. Even he can't discount the growing threat. "There must've been more than we realized."

"We can't win, can we?" I whisper. "Not even with the snow pirates or your sister's magic."

Behind us, both of our guards have come up to look out the window too. The tension and worry glues to each one of us, sticking to the silence as we watch.

The snow pirates, the Elites, Fourth and Third soldiers…

we're getting overwhelmed. It's not enough. After all our plans, it's not—

Suddenly, a horn blares.

From up on the slope where the Red Raids first appeared, an army crests.

My hand snags onto Manu's arm, fingers squeezing. "Who is *that*?"

I squint, and I just barely make out two things: a banner of two converging suns and another one of the serpent king's sigil.

"First and Second Kingdom?" I ask breathlessly. "I didn't know they were coming to help!"

"They weren't," Manu admits, glancing down at me with surprise. "We didn't know they would be here. We sent missives to Second Kingdom, but we didn't know... The prince must've sent soldiers on ships and met King Thold at Breakwater. And they must've just come straight here."

Hope locks itself around my heart. Then my eyes widen when I see King Thold standing, green cloak snapping in the wind, wearing armor of green and black and a crown on his head. His Elites are with him, and all at once, he raises his sword and lets out a battle cry, sending First and Second soldiers to sprint down toward the fae.

Then the king raises both arms, and the ground rumbles and foams, seeming to bubble up...and a torrent of serpents bursts through the snow. The snakes pop up, their bodies long and white and huge.

There are dozens of them, and King Thold sends their zigzagging bodies to slither down the slope. They start attacking the fae with viciousness. Big jaws unhinging to clamp over legs and torsos. Long lengths wrapping around entire soldiers and constricting them so tightly the fae drop to the ground.

"Oh gods..."

The new arrivals of both snake and soldier now flood the

battle scene. From our vantage point, it looks like the snowy landscape is an ocean of white. Snow serpents continue to burst up every few feet like choppy waves coming to snatch at the fae and drag them under.

The soldiers from Second and First Kingdom have reached Fourth and Third's Elites, backing them up and pushing at the influx of fae.

In the air, timberwings swoop down in deadly arcs, talons snatching fae and tossing them down again, making them plummet to their deaths. Snow pirates fight, fire claws rampage, and my heart beats so fast in my chest I think I might pass out.

But I don't dare miss a thing because the fae…the fae are *losing*.

"It's happened, Lady Rissa," Manu says beside me, his voice strangled.

"What's happening?" I ask, just as tightly.

"We don't need a rotting ground," he tells me as he looks over with the ghost of a watery smile. "Because Orea has finally united. We're fighting…*together*."

The guards don't let us leave until the battle horn blows.

As soon as they deem it safe, I tear out of the noble's estate with Manu right behind me. We head out onto the slick street, all of us racing toward the castle.

The battle is over.

A bit of sunlight has pierced through the clouds, and it's stopped snowing, but I'm still frozen.

Cold fear has taken root.

My body trembles, but I say a silent prayer to the Divine as I race down Ranhold's empty streets. We pass corpses and charred buildings, but my eyes stay straight ahead.

We won the battle. Manu and I watched as our forces took

GOLDFINCH

out the fae, but this noose around my throat won't loosen. Not until I see if Osrik is okay.

If he *lives*.

When we get out of the city and come to the stretch of land in front of the castle's destroyed outer walls, I skid to a stop, my breath panting in and out.

It's so much worse seeing a battleground up close than it is from a tower window.

Placing my hand over my nose and mouth, I gag at the sight and smell of bloodied bodies and entrails spread around and staining the snow. Seeing the faces of the dead is probably going to haunt me forever.

But I look.

I look for every armored soldier clad in black metal chest plates and fierce helmets. I search through them, while Manu breaks away, running to a soldier from Third.

Cran sticks to my side, but we stop when we find a Fourth soldier. He sinks down to his knees and turns the man over and then yanks off his helmet. Unseeing eyes stare up at the sky, and Cran lets out a shaky breath, his face going pale.

I kneel down in the snow next to him. "What was his name?" I ask quietly.

"We called him Tipper," he chokes out. "Never could hold down his henade. Always tipped over whenever he tried to walk home from the taverns."

Even though I didn't know him, I feel my chest tighten. "I'm sorry."

Cran shoots out a breath and stands, gaze scanning the battleground where so many more bodies lie. "We fight, Lady Rissa. But even if we win, we still lose."

My jaw aches with emotion and I want to sob, because he's right. I'm terrified I'm going to lose too. I'm terrified to keep searching the bodies.

But I have to face it. I have to know.

So together, we keep looking, while groups of Second and Third soldiers seem to be doing the same. Cran and I find another six of Fourth's Elites dead.

None of them are Osrik.

We pass by so much gruesome death that once my tears start falling, they won't stop. Timberwings, Elites, soldiers from every kingdom, pirates, and fire claws. They all lie here amongst the bodies of the fae in a terrible ice-cold graveyard.

My heart feels ripped apart and stomped on by the time we make it to Ranhold's outer wall. Only a small part still stands, the rest of it left in rubbled pieces along the snow.

I feel like my heart is a rubbled ruin too.

But then I hear a voice.

"Rissa?"

My gaze jerks up. I can barely see him through the tears in my eyes, but Osrik's bulky body is unmistakable. He has his helmet off and his arms are bare and littered with slices. His black armor is dented and singed, and there are splatters of blood on his face.

But he's alive.

My entire body jolts, and I'm running before I even realize it. I slip and slide in the slick snow, barreling past the broken stone, but then I reach him and *jump*.

Osrik catches me beneath my arms. He lets me hang there in front of him awkwardly while he looks me over, his expression intense, brown eyes wild with worry.

"You okay?"

"I'm fine," I say with exasperation. "I was trying to leap into your arms!"

"You *are* in my arms," he says, giving me a little shake.

"Stop holding me out like this! This is the way you hold a stray cat you're worried is going to claw you!"

"I'm filthy," he warns.

"I *don't* care."

The next instant, I'm finally crushed against his chest, and he holds me the way I want, with his big hands firmly at my ass and his beard against my cheek.

"Are you okay?" I ask shakily, leaning back to get another look at his face that's streaked with blood. "Is any of this yours?"

"I'm good, Rissa. I have you."

A sob escapes me and I bury myself against him again, trying to stop my full-body shakes. "I was so scared," I admit, my breath hot, my tears scalding.

He squeezes me against him, one hand rubbing up and down my back in comforting strokes. "I'm okay. *You're* okay," he rumbles out. "We won."

I nod and turn to kiss him, my lips wet with my tears. Then I pull away and press my hands on his cheeks, my eyes darting between each of his. "You gave Manu the better house."

He frowns. "What?"

"Manu. He had the better house. So I went there so I could watch. He had a *tower*, Osrik," I lecture.

He pauses, his jaw muscles jumping. For some reason, that sight makes my stomach warm. "You were in the same room as the fucker who almost got you killed?"

"I didn't get a tower. I needed to see."

He opens his mouth like he wants to start lecturing me back, but then he lets out a thick sigh. "You know what? Fuck it. I'm just glad I have you in my arms."

Osrik kisses me again, his tongue insistent, teeth biting at my bottom lip and filling me with warmth that finally makes my shakes subside. "You exasperating fucking woman of mine," he mumbles against me. "Always trying to see if I'm okay."

I tug at his beard. "Well, stop putting yourself in danger and I won't have to."

His hand squeezes my ass, making my stomach spin. "That's the end goal, Yellow Bell."

After a moment, he sets me back down on my feet, keeping me tucked to his side. Everyone else is gathering in this courtyard area too, and I look around, trying to see who else is alive.

"Your commander? The captains?" I ask, because I know how much he cares about them.

He nods. "They're good too."

I breathe out a sigh of relief.

My gaze darts to the wall just as Manu and his queen sister pass through. Call me crazy, but I'm actually relieved for him. He looks across the courtyard, and when he sees I'm with Osrik, he gives me a small smile and a nod.

Osrik tenses next to me, but I tap his arm and look up at him. "It's fine," I tell him. "Sharing that tower window was good for me, I think."

"Killing them would be good for me," he mutters.

I laugh and pat him again before wrinkling my nose when I see all the blood I got on my hand. I wipe it off on his armor. "You just killed, like, a hundred fae," I point out.

"Actually, *I* killed a hundred bloodthirsty fae," Judd says cheerfully as he walks by, strutting like a peacock and tossing back his sweat-slicked hair. "I practically won this battle single-handedly!"

"You did not," Captain Lu shouts back as she appears.

"Aww, don't be jealous, Lu-Lu," he tells her as they meet up. "You helped a little. Right, Dig?"

Auren's old guard shakes his head at Judd. It's strange to see him in black armor instead of gold. Right behind him is Commander Ryatt. Every single one of them looks just as bloodied and battle-worn as Osrik.

But alive.

Second Kingdom's soldiers gather around too, their copper-hued armor stained with blood, and I can't help but notice there are fewer of them than the number that first crested the slope. I wonder how many they lost. I wonder how many all of our kingdoms have lost.

Like Cran said, even if we win, we still lose.

King Thold enters the ruined courtyard with some of his guards trailing after him, and he heads straight for Queen Kaila and her Elites. He still has a snow serpent dangling from his neck, the snake's tongue darting out and tail flicking against his side.

"Where did the rest of the snakes go?" I whisper to Osrik.

"He sent them back under the snow."

I glance down at the ground, barely stopping from picking up my feet. "That's...unsettling."

Osrik chuckles.

Judd breaks off to speak to a couple of Red Raids, their blood-colored cloths still tied around their faces. In the distance, some of their ships are smoking and ruined, their fire claws roaming free to feast on the fallen.

My stomach turns and I yank my gaze away.

A shadow suddenly casts over us, and I look up to see a timberwing landing. Commander Ryatt strides forward, stopping right in front of where the bird lands.

"Tyde?" he asks.

The Elite on the saddle has a bandage around his arm, and he holds himself stiffly. Beneath his armor, I can see the bulge where I know his chest is also wrapped. He was injured at the battle of Cliffhelm, but he didn't want to be left behind. His power of sight is so helpful that Osrik and the others didn't argue.

Tyde pulls down his face mask and wipes away the frost at his eyes. "I tracked them. There are still a few battalions between here and Breakwater."

An Orean with a copper breastplate steps forward. "Second Kingdom will defeat them. We have another ship landing at Breakwater soon. We will trap them and end them," he declares.

Everyone nods, and Tyde speaks up again. "Commander, I also tracked another group. Stragglers that fled back toward Sixth Kingdom. And there's still the fae who took Highbell."

"Then we take it back," the serpent king declares, his expression firm. "We go to Highbell and then to Seventh Kingdom too. We chase every fae all the way to the edge of the world."

Queen Kaila looks at Manu before stepping forward. "Third will help. Let us rid Orea of the rest of these fae," she says, her voice strong, her braid of black hair still perfectly in place and her silver armor gleaming.

Commander Ryatt exchanges a glance with Osrik, Lu, and Judd, and they seem to communicate silently. "We will track down the stragglers and meet you in Highbell," he says before he looks to Kaila. "Like Her Majesty said, let us rid Orea of them. Once and for all."

Everyone looks around at each other, the weight of this battle, this win, settling in. Orea was victorious. Through luck and strategy and uniting together, we somehow won against a devastating force. But it's not over.

Not yet.

King Thold nods. "For Orea."

Commander Ryatt is the first to repeat it, and then they all do. It falls from my own lips too, just as I hear Osrik rumble it out.

Even if we win, we still lose…but we do it for Orea.

For each other.

"We've won three battles," Lu announces, her dark skin streaked with bright blood. "Now, we have to win the war."

# CHAPTER 46

## COMMANDER RYATT

As soon as we land at Highbell Castle, Lu hops off and rips down her face covering. "Well, I guess the *where the fuck did Slade go* question is partially answered," she says. "He's definitely been here."

"Yeah," I say, still reeling at what we saw from the air. There was a huge patch of snow right outside Highbell City that was decimated with rot. The mountain was much the same, and the scent of death seems thicker in the direction of the castle.

Not looking forward to seeing what's inside.

I leap off the back of Lu's timberwing as the others land in the courtyard with us. When Lu pets her beast, a pang goes through me. Kitt was a good bird. I hate that her corpse was left in the cold to gather frost. She deserved better.

When all this is over, I'm going to build her a proper pyre, along with all our soldiers back at Cliffhelm. Make them a fucking monument for their sacrifice. Ensure I pay proper respects.

Especially for Maston and Finley, because we owe them everything.

I sent word to Isalee and Warken, making sure all of their remaining family members have more gold than they know what to do with so they're taken care of.

Judd dismounts his timberwing too, fingers working to unhook the pannier between his and Osrik's beast. "Did you see that?" he says with an impressed grin. "The whole land was rotted!"

"How could we not fucking see it?" Osrik grumbles before he reaches up and plucks Rissa off the back of his timberwing and sets her on the ground beside him.

"Maybe he's here," Judd says, as Digby unbuckles from Judd's saddle and lands next to him.

The guard starts helping some of the Elites out of the panniers, but I notice he's pale as a sheet. I inwardly curse myself. I didn't even consider what it might be like for him or Rissa to be back here. Especially in these conditions.

Highbell is ruined. The whole city charred, the forest burnt to a crisp. Every inch of it empty and rotted. It must be difficult to see it like this.

The castle doors open, and out walks Manu with a couple Third guards. They reached Highbell before us, while the Wrath and I tracked down some stragglers trying to hide.

They were easy pickings.

"How many fae did you have to deal with?" I ask, though I already know the answer.

"Surprisingly...none," he says, just as Lu comes up to join us. "We spoke to the survivors inside. Apparently, King Ravinger came through and cleared out the city before he and Queen Malina left."

My attention sharpens. "Queen Malina? The two of them went to Seventh together?"

Manu nods. "That's what the people inside said."

"How long ago?"

"I'm not sure how many days exactly."

Lu's gaze flicks to the castle behind him. "How many survivors are here?"

Guilt spreads over his face. "About a hundred."

My guts twist with the implications. Highbell used to be home to hundreds of thousands. Just like Ranhold, the fae have devastated this capital. Wiped out the whole city, taking out entire family lines.

Generations of Oreans, gone.

But we are fighting back. With the battles at Breakwater, Cliffhelm, and Ranhold, Orea has managed to come together and beat them back.

And here in Highbell, where we expected great difficulty in encountering more of their army, where we'd expected a firm fae foothold, we've arrived to see they've already been knocked away by my brother.

There's no time to waste. We have to keep pressing in, keep fighting back. Because against all odds, Orea is actually fucking winning.

The rotten trail of breadcrumbs Slade has left is a balm to my scorching worry. He was here. I don't know what the hell happened, but he was here, so I'm going to pray that he made it across the bridge. That he's found our mother and Auren and he's bringing them both back.

Hope has started to billow.

"Did your sister and Thold decide when we leave for Seventh?" I ask Manu.

"Early tomorrow morning. I'll send someone out to get your timberwings fed and watered in the perch. And despite the lingering stench, the castle has already been cleared and cleaned. There are plenty of rooms for everyone to rest until we leave."

I nod and look back at Lu. "I'm going to go speak with some of the survivors."

I'll feel more reassured once I get confirmation with my own ears that Slade was here. That he did actually head for Seventh. I know he's the most powerful person in Orea, and I've been trying to tell myself that he's fine, but it's a fucking relief to have proof that he's not dead in a snowy ditch somewhere. Something had to have happened for him not to have shown up to Ranhold, but even so, he made sure to help rid us of the threat here.

"I'll meet you all in the dining room at dawn," I tell Lu. "Get some rest."

"You too, Commander," she says, and then I turn and follow Manu into the golden castle.

"Alright, I'll say it," Judd drawls from where he's plopped on a dining room chair with a plateful of food in front of him. His yellow hair is still wet from washing. Everyone, him included, looks so much better now that we've all had a full night of sleep without danger banging down our doors. "Highbell Castle actually looks pretty fucking amazing."

Lu snorts from where she sits next to him, mouth nearly bursting with a huge bite of food.

"Look at it," he goes on, motioning a hand around the room. "It's all so…*gold*."

"What did you think it was gonna look like, asshole?" Osrik says as he keeps piling food onto Rissa's plate. Her blonde brows go higher and higher with every spoonful he shovels on until she elbows him and makes him stop.

Judd looks over at Digby where he sits at the middle of the table. The guard keeps shifting in his chair, like he's uncomfortable to be in the formal dining room. Not that there's much *formal* about it anymore. Chairs are mismatched, flatware missing, curtains ripped off the walls.

It looks like the looters managed to make off with quite the stash.

"Dig, how long did it take Auren to gild this whole place?"

His brown eyes flick around the room, and Rissa watches him, thoughts seeming to churn through her eyes. "A long time, I suspect," he says quietly. "I should have recognized it was her doing it. Midas was always secretive, rooms always closed up when he worked on them."

"The cage was probably a tip-off," Judd replies, gnawing off a hunk of bread.

"It should've been," Digby replies grimly.

"It's disgusting, what he did to her," Rissa says, her mouth pinched. "How she was treated…"

I don't think she's only talking about Midas.

"It's alright. Gildy got the last laugh. Midas is in a nice little golden tomb for all of eternity," Judd says jovially. "I'm going to make it my holiday trip to go see him every year and laugh my ass off." Rissa smirks at his words as he gets up from the table. "Alright, I'm going to go make sure our Elites are ready to go," he says before swiping the goblet in front of Lu and draining it down.

"Hey!" she says.

He gives her a salute. "Too slow, Captain. Which is why I always win."

"You do *not*."

Judd hums. "Say that to the wine barrels. And the fight circle matches. My numbers are far superior."

"You padded those numbers," she argues, getting louder as he heads for the door. "And I'm the one with the longest running barrel time, and you fucking know it!"

His laughter echoes in the room as he walks out.

Lu groans and frowns into her empty cup. "He's going to be insufferable."

"When is he not?" Osrik says with a cocked brow.

Chuckling, I push away my plate of food and then glance around at everyone. "Listen," I say, sobering. "We've had strategy, timing, and fucking luck on our side so far. But we don't know what we're walking into when we get to Seventh."

They chew on my words as much as their food.

"But even though our numbers are down, we're in the best possible position we could be in. We're so fucking close I can taste it. If we can pull this off, then the rest of Orea won't become what Highbell and Ranhold have."

Osrik shrugs. "Then we fucking pull it off."

Everyone nods and I lift my cup in a toast. "We fucking pull it off."

Because if we don't, all of this was for nothing.

When we gather at Highbell's barracks, the yard is already full of growling, antsy timberwings. King Thold is with his Elites, Queen Kaila with hers. The Wrath with ours. A group of Second soldiers decided to stay with us too, with their fleet of beasts.

Everyone is dressed in full armor, save for Manu, who's staying behind here in Highbell with the rest of the survivors.

I've counted heads multiple times. We're nearly a hundred strong, and we're lucky we've managed to scrape together this much after all our combined losses. But a hundred isn't a lot. Unless Slade managed to clear Seventh too, we could be vastly outnumbered. Especially considering we're traveling to the source of the invasion.

I don't know if it'll be enough. But we have to *make it* be enough.

Like Osrik said, we fucking pull it off.

And we do it with what we've got.

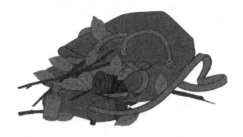

# CHAPTER 47

## EMONIE

A sudden lurch beneath me makes my eyes pop open in alarm, and I become instantly awake. I'm nearly sent sprawling as someone hefts up the back of the prisoner's cart.

I start to roll, but I reach out and grip the metal bars to stop myself before I slam against the other side. I hold on until the cart is dropped back down, and I curse beneath my breath from the jolt.

I've been in here for a couple days now, and my body is sore all over. I look over at the fae who knocked me around so unceremoniously and realize he's hitched the cart to a pair of harnessed horses.

Things stalled after the veined fae died, so everything was at a bit of a standstill. The king has probably been figuring out how to deal with Lydia and Orea at the same time. But maybe this means the contingent is finally going to be heading back toward the capital like he wanted.

I eye the fae as he checks the horse's harnesses, and when he starts to leave, I call out to him. "Hey, I'm hungry, and I need some water."

At least they let me out to relieve myself a couple times, but that's been the entirety of their hospitality.

The soldier turns to look at me and then comes over. "Yeah?" He stops in front of me, leering at me in my revealing dress. Then he spits in my face, almost right into my mouth.

Lovely.

"There," he says as I flinch in disgust. "Enjoy." He turns and walks away with a laugh.

"What a complete bastard," I grumble as I wipe his spit away.

I hear noises ahead, and sure enough, it looks like I'm at the very back of the gathered Stone Swords who are starting to march toward Lydia.

They're taking me with them, and that part is quite convenient, since it means I'll be back in the city with the Vulmin. But they're taking me to be *burned alive*, and that part is not so convenient.

But it's just an obstacle I have to figure out how to get around. Simple. Easy.

I can handle this.

Chewing on my lip, I look around, watching the camp, trying to come up with a plan. After a few more minutes, a burst of voices draws my attention toward the buildings, and King Carrick comes striding out. Unfortunately, all my finger crossing was for nothing except a cramp in my hand. The goddesses have not, in fact, blessed us with his demise.

Shame.

However, Carrick is yelling and he does *not* look pleased.

Which pleases me.

"You're telling me that one single Orean managed to wipe out every one of our soldiers at the bridge?" he shouts,

434

rounding on the twins who are following behind him like chicks to a mother hen.

One of the twins replies, but it's much quieter. He looks like he's trying desperately to placate the furious king, though he really seems to be doing a terrible job at it.

"What do you mean there's now a barrier? What kind of barrier?"

I'm not certain, but I think the twins say something about ice.

"Orea is pathetic. We should have crushed them all by now! And you should have been checking in on the bridge!"

This time, I hear the reply. "Sire, we have made great strides."

"And yet, you two have also just informed me that you have not received word from our soldiers at the gilded castle nor an update on the next frozen kingdom," the king seethes. "Your *strides* are failing, and that is unacceptable!"

A soldier steps forward, one of the higher ranking Badges. "Our contingent to Lydia is on the move," he informs the king. "But I can immediately gather another battalion and go to the bridge. I can get you a full report—"

Carrick interrupts him with a furious look. "No. It is obvious that the incompetence in Orea needs to be remedied. I will go to the bridge and handle it myself since everyone else seems to be inept." Carrick glares at him before moving to the twins, his face hardened and terrifying. "You two will bring me back at once. I'll take care of this *barrier*." Then his head snaps to the army camp. "I want every other soldier not leaving for Lydia readied immediately. We leave for Orea *now*. The full second wave!"

He turns and strides away, while the rest of them exchange looks and start to scramble. The camp was busy before, but now it becomes downright hectic.

Everyone hurries around, readying to leave. The Badges

shout orders left and right to the Stone Swords, every single soldier armoring up and getting outfitted with their weapons.

Longingly, I watch some of them gnaw on food and chug down water. My mouth aches with thirst and my stomach growls. I blame both the Stone Swords for not giving me any provisions and this cursed deadlands. It feels like it's sucking me dry.

Oh well. I'll have to do this without sustenance too. I can handle this. I'm a Vulmi, for goddesses' sake.

A couple minutes pass and then I see my jailer come hurrying over. I perk up, a plan forming in my mind.

I scoot forward, knees tucked beneath me, and I sit up straight. Shove my breasts up a bit. "Oh, thank goodness," I exclaim, breathing out a sigh of relief. I start hiking the gold dress up my thighs too, and his eyes widen when I go higher *and higher*... "I really need your help," I tell him in my sultriest voice—and I'm quite good at the sultry voice. Years of practice.

When he's just a step away, I let my magic pour over me. Bones shift, cheeks spread, lips thin out, scalp tingles, and my eyes water. Within a blink, my glamour magic has changed me into him.

He really should've been careful when shoving me into this cart.

I clear my throat just as he stops in front of the door, and he glances up from my exposed legs to my face—well, *his* face.

His eyes go wide. "What—"

I strike before he can finish his sentence.

My hands lash out and I grab him by his neck and yank him forward, smashing his skull into the bars as hard as I can. He makes a noise like a carpet being rolled up, a stuffed breath escaping his tight throat. Then the jailer crumples, but I shove my hands beneath his arms to keep him up.

"Goddess, you're a heavy asshole," I say between my

teeth as I shift him so I can hold him up with one arm. With my other hand, I fish at his buckle where the keyring is.

My fingers bungle around for a moment, my back and arm straining to keep him up. I give a quick look around, but the camp is so hectic with everyone rushing around that no one is noticing what's happening.

As soon as I have hold of the keyring, the jailer nearly slips out of my hold. I manage to catch him, while struggling to curl my hand back toward the lock. Since I'm doing it one-handed, I fumble several times. Sweat gathers at my neck, my whole body going hot with nerves.

"Come on…" I curse the lock and my blundering fingers, casting another nervous glance around. I've gotten lucky so far, but none of it matters if I don't get this damn key—

In.

I turn the key, making the bolt jump open and fall to the ground. As soon as it does, I let the jailer's body drop too. I shove open the door and leap to the ground a second later. My heart pounds in my chest, adrenaline rushing over me like a downpour.

I climb under the cart and pull the jailer with me, which takes every lick of my strength. Dragging a deadweight body while crouched under something is way more difficult than I thought.

Using my feet braced on the ground in my crouched position, I heave him under until his feet no longer poke out. We're not totally hidden, but the two wheels are large enough that we're somewhat concealed on both sides. I dart a glance around again before I get to work.

"Sorry about this," I tell the unconscious male. "I won't look."

I waste no time since I have none to spare. I start stripping him, but this part goes quite quickly. "I wish I could say you're the first fae I've had to knock out and strip, but alas, you're not," I mutter.

As I work, I also use my magic to glamour more of my body too. Just enough to make me fill out more so I look less like a slim female and more like a bulky male. I can't take on his entire body—not that I'd want to, but definitely not with the stone around my ribs. The best I can do is fill out a bit more so his clothes won't hang off me.

After I free him of his clothing, I yank on the pants and then take off my dress before pulling on his shirt and armor. It's a tight fit because of this awful stone band around me, but the long sleeves and trousers hide my stone cuffs very nicely.

Then I lay my gold dress over his groin so that he's not so exposed. It's the least I can do, really.

Though, to be honest, there isn't much to cover up.

I'm out of breath by the time I crawl down to his feet and yank off his boots. I immediately get hit in the face with his stench. "Oh, great purple skies, your feet are disgusting!" I hiss at him.

This smell can't be normal. Surely, he has something growing there. I hesitate, wondering if I could forgo his shoes and try to filch someone else's, but I know I can't risk it. Cursing him under my breath the whole time, I pull on his boots and lace them up. "If I get a foot rash after this, I am going to be very annoyed," I tell him.

Finished, I crawl up to the wheel and peer between the spokes, making sure no one is looking this way. Then I slip out from beneath it and straighten up. My pants and boots are covered in gray dust from the ground, but there's nothing I can do about that.

Trying to act natural, I walk up to the hitch, eyeing the horses. The last thing I want is for them to take off and expose my unconscious friend. I can't lift him into the cart, and I don't want to waste my power having to glamour him either. So he's staying right there, for as long as he naps.

GOLDFINCH

At least I'm letting his feet air out. Honestly, he should be thanking me.

The camp is nothing but noise and rush. Dust kicks up into the air as the soldiers behind me get ready to go to the bridge, while the convoy ahead is on the move for Lydia.

I'm *really* lucky that the prison cart goes last. Or in this case, doesn't go at all.

My pulse is racing, but I force myself to act calm. I work my way up to the moss green horse, smoothing my hand over his flank. "Easy, pony," I murmur when he twitches. "Me and you are going to go for a little ride, okay?"

His green eye rolls toward me as I come up to his neck. "No more pulling prison carts for you. You're better than that."

He chuffs.

"Good pony," I say as I move to his side harness. I need to detach it from his saddle so it's not totally obvious that he was supposed to be hitched to something. "There we go…"

"Soldier!"

I startle so badly I nearly take out my eye on the buckle when I flinch forward. Spinning around, I face the male striding over to me. "What are you doing?" he demands.

"Just securing the saddles, sir," I lie, dropping my voice as low as I can. It would be nice if I'd had time to come up with something better than that, but I'm working on my toes here. In a pair of very smelly boots.

At least I manage to say it with complete confidence, because usually, that's all you need to convince someone. I'm also very good at sounding like a male. Years of practice with that too.

But the soldier's eyes move from me, over to the cart, and I start sweating. Profusely.

*Don't look down. Please don't look down. There's definitely not a naked body behind the wheel.*

"Where's the prisoner?"

My heart just might fall right out of my chest.

"Uh—Had to move her to the other cart, sir," I say, jutting my thumb toward the marching convoy. "They didn't tell me why."

It's an army, someone higher up is always telling other people what to do, right? Right. I just *really* hope there is another cart, or I'm dead.

The soldier grits his teeth, glancing over. "Fucking Revi, always pulling this shit."

I try not to collapse in a fit of relief.

Instead, I scoff in agreement. "Yeah, it's always fucking Revi."

Poor Revi.

"Fine," he says. "Since you're not needed in Lydia, you come with us."

My mouth pops open in surprise, eyes widening before I can catch myself. "But…uh, sir…"

"Get a helmet and sword," he orders. "And get that horse up to the king immediately. He doesn't like the ones we already brought him."

*Shit on a saddle.*

Near the king is the *last* place I want to be.

But I don't dare push my luck. The goddess of favor and filch has already blessed me with my pilfered body and the fact that I got out of that cart in the first place.

So I say, "Of course, sir," and then I quickly turn around and continue unhitching the horse.

I'm hoping the soldier will walk off and leave me to my escape plans, but instead, he hollers at another soldier, and the two of them start talking right beside me, making it so I can't sneak away.

I really hate this male. Why is it always the aggravating ones that stick around?

Chewing on a silent curse, I take the horse and start leading it through the barracks, stealing a few looks back as I go. I'm sweating buckets now. All it's going to take is one soldier to look under the cart or move it.

I need to put distance between us.

I eye the camp, and I manage to swipe a helmet from the ground and shove it over my head. I don't see any spare swords lying around, but I do manage to grab someone's waterskin and then steal a piece of meat off the skewer that was left by the fire.

I bite into it as we walk, barely chewing as I swallow the fatty pieces down. Delicious. Then I drain my entire waterskin before tossing it aside. When I wipe my mouth, I try to figure out what to do next.

I need to get rid of this horse.

Just as soon as I have that thought, I start looking around for a soldier I can try and catch unaware so I can pass the horse off to them instead. Then I can run into someone, steal another face, and try to catch up with the Lydia-bound soldiers. Then I can warn the Vulmin.

I can still pull this off, I just need—

"What took you so long?" a soldier barks as he comes up to me. He yanks on the horse's rein, signaling me to move faster. "Go!"

I get swept into a press of bodies as soldiers line up in formation. My eyes shoot ahead, and there's the king, dressed in his own stone armor, looking formidable as he stands with the twins.

I want to run in the other direction as fast as I can. My adrenaline wants me to do that too, but I can't.

So I force myself forward until I'm behind King Carrick, and then I hold out the reins as I bend at the waist. "Sire, your horse."

Even though I'm in complete glamour, my nervousness

spikes, and the stone bands around my body practically burn through my clothes.

*Can he sense stone? Will he know it's me?*

A wordless prayer to the goddesses blares in my head.

The king doesn't even spare me a glance. He snatches the reins from my hands and eyes the horse before mounting himself onto the saddle.

Behind him—behind *us*—the army is forming more and more perfect rows of soldiers. And I'm right here, at the front. With the Stone King.

Not good.

As soon as he's on the horse, he turns to one of the Badges. Beside him, the twins sit on their own horses, waiting.

"Fassa and Friano will take me through. Lead the army to the bridge," Carrick commands. Then he pauses. "The faction is waiting?"

I see the Badge give a tight nod. "Yes, Your Majesty. We confirmed that they just arrived."

"Good. Meet up with them and ensure they fall in line. I want them bringing up the rear. They can enter Orea after we've cleared the bridge."

"Of course, my king."

I watch Carrick and the twins take off on their horses, steering deeper into the deadlands. I frown, wondering where they're going.

The Badge turns to the soldiers lining up, which unfortunately, includes me.

"Forward march!" he shouts, voice rattling through my brittle nerves and making them snap.

Everyone starts to move in their neat rows, while I'm stuck in the front lines. As a Stone Sword soldier. Marching toward the bridge of Lemuria.

Unless I can get away, I'm going to *Orea*.

I'm quite certain it's the pounding panic that's messing

up my thoughts, but all I can think about is how badly my feet are going to smell once I get there.

Badly.

Very, very badly.

# CHAPTER 48

## QUEEN MALINA

I'm jolted awake by a deafening crash.

I tear my eyes open in a panic, and Dommik jerks upright beside me. My heart slams inside my chest, and we take one look at each other and start yanking on our clothes as fast as we can.

Fear grips me around the throat, crushing it under its merciless hold.

The ice walls of the house have frosted over, making everything opaque. It's stopped snowing, but the morning air is chilled and stark, which for some reason, seems to make the noises in the air extra sharp. As soon as we're clothed, Dommik grips my hand and we slip out of the open doorway and around the stone part of the wall.

"It's the bridge," I say, shaking my head with utter dread. "We need to get back now! We never should have left."

I can tell by Dommik's darkening expression that he

doesn't like to hear me say that, but it's true, and we both know it.

That cracking noise is unmistakable. The fae are breaking through my barriers, and I'm not there, because I selfishly took the opportunity to come out here with Dommik last night. I should have stayed closer to the bridge. Monitoring it and making sure I was ready. Instead, we've been caught unawares.

I'm so angry at myself I could scream.

"Hurry, take me there. I might be able to defend the barriers before they break through them all!"

He pulls his shadows in and then begins to leap us in that direction. We stop just outside the castle walls, standing in view of the bridge.

The bridge that's full of fae soldiers.

Fear and anger burst through me, and ice crystals stab up through my palms.

I follow their trail on the bridge to the mouth where my barriers begin, and my stomach drops like a brick in a bucket. In front of it, not behind it, stands the Stone King, his formidable form unmistakable.

My body impulsively tightens with muscle memory, as if reliving the way he pinned me beneath the weight of the stone table and threatened to squish me like a bug.

I have a feeling he's come back to finish what he started. Not just crushing me, but all of Orea.

There's another resounding crack, and the third layer of my barrier crumbles. The king is here, on Orea's side, using his magic to rip through my barriers with boulders.

"Take me there now!" I say frantically to Dommik.

When he doesn't, I start running, but after only a few strides, Dommik snatches me up from behind. "No!" he growls in my ear as I flail. "It's too late!"

He's right. I watch as the fae king's magic starts smashing

through every layer of my defense. Through every layer of my hope.

I'm not good enough. Everything I've tried to do has fallen short. I'm not as powerful as them. Not as skilled or knowledgeable in magic. These fae make it seem like everything I attempt is child's play.

Tears fill my eyes, but Dommik suddenly jerks behind me, his arms going lax. We both fall, pitching to the ground. The breath gets knocked from my ribs as he lands heavily on top of me, but I manage to roll out from under him. When I push myself up, I see he's face down in the snow, unmoving.

Alarm clangs against my chest, and I shove him on his side. "Dommik!"

But then I freeze when I see two familiar fae standing over me.

The twins, Fassa and Friano. Thick black hair past their shoulders, brown eyes and smooth faces—faces that used to look at me with charming attention but now stare down at me with disgust.

"Queen Malina," Fassa says, the mole on his right cheek indenting in with his sneer. "We thought we might see you again. We were sure to be ready, in case you returned."

I hold up my palms to attack, slices of ice springing up, yet he grips my wrist and clamps something over it. My arm drops with the abrupt weight, and the magic that was collecting in my hand shatters away.

There's a sensation of a heaviness pressing over me. As if something beneath my skin is damming up the access to my magic. The suppression radiates from this smooth gray cuff he's placed on me.

Desperately, I try to pull it off, but I can't slip it past my hand.

"Who's this one?" Fassa says as he kicks at Dommik's unconscious body.

"Don't touch him," I hiss, but when I try to lurch forward, Friano stops me, gripping the back of my neck like a collared dog.

"You're the reason for this little frozen blockade?" Friano tsks, while the sound of cracking and crashing continues behind us. "You are a nuisance. The king isn't pleased."

My eyes narrow. "How are you on this side of the bridge?" I demand, glancing back toward it. The Stone King is making quick work of the layers, but that doesn't explain how they're already on Orea's side.

He ignores my question and, instead, pulls me upright. "Let's tie them up," Friano says to his brother. "Then we'll find out what the king wants to do with them."

I try to wrench away, but he's so much stronger than me.

To my utter disappointment, Fassa snaps another one of those shackles around Dommik's wrist too and then bends down to haul him up and over his shoulder. With Friano's grip on my arm, we are dragged into Cauval's ruins and bound to a cracked and fallen pillar.

The stone digs into my back as Dommik gets tied on the other side. I can only see him if I strain to look over my shoulder. The twins search Dommik's lax body, yanking out his weapons one after the other, while they ignore my attempt at getting myself free.

They've bound me with thick leather straps that look like horse's reins. I struggle to get out, but the reins bite into my skin. No matter how hard I try, I can't call up my magic either.

When they're finished, they walk out, just as another crack crashes through the air outside. Deep in my bones, I know that sound marks the final barrier breaking.

Orea is wide open.

If I'd been here right at the beginning, if I'd had time to see them coming, Dommik and I could have attacked. I could have been ready to fortify, to throw ice magic at them from this side.

Instead, I was tucked in Dommik's arms, sleeping with a peace I did not deserve.

*When will I stop failing Orea?*

I glance over my shoulder and call Dommik's name, but he doesn't stir. Worry mangles my insides. What if they hit him too hard and he doesn't wake again? What if they struck him so hard they killed him?

My worry turns into panic. "Dommik!"

He stays slumped, his hood thrown back, but then I see his shoulders lift slightly with a breath, and I exhale in relief.

I try to get myself free from the bindings again, but the straps are looped tightly around me with barely any give. Instead, I focus on the strange cuff around my wrist that seems to be affecting my magic.

Both my arms are pressed against my sides, so it takes some maneuvering before I'm able to wrench my hands together in front of me. As soon as I do, I start tugging at the cuff as hard as I can, spinning it, trying to squeeze it over the bones in my hand. I even pick up some of the snow beneath me and shove it under the cuff, hoping it will help, but it doesn't.

It won't come off.

When the fae king comes striding in, I nearly jump right out of my skin.

Dressed in stone-plated armor and a marbled crown, his granite eyes land on me as he comes to a stop. I can't move. I'm stuck in place, fear freezing me.

"The *Cold Queen*. You thought you could keep us out with a few shards of ice?" he asks, and while his words are mocking, his tone is hardened.

Anxiety stomps down my nerves as he regards me, and though no stone presses down on me, my breath feels tight. Suffocated.

"Are you responsible for the death of my soldiers?" he asks.

My heart beats wildly, but I don't reply.

The king takes another step so he's looming over me, watching me like one might study an insect that lost its leg. Deciding if he should step on me now or leave me to struggle.

I lift my chin, looking back at him without falter. I have learned to look men like him in the eye when they wished me to drop my gaze and bend my neck in submission.

My gaze tells him the same thing as my silent mouth: I won't submit to him.

I am a queen, and cold does not cower.

The two of us stare at each other, while the twins stand several paces behind him. Outside, I can hear the wind shuffling, can hear soldiers shouting as his army breaches Orea.

Again.

Still, we watch each other.

Within this overbearing glare between enemies, there is a push of wills. A push of *worlds*.

He is so very fae, and I am so very Orean, and though I am not yet forty years, I can feel centuries' worth of hostility emanating from us both. As if I hold the blood of every Orean who has ever been betrayed by a fae, and he holds that of every fae who has hated an Orean.

He wants to crush us, I want to be rid of them, and it's obvious that a broken bridge and even a barricaded one was only a temporary respite. So long as our realms are tethered, death and threat will always have a way to return.

Perhaps Dommik was right. Perhaps the bridge to nowhere was a lie and that track of land *did* lead somewhere else. Somewhere far from the fae, so that the Oreans who crossed it went somewhere new, somewhere better.

The bridge was never supposed to connect us. I see that as clearly as I see the grooves of granite in the fae king's eyes and the chiseled lines of his jaw.

The girl who crossed into Annwyn, who married a fae and bound our worlds together, perhaps she was the true villain in all of this. For all that's happened since then is betrayal and war and, now, annihilation.

Our worlds were never meant to tether.

So the fae king can look at me with hate, and I can look at him right back, because none of this should have ever happened.

King Carrick tilts his head, as if it's tipping with the thoughts weighing down his mind, and I wonder if perhaps he was thinking similar things to what I was.

"No," he finally says, answering some unspoken question. "You're far too weak to have killed my soldiers. You weren't even able to successfully block the bridge."

Humiliation and anger scrape against my insides, rubbing my shortcomings raw.

Satisfaction pulls at his face and he leans closer to me. "This is why you're losing your world, Orean queen. Because you are not strong enough to keep it."

He starts looking around the ruins, critical gaze taking in the disintegrating structure. "This is your great history of Orea?" he asks with a disparaging tone. "This is *nothing*. So insignificant that it wasn't even worth my time when I first arrived."

Then he lifts his hands, and the entire structure begins to shake and shift, the very ground trembling. My heart pounds past my ribs as the walls start cracking. Then they start shifting and smoothing, stretching and realigning.

He smiles cruelly. "Let me show you how quickly your Orea will be forgotten."

I watch in stunned silence as he uses his magic to transform the ruins into a sturdy, solid castle. Using immense power as if it's *nothing*.

For centuries, Cauval has laid here in frozen waste, and within seconds, a single fae transforms it. *Erases* it.

451

There's so much power in the air I can taste its dust, as if it's signifying the ashes of Orea itself blowing away.

No longer are the walls reaching for an open sky. They stretch and close, the stones groaning and grinding as they move. The stone melds into an arched ceiling upon solid brick walls. Beneath me, the floor rolls with stonework that flows over the snow like roughened ripples.

Then the pillar we're tied to moves too, tearing a frightened screech from my throat as Dommik and I are lifted with it. The pillar stands upright, making our bindings slip down until we crash upon the floor.

I jerk my body up, trying to fix the bindings that hold me sideways, adjusting until I can sit upright. On the other side of the pillar, I can see Dommik's legs sprawled out, head lolling upon his chest.

The noises stop as every crack and crevice is filled in and smoothed, and then the stone becomes inanimate once more.

The king looks at me with triumph.

"See how quickly Orean history is replaced?" he says, hands dropping down to his sides. "See how easy it is for fae to lay claim? The stronger, better species will always win."

He walks over to where I now sit, and the cavernous hall echoes the sounds of his footsteps bouncing against the solid gray walls. "You see now, don't you, Cold Queen? Fae are superior. You've always known that. It's why you wanted our magic in your veins."

I swallow hard as I look up at him, seething and shaking all at once.

"Oreans can never win against the might of the fae."

After he makes sure his words have sunken in, he turns, and the stone doors he's created scrape open.

It feels as if something inside of me has been scraped open too.

"Leave them," the fae king says to the twins. "Make sure

she can hear every soldier that marches through. Let her lay witness to our victory until she is nothing but bones and frost. Let this be her living tomb, where she's left to die while fae thrive." Then he strides out of the building, leaving my teeth to chatter in his wake.

Outside, I can hear the army march in, just like he wanted me to.

I glance around, but the inside of this new castle he's built is nothing like what Cauval used to look like. Anger stabs like chips of ice behind my eyes as I stare at the twins.

Pruinn is dead at Ravinger's hand, but I wish he'd been able to kill these two off as well. I wish more than anything that he was still here. Stone wouldn't win against rot. I'd take great pleasure in seeing Ravinger decay the fae king's flesh from his bones.

But he's not here, and the twins stand over me with a condescending curiosity that enrages me. If only these two had been a part of the casualties Dommik burned. If only he'd killed them before I'd been such a fool and willingly let them slice open my hands and let my blood drip.

I've had so many failures.

"How did you get here?" I ask, my voice hoarse. "You and Pruinn. You three were in Orea when he lured me here. How? The bridge was still broken."

They shake their heads in unison.

"How were you and the king here right now?" I go on. "How was he on this side to break down my barriers?"

Still, they stay silent, their identical expressions filling me with an outburst of anger. "I'm here to die," I spit. "What does it matter anymore?"

"All of it matters," they say together.

I strain against the bindings that pinch into my arms, the unrelenting pillar at my back a reminder of just how stuck I am. "Or perhaps none of it does," I argue coldly.

None of what I've tried to do has mattered at all.

They walk closer, their steps sounding hollow through the empty building.

"Did you know why Pruinn chose you?" Fassa asks, cocking his head as he studies me.

"Because I'm an Orean royal."

"You're *the* Orean royal," he corrects, making me pause. "The Colier bloodline consists of the longest-ruling monarchs in all of Orea."

"I know that," I snap. "You think I don't know my own family history?"

The twins walk around the newly constructed castle, their long black hair giving off an ethereal shine. "What we think is that you were a fool, Cold Queen. Easily tricked with illusion and compliments," Friano tells me.

A hammer of guilt slams into me, because he's absolutely correct.

"Are you going to trick me again now?" I challenge, my tone full of sharpened ends. "Use your magic to make it seem like this place is something other than what it really is?"

"You would only see through illusion now. Your eyes are open."

A part of me wishes they weren't. Wishes I could still scent the drugging blossoms and hear lilting music and let the lies lull me into a false sense of peace. Anything but this crushing, fatalistic failure.

"Blood matters when it comes to magic, Queen Malina. Just as sacrifice has always been the price for our own tandem power, willingness has always been the price for the bridge." Friano smirks at me as he eyes my restraints. "You aren't willing right now, are you?"

The two of them laugh together as they walk out, leaving Dommik and me behind. Leaving us caught.

With Dommik still unconscious, I have nothing but the sounds of the army to accompany me.

Only that, and the twins' lingering words.

For long minutes, they repeat in my head. Over and over again. Like a defeatist mantra left to stifle me.

Except...as I go over what they said, a dawning realization starts to rise within me. All because of one single word.

*Willingness.*

Like a bucket of water poured over my head, the truth is there, soaking right into my skin. I stare, though I'm not seeing. Breathe, though not feeling the air.

*You're* the *Orean royal.*

*Blood matters when it comes to magic.*

*Willingness has always been the price for the bridge.*

I cannot say I've ever felt what I feel now. I never knew I *could* feel such opposite emotions at once. Such heights of empowering certainty that have risen inside of me... With such depths of devastating understanding.

"Malina?"

My head jerks to the right as Dommik wakes, already trying to strain forward.

"I'm here," I reassure him. "We're alone."

His head moves, gaze probably roving over the building so he can gain a sense of his surroundings before he looks over his shoulder to me. "Are you alright?"

I swallow the lump in my throat. Swallow the truth.

"Yes. I'm alright."

He tries to use his magic, cursing when he realizes he can't. He starts tugging at the gray cuff at his wrist. "What the fuck is this?" he hisses, his hand losing blood flow as he strains to shove it down his hand.

"You're going to hurt yourself," I say in light reprimand.

He growls. "Can you use your magic at all?"

"No," I say, trying to lift my wrist. "It's these gray cuffs. I don't know how, but they're blocking our magic."

Dommik lets out another curse as he looks around the new castle that the king erected. It's a slap in the face, to have taken ancient Orean stone and made it into such a perverse show of fae power.

"The king made it," I say numbly. "To prove how easily fae can erase Oreans."

Silence stretches between us. I wince at the sound of the soldiers outside.

"Tell me what's wrong."

Pulling my gaze away from the ceiling, I blink at Dommik's question. "Aside from the obvious?"

"Yes, aside from that."

I stare straight ahead. "Well, I was foolish at the bridge, an army is marching, the fae king made threats, I'm captured in Seventh Kingdom, and I'm trapped here with a shadow assassin. My history is repeating itself." I laugh bleakly. "Although, that last one isn't quite so bad this time around."

He doesn't join in with my attempt at dry humor. Instead, I feel him straining to look over at me, his silence filling the already quiet castle. He's deciphering me the same way he always has—as if he's delving down past my top layer to root around in the parts I've buried.

My eyes drop to my hands, and I drag my finger over the slice down my left palm. No shards of ice are gathered there now, just the faintest blue stains down the unsealed gash.

"There's something else," Dommik says quietly. "Tell me."

I go still for a moment.

The intensity of his tone tells me he's not going to drop this. So I swallow, placing my shaky hands back to my lap. "It was only something those fae twins said."

"What did they say?"

A torn-away sigh escapes me, the end jagged, the taste bitter.

"They pointed out the Coliers are the longest-ruling monarchs in Orea's history."

Dommik waits for me to keep going.

"The longest-ruling. An ancient royal bloodline flowing right here in my veins," I say, jerking my hand up to view the blue lines that run beneath my pale skin. "And I've ruined it. I've failed."

Tears spring to my eyes as my throat tightens. "Willingness," I murmur. "That's what they said. The bridge has always been about willingness."

Looking around the pillar, I focus on his intent face. "It wouldn't have worked," I say quietly. "My blood. Not if I hadn't been willing. That was the key, Dommik. That was what damned us all. How willing I was."

A tear drips over my cheek, and a shiver runs along my spine. I glance down where my sleeves have rolled up, at where goose bumps litter my arms.

"You feel cold?" he asks, his tone tinged in shock. "You *never* feel cold."

The Cold Queen who never felt coldness, yet now, I'm chilled through.

All because of that one single word.

*Willingness*.

# CHAPTER 49

## SLADE

M ore Vulmin arrive in Lydia ahead of Wick's estimation. A collection of fae who have traveled from all over Annwyn. And each one of them bears the mark of their cause: a broken-winged bird sigil worn boldly on their bodies.

This influx has made more citizens of Lydia brave the streets, curiosity and a demand to know what's happening to their city overcoming their fear of the rumored dragon running rampant.

Everyone has gathered outside our building, demanding answers.

"This seems tentative," Auren murmurs beside me as we look down from the balcony to the street below. "They could turn on each other."

"They could," I agree as I watch Wick.

The minute we were informed of a crowd gathering outside, the Vulmin leader went out to the street to meet everyone. He's on the ground with them, standing on the stoop. More fae have gathered upon the rooftops and the branched walkways of the twisting trees, and every building within sight is also filled to the brim with fae watching and listening out of open windows. I even notice Hare and Fang down there in the throng.

"The anti-Turley and Vulmin propaganda has instilled some deep-seated mistrust. I'm surprised the Lydians are even standing here listening to him. What if someone attacks?"

My lips twitch. "They won't."

"How do you know?"

I look at her pointedly.

"Oh, right. No one would *dare* attack with you standing here since they're worried you'll manifest a dragon," she says with a smirk.

But I shake my head. "I wasn't talking about me."

"*Me*?" she says in surprise.

"Yes, you. Look at them," I say, stepping behind her slightly. "See how the Vulmin keep stealing looks your way? They fucking worship you. None of them would stand for you to be hurt. Every Vulmin guard down there is watching the crowd with a very keen eye, and every new Vulmin that's arrived can't stop staring. And Goldfinch, they heard what you did. You chased away the *king*. They know how powerful you are. They wouldn't dare attack."

The most endearing flush darkens her cheeks while Wick's voice drags on in the background as he answers question after question from people in the crowd.

"Oh," she says, turning back around.

I reach down to squeeze her hand. "Yes. *Oh*."

"The most important thing is that Lydia is safe!" Wick calls out. "The Vulmin aren't enemies to Annwyn. We aren't *your* enemies. We are against the very violence that the crown has been doling out."

"The king said you're all traitors!" an older fae male shouts from an open window across the street, his face wrung out with wrinkles.

Wick shakes his head. "The Carricks are the ones who betrayed our world. Since wearing the crown, they have done nothing but reach for more power, more control. They have raised our taxes, taken our homes, demanded our fealty, spread hate toward our fellow fae and Oreans who have done nothing but exist. And the Stone King has drafted every available fae for a war to invade, without even telling his own people that's what he was doing!"

The Lydians glance around with frowns and confusion that Wick latches onto.

"Yes. The Stone King has drafted our people into an invasion of *Orea*."

Voices blot out the silence in patches strewn around the street. People denying his words, arguing, asking questions, reacting with anger or shock or challenge.

"It's true!" Wick declares. "Carrick is more than willing to sacrifice our lives for his greed for more power, with a war we did not agree to. He has to be stopped!"

"Lyäri!" one of the Vulmin suddenly yells. "I want to hear from the Lyäri Ulvêre!"

The crowd goes quiet, every eye swinging up to her, and Auren stiffens beside me. Though they can't see it, I watch the way her aura flits about anxiously, the golden light and thin tendrils of black darting around her with the flare of her quickened pulse.

"You can do this," I murmur at her side.

Behind the railing, her ribbons twist along the floor of the balcony, but the people don't see that or hear the way she takes a steadying breath. She keeps her expression perfectly calm, and pride fills me as I watch her step forward with her head held high.

"Lyäri Ulvêre," she repeats, eyes casting over the crowd. "Golden one gone, you called me. But I think you can see that I'm not gone anymore," she says with a warm smile. "And while I haven't been back for very long, during my time here, I've been hunted, hated, threatened, attacked, imprisoned, and impersonated. I have done *nothing* wrong. King Carrick had my parents killed. Wanted *me* killed, even when I was only a girl, which is how I ended up in Orea for most of my life."

Whispers scatter like rolled dice.

Auren's voice grows stronger. Her demeanor more sure and confident. My pride swells at watching her.

"Oreans are not our enemy, and we aren't enemies to each other either," she tells the crowd. "Those are just lies that have been crafted carefully for centuries so that the crown could justify cruelty toward Oreans and, eventually, invade their world. The fighting and hate is needless, and it has to stop before more people are killed."

Nerves no longer twist through her ribbons or make her aura flicker as she speaks. Everyone watches her with rapt attention, and she seems to gleam in the sunlight.

"I stand before you not just as a Turley, but as a fae *and* an Orean," she says, and I swear everyone on the street looks at her blunt Turley ears. "Wick was right. We can do better. *Annwyn can be better*. But we have to unite, to come together as people, and it has to start right here and now," she announces. "A new dawn must rise."

The Vulmin below grip their pins or buttons or stitchings with their sigil and hold them up. "Dawn's bird!" they chant. More voices join in, repeating the meaning for their symbol— that even a broken-winged bird will rise like the sun.

The truth of that shines out as Auren stands here.

Even if my father had never taught me a single thing about the Turleys, had wiped them away from importance like so many other Carrick followers, I wish I would have known enough to put two and two together. Wish I would have known the significance of her golden skin. Because the first time I saw her, I knew she was extraordinary. And seeing her here and now, it's so obvious what she is.

A queen. Gold-touched and blood-blessed. And for some reason, paired with me.

She steps back and takes my hand again, her fingers immediately twisting through mine and holding us together. She looks over at me as the people chant and clap and cheer.

"You are magnificent," I tell her.

Her pulse quickens. "I'm just me."

I nod. "Yes."

Exactly.

Her eyes soften, fingers squeezing again, and all I want to do is pull her in close and have her to myself, but that's not how it is anymore, is it? Auren isn't just mine. She's found a place with all of these fae. They look up to her. Stand in awe of her. She means something to everyone on this street. Her very presence impacting them.

I'm so fucking proud of her.

Things start to die down, the coldness between Lydians and Vulmin seeming to warm up purely by Auren's glowing presence until things seem not quite so tentative anymore.

I relax a bit, but only for a split second. Because my mind drifts to my mother. It's a constant worry that gnaws on my gut. I feel my expression pinch, and Auren notices instantly.

"Are you okay?" she asks quietly, but then she seems to read the answer in my eyes, and her own expression turns determined.

"Let's go," she says. "We should be able to get through the crowd now. We'll have Wick show us where the Oreans are. We'll go talk to them and see if they have any information about Elore."

I nod and take in a tight breath. Just the thought of my mother being in my father's clutches makes a cold sweat break out over my skin. I need to find her and get her safe. I can't stand to think about what she might be enduring.

"My father is a fucking snake," I say as we both turn to go inside. "He'll be keeping her close."

"We'll find her," she promises, her voice steely.

I nod and press a kiss to the top of her head. "We will."

And this time, I won't have to rip into the world *or* rip myself. My father will be the one ripped apart.

"His eye," she begins. "I meant to tell you—I think you rotted it."

I pause, looking over at her. "His eye?"

She nods, a wicked smirk curling her lips. "Yep. He wears a patch over it, but I think you must've rotted it partially all those years ago when you fought. I could see the veins."

"Good," I growl, feeling a hint of satisfaction. He probably hated that I was able to do that to him. That it destroyed part of his face. "The next time I see him, I won't just rot one of his eyes. I'll crush his fucking skull."

Her ribbon grazes over my arm in comfort as we head for the staircase. The Vulmin inside stop and tip their heads as we pass, and Auren offers them a smile.

When we get to the stairs, she glances over at me. "Do you think everyone was able to stop the fae army at Ranhold?"

"I don't know for certain," I answer honestly. "But I stopped a lot of them, and King Thold's magic is impressive. He's formidable, so King Fulke wouldn't dare deny him. Fifth has a good-sized army too. With Lu, Judd, and Digby there, I'm sure they were able to prepare Fifth and stop the fae in their tracks."

Her head whips over. "*Digby* went with them? To Ranhold?"

I pause. "Did I forget to mention that?"

"Yes. You did," she says, voice taking on a nervous edge. "But it's dangerous. And he was badly hurt…"

"He's healed, and it was important to him. When he heard what the army did to Highbell, he was fucking devastated. I couldn't deny him the right to go help."

She lets out a sigh. "Of course he wanted to go." She pauses. "What about Queen Kaila? Do you think she showed up to help them?"

"I told her what would happen if she didn't."

Auren hums. "I'm surprised you didn't kill her."

"Despite what I told her, I will kill her. Gladly. You just say the word."

"No. You were right to let her go. Killing her would've only divided Orea more. Three kingdoms are already in turmoil. You needed her alive to help fight this war."

"And she'd better be fucking fighting," I say. "But if not, I'll deal with her."

*After* we deal with everything here.

I brace myself to go see the Drollard villagers. To come face to face with the torment they've suffered since they got here…and for what they might say about my mother.

Auren stops at the bottom of the stairs and looks over. She's so incredibly attuned to me. "We *will* get her back, Slade," she reassures me again. Just like she has multiple times, because she knows how heavily this is weighing on my mind. "Nothing will stop us."

My chest goes warm at her protective vehemence. At how fierce she is on my mother's behalf. "I know."

We go through the corridor, aiming for the entry that serves as the storefront. When we get to the front door and walk out, the street is still busy, but Wick's been able to move and is talking with people in smaller groups. Other Vulmin appear to be doing the same.

As we make our way onto the road, the crowd parts,

people murmuring *Turley* and *Lyäri* and *dragon* as we go. I watch everyone like a hawk, but they keep a respectful distance from Auren, though I still keep my guard up, my protectiveness urged on by the pair bond.

Her ribbons trail behind her like the fabric of a gown, though they twist and twirl, lifting around her—and me. One of them is always touching me.

I smirk down at one as it wraps itself around my wrist, tugging me closer. I watch her ribbons, watch her, seeing her smiling at the fae and them smiling back. Seeing the reverence in their eyes and the way this land seems to glow around her. It makes my heart full—and makes my heart hurt.

Because this is where she belongs.

She was always glorious, but here in Annwyn, it's as if her soul sings, lit up by the sun and gleaming from the inside out. People in Orea either wanted to exploit her or suppress her. But seeing her here, this is where she *fits*.

She deserves to breathe in the air of home, to walk amongst fae who are in awe of her. She deserves to have the land sing just from her presence, and the sun stream down upon her gilded skin.

Auren was always too bright for Orea.

When you're surrounded by jealous shadows, all they want to do is put you out.

But she didn't succumb. Against all fucking odds. Against Oreans and fae alike, against monarchs and cruelty, she's here. She's not only survived, but overcome.

And now she burns brighter than ever.

Which means we will have a lot to talk about when this is all over.

Wick notices us as we get closer, so he breaks away to give us his attention. It's strange for me to think that this is Auren's relative. I'm sure it's even stranger for her.

But I watch him like a fucking hawk too.

"We'd like to speak with the Oreans now," Auren tells him. "We need to see if they can tell us anything about Slade's mother."

Wick nods and turns toward the left. "Alright. I'll take you to the house they're staying at. It's just down—"

"Wick!"

We're interrupted by a Vulmin running down the street. He squeezes past people, forehead slicked in sweat. His anxious energy immediately makes me tense as he reaches us. "Stone Swords! They're setting fire to the city!"

Gasps ring out.

"Why would they set fire to our city?" a Lydian cries.

"We should've turned in the Vulmin! It's their fault!"

"But this is the capital! Why would they burn it? They know there are innocents here!"

Wick jumps up onto a house's front steps to shout across the crowd before they grow too frenzied. "King Carrick doesn't care about innocents. He's willing to sacrifice everyone here. This is why we need to come together! No more Vulmin against fellow fae! We are all people of Annwyn, and we will not let a tyrannical monarch destroy us! It's time to work together!"

His proclamation seems to catch, the doubters and naysayers quieting.

"Make sure all the children and infirm are taken to the canals! Bring only supplies that you can carry and go downstream." His gaze casts across the street. "Any Vulmin or Lydian willing to fight or deal with the flames, come with me!"

We race with Wick down the street, and people either join us or rush toward buildings and boats. He knows the way, taking us down different bridges and walkways, heading for the entrance of the city as more fae come with us to help.

"Is the king with them?" Wick asks the Vulmin.

"No. I heard them say the king went into Orea."

Slade and I exchange a look.

"Make sure everyone is armed!" Wick calls out before he turns to us. "Lydia might be teeming with waterways, but it's also full of trees that can catch and burn."

"Carrick won't burn another city to the ground," Auren replies darkly.

I know she's thinking of Bryol. Of what they did to her home, her parents. She won't let it happen here.

Wick looks at her as we hurry over a covered bridge. Throngs of knitted smoke are now weaving into the air in thick sheets. People are running away, and others are jumping into the canals. There's shouting and fighting ahead.

A Vulmin rushes over, his face streaked in ash, breath coming in coughing spurts.

"How many soldiers?" Wick asks him.

"So far, two hundred strong. I don't know if there are more coming. They've got magicked fire-users too."

A grim look crosses Wick's face as he pulls out his sword. "Enough to take a city that has no outer walls, no towers, no defensive protections whatsoever…"

But Auren shakes her head. "No. They can't retake the city. Not with us here. They don't stand a chance."

Wick blinks over at her, as if he's suddenly remembered her power and my own.

We turn the corner around a bricked building, and then we stop to take everything in. The city's arch is barely visible through the smoke. There are Stone Swords gripping torches and swords, fighting Vulmin and lighting up anything the flames are willing to devour.

I spot two soldiers using fire magic—one that blows out a thick stream of blue flame, and another who tosses sparks from his hands.

Above us, animals and birds stream from the trees that have caught fire, the flames spreading up the plaited branches and licking down the leaves. Already, the fire is polluting everything with heat and smoke, and starting to consume several buildings closest to the entrance.

I can feel Auren's anger prying open and showing its teeth. It makes her aura burn deeper.

"The fire is spreading fast!" the Vulmin says, yanking up his shirt to cover his mouth in order to block the fumes.

"Anyone with water magic?" Wick asks.

"You don't need water magic. You have me," Auren tells him.

Pride fills my chest at the ferocity of her words.

Gold starts flowing from her hands and gathering thickly at the ground, thin veins of black rot branching through it. She lets it pool, and the fae with us back up, eyeing her with amazement.

Stone Swords across the way spot Auren. "There's the gilded Turley!" one of them shouts, and the fire-breathing fae steps forward. "King Carrick wants her burned alive!"

*Burned alive?*

As soon as I hear those words, my dragon tears free.

No warning. No build up.

The threat made to Auren makes the manifestation happen with an intense suddenness that yanks the breath from my chest as shadows surge out of me.

The dragon forms, body rippling as it solidifies with wicked teeth and curved spikes, and golden scales gleaming down its chest.

It's massive and it's fucking *pissed*.

Auren doesn't move an inch as it solidifies, but Wick and the others cry out in shock and leap out of the way.

When the dragon's mouth opens with a furious roar, Auren sends her gold rushing out. The terrified Stone Swords take one look at the dragon and her power and turn to flee.

But her gold is faster.

Like a mudslide, it floods the ground before rising and crashing over the soldiers like a tempestuous sea. They're knocked down and trapped beneath its hardening weight, their screams louder than the snapping teeth of the flames.

She controls her power flawlessly and with astonishing ease. It goes after every soldier, while avoiding everyone else. With precision, she also drags it up like spreads of paint, stretching up the buildings and into the trees to douse the flames.

Fucking magnificent.

She turns to me, hands still outstretched, still pouring with power. "I've got it here. Can you go take care of the soldiers outside?"

A dark grin twists my lips. "Absolutely."

While my aggravated bond wants me to protect her, I also recognize how fucking strong she is, and how much she needs me to *acknowledge* that strength. How it will empower her even more because I have complete confidence in her.

I stroke at her ribbon that's wrapped around my arm before it tugs away, and then I turn toward the dragon, looking it in the eye. The terrifying creature blinks at me with an innate sense of familiarity. Manifested from me, but its own entity.

I use the spikes down its leg to climb up, and the scaled creature rumbles beneath my hold. I settle on its back, right into a notch behind one of the sharp black spikes.

Then we lift into the air. I look down, watching Auren walk calmly forward, her magic eating up every enemy in her wake as gold seeps over the flames, snuffing out the fire with its viscous spread.

The king thought he could burn down this city? Burn her?

She burns brighter than anything else ever could.

My dragon lifts higher, snapping branches from the giant trees as it breaks out from the covering and into open air. When it spots the Stone Swords gathering on the road just outside the city, it snarls.

I grin.

The creature swoops down, and soldiers shout and start to flee in terror. Some of them toss magic our way, and flares of sparking light land against the dragon's chest and belly. But it does nothing except bounce off the gilded scales.

That, and angers the dragon even more.

It opens its fanged maw and roars out rot. Like black flame that writhes with roots in a poisonous spew. It descends upon the running soldiers, consuming them in sprays of death.

The dragon flies lower, reveling in the destruction, and I revel with it. After the threat made to Auren, my aggravated bond craves retribution with bloodthirsty demand.

It swoops down with another air-splintering roar, opening its mouth to spread carnage. The Stone Swords fall, some caught up close, getting so much rot blasted at them that their bodies disintegrate into dust the moment they hit the ground. Others try to run, before their bodies succumb to the noxious fumes and they're left to fester.

We circle, and the monster yanks up the dying, swallowing them down whole. It decimates the entire contingent, turning the ground a sickly yellow, leaving nothing in its radius alive.

Auren comes walking out, stopping just beneath the archway. There's a gold-slicked street behind her, and remnants of smoke in choked-off tendrils rising from the crisped trees.

Fae gather at her back, and my dragon circles once more before we land in front of her. Everyone else backs away, but not her.

She strides confidently forward, stopping right in front of the creature.

I have no fear, and neither does she. Both of us know it won't hurt her. She's as much a part of me as this manifestation is.

Her ribbons curl in front of her armor-clad chest, lifting

up to stroke the creature's maw. Everyone seems to hold their breath as it blinks, watching her.

Then the dragon lowers its head as a subject might bow for a queen.

I'm reminded suddenly about what my father said—about how if I manifested a dragon, I would be king of the skies.

But he was wrong.

Because my dragon drops in supplication to her. She's the one who rules, and I couldn't be more fucking proud.

The sight affects the Vulmin and the Lydians too. They all stand in gaping awe, watching this golden Turley stand here, as a dragon, the most ancient of powers, *bows* to her.

I climb down its back, leaping off the last few feet, my boots kicking up dust from the decayed soil. I go to her, and the two of us share a look before we turn back toward the city's arch.

Where everyone suddenly drops to their knees, repeating one thing.

*Lyäri Nōhcra.*

No longer the golden one gone, but...

The golden one who *rules*.

# CHAPTER 50

## AUREN TURLEY

The veneration coming from the fae is both exhilarating and intense. My ire from the threat of the flames and the Stone Swords bleeds away, and in its place is this display that I'm not sure what to do with. Plenty of people have wanted me to bow to them, but I've never wanted anyone to bow to me.

I definitely never expected a *dragon* to do it.

"Nōhcra," I say to Slade. "What does that mean?"

"My old fae is rusty, but I believe *Nōhcir* is to rule."

My heart skips as I look over at him, my brows pulling into a frown.

His dark green eyes meet mine. "Lyäri Nōhcra—the golden one rules."

My gaze jumps from him to them and back again. "To *rule*? I'm not a queen."

"And yet...they bow to you."

I swallow hard, nerves pinching throughout my stomach. I'm not sure what to say to them.

Slade presses his hand at my back, his touch trailing over my ribbons. "I'm going to take the dragon around once more. Make sure I didn't miss anyone further down the road. If I did, I can question them."

Turning, I leap at the chance. "I'll go with you."

His black brows lift in surprise. "Don't you want to speak with them?" he asks.

"Not yet," I admit.

"You're sure?"

I nod. "Yes. Besides, you think I'd miss my chance at riding a dragon? No way, Lord Rot."

I turn back to the monstrous dragon. It stands fifty feet tall at least, its scales as dark as a pitch-black night, except for the gilded ones that scrape up its chest. It's the same color as the one over Slade's heart. The same color as the one at my neck.

Its iridescent eye blinks at me, a low noise rumbling from its chest that makes me stop. "It won't hurt you," Slade says quietly.

"I know."

I lift my hand slowly, watching the beast watch me. Then I gently place my palm against its snout. It thrums with power. With darkness and death. But it thrums with the familiarity of Slade too. Terrifying and comforting all at the same time.

"He feels like you," I murmur, glancing over at Slade. He's watching me, not the dragon, and the look in his eyes makes my breath hold still, stuck in place. He looks at me like I've hung the sun in the sky.

"From what I understand, dragons manifest from power *and* soul. So it will feel like me…just as it also feels like you, because our souls are rooted together."

I drop my hand to turn around. "So what you're saying

is, this is your dragon...but it's also kind of *my* dragon," I say with a playful smirk.

He drags his hand over the top curve of my ass and then taps playfully. "That's exactly what I'm saying. Now get on, Goldfinch, and let's fly."

I spin around in excitement, and Slade offers me his hand to help me up. I brace my feet and start to climb the spikes. The dragon puts its leg out straighter, as if to help me, and then Slade follows. We settle on its arched back, and I grip the spike in front of me as Slade sits right behind me.

He puts his hands at my waist, squeezing. "Hold on."

I take a breath, and then we're in the air. Powerful reptilian wings stretch out and take us up higher and higher. The fae gathered below wave and cheer as we lift into the sky.

My stomach dips even as my heart soars.

"This is incredible!" I shout back to Slade, my ribbons curled between us.

My back rests against his chest, and feeling his solid, warm presence behind me is a comfort all its own.

"*You* were incredible," he says in my ear, making butterflies swarm in my stomach.

"So were you."

One of his hands comes around me, pressing against my abdomen. I lean into his embrace, letting myself take a breath, letting the tension melt out of my muscles.

I watch the dragon's shadow as we fly over the land below, taking in the contrast of rotted land and lush greenery.

"Is it strange? For you to be back here?" I ask as the wind whips past us.

The dragon circles wider, taking us higher, as if it knows we need a moment alone.

"It is," Slade admits. "But it's also not."

"I know exactly what you mean."

From this vantage point, I have a much clearer view of

just how many soldiers the dragon decimated. "I don't see any survivors."

"No," he agrees. "The dragon was pretty fucking thorough."

"Wait until the others see your dragon," I say with a grin. "Judd is going to be the first one to ask for a ride."

Slade chuckles and I feel his amusement rumble through my back. "I have a feeling this creature will only ever tolerate you and me."

"Judd will be very disappointed."

"So long as I never disappoint *you*, Goldfinch."

"You never could," I reply before looking back at him teasingly. "And I'll tell you a secret."

His eyebrow cocks up, waiting.

"I've always loved hearing you call me Goldfinch."

His hand tightens around me while his eyes soften, gaze delving into me with meaning. "Believe *me*. Being able to call you Goldfinch means more to me than you know."

My lips curve into a smile, and he presses a kiss against my temple before I turn back around.

I move my gaze over to the plateau where Glassworth Palace sits. Then my eyes skim just to the left of it, where a row of blocks are set into the side of the cliff.

"That's where the underground dungeons are," I say, pointing. "Where I was kept."

I feel more than hear him growl, but then his dragon growls too, and I definitely hear *that*.

My hand comes down to his thigh that's pressing against mine. "I'm okay," I tell him. "I made it."

"Yeah, you did. I'm fucking proud of you, Goldfinch. For all of it."

I'm proud of me too.

I eye the green blocks set into the cliffs—the same green as Slade's eyes. That block fed light into my cell like a barred window, though now, I can see just how thick and deep the slab is. I shudder as I remember what it felt like to be trapped on the other side of it.

One king caged my body. Another tried to cage my mind. The first is dead by my hand, and the second is due for a reckoning.

He'll get what's coming to him.

Dark satisfaction settles in my chest at the fact that Una's body is rotting inside that dungeon. That her horrible magic can't eat away at anyone else's mind ever again.

"You're not there," Slade soothes, as if he can sense the emotions thrumming through me.

I'm not in Midas's cage. I'm not trapped within the holes of punctured memories. I'm back in Annwyn, reunited with Slade, in total control of my mind and power. And nothing can stop me from making sure we get all of our joy-filled *one days*, because we deserve it. *I* deserve it.

After a lifetime of trauma and emotional manipulation and abuse, I have finally healed and grown enough to realize that. To say it to myself.

I deserve happy, and so does Slade.

My heart aches to think of all he's endured. Of what he's still enduring, because until we find his mother, those shadows can't leave his eyes.

But he doesn't have to shoulder these things alone anymore, and neither do I.

That's what I feel the most through our paired connection. A sense of belonging. Cohesion. Devotedness. Love incarnate. A connection that strengthens me from the inside out, but that doesn't surprise me.

Because Slade has been doing that since the moment we met.

The dragon turns from the plateau, passing by the mist of the waterfall. Facing this way, we have a clear view of

Glassworth. It looks stunning in this light. Every inch an architectural feat of both labor and magic. Smooth white walls and hundreds, maybe thousands, of stained glass windows casting off an array of colors.

A pretty palace for an ugly king.

And his reign is toppling. I think everyone can feel that the energy of the Vulmin is mounting. Growing. It feels so different from before. They're no longer worried about hiding in the shadows. We're past that now.

Change is coming. It's already begun. We're so close I can taste it.

So close, and yet there's still so much to do.

"We should get back," I say, even though I'd love to be able to fly all day with him. To let day bleed into night and watch the stars salt the sky.

One day.

For now, we need to make sure no one was hurt from the initial fire. Then we need to speak with the Oreans and make a plan to find Elore.

Whatever inherent understanding there is between Slade and the dragon makes the creature start to turn back around to head for Lydia. But something catches my eye at the palace.

"Wait, what is that?" I point ahead, and I can feel Slade turn to look in that direction too. I frown, squinting. "Are those soldiers?"

He pauses. "It does look like soldiers coming out from the gates."

I turn to look at him over my shoulder. "Do you think King Carrick is there instead of Orea? That he's sending those soldiers down to Lydia?"

"Seems bold when they can clearly see a dragon in the fucking sky."

"Believe me, Carrick is arrogant enough to do it," I reply. "Let's get a closer look so we know what we're dealing with."

Slade's dragon changes trajectory, devouring the distance with every beat of its wings. We follow the road that leads up the steep path to the plateau, right up to the palace gate.

My attention is locked on the gathering of soldiers I can see just outside, but I frown when I realize something is off about them, though I can't put my finger on what.

Magic crackles through the air suddenly, and a second later, something shoots up, aiming toward us like a razor -sharp bolt of glass.

"They're attacking!" I cry.

We bank to the left, and the sharp arrow zips by. I feel a low growl come out of the dragon, the noise traveling all the way up its body and echoing my own anger.

But when I look up, I see the threat wasn't done.

The sharp bolt is arcing back down, aiming for us again. Before it can strike us, I lift my hand, and a stretch of gold releases in a wave.

The liquid metal wraps around the weapon, and I feel the tug of power, feel whoever is controlling this projectile trying to fight against me.

It doesn't work.

My magic turns the bolt solid gold, giving me full control, and I send it falling to the ground.

My ribbons twist around my torso while I palm more gold, ready in case another one of those magical arrows tries to hit us again.

Anger radiates from the dragon and it flies down lower, a roar building in its throat, ready to rot them all through.

We're so close to the palace now that I can see all the different colors feeding in from the windows. I can see the decorative gate in front of it, see the soldiers gathered...

And then it clicks. Why something looked off.

It's because these soldiers aren't Stone Swords.

I jerk my head over my shoulder just as the dragon opens

its mouth and starts roaring out power to strike the soldiers below.

"Slade! Those aren't Stone Swords! Those are—"

*Snap*.

The sound is so awful it makes me physically recoil.

The main bone of the dragon's wing breaks, and we start to fall. Its spewed rot chokes off, its roar turning into a scream. Behind me, Slade jolts and goes stiff.

"Hold on!" he shouts, though his voice sounds strained.

His hands lash out clumsily, and he wraps his arms around me and the spike I cling to, trying to keep me stable.

I reach out on either side of the plummeting dragon, forcing out gold as fast as I can. "Come on, come on," I say, teeth gritted, fear pumping through my veins as wind blows and the ground rushes up.

It's not enough, not for how big this dragon is. But the gold I manage to pour out comes together in a viscid wave. It stretches up, bracing against the ground, just barely solidified enough to catch us and break the worst of our fall.

We crash into it, and my head knocks against the dragon's spike as the liquid metal splashes around us on impact.

The dragon roars out in pain from its wing, and Slade picks me up and leaps off the back of the beast. He sets me down on the ground and then puts his arm in front of me protectively as a growl tears from his throat.

We're surrounded by soldiers.

But not a single one of them wears the Stone Sword armor. No, they're in red and black, and I've fought them before. Because these are Cull's guards.

Slade's father is here.

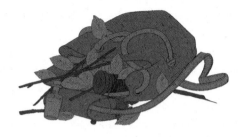

# CHAPTER 51

### EMONIE

The walk from the barracks to the bridge didn't take nearly as long as I'd have liked. But it was enough for me to slip further back in the lines. A little shifting here, a slowed step there, and one by one, I was able to put more space between myself and the front so I could breathe easier.

The other Stone Swords sent me plenty of irritated looks. I was also elbowed once or twice, but no one confronted me or shoved me forward again. I was hoping I could sneak out somehow and head in the other direction, but I realized pretty quickly that just isn't possible.

The higher ranking Badges keep moving their horses up and down the lines, barking out commands and corrections. I might've been able to sneak further back in the rows, but there's no way for me to slip out completely.

We march through the deadlands, and the further we go, the worse it is. The crippling, scorched earth looks like it's been sucked dry of life. Then we reach one of the dead cities, which is nothing but rotten wood and ash-riddled rubble.

And it's supposed to be empty.

It was abandoned long ago, but right now, it holds soldiers.

I can feel the other Stone Swords around me grow tense as we take them in. A few of the Badges move ahead to meet with them just off the path, and unease curls up in my nerves as I get a better look.

Those soldiers waiting in the ruins aren't Stone Swords.

This army wears armor that's stained with both old and new blood. The front of their helmets are in the shape of a blade, leaving their noses and mouths exposed. And hanging from black chains on their belts are…

I can't help it—my hand flies to my mouth, eyes widening in shock when I realize what it is. What *they* are. My steps stagger as I take in the fillets of flesh that hang from their chains. Bits of hide dried out like strips of jerky that they're wearing as trophies. If it weren't for the soldiers surrounding me, I'd run the other way.

Because I know exactly who these fae are.

*Gore*.

They're a faction of fanatics. The lowest of the low. Last I heard, they were banished to an island, kept away from the mainlands and left to kill each other off.

Either that was a lie or they've severely multiplied, because there are *hundreds* of them gathered in this dead city, and they look terrifying.

Dread fills my stomach until I'm drunk with it. I'm so frightened I can barely march straight. These aren't fae, they're monsters.

They don't belong here. They were banished for a reason. That reason being they devour the flesh of their fellow fae.

It goes against every moral, every ethic, against nature itself. But they do it for power.

*Conquer and consume.* That was their mantra. They believed that consuming the flesh of other fae made them stronger. More powerful.

I think it just made them depraved.

I stand in the corner of belief that Annwyn has cursed them for their corruption.

That's why they have hair like limp strings. That's why their lips have pulled back from their mouths, and their teeth are sharpened into points. That's why they've gone mostly blind, save for the shadows they track, aided by the sense of smell that's far and above what anyone else is capable of scenting. And that's why every single one of them has a tinge of red to their skin tones and they reek of blood.

It reveals the truth of the forbidden flesh they've consumed.

Some of the Gore soldiers stand ready, mouths in permanent snarls, sharp teeth stained pink. I feel their eyes on our procession, and my skin crawls. They're an abomination.

I see the Badges talking to a small group of Gore, probably higher ranking based on how heavy their chains are with their multiple slabs of flesh hanging down.

"King Carrick wants you to bring up the rear, after we've cleared the bridge."

I don't hear what the Gore soldier replies, but another one snarls and jerks forward, making the Badges flinch. Guttural, aggressive laughter spreads through the Gore. The Badges quickly turn and head back with strained faces before remounting their anxious horses.

If our own battle-trained horses won't go near the Gore, that should tell us something.

The army continues to move past, and I'm grateful I'm not on an outside row, that I have some buffer between me and the glaring Gore. But I wish I had an even *bigger* buffer. Like an ocean. Like them being on that abandoned island with an entire sea between them and civilization where they're *supposed* to be.

King Carrick is an absolute idiot if he thinks they're going to be loyal to him. Gore aren't loyal to anybody. They only answer to flesh and power.

And yet he's just going to…let them loose. In Orea.

They already do unspeakable things to their own faekind. I don't even want to imagine what they'll do to Oreans. The very thought makes me shudder in fear.

I glance around, wondering where the hell Carrick went and what's going to happen when the Gore get done with everyone in Orea and decide to turn on us. Wondering how I'm going to make any sort of difference when all of this has gotten way bigger than me.

My worry grows with every step, until all too soon, our destination comes into view and my breath catches.

The bridge of Lemuria.

It's famous. Everyone knows the story of how our fae prince came here, at the edge of our world, and used his magnificent power to tether it with his princess's home realm. A wedding gift, from him to her, and a display of power that Annwyn had never seen before.

I don't know how it worked, though stories have been passed down for generations. All I know is, Orea had a bridge, and the prince somehow connected it to Annwyn.

But now that I see it in person, I'm amazed at how… utterly plain it is.

Fae are known for elaborate buildings and ostentatious designs. We like flare and beauty and adornments. But this bridge is simple.

Just a pair of white pillars and rustic rope stretching from them, wrapped around short balustrades beyond. The bridge itself is stark as well. Only gray dirt along a narrow path that disappears after a few feet, swallowed by a thick fog.

I don't want to go into that fog.

And yet the army keeps marching. We have to shift,

narrowing our lines to only three per row, and I get shuffled back even more. Up ahead, the front lines have already disappeared.

A hush falls over the army. Even the Badges have entered the lines, horses nickering and snorting with unease. I get closer and closer, and my nerves twist tighter.

"It feels wrong, doesn't it?" I mutter to the male to my left. "Like we should turn back around?"

He ignores me, and I refocus ahead, though I have a terrible feeling in my stomach. Every ounce of intuition is a weight that's trying to get me to stay. To not take another step forward.

But I can't.

My footsteps falter as I reach the pillars, but I'm trapped. There are soldiers behind me, beside me, in front of me. Gore at the dead city just a mile away.

There's no way out.

"This feels strange..." I say again, but still, no one replies.

Don't they feel it? Annwyn doesn't want us to go there.

I suck in a hurried breath, and then my feet leave the dead soil, and just like that, I'm on the bridge.

My nerves pound with unease. The sound of the soldiers marching onward in synchronized steps fills the air, making everything so much more ominous.

Then I enter the thick, swirling fog too, getting swallowed up in it...

And I realize instantly that something is terribly wrong.

There's a pressure that builds up beneath my skin. As if I'm nothing but soap and air, filling into a bubble. It strains within me and then, in the next second—*pop*.

My glamour magic disappears.

It wasn't even the usual shift of draining away. Instead, it was there one second, gone the next, just as I'm swallowed by the fog.

I've lost a few inches of height, my hair is auburn with

orange tips again and scraping against my neck. The uniform and armor swims on me, the boots so big I nearly trip.

Pure panic floods my system, and I quickly duck my head. My entire body breaks out into a cold sweat.

My glamour is gone. Just *gone*.

I frantically try to call it up, to make my skin tingle and smear, but it doesn't work. I can't even change the tint of my hair.

Someone is going to see me. Someone is going to notice.

Why did I open my big mouth and talk to the soldiers next to me? I shouldn't have drawn attention to myself. Now, they're even more likely to notice I've changed into an entirely different person.

Desperately, I try to call upon my magic again and again, but it won't work. It's this bridge. It has to be.

*Why did I come on this damn bridge?*

I should've just taken my chances and run like my ass was on fire. Right now, I'd prefer my ass *was* on fire.

This is not good.

I glance around surreptitiously, wondering if any other fae is feeling these effects, but none of the nearby soldiers are wearing the pin that marks them as magicked.

Is the king unable to use his stone power on the bridge? Is that why this information isn't public? Is that why he didn't travel with us?

That would have been a massive breach in his defenses if anyone were to know. Perhaps only the magicked soldiers get briefed on this little tidbit and are sworn to secrecy? Unless only my magic is being affected for some reason...but I have a feeling it's not just me.

Which means the king is vulnerable on the bridge. So am I, sure, but more importantly—him.

My thoughts spring around, bouncing off the walls of my skull as I try to come up with a plan. But being on the bridge is suffocating. I've never done well in confined spaces, and even though we are literally walking over an endless void, I've never felt so trapped.

The mist wraps around me like thick blankets, making me wish I could shove them off. It should feel damp, but it's completely dry. More like smoke than fog, though it carries no scent.

I hate it, but it's the only thing concealing me. The bridge exposed me and veiled me all at once.

I'm still working out how I can use this information to my advantage when I feel a distinct chill in the air. A second later, the army procession stops.

We stand here, not moving, just waiting and listening while my nerves tighten. I lick my dry lips, eyes darting around the haze, but I can barely even see the soldier in front of me.

I hear dull thudding ahead, but the sounds are distorted. I wonder what's going on. After a couple of minutes, I start to squirm in place, my toes swimming within my boots. Without being too obvious, I try to hitch up my pants before they fall around my ankles.

Standing still in the fog makes me feel even more vulnerable than moving in it. I just want off. I want to get off this stupid bridge and—

*CRASH!*

A deafening noise ahead makes me jump, and I accidentally bump into the soldier to my right. He glances over at me, expression dripping in annoyance...until he takes me in. Even within the haze, he can see that I'm not the soldier I was before.

He glances around, at a loss, like he thinks the fog might be making him see things. When he focuses on me again, his eyes narrow. "Wait, I recognize you."

My eyes flare in panic, and for some stupid reason, I shush him, as if that's going to shut him up. At the other end of the bridge, more sounds of cracking and smashing rip through the air.

But to my ears, the male's accusing voice is louder. "You're that pris—"

I act on pure instinct, and my foot shoots forward, swiping his leg out from under him. His words cut off as he loses balance, eyes widening when he tilts sideways. We lock gazes, both of us realizing at the exact same time that he's pitching straight over the edge of the bridge.

I fling my hand out to catch him, but it's too late. I've already done the damage.

The soldier tips right off the side, bounces over the rope, and falls.

I lurch toward him, and other soldiers nearby shout and try to reach for him, but no one has a chance, and no one wants to risk falling too. All we can do is watch him plunge into the mist as he lets out a piercing scream that stabs straight past my eardrums and into my heart.

That scream seems to stretch and stretch, until I'm certain it's never going to end. Guilt drags through me as I stare at the air in shock.

I've killed him. I didn't mean to, I just reacted, and he fell off the bridge. Fell into a void we have no concept of. A void we can't even comprehend.

*What if he falls forever?*

"What's going on?"

I jerk around and see a shadowed silhouette ahead shoving soldiers aside, stomping this way. Stone Swords shuffle over to make room, and then the Badge stops and looks out over the rope.

My heart sprints through my chest. I start backing away, maneuvering past the soldiers while they're still distracted. They're swarming around the spot where the soldier fell, leaving room for my retreat. I hear them murmuring, listening to the fading scream.

The Badge turns and looks around. "What happened?" he demands.

Nobody speaks up at first, just murmurings I can't hear past the pounding in my head.

But then, words like *pushed* and *tripped* start bouncing around, and I have no idea which one is going to land. Have no idea if through the thick fog, one of the nearby soldiers saw.

"Who was in line with him?" the Badge asks.

I drop to the ground.

The fog is even thicker down here against the gray dirt, and I narrowly avoid soldiers' legs while also avoiding falling over the edge myself.

I scramble like a rodent searching for a hole to hide in. Luckily, I manage to pass a group huddled near the rope, leaving a spot for me to squeeze by.

But with the questions from the Badge being tossed like darts, I feel like I have a giant bullseye pointed right on my face.

I also don't dare look over the edge. I know all I'll see is fog, but already, vertigo is threatening to tilt my brain. Panic is just a breath away.

When I find a cluster of soldiers with a space behind them, I nearly cry in relief. I scuttle behind them and then pop back up as quickly as I can, pretending to have been there all along.

I stay behind the taller group, hastily shoving the ends of my hair up into the too-large helmet and rolling up the waist of my trousers so they stay on.

Another resounding crack fills in the air.

My entire body is covered in sweat, and I'm bracing myself for everyone to turn around and look at me. I'm waiting to get dragged forward and found out.

Guilt seeps through my pores as much as my anxiety does.

I'm going to be caught.

*What if they toss me over too? What if they give me to the Gore?*

A shiver runs down my spine. I think I might be sick.

When the Badge shouts out, I flinch, bracing...

"Everyone back in formation! And stay the fuck away from the edges!"

I blink, shocked and frozen. I hear shuffling, and then I'm pushed around as soldiers hurry to reform the rows. In a daze, I force myself to get in line with two other soldiers, when really, all I want to do is dissolve into a puddle of relief.

That was a close one.

The army procession starts to move again, and I move with it, like a piece of seaweed caught in the ocean's tow. I'm still shaking when the fog lifts, like the foam dissolving upon the sand, and then, we flow out onto a white shore of snow.

*Orea.*

My eyes widen as I take in the new world.

The land is vast, empty with snow and ice and fissures through the ground. The only structure that stands is in ruins to my right. An ancient castle long since crumbled.

The landscape is so different from Annwyn. There isn't a single place in our world that's covered in such cold. It's actually quite beautiful, if it weren't for the ruined ground broken up and split.

The sky is as colorless as the bridge, yet the air holds a scent that makes me want to gag.

Okay, so Orea *reeks*.

They didn't say that in the history books.

Off in this distance, I can see trails of smoke rising, so that must be part of the stench. I'm really hoping that the veined soldier didn't die from breathing the air.

Hopefully, it's not poisoned.

As soon as I step off the bridge's dirt and onto the snow, I feel my magic come whooshing back. It takes me unawares, my body puffing back out, straining against the stone banded around me, feet filling out my shoes, face morphing, hair darkening and shortening.

I nearly trip on the slippery ground as my body tries to readjust to my changed limbs and weight. With my feet no longer swimming inside the overlarge boots, I manage to stay upright as I track through the snow. Barely.

I pass by remnants of thick walls of ice now crumbled to pieces. I guess that explains those crashing sounds. This is the barrier the king was informed about. Now, it lies broken and useless.

We're through. Pouring into a frozen world that feels utterly different from Annwyn. I look around, trying to find the king, when suddenly, the ruins to the right start moving.

*I guess I found him.*

Stone lifts and shifts, and the whole army stops, watching the might of the king's power as he moves entire walls and erects new ones, changing the relic into a completely new structure.

His magic transforms the ruins into a blocky castle that looks more like a fortress, with a single square tower at the front and a pointed roof that reaches up like it wants to stab the sky.

When the building settles, something heavy settles in my stomach too. I glance behind me, watching more soldiers flow in from the bridge. Up ahead, Badges are shouting for the army to form around the new fortress, probably waiting for the king's next orders.

They're talking, some gathering around the burning piles where the smoke is coming from. At first, I think it's to keep warm, but then I notice the shape of those smoking piles, and I realize they're…bodies.

No wonder it smells so bad.

I swallow down a gulp of bile, my eyes moving to the new building. The king is in there right now. All I'd need is *one* opportune moment. One second of him being caught unawares.

A stupid, terrible idea, but…I can't simply leave. For one, I'd most definitely be caught by flesh-eating Gore monsters. And two…what about Orea? What if I have a chance to kill the king and end this?

"Dammit," I mutter beneath my breath. Why did my Vulmi parents raise me to be so damn honorable?

My eyes dart around, and when soldiers start breaking off in different directions, I make my move. Not back toward the bridge, but toward the fortress instead.

I'm either going to somehow kill a Stone King, die trying, or…hopefully some third option that I haven't quite thought of yet, but one that doesn't involve getting murdered or eaten alive.

I'm particular about the not getting eaten alive part.

I shoot up a quick prayer to Dronidylis, the goddess of favor and filch. Because if I'm going to somehow steal the king's life, then I'm going to need all the favor I can get.

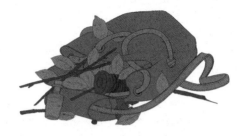

# CHAPTER 52

### EMONIE

The fortress Carrick built is just as gray as the sky. It doesn't surprise me that the king felt the need to make it. He's always been a show-off when it comes to his magic.

Fae love power, and we also love judging power. We can be quite critical about it. Even now, when so much of our population's magical ability has dwindled.

But there's no denying that King Carrick has the magical might, just like there's no doubt he wants to show it. To stake his claim on this world.

Except…he's not the only one with magic.

I might not be as flashy, might not be able to shove around a bunch of rocks and build a fortress in the middle of nowhere, but my glamour magic has helped me plenty of times over the years.

I'm hoping it can help me now too.

I dart around the back of the fortress. The snow is deeper

here, so my footsteps sink down, forcing me to slog through and leave an obvious trail behind me.

Can't do anything about that.

When I get behind the building, I glance back at the bridge, watching the slow but steady stream of Stone Swords filing in, some of them slipping as they make the transition from dreary gray to icy Orean ground.

I'm not sure exactly how many Stone Swords Carrick is sending—I wasn't able to get a clear count while in the prisoner's cart. But so long as these soldiers are coming down the bridge, it means that the Gore aren't yet. And that's a good thing.

It's going to be a very *bad* thing the second they're unleashed into Orea, but maybe I can stop that from happening.

Turning back around, I eye the edge of ground to my right that looks like it's been torn right off. As if a goddess was once here, and she took the entire world and ripped it like a sheet of parchment, leaving behind the jagged edge of this frozen land to float with the fog. Maybe the other torn half floats somewhere else.

If it does, I really hope they don't have a stupid Stone King. One of him is enough.

I rush to the far corner of the fortress and then peer around it before I start making my way up its side. I sidle past the tower and then carefully look around the corner. From here, I'm blocked from view of the bridge, but I'm able to see all the Stone Swords converging into organizing groups.

The door of the fortress scrapes open, and I lurch back just as Carrick comes striding out. As he goes, he moves his hands, and stone erupts in front of him from the snow. I nearly fall from the shake of the ground, hand scrabbling to hold myself up against the wall.

He yanks up stone from the earth that looks like layered cake. He makes a rocky path to walk upon so his polished boots don't sink in even an inch of snow. Then pillars start to erect ahead of him, making soldiers rush out of the way.

Ten pillars lift up to the sky, more stone flattens on the ground between them, and then a pitched roof forms above with the sound of grinding stone and cracking rock. He's made a large pavilion, presumably for some of the soldiers to stand beneath, getting somewhat of a reprieve from the elements.

Carrick keeps walking and then stops at the edge of the structure. Then he lifts his hands again, and the earth shakes, some of the rifts widening as he pilfers from the land's depths.

From the snow, more pillars of stone rise. About as tall and wide as himself this time. A dozen of them form. Then two dozen. Three. A hundred. Maybe more.

I frown at the sight. *What is he making?*

My frown turns into a wide-eyed look when he stops jutting up more stone and instead starts to form them. Their bulk shifts, the sounds echoing as the rock twists and morphs, until a hundred stone soldiers stand like armored statues in the snow.

My breath hitches in my chest.

The king seems to test these new forms, his hands controlling them, making them move in unison, longswords clutched in their granite hands.

*Shit. This is not good.*

The other fae soldiers stand around, watching these new statues in a combination of awe and wariness as the stone figures move and shift. I had no idea the king was able to do this with his magic.

Orea is in big trouble.

Whatever win they managed to have here isn't going to matter. Not if the king can just pop lifeless soldiers up from the ground. The Oreans are going to be leveled. Completely decimated. How can they go against soldiers that don't bleed?

That don't feel fear or pain? How do you even destroy one of these hewn bastards?

More dread grows in my stomach, like spreading spores of moss that latch on. King Carrick has to be stopped. He *has* to, and there's no one else around in this sea of soldiers—both real and rock—except for me to do it.

*Really* unfair that it's only me.

But no time to feel sorry for myself. Ludogar died by King Carrick's hand. My parents too. Just like so many other Vulmin and Oreans have been killed, all because of him and his predecessors.

Determination stiffens my back, and I harden my features as I watch Carrick settle his creations and then erect one last building on the other side of the pavilion. He disappears into its walls before the roof even starts forming. A trail of Badges follow behind him, probably to make more war plans.

I need to get in there. But first, I need a weapon…or three.

Time to go foraging.

Straightening up, I stride ahead, marching forward as if I'm nothing but a simple soldier with a simple task. The glamoured features I'm borrowing are perfectly plain, so no one pays me much attention. I pick my way through the frozen terrain, carefully avoiding the open clefts and patches of ice and browned veins that run through the snow while I walk amongst the others.

I pry a cloak from someone's open pack. I swipe a small dagger from another male's belt while he stands in a circle, talking to other soldiers. I even manage to steal someone's sword while the unsuspecting fellow is squatting behind a snow bank, straining out some sludge.

I wrinkle my nose as I pass. He had better bury that when he's done.

Now armed, I feel much better. My fingers itch to grab more things, but unfortunately, I'm without my beloved foraging pouch, so this will have to do.

I feed my stolen sword through my belt loop, and palm the dagger up my sleeve, securing it against the stone shackle. Then I clasp the cloak around my neck and pull up the hood, because even with my adrenaline burning hot, this place is absolutely freezing.

When I turn toward the pavilion, I see someone walking out from the other building the king created—the one he's still inside of.

I dart for the person, matching his trajectory, walking as quickly as I can without being too fast to gather attention.

If he was in there with the king, he can go in there again.

Or, *I* can, with his face.

I sidestep around groups of soldiers and stuff the end of my cloak clumsily into my waistband.

But as I'm maneuvering over the uneven terrain, I realize too late that this fae isn't wearing armor. My stomach drops when I recognize the shiny black hair that hangs down his back.

It's one of the twins that met with the king back at the army camp. I can't tell one from the other, so I have no idea which it is.

I falter, steps slowing as I consider what to do. I could stop and abandon this plan, but I might not get another chance, and I have no time to spare. Every second is already spent.

I let out a breath. "This is fine," I mutter to myself. "Completely fine." I was hoping this was a random Badge, because the twins seem more important, but this could still work.

Keeping to the plan, I match his stride and determine where we're going to cross paths. When I'm only a handful of steps away from him, I put my head down, pretending to yank on the cloak like it's caught in my trousers, and—

*Bam.*

The two of us crash together.

We collide hard enough that he tumbles to the ground, the

both of us landing in a tangled heap. He cries out in surprise, shoving me while I scramble, trying to unhook my limbs from his, my movement a flurry of panic.

"Get off me!" he snarls when I nearly knock him face-first into the ground.

I wipe off flakes of snow stuck to him. "Sorry, sir!" I say frantically.

He shoves me away and gets to his feet while I spring to mine.

"Are you alright?" another soldier asks, a group of them walking up.

"Fine," the fae grits out as he shoots me a furious look and dusts himself off. "Watch where you're going!" he snaps at me.

My head bobs in an exaggerated nod. "Of course, sir. Sorry again, sir."

With a huff, he turns and marches away, and the other soldiers who saw the whole thing eye me as I sheepishly walk in the other direction with my head down. I hear them snickering as I go, while I do my best to look embarrassed.

Inwardly, I'm preening.

That worked better than I'd planned. A swipe of hand here, a purposeful shift there, and through it all, I digested every part of him that I need to take on his features for my glamour.

I walk as I do it.

As soon as I reach the pillars of the pavilion where a big group of soldiers are gathered, I force a glamoured change, one feature at a time. One change per pillar I pass.

Eyes, face shape, skin, height, hair. Luckily, the fae is quite slim, so I can give myself more breathing room beneath this horrible stone band still caught around my back.

By the time I reach the other end of the pavilion, I'm glamoured into a different male. The unfortunate part is, I'm in armor, and the twin was not.

I yank off my helmet, leaving it behind in the snow, but I can't strip down the rest. I clasp the gray cloak around me tighter, just to try and make it less obvious that I'm wearing a chest plate beneath.

My eyes scan the stone statues as I pass them by. Their chiseled bodies and fae-like faces are all eerily the same and completely still. The rock they're formed with is in layers of gray, and frost is gathered on their smooth heads like clumps of hair.

As I pass them row by row, I get the uneasy sensation that their motionless, pupil-less eyes are following me, even though I know they aren't.

Still, I hurry forward, aiming for the building ahead, where the king and his army advisors are gathered. My heart beats like a hammer against my chest as I make my way closer, but I force my borrowed face to stay calm and expressionless while I inwardly give myself a pep talk.

Go in. Get close to the king. Kill him. That's it. Three easy steps.

I can do this. I'm a Vulmi. I've done lots of difficult missions.

And if I succeed, I could make the difference for thousands of Orean lives.

Fear sticks to my spine, but I force my shoulders back. Shaking my arm slightly, I shift the dagger caught up my sleeve. Its presence makes me feel better.

Sweat drips down the side of my face, but then I'm only a dozen steps away.

I can hear voices inside. One of them is King Carrick.

My self-preservation kicks in, screaming at me to turn around and get as far away as possible, but I ignore it.

I'm a Vulmi, I tell myself again. Just like my parents were. Vulmin don't tuck and run. We rise with the dawn and we fight.

*Here goes everything.*

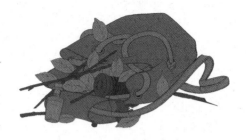

# CHAPTER 53

## EMONIE

J ust as my boot hits the first step leading up the building, someone comes out through the doorway.

I freeze.

I don't know what I did to piss off Droni, my favorite goddess, but she is clearly *not* favoring me right now.

Because the person that comes out is *the other twin*.

My eyes go wide for a split second before I can stop myself and move out of the way. "What are you doing back already?" he says to me, barely looking in my direction.

My body flushes with hot panic, and for a moment, I don't know what to do. But instinct takes over and I turn on my heel and walk beside him, because it seems like that's what he expects.

I steal a look over my shoulder at the building as I get further away from it.

*Dammit*!

Inwardly, I'm panicking so much that it takes me a couple

seconds to realize he's speaking. "…shouldn't do. Because now, we'll have to test out our power on that as well. *While* maintaining our current hold. It won't be easy."

I say nothing, because while I can grit through a male impersonation, I'm sure this fae knows his brother's voice better than his own. Or maybe it's his own voice too since they're twins? Something to ponder.

Silently, of course.

"He may want us to go with him. But we're close now, Fassa. Once this is over, we're going to be the richest fae in Annwyn for our service to the crown. We'll get our choice of land here in Orea too." He pauses. "Pruinn is probably dead. But no matter. That means we won't have to split the pie with him any longer."

I bob my head in agreement, though I have no idea who Pruinn is.

"What's wrong with you?" he suddenly asks as we begin to walk beneath the pavilion. I almost stumble with nervousness, but I shake my head, trying to play it off.

But he grabs hold of my arm, wrenching me to an abrupt stop. I go still, panic flaring as he faces me.

His eyes narrow, gaze dropping down. "What are you wearing?"

I open my mouth to say something, but I don't get the chance. His gaze slams back up against my borrowed face.

His expression darkens with sudden menace. "You're not my brother."

The sentence is like a death toll. Each word ringing in my ears.

Trying to salvage my disguise—my life—I shake my head. "What are you talking about?" I grumble out. "Yes I am."

His eyes flare, and quicker than I can react, the other twin—the one whose features I'm wearing—comes up beside us. "Friano?"

502

*You have got to be kidding me.*

The moment his gaze travels from his brother to me, I feel a noose tighten around my throat.

"What is this?" he hisses.

All around us, other Stone Swords have stopped to look in our direction as they realize something is happening.

I'm thoroughly caught. Like a mouse in a trap, surrounded by hungry cats.

The twins—the real ones—share a look, and then both of them slap their palms against my chest without warning. Magic spews from their fingers, leaving me itchy all over.

My glamour suddenly peels away, like one long strip of skin yanked off, leaving me raw and chafing.

"Restore something," one twin says.

I stumble back, a pained grunt escaping me as my hand flies up to my ear. My fingers find the source of the sharp stinging sensations, and my eyes go wide at what I feel.

"And instill something," the other one finishes.

The top of my left ear had been sliced off from King Carrick's orders, but now, something has sprouted from it. Like thin, curved branches, it comes out of the cut cartilage to curl around the entire shape of my ear. Curling like…

"Looks like the little changeling has sprouted an antler," the twin I'd pretended to be—Fassa—says. "And it draws attention to what she really is," he goes on, staring at my cut ear. "A traitor to her own kind. Vulmin, an Orean-loving scum."

Noises of disgust ripple out from the other Stone Swords, and my stomach twists into knots.

The other brother takes a threatening step toward me that makes me flinch. "You think I wouldn't know my own brother? I could sense him even if I were deaf, blind, and magic-less. We are connected by more than power or blood. Twins have a sixth sense with one another."

"Seems tedious," I mutter, dropping my hand from my ear.

He doesn't find that amusing, and his anger seems to stir up the soldiers, because I feel some of them behind me move closer. Anxiousness skitters through my limbs, my gaze flicking every which way as my body tenses.

"What do you want to do with her?" someone asks.

The twins look terrifying now, and I shift my body ever so slightly as they answer in unison. "Teach this Orean sympathizer a lesson."

The soldiers move to pounce. I only have time to yank out the sword from my belt and swing. I slice through the arm of the closest soldier, and then pivot, aiming for the twin's chest, but he's pushed out of the way by his brother.

The Stone Swords descend upon me like rabid wolves.

There are far too many.

Someone slams their arm against my wrist, making my hold on the weapon falter. I flail and swing around, trying to stab someone, *anyone*, and I feel my blade hit someone's armor with a rocky scrape. But then the sword is wrenched out of my clawed fingers, with a simultaneous kick to the gut.

I start to fall.

Everyone knows when you're in a fight, it's a death sentence to fall. The moment you're on the ground, it's over. So when my knees hit the stone and the kicks start coming, I know I'm dead.

There's no coming back from this.

Pain showers down on me like pellets of punishing rain. The ominous press of bodies that surrounds my fetal form just oppressive clouds of gray. They land hits and kicks so savagely it steals my breath. Cracks my ribs. Boots stabbing into muscle and organs, limbs viciously butchered with slices of blades that hit like whips.

I curl up into a ball, head tucked, knees up, and endure. There's nothing else to do.

My body is pelted with brutality. My clothes are torn,

boots kicked off, hair ripped from my scalp. There is no source of pain, because it's everywhere, all at once. There's no breath, no thoughts, no anything, except this downpour of agony that I know is going to kill me.

Tears leak from my eyes, burning as they land on my arm, while the deluge floods my system, soaking me through with its torture.

A kick to the temple has me blacking out for a few seconds, my mind heavy with resentful consciousness, though I know my body can't take much more.

Grief and terror are my inner torrent, but when I nearly black out again, everything suddenly stops. Or maybe it isn't so sudden, because time feels like it's been fastened. Holding on with a grudge.

I look up blearily, body floating, and it takes me several seconds for my mind to connect the faces of the twins standing over me.

They look at me with hate, and then I'm pulled away, body caught at the ankles. I'm dragged off the stone pavilion and through the snow, but I don't try to struggle or move.

I can't.

The snow is actually a reprieve, since the cold offers a numbness I long for.

My eyes are nearly swollen shut. My sides scraping out soggy breaths. I'm hurting in so many places, I can't track them all.

They leave me lying on a hard stone surface against a shadowed wall. I blink, trying to see where I am, and see two soldiers laugh as they walk away, following the trail of blood I've left behind in the snow.

For several seconds, all I do is stare and breathe, but even that is difficult.

Pain is *everywhere*.

"Hello?" a feminine voice echoes, and I look up at the cavernous ceiling. Maybe I've died and I'm in Dronidylis's temple. If I am, she needs a new decorator. Didn't take her for someone who liked the cold.

"I said are you alright?"

"Annoying goddess," I say around a bloodied tongue.

"What?"

My eyes roll, shifting to look in the direction of the voice. Just my luck, it's not a goddess. It's a woman tied to a pillar. I'd laugh if I didn't think it would crack a rib.

"Who are you?"

"I can be anyone," I mumble.

"*What*?"

*Great skies, why can't I just die in peace?*

"Hello?" she snaps again.

With a grunt, I force both eyes to fully open past the swell and shove myself up to a sitting position. I gasp in pain, but I think, by some miracle, my ribs aren't actually broken. It's the stone band around my back that's been snapped, and its rough edges are digging painfully into my ribs. Maybe this thing protected me a bit.

I reach up and tear one of the pieces away, though I nearly black out again at the pain it takes to move.

I'll just get the other piece…later.

My head swims for several seconds before I'm able to focus on the pillar on the other side of the room. The female tied there has pure white hair and fair skin. On the other side of the pillar is a male with a darker complexion except for a pattern of light skin around his mouth and nose. Even from here, and even with swollen eyes, I can see one very important detail about them.

Blunt ears.

"You're Oreans," I slur, body braced against the wall behind me.

"Shouldn't be that surprising, since we're in *Orea*," the man retorts.

"Why were you beaten?" the woman asks.

# GOLDFINCH

"I was beaten?" I rasp before spitting out a glob of blood. "Huh. That explains the agonizing pain."

They stare at me. "You should see the other guys," I say, but when I try to smile, I notice that my lips are split, so it just makes them split more.

No smiling. Add that to the list right under no walking, no breathing, and no moving. That should cover it.

"So, who are you?" I ask.

"Queen Malina Colier," the woman says, and despite her disheveled and bound appearance, I believe her. There's just something regal about her. I mean, who else but a royal would be sitting up so straight while tied up? Her posture is excellent.

"An Orean royal," I muse, voice raw. I must've screamed while I was being beaten. I don't really recollect.

Heaving in as big a breath as I'm capable of, I start edging my way over to them in very, *very* slow increments. Inch by inch, they watch me warily while I try really hard not to pass out.

By the time I make it in front of the woman, I'm dripping sweat despite the cold, and I'm panting so hard my ribs are getting bruises on top of their bruises.

"What are you doing?" she asks sharply when I palm the dagger that's still blessedly caught up my sleeve.

Behind her, the man strains against the bindings, looking like he wants to tear free and strangle me. "Stay away from her, fae filth!" he spits.

"This one doesn't like me," I mumble before glancing at the woman. "Don't worry, I'm a Vulmi."

"What in the world does that mean?"

"It means we protect Oreans."

My fingers ache, but I manage to grip the hilt of the dagger, and then I start to saw at the thick bindings around her. It's not easy or quick, but I know I need to get them out of here, so even though every drag hurts, I grit my teeth and bear it.

Because if I can just do this *one* thing…then at least I

won't die for nothing. At least I'll have helped, even if only a little. I didn't kill a Stone King or save thousands of Oreans, but I can set these two free and give them another chance. If I do that, the goddesses will know I tried my best. Maybe Droni can give this Orean queen a little bit of favor instead—that would be alright with me.

I saw harder and harder, eyes watering from the pain in my beaten body, but finally, the strap slices apart. The woman tears off the bindings the rest of the way and then takes the dagger from my limp hand.

Fortunately, she doesn't stab me with it. She races over to the man and gets him free next. She doesn't manage to do it any quicker than I did, so that gives me a little confidence boost, which is lovely.

When they're both free, the man comes around where I've flopped against the pillar.

"How do we get these off?" he demands, shaking his hand.

My eyes drag up to the gray cuffs around both their wrists. I saw those same cuffs on Wick and Auren. Some sort of magical cork, keeping their powers plugged up.

"I don't know," I admit before peering at them. "You two have magic? What kind?" I ask croakily.

Even though I've released them, they don't answer me. Fair enough. Even though I'm a Vulmi, I *am* still fae. Judging on how I found them tied up, and that our kind is invading their world, they're probably not too keen to trust me.

I notice the Orean queen doesn't give me back the dagger either. Instead, she opts to tuck it into the pocket of her pretty dress.

Good for her.

"Can't help with the cuffs, I'm afraid," I tell the man before I cough up a little blood.

That's probably not a great sign.

For some stupid reason, I start to drag myself up to my

feet, though my vision blots out halfway there. I only stay upright because the woman comes over to steady me.

"Thanks," I pant out between labored breaths. I'm sweating so much my hair is stuck against my temples. "Alright, come on."

Queen Malina watches me shuffle forward a few steps. "What are you doing?"

"You need to get out of here," I say without looking back. "Right now. There's no time to waste. I'll make a distraction if I need to so that you two can get away."

"You can't even walk."

"A bit rude," I mumble before I motion them forward. I have to lean against the wall to keep myself up. It's only pure fear for them and determination to do something useful that keeps one foot moving in front of the other. I can wallow in pain after they go.

They're still moving far too slow, though. Whispering back and forth as I finally make it to the doorway.

Then a sound stops my heart. Roaring voices coming from the void.

With my head craned past the door, I look toward the bridge at where the sound is coming from. My blood runs so cold that I stiffen and stagger. Going dizzy, I fall back, landing on the floor in a painful heap that makes me gasp.

The queen crouches down to help me back up, but instead, I latch onto her wrist. "Listen to me," I say frantically. "I know I'm just a fae, but trust me when I tell you that you need to get as far away from here as you possibly can. Because what's coming down that bridge next is something you can't survive. None of you can."

Her icy blue eyes flash at my frenzied tone. "What's coming down that bridge?"

I shake my head as fear lances through my stomach and threatens to drain me out. "Death," I tell her honestly. "The fae coming next are monsters. They will pick the muscles from your bones and eat your flesh while you're still alive. They will defile everything. There will be no escaping them once they're unleashed into your world. And they're coming," I press urgently. "Right now. So you need to go!"

The queen shudders visibly, and I can see the grim expression on the man's face despite being partially obscured by his hood.

When she tries to help me up again, I shove her away. "The Stone Swords are distracted already. Go!" When she still hesitates, I harden my expression. "I'll only slow you down. Hurry up, Orean queen. Don't waste your chance."

She swallows hard, and then the man grips her by the arm and drags her out of the fortress. I watch as they run the length of the wall while my pulse beats wildly.

Only when they disappear around the corner do I let out a breath. I stay slumped in the threshold of the doorway, feeling dread for Orea and crushing failure.

I couldn't kill the king. I couldn't stop what's coming… but at least I got them away.

And maybe that will count for something.

# CHAPTER 54

## QUEEN MALINA

Dommik and I race out of the castle, leaving the fae woman behind. I steal one last glance at her before I go. She's in a terrible state. So badly hurt that I couldn't even tell what she really looked like, other than auburn hair with orange ends and a strange reddish tint to her eyes.

I've no idea why the fae have beaten her so severely, but if she hadn't been dumped in there with us, we wouldn't have been able to get out. Leaving her behind seems a poor way to thank her.

Even if she is fae.

"Wait," I say after Dommik and I run around the corner. We press our backs against the wall, temporarily hidden from view from the army collecting at the other side. "We can't just leave her."

"We have to. You know we do, Malina. She can't walk,

let alone run." He grits his teeth, straining once again to shove the cuff off his hand, cursing when he still can't do it. "We need to go, and I can't use my shadows. You heard what she said. Something is coming. We need to run."

He points straight ahead in the direction where we found that ruined house and spent one blissful night together. That seems such a long time ago.

"It's a clear shot. None of the army is in this direction. If we run, they might not see us."

A sudden sound erupts from across the land, but not in the direction of the bridge. Still, I can't help but remember what the fae said.

*What's coming down that bridge next is something you can't survive.*

My stomach twists.

When he reaches for my hand again, I pull away. "Dommik…"

Fearful exasperation fills his face. "Malina, we can't bring her, dammit!"

I look over his handsome face with a despair that clings. It latches onto me, squeezing my skin, cinching my throat.

As I stare at him, at a loss, his expression falters. "Malina?"

"I…"

A Stone Sword comes from out of nowhere.

He lets out a noise of surprise when he notices us, but quickly recovers and moves to attack. With his sword raised, he flings himself forward, so it's very fortunate that my assassin is so skilled.

Even being caught unawares and without a weapon, Dommik reacts in the blink of an eye. Body swiveling, he turns, blocking me from harm and jerking to the right so that the sword's trajectory misses.

Turns out, Dommik doesn't need his shadows to

assassinate, because his movements are fluid and wickedly fast even without them.

I can barely track him as he ducks and spins, avoiding another swing before he turns and kicks out the soldier's knee. The soldier cries out in pain and falls to the snow, and Dommik launches himself at him.

Dommik wrests away the sword from his grip, and I start backing up several steps, looking away as he slices the fae's throat.

When it's done and the soldier lies bleeding out on the snowy ground, Dommik turns and looks at me. "Queenie?"

It takes great effort for me to speak past my fisted throat. "If I commanded you to do something, would you do it?"

A frown forms between his brows as he pants out breath. "What? No."

My heart fills with desperation. "If I *asked* you to do something, would you do it then?"

He takes a step toward me, but I take another one back. His gaze drops to my feet before flicking back up. "What are you doing, Malina?"

I shake my head. Tongue thick, I drag out the laden words. "Please," I beg. "Go get her."

His eyes flare with frustration. "I told you, she can't come with us! Not without my shadows, and not if we have any hope of getting away!"

"Please!" I shout, my voice gone shrill, drowned out by the wind that's begun to whip. "*I need you to go* get her!"

"Fine!" he hisses through clenched teeth and glaring eyes. "You stubborn, foolish fucking woman. I'll go get her. Wait here!"

He turns and hurries back the other way, and I hold my breath as I watch him go. He pauses for a moment as he peers around the corner. Then he shoots me a look over his shoulder and darts away.

I turn and run.

I'm entirely aware that I only have mere seconds, which is why I don't hesitate. Dommik will be confused when he comes back and I'm not here, and then that confusion will turn into fear.

But I couldn't allow him to follow me, and no amount of explaining would've deterred him. He wouldn't listen to me if I asked him to stay behind.

This is the only way, and this is my only chance. The fae told me, *don't waste your chance*, so I won't.

*Forgive me, Dommik.*

My vision blurs, but I run through the snow faster than I've ever run before, making it to the back of the castle and then darting around the corner. I don't let myself think, I just go. Racing alongside the edge of the world as the fog rolls like clouds of threatening thunder.

Straight ahead, I see the bridge, see the Stone Swords now cleared away from it, the army giving it a wide berth. With my heart pounding in my chest, I leave behind the cover of the castle and start sprinting out in the open, aiming straight for the entrance.

The fae spot me.

Their heads turn in my direction, their shouts tossing into the air. Panic and pressure build up inside me, pushing me to go faster. To not be caught.

Because I *can't* be caught. If I am, then it's over. If I am, *Orea* is over, and I can't let that happen.

Suddenly, the terrible roaring we first heard inside the castle erupts again, coming from the bridge. From inside the thick fog.

I can taste bitter fear at the back of my throat.

*I must go faster.*

The woman's warning pounds beneath my temples.

*The fae coming next are monsters. They will pick the*

*muscles from your bones and eat your flesh while you're still alive. They will defile everything. There will be no escaping it once they're unleashed into your world.*

That's what's coming. An evil that celebrates its own vileness by roaring threats into the air.

Shouts sound to my right and I see soldiers running for me, their feet slipping in the snow. Yet my steps are steady, my arms pumping, gaze determinedly set.

I make it to the entrance of the bridge before anyone can get to me. Hand curling around the white pillar, I swing myself down the path of the bridge.

The fog swallows me whole.

As thick as the wool of my dress, it envelops me, closing me into its shrouded embrace. I look over my shoulder at the shadows of soldiers who start to follow me in, but I keep running despite the thick air. Despite the terror in my wide-open eyes.

Then that chilling sound of a thousand joined voices in vicious roaring erupts again, and the other fae soldiers scatter, leaving me behind. Abandoning me to the mercy of whatever kinds of monsters are making those terrible noises.

If the Stone Swords won't even risk meeting up with the fae coming down this bridge, then Orea truly is doomed.

Unless I stop them.

# CHAPTER 55

## COMMANDER RYATT

I haven't been all the way to the end of the world before this, but Seventh Kingdom is just as vast and desolate as the stories.

I ride a borrowed timberwing from Second Kingdom's fleet, while everyone else rides around me like a flock. The Wrath take up the front, King Thold and Kaila in the middle, and Second Kingdom takes up the rear.

Fifth and Sixth Kingdoms are cold, but Seventh? It's fucking arctic. So frigid that it even hurts to breathe. Like ice just slices down my throat with every inhale.

At first, I'm so focused on trying to get my desert-native beast to keep flying despite the elements, that I don't notice anything else other than the freezing clouds we fly above.

But the closer we get, the more I feel it. A buzz in the air, like when you accidentally walk right in the middle of a swarm of bees. A hum that vibrates against my skin with threat.

I can see the other soldiers and even timberwings growing antsy and confused. But none of the Wrath does, and neither does Kaila or Thold. Because we recognize what that buzz in the air is.

Magic. *Powerful* magic.

My pulse climbs as high as our altitude as we continue on. I don't know what kind of magic we might be flying toward, if what I'm feeling has to do with the fae or the bridge, but it sets my teeth on edge.

A shout has me whipping my head around. It's Tyde, mouthing something at me from the back of Gideon's timberwing, but I can't hear what he's trying to say. He rips off his face covering and points down as he shouts again, but I can't hear a word. Not with how fast we're going, not with the whipping wind tearing away his words.

But a second later, a blast of light shoots up at us from the sky below, startling the shit out of my bird and me both.

I have time to jerk my head forward and hear timberwings screeching, and then the light breaks apart into hundreds of crisscrossing lines and slams into us.

It's a net of lightning. An electrocuting, blinding web that catches nearly a fourth of our group. I'm one of them.

I'm jolted from the flare that's both solid and not, both passing through us and catching hold. My body goes rigid, my skin crackling with light and pain.

Beneath me, the timberwing goes stiff too, wings paralyzed, and we fall. We fucking *plummet*.

The net falls with us, dragging us down, and I can't breathe or blink, can't move within its confines. My teeth are clenched, wind whipping at my exposed face, and just when I think I'll pass out from lack of breath, we slam to the ground.

The net sizzles away, and I suck in a gulp of frantic air. I'm buckled to the saddle, but the timberwing is panicked, wings flapping, trying to buck me off.

All his jerky movements do is nearly knock my skull off my spine, my bones threatening to snap with how hard he's tossing me around.

There's nothing I can do but hold on.

Then a blade comes down and slices the strap holding me hostage, and I go flying off the beast's back. As soon as I do, the timberwing takes flight with a roar, leaving me behind as it flees.

But Judd helps me to my feet, the dagger still in his hand from cutting me free. He smiles, albeit shakily. "See, that's twice I've saved your—"

His body jolts.

We both look down at the same time. Both see the sword stabbed clean through his chest.

Denial pounds in my skull, and my vision tips. That didn't happen. It isn't happening…

Judd's head lifts and his hazel eyes latch onto me. "*Shit*," he says, his voice garbled.

"No…"

I hear Lu *scream*. "JUDD!"

Horror blares through me, and the sword sticking through him is suddenly yanked back out. Judd cries out in agony and then hits the ground hard.

I'm so fucking stricken that I nearly don't react to that blood stained sword now swinging in my direction. Somehow, I manage to yank my blade from my scabbard just in time to meet it before it takes off my head.

But the force of the hit sends me flying backwards.

I land on my back in shock. *How strong is this fae?*

Around me, I hear other fighting going on. From my peripheral, I see Lu skid in front of Judd. Timberwings roar, and the clash of weapons and shouts erupt all around us.

But my pulse drums even louder.

*Judd. Judd. Judd.*

All I can see is that sword plunging through his body. The look of shock in his eyes.

And the way Lu *screamed*…

Stunned fury radiates within me and then a rage-filled battle cry rips from my throat. Judd.

They did that to *Judd*.

I shove myself upright and pick up my sword from the snow, head whipping up to see the fae is coming for me again, but instead of a battle cry of his own, I hear a sound like grinding rock.

He swings at me, but I duck this time and pivot around. I lift my foot to send a kick to his knee…and nearly break my damn foot. My body jolts.

*What the hell?*

His sword comes at me and I roll. I hear the hit land in the snow instead. One look to my left, and I see how deep the divot is that he made in the ground. The force he's swinging with would've cleaved me in two.

Fae are strong, but not *that* strong. And his leg didn't move at all when I kicked him.

The soldier moves stiffly, and I finally have time to get a good look at him. I thought he was just wearing full body armor, more intensive than the other Stone Swords we've seen, but no. It isn't the armor that's stone. The whole body is *stone*.

I'm fighting against a godsdamned statue.

It's relentless. It comes at me again and again, and I can't overpower it. It has no muscles. No bones. No eyes or jugular. There are no weak spots because it's not a body. It's like fighting a moving boulder.

The edges of my blade are getting blunted, my armor damaged. All around me, I hear the struggles of more fights. Hear the unmistakable sounds of death.

The statue soldier sends a fist against my armor and

sends me flying again. I'm stunned from the pain that flares through my chest, my armor dented from the impact of his hit.

I get up, breath still knocked out of me, but look around and see dozens of them surrounding us, and more coming. In the distance, I can make out a castle, and the bridge, and between us, hundreds more fae soldiers.

My stomach doesn't just drop. It plunges down into a void.

We can't win this.

The realization hits me harder than the stone statue ever could.

My gaze swings around in a daze. There are bodies of people and timberwings lying dead in the snow. More fighting, everyone being overpowered by these hellish statues that we can't defeat.

I can't see Judd, can't see Lu. Have no idea where Osrik or Digby are. We're outnumbered, caught unawares. All our strategy and luck and heart just battered right the hell out of us in an instant.

Queen Kaila is in the air, her timberwing narrowly missing another one of those nets of electrocuting light. Her magic screams through the air, threatening to burst my eardrums, but it doesn't affect the statue I'm fighting since it has no fucking ears.

King Thold is on the ground with his soldiers, and I see Second Kingdom too. But we're falling left and right like felled trees.

Even the serpent king's magic isn't doing any good. Fangs and venom and constriction are useless against moving rock. The snow serpents that rush out of the snow do nothing to slow our opponents.

But…this is the Stone King's magic.

My mind claws with desperate nails, trying to latch onto a plan.

If we can take the fae king down, we can take down these statues too.

When the statue comes for me again, this time, I race toward it. As soon as it raises its arm to swing its weapon, I shift my body and use the slick snow to my advantage, sliding right beneath its arm.

Then I sprint. Focused only on the need to outrun my opponent and find the king.

There's so much fighting going on that I can't track it all. My pulse is erratic, my breathing labored, and behind me, I hear the sound of grinding rock from the statue as it chases after me.

But then I hear someone cry out hoarsely, and my head whips around as I see Digby fall into the snow. His head knocks back into a snowbank, and his helmet flies off. He struggles to grab the sword that fell just out of his grip, but one of the statues is bearing down on him, moving its weapon to strike.

To kill.

I pump my arms, legs racing as fast as I can to get to him, but I'm too far away.

Too fucking far.

Panic bursts through my stomach and burns up my throat. First Judd, and now I'm about to watch Digby get struck down too.

I try to push my body, to eat up the distance, but the statue raises its sword and starts swinging it down, and my heart stops as Digby raises an arm in front of him, fear flashing over his face where he lies on the snow.

But suddenly, a timberwing swoops down from nowhere. The big beast slams its outstretched talons against the statue, gripping it by the arm. With a roar, the bird flings it at another statue, causing them both to crack and fall.

"Digby!" I reach him in five more steps and then wrench him up from the snow.

He swings his head to look at me, but then his eyes shift over my shoulder and go wide. "Duck!" he bellows.

I drop to the ground without pause, and I feel the air shift above me, hear the whistle from a sword swinging where my head just was.

*That was close.*

Spinning around on the ground, I sweep my leg and knock the statue's foot out from under it. The walking rock goes tipping back, falling hard, its weight making it sink deep into the snow.

I waste no time in leaping to my feet, just as the timberwing lands next to Digby and me. That's when I recognize the bare-backed beast.

It's *Argo*.

"Fuck, you're a good bird," I say to him.

Behind us, another two statues have locked their attention on us and are coming at us fast.

"Get on!" I shout to Digby, and he jumps up onto Argo's back a second before I do.

As soon as we're both on, Argo launches into the air, roaring at the statues. His wings flap hard and he lifts us higher. I look down as the statues stop, unable to look up, and then they start stalking toward someone else instead.

We have to stop these things.

I dig my hands into Argo's feathers at his sides to hold on. "The fae king is controlling these!" I shout at Digby. "We need to find him!"

"Got it," he says before he moves his grip at the sides of Argo's neck to direct him.

The beast circles while I focus on holding on, my head turning as I try to search for the king. I have no clue what he looks like, but he wouldn't be far, right? He must be close by so he can control these things.

"There!" Digby shouts, and I follow the line of where he's pointing and see a man standing on a piece of pillared rock that's jutting up from the ground. He's up high, probably so he can have the best vantage point, and his hands are stretched in front of him, like he's pulling imaginary puppets on strings.

He's not even trying to be inconspicuous.

Then again, he's powerful enough that he probably doesn't think he needs to be. Sometimes, arrogance like that can be exploited and turned into a weakness.

"Get me above him!" I yell.

Argo pivots, the speed of his flight unmatched as we fly toward the king. I inwardly brace myself.

There is no time to hesitate or calculate or run through the scenarios. I am outmatched against the fae king in every possible way.

Every way...except taking him utterly by surprise.

The moment Argo gets me above him, I launch myself down.

No hesitation.

I force my mind to blank, my emotions to clear. The only discernible effect of my inner fear comes from my pounding heart as I free-fall.

There's a very slim margin for my drop to strike true, and there's an even slimmer chance that I succeed even if I do land on the right spot.

But while I may not have magic, may not have anything that this fae considers powerful, I do have one thing.

Loyalty.

I am so fucking loyal to Orea, to our people, that I will do whatever I need to. My life is forfeit to the cause. I am willing to do anything and everything to save it. But the fae king wants our world for himself. Which means he has to have a *self* in order to reap the benefit.

I just want to save Orea. If I die to achieve that goal, so be it.

Fucking pull it off. Whatever it takes.

My body drops.

Gravity reaches up and grabs hold of me in its iron fist. Forward and backward, tipping, reaching, I aim to hit the stone platform so I don't go skidding right off and land in a broken, useless heap.

One chance.

I suck in a breath as I lean into the fall, arms stretched out...

And I slam right into the fae king.

The force of my hit makes both of us fly off the raised platform. We crash onto the ground below, sinking into the snow.

The difference between the two of us is immediately apparent. He has a crown and pointed ears and immense magic, but he's not a soldier. He's not used to taking a hit. It's obvious, because when we land, he's stunned for too many seconds. Seconds I'm able to take advantage of.

He has his power, but I have my fucking fists.

I start pummeling him. I pin him down, my punches landing again and again, everywhere I can hit. My knuckles crack, fingers shooting with pain because of how rigid his skin is, but I ignore it, not even letting a second pass before I'm hitting him again.

My fury is my fodder. It feeds me with gluttonous force, while I take out all my anger on him for what he's done to Orea. To our people. To *Judd*.

My vision has gone red, stained darker with the blood I make burst from his skin. I don't know how many hits I manage to land, all I'm aware of is each brutal contact my fist makes with his body before I'm ripped away.

I'm tossed in the snow by another fae, but I'm pumping with adrenaline and rage and battle lust, so I roll and leap right back up to my feet. The soldier who tore me away from his king yanks out his sword threateningly...but then he's mowed down by a line of stone statues.

He just saved the king from a beating, and in thanks, he gets trampled.

I look to my left, seeing the furious king stepping up out of the snow, his hateful eyes staring right at me. The stone statues span out and I turn, trying to keep them all in my sights.

But they circle around me. *Surround* me.

My breathing is hard and fast, and I can't get past them. Their chiseled forms close in, layers of rock sculpted into bodies that bear down on me with faceless glares.

They don't even raise their weapons. They just march. Closer and closer with threat.

I'm penned in and I realize the fae king is going to make them crush me to death between their solid mass. I turn around, panic building as I desperately look for a spot to dart out, but there is none.

I'm trapped.

Claustrophobic.

My eyes swing around wildly. I grit my teeth, my pulse hammering, but reality settles in. I'm going to be crushed to death right here.

I watch as their rigid, unrelenting forms close in.

And in.

And in.

I have one more second. One moment, before I'll be pulverized. I can't even turn anymore. I feel them press in on all sides, about to immobilize me.

In a final, desperate bid to live, my knees bend, legs poised, muscles tensed, and then I launch myself as high as I possibly can.

I get three feet up in the air and then kick out, bracing my boots against the statues, using their bodies to climb out from their pressing tomb.

Without minds of their own, they're beholden to their puppet master, so they can't react quickly enough. I scale them, hands grappling, digging in to every foothold, and then some-fucking-how, I make it onto their shoulders and fling myself out of their claustrophobic circle.

I land hard on the balls of my feet, pain shooting through both ankles, but my head whips up to face the Stone King, and our eyes meet.

His gaze widens as I lift my blade—metal. Not an inch of stone on me that he can control. And with my momentum fueled purely by near-death panic and unadulterated rage, I swing my sword.

Right through his neck.

Metal slices through him, and the moment his head hits the snow, so does every single statue. All at once.

Lifeless. Unmoving.

Useless rock.

I land hard on my knees, heaving breath, the head of the fae king rolling to a stop to my left.

Dead.

I glance up, my heart hammering through my chest, and elation runs through me.

But then I hear the war drum and battle cries as the Stone Swords descend like vultures, ready to pick us off, and horror washes over me. Fatal comprehension.

Because I killed their king. I killed the person who ordered this invasion.

But it doesn't fucking matter. The war didn't end with him.

The fae are going to slaughter us anyway.

# CHAPTER 56

### QUEEN MALINA

When I'm sure that the soldiers aren't following me anymore, when I'm sure they've left me to my fate, I skid to a stop on the bridge.

I stand upon the gray dirt, panting, hardly able to see more than the hand in front of my face with how thick the haze is.

Inside this vaporous shroud, sound is muffled. I no longer feel the lash of the wind or hear the Stone Swords or whatever commotion was coming further away from the castle. I can't see any part of Seventh Kingdom either.

It's as if I'm in a different world. One where I'm utterly alone.

With one hand, I reach blindly forward until I grip the rough rope that hangs between the balustrades, needing it to steady me.

Then I slip my other hand into my dress pocket and take

out the dagger I stowed. I stare down at it, and my hands start to shake.

I feel the tender slices down my palms. A vivid reminder of the night the fae twins cut them and how I let my blood drip down to fuse with their magical ceremony.

*Do you know why we chose you?*

They chose me because I was the right royal.

They chose me because they couldn't re-form the bridge alone.

They chose me…because blood matters.

*I thought it was a good idea to sneak into the atrium to hide. My scholar can't come all the way up these stairs with his knobby knees to find me, anyway. He'll be looking all over. That will teach him to strike my hands with his switch.*

*Except when I come into the glass room, I hear voices. I start to back out, but I stop when I recognize my mother talking. My stomach dips though, because it sounds like she's crying.*

*Why is she crying?*

*Spinning around, I duck between the trailing plants and follow her voice. I spot her sitting at the water fountain. She's wearing a pretty blue dress, her dark blonde hair braided around her head. White blossoms and dark green leaves surround her while the fountain flows. It usually makes her happy to be in here, but right now, she's not happy. Her cheeks are wet and her eyes are red.*

*She's with Mender Fyce, and I freeze when I see him taking a needle out of her arm. Blood drips out of the spot and he murmurs something to her. My stomach gets a bit queasy. I don't like seeing blood.*

*"Mother?" I call nervously.*

*Her head snaps over and her brows lift. "Malina, what are you doing up here?"*

*I skitter over and stop in front of her, watching as the mender quickly dabs at her arm, cleaning up the wound. "I will dispose of this, Your Majesty," he says, holding a big vial in his hand. "Try to rest today."*

*My eyes widen. "Is that your blood in there?"*

*"It's alright, darling," she says to me, distracting me from the vial before she turns back to the mender. "Thank you, Fyce."*

*He bows and then walks away, leaving the two of us alone.*

*"Why did he take your blood?" I ask anxiously. "Why are you crying?"*

*My mother looks pale and sad, and I don't like it at all.*

*"Come here," she says, patting her knee.*

*I jump up, but when she winces, I know I've hurt her, and it makes me want to cry. "What's wrong, Mother?"*

*She rocks me a little bit and rubs my back. "I've been feeling a little ill lately. The menders are helping, that's all."*

*"Ill?" I say, worried. "Like a tummy ache?"*

*"A little bit like that."*

*"Is that why you've been sleeping so much?"*

*She presses her finger into my side, making me ticklish. "Well, I've got to keep up with you! And you have so much energy, so I need to sleep extra long in the mornings," she teases.*

*My giggle from her tickling fades away as I look at her. "Are you going to be alright?"*

*"Yes, of course," she says before kissing me on the forehead.*

*"If your blood's no good, I could give you some of mine," I offer, holding out my arm. "Maybe it will give you some of my energy?"*

*She smiles, but her eyes go shiny. My bottom lip wobbles, because I worry I've said something wrong.*

*But Mother takes my offered arm and presses a kiss to the inside of my wrist. "Your blood is far more precious than mine, my darling."*

*"Your blood is important too!" I insist. "You're a queen!"*

*She taps a finger to the tip of my nose. "Ah, but you are a Colier by blood," she says before petting over my white hair. "And you will be queen one day."*

*I consider this. "Am I going to be tired too?"*

*Mother laughs, the sound filling up the atrium, but I chew on my lip nervously. When she notices, her expression softens. "Queens do get tired, but we push through."*

*I frown. "But why?"*

*She pauses for a moment, looking me over. "Do you remember how I've told you the stories about when you were a baby? When I would hold you all hours of the night because you wouldn't stop crying and you didn't want to be put down or be held by anyone other than me?"*

*"Yes."*

*"Being a mother to a baby is a bit like being a queen," she explains. "We have to care for others, we have responsibilities, and we have people who depend on us. We may be tired or sad or perhaps even ill, but a queen makes sure to take care of her people just as she'd take care of her baby."*

*I play with the frills at her collar. "I'm sorry I made you tired when I was a baby."*

*Maybe if I hadn't, she wouldn't be so tired and ill now.*

*"Don't be," she says with a smile as she brushes a warm hand across my cheek. "To be a queen and a mother is an honor. I give all that I can because I love this kingdom, and because I love you." She reaches down and squeezes my hand. Hers looks so strong and pretty next to my small and stubby*

*fingers. "One day, you'll be a queen and a mother, and you'll be far better at both than I am."*

*My eyebrows drop, because I can't imagine such a thing. "But you're a wonderful mother, and you're a perfect queen. Everyone says so. I don't think I could ever be as good as you."*

*A tear suddenly drops down her cheek, even though she's still trying to smile. It makes me want to cry too. I keep saying the wrong things. I'm not making her feel better at all.*

*"Ah, but you have this strong, precious Colier blood, remember?" she says, tracing a finger down the lines of the blue veins on my arm. "This will help you in both roles. You're going to be the greatest queen Highbell has ever seen."*

*"How do you know?" I ask nervously. I want it to be true, but I'm not sure I could ever be as good as she is. Everyone loves her.*

*Mother cups my face with both hands, her gray eyes looking between each of mine. "Because unlike me, you were born for this. You're going to be exactly what this kingdom needs, Malina, because it's in your blood."*

*She kisses me on the hand and then settles me back onto the ground. "Now run back down and return to your lessons before your poor scholar walks himself into a limp looking all over for you."*

*I nod reluctantly. "Are you sure you're alright?"*

*Mother gives me a little smile. "Of course I am, darling."*

She died four months later.

That memory blows out as quickly as it sparked. A brief flash, gone in a blink. Tears coat my cheeks, freezing with the frigid air. My mother was wrong. I wasn't a great queen for Highbell. I didn't become what it needed.

I became its downfall.

Yet despite my failures, I *do* have the right blood. So now, I need to use it to right the wrong I committed when I willingly let this bridge be remade. Perhaps, by doing this, I can *finally* be who she believed I would be. Who I should have been from the start.

By standing here and giving Orea my everything. By giving the bridge one last offering.

An offering of blood. And willingness.

Because that is what the twins meant. They gave me the answer through their mockery. It's what the bridge represents, and that monumental knowing has given me crystal-clear clarity, even here, within the veiled air.

Down the bridge, distant wind churns the fog. Down in my chest, my heart drips.

I swallow past the lump in my throat and then lift the dagger, but my hand shakes so badly that I can't hold it still.

Tears leak from my eyes, and my teeth chatter. My body has finally thawed enough to feel the chill, only for me to stand here and freeze. To let the warmth I've earned drain right back out.

Such a sad thought.

"Malina!"

I flinch in surprise as Dommik appears out of the thick fog like a wraith. His eyes are wild, hood thrown back, face full of fear.

"What are you doing?" he shouts, and I notice he's covered in blood spatter. That he's probably had to fight his way through to get to me.

"You shouldn't be here, Dommik!" I yell desperately.

"Let's go!" He tries to take my arm, to pull me away, but I don't budge. "What are you doing?" he demands again.

I hate hearing the panic in his voice. The terrified confusion.

Swallowing hard, I look him in the eye. "I can't go, Dommik."

"What the fuck do you mean?" he growls out.

"Blood matters," I say urgently, except how could I begin to explain? Yet I have to, because now he's followed me here and I have to tell him the truth.

So I do. With heavy words that stack up only to weigh me down.

"It *has* to be me."

His eyes flare as they search for answers in mine. Answers I tried to shield him from. But it seems I can't hide from an assassin who travels in shadows.

"This is what was wrong. When I asked you before," he says, piecing it together. "What did those fae tell you? They're tricking you, Malina!"

His body is tense and poised, his survival instincts spiking. I can see he wants to rush, to run. I can see that he thinks there's still a chance for that.

But he doesn't understand yet. This was the bridge to nowhere.

Until a girl willingly walked it and went into a different realm. Until a fae came and bound the worlds together, because the two of them, Orean and fae, willed it so. Because a different fae then willed it to break. And because I willed it to repair.

"*Willingness*," I say thickly, trying to make him understand. "Willingness has always been the price for the bridge."

"Malina, please. Let's get off this bridge. Let's go and talk about this…"

I shake my head and grip his hand firmly. "It has to be me," I say again, tone pleading with him to understand. "The moment I willingly gave my Orean blood to repair what the fae had broken, the bridge's life…tied to mine."

He gapes at me, blood draining from his face.

I swallow hard, unable to stop my tears as they fall, as my hand shakes where it grips him. "But I can end it, Dommik. Not block it. Not break it. I can *undo* it."

His eyes widen as understanding fills his face. "No…" he says, shaking his head in denial. "We could…we could win. We could beat them back. If King Rot returns, maybe—"

"It doesn't matter," I say, cutting him off. "It doesn't matter if today, or even a hundred years from now, we manage to win. Unless we end it for good, history will always repeat itself. Even if we lived centuries in peace, that peace would fail just like it did before. Eventually, fae and Orean will always clash."

"Malina."

This utter grief in his voice is laced with his terror. It consumes me. Threatens to topple me. But I hold firm. Give him the smallest smile, even as my blue eyes pour.

"It's alright," I murmur. "I'm finally going to be the queen that Orea needs me to be."

Moisture runs through his gaze.

"So, please," I breathe, voice trembling. "I need you to go."

But the stubborn man shakes his head. "I'm not leaving you."

A sob breaks my throat. Shatters my tongue.

Down the bridge, a joined roar erupts and shakes the dirt I stand on, screaming out its threat. It fills me with terror. With determination.

I raise the dagger to my chest as tears drip off my face, and I hear my mother's words. *You're going to be exactly what this kingdom needs, Malina, because it's in your blood.*

This time, I can give *Orea* my blood. This time, I won't fail.

With wet, burning eyes, I look straight at Dommik and I plead. "I wish you'd go," I cry, my hand shaking so badly I can't keep the dagger lined up with my heart. "I wish you'd *live*."

He lets out a choked breath before he reaches up to hold my face. Runs a thumb across my cheek. Kisses me softly.

"I'm your assassin, remember? I'm in charge of your death. So if it has to be you, then it has to be me too, Queenie," he says quietly. Heartbreakingly.

Then he reaches up and steadies my shaking hand, his fingers curling over mine where I'm gripping the hilt. "You don't have to face death without me. You don't have to go alone."

Despair flows past my thawed heart and drains out into the gray.

The outside world is closing in. I can feel the bridge vibrate with thousands of footsteps. The fog no longer able to muffle the roars of Orea's impending peril.

There's no more time.

My whole body quakes. When I glance down at the dagger with terror, Dommik takes my chin and makes me look back up at him.

His dark eyes make everything else disappear.

"It's only us. Just a Cold Queen and an assassin," he says quietly, and my throat squeezes.

"I wish we could've had longer together," I whisper brokenly.

He brushes the hair away from my face tenderly and stares into my fracturing eyes. "But we will have death together, and that is endless."

Heartache drowns me. Makes my words a hitching rasp. "I love you, Dommik."

His gaze bores in. "You own my heart, Malina."

We shiver beneath our shaken confessions.

The fog starts to dissipate, like it's being forced to pull back. From the corner of my eye, I see them. The monstrous fae come to spread their evil.

"They can't touch us," Dommik murmurs, gaze unwavering, touch calm and still. "Keep looking at me."

I nod, and then I let the terror exhale away. Let my mind go still. Because I am exactly where I need to be. Where I want to be.

*Willingness.*

"I'm ready."

I close my eyes with a sigh. I hear Dommik suck in a sob.

And then, with my assassin's help, I push the blade straight into my heart.

It pierces, cold and utterly agonizing.

The most fatal pain I could ever comprehend.

My breath yanks out of me. Eyes flare open as I rip the dagger back out.

The fatal pain storms. Icicle shards pouring out with the puncture. Damning damage of my life left to flood.

Time stops with my frantic gaze. Frost gathering at my lids and lips. Words caught in an icicle throat while snow flakes from my skin.

I stare at Dommik with wide eyes…and I feel my organ begin to fail.

Last beats, beating for my people. To do this *one* thing right.

To be exactly what my kingdom needs.

My knees crash to the ground, and my blood spills over the gray bridge. It hisses and steams on impact, even as shards of ice fall from my palms.

Dommik goes down onto his knees with me. Tears running down his dappled face. Then he wraps his hand around mine where I'm still holding the dagger, and he plunges it into his heart too.

When the roaring fae are only feet away, when my blood has soaked the surface and Dommik takes his last breath, the bridge suddenly *explodes*.

It shatters like ice. Obliterating in a blink.

The bridge doesn't break this time. It *unmakes*.

It's blaring and blinding. Light and mist and sound and void—all of it erupting out and sucking in.

Dommik and I are thrown off the gray surface that no longer exists. Leaving life behind with the final drops of our unbeating hearts.

With the last spot of vision, with our bodies wrapped tightly around each other, Dommik and I fall into the void.

Into the death.

*Willingly*.

As shadow and freeze, we embrace it together.

Then, the bridge is no more.

And neither...

are we.

# CHAPTER 57

## COMMANDER RYATT

The army of fae rushes in for attack, and the sound is deafening.

Movement next to me has me turning, and I'm shocked as Lu comes up beside me. Osrik too. Digby and Rissa on Argo. A dozen Second soldiers just behind. King Thold and a few of his men. We tighten into formation, readying ourselves.

One. Last. Stand.

With blood and sweat and pain and rage and defiance. We stand here, when we know it's going to be a slaughter.

Lu, Osrik, and I share a glance. It's heavy. It's fucking *wrong*. Because Judd isn't with us. He should be standing here with a shit-eating smirk on his face, ready to throw himself into the battle and lift our spirits all at the same time.

But he's not standing. He's lying on the ground somewhere, gone where Wrath can't reach.

So even though the fae are charging, shouting, ready to swing the final blade of death, we stand tall.

I'm going to be cut down, but I'm going to take these fae down with me—as many of them as I can.

"For Judd," I say as I grip my sword, muscles tensed and ready.

Lu and Osrik both nod. "For Judd."

We face forward, weapons in hand, and our Wrath charges toward Death.

But before we can reach the front lines, a booming sound rips through the land. Like the side of a mountain breaking free and toppling. Like an entire city's worth of buildings crashing down all at once.

Everyone stops, Orean and fae alike, looking around in shock.

When my gaze lands on the source, my eyes go wide. My heart stops pumping. Because the fog around the bridge of Lemuria suddenly parts, like something in the air *swells*. Shoves.

For a moment, this force, whatever it is, sucks away all the thick fog that was obscuring the bridge, clearing it for view. At the far end, I can see fae soldiers in blood-red armor. But at the middle are two figures. Not soldiers—I can see that even from this distance.

As I squint, trying to see who it is, trying to figure out what's happening, the bridge suddenly bursts.

I thought the sound before was loud, but no, this explosion is *deafening*.

World-altering.

The fog, the air, the land, the void, it all seems to rupture in one cataclysmic event. The entire earth shakes. The skies above thunder. Fatal magic fractures the realm.

I'm knocked to the ground, right along with everyone else. Lu and I land beside each other, and we share a stunned look.

"The bridge just fucking exploded..." she breathes out.

"It can't have," I blurt, even though I know it's nothing more than pure denial bullshit.

Because it can.

It fucking *has*.

Then the shaking stops and seems to settle. I look around, thoughts spinning. "We—"

I was wrong. It's not settling. It was just the inhale before the blow.

The land where the bridge was starts to give way. With booming cracks, the ground begins sucking down into the void, like it can no longer stay up. Like whatever force just destroyed the bridge is going to destroy the land too.

The stone castle starts to crumble, and in a second, disappears entirely in a rush of dust and snow.

I blink in shock, mouth gaping, fear galloping through my chest.

It's like I'm watching an invisible mouth gnawing at the earth's crust, biting it off chunk by chunk. And it's spreading. *Fast*.

Osrik suddenly bellows, "*Run!*"

It snaps me out of my stupor.

Lu and I leap to our feet, and we turn and start sprinting, just as the whole fae army tries to do the same. Everyone runs, screaming as the earth breaks away. There's nothing but pure panic in our shared consciousness, as if we've become one giant herd.

"Digby!" Osrik roars, and I look over as Digby launches Judd's timberwing in the air with Rissa clutched in front of him.

Rissa screams, reaching down for Osrik, horror on her face and his name wrenched from her lips.

But they fly up, just as more timberwings scatter. "We need a bird!" I shout, but the beasts are panicked, some taking off without a rider.

We have none to get on.

The threat of mortal danger licks at our backs like frenzied flames, singeing us with the promise of our own peril.

Snow and fog churns from the earth that rips away, the collapsing land polluting the air with the ghost of the ground. My lungs burn, my heart feeling like it's going to burst, but I keep running as everyone else flees too.

But I hear it closing in on us. Hear hundreds of screaming fae start to succumb to the fall.

The rumbling gets louder...closer. The ground shaking harder.

"We're not gonna make it!" Lu shouts desperately at my side.

It has to fucking stop. It won't just keep disintegrating all of Seventh Kingdom—all of fucking Orea...will it?

The bridge is obliterated, but what if it obliterates everything else too? What if there *is* nowhere to run?

Fear cuts into my heart and starts draining me dry.

The land just behind me starts giving way. People fall in. Terror overwhelms me when I feel the ground beneath my own boots start sinking.

This is fucking it. This is it. This is—

Lu trips.

I spin to catch her, hand snatching at her arm as she falls with the dropping land. Her body jolts as I catch her, but the ground cracks beneath my feet, the snow giving way for me too, and our eyes meet in horrified acceptance.

And then. It...stops.

I stand frozen while Lu hangs over churning air, held up only by my grip.

I pant, eyes wide, staring past her down to the abyss. The void swirls with fog and snow and darkness, carrying the echoing screams of thousands who've fallen.

It's like I'm in a dream, or a daze. I can't move. I just keep staring.

"Pull me up!" Lu screams frantically. "Ryatt! Snap out of it and *pull me the fuck up*!"

I blink and wrench my attention to her. But I'm scared to fucking move, scared the ground beneath me will crumble if I dare.

"*Ryatt!*" Lu yells again.

Osrik appears beside me. With his massive strength, he bands an arm around me and hauls me back, while simultaneously reaching down to fling Lu up and over.

I fall backwards a couple of feet away, while Lu lands in a heap beside me. Osrik hurries over and yanks us back to our feet and we all back away.

My pulse is on a rampage, breath panting as I look out at the landscape. Or…what *used* to be a landscape.

Seventh Kingdom looks like a split seam. Where the bridge was, the ground has torn away in a line, stretching all the way to where we stand. The void has made a V, stolen the bridge, the castle, maybe a couple miles' worth of land across the edge.

The seam grew narrower as it reached toward us, but it still extends with a quarter of a mile gap right here at its end. Seventh's land stretches precariously to my left and right, and I see just how fucking lucky Lu and I are. We were a step away from being sucked down into the void.

Just like all the fae soldiers were.

"Fucking hell," Lu pants beside me, her hands visibly shaking. She glances over. "Thanks for catching me."

I nod numbly, and she looks at Osrik. "Thanks for pulling me up, Os."

He doesn't reply. He's searching the sky, watching the circle of timberwings. Some are chasing down the riderless birds, snatching up their reins to bring them back.

I turn and look at everyone on the ground, counting heads, finding faces. There are too fucking few. We walk further away from the edge and gather together, and I start cataloging everyone as the timberwings land and we all converge.

Digby with Rissa. King Thold, but I only see two of his soldiers with him, and both are bloodied, their green-clad armor

545

stained with spatter. Queen Kaila lands with a dozen soldiers of her own. I count only twelve men from Second, some of whom are grievously wounded. No fae stand with us.

My chest hammers like it's being pelted with hail. "Judd…" My voice is thick, my jaw tight.

Lu meets my eyes, hers red-rimmed as she shakes her head and says the most devastating words. "He died in my arms." Her voice is broken, misery punching straight through.

He died, and then his body fell into the void. We don't even have his fucking body to bury. Osrik lets out a roar of anguish, knees hitting the ground, head hanging in fury and grief as his fist hits the snow.

Misery and shame strangle me.

Judd died because he was saving me. Cutting me off that timberwing because I was stuck. It would've been my chest that sword had stabbed through if he hadn't come over to help.

And now he's dead. Gone. Fallen away with the disintegrated land.

Rissa rushes over to Osrik and kneels with him, arms wrapping around his bulk, her head nestling against his side.

Emotion thickens in my throat.

"It's over…" Queen Kaila says from the back of her beast. Her face is pale. Eyes haunted, but her voice holds hope. "The bridge is gone—our worlds severed. The fae have actually been *defeated*."

King Thold's grim face looks at the broken land, at the wounded soldiers. "At great sacrifice."

The threat of the fae, the one thing that was driving me forward, has been wiped out in sudden seconds. Yet while the others are reeling with bittersweet relief, I'm just reeling.

Yes, the fae are defeated. Yes, Orea is safe.

But…the bridge is gone.

Which means there's no way for Slade, or my mother, or Auren to come *back*.

# CHAPTER 58

## SLADE

The moment my dragon's wing snaps, I jolt with excruciating pain that radiates down my arms. The sensation steals my breath and overloads my mind. I'm stuck in shock for a moment as we begin to plummet from the sky.

The ground rushes up faster and faster as my dragon roars in agony, but at the last moment, I manage to take hold of the spike in front of Auren to brace around her.

"Hold on!" I shout.

Through strained eyes, I see her hands flash out, and then gold pours from them. Somehow, she manages to break our fatal fall as we crash into the front of Glassworth's courtyard, her magic sloshing between us and helping to soften the landing.

Our bodies knock together in the teeth-jarring crash. The dragon bears the brunt of the collision, and even with Auren's gold, the fall still stuns it. Stuns *me*.

I don't know exactly how the manifestation magic works between creature and keeper. I have no idea if it can actually die or not. But it's very fucking clear that it can feel pain and that *I* can feel echoes of that pain too.

The face of the palace glares down at us through hundreds of different stained glass windows. Right before we started to fall, Auren tried to warn me that these aren't Stone Swords gathered, and she's right. The soldiers rushing over are clad in black and red.

Apprehension grabs hold of me as I realize who they are. Who they serve.

My father.

Rage sparks to life and starts ranting against my ribs.

I grasp Auren and then leap us both off the back of my dragon, my boots splashing in the liquid gold as I set her down.

"Great Divine," Auren chokes out, looking horrified at the grotesque break in the dragon's wing.

When the soldiers start to surround us, the dragon tries to stand, but before it can, its back leg suddenly breaks too.

The sound of the bone is like a snapped tree, and the courtyard echoes with it. The dragon roars out in agony, and I stumble against Auren as that ripple of pain goes through me. I gasp, knowing my father is doing this, and I whip my head around, but I can't see him. The fucking coward is *hiding*.

Auren cries out with alarm as she braces me to keep me from falling.

I grit my teeth and push past the pain and make my rot surge out, hooking it into the nearest soldiers in a wave of wrath that attacks them from the ground up.

Out of nowhere, a net falls over my dragon's head, and I whirl. The beast bellows with its own fury at suddenly being held down, and its sharp teeth try to snap at the bindings.

But the net is too strong; it doesn't so much as fray a

single cord. And the corners are somehow secured to the ground, not allowing the dragon to rip it up and get free.

I lurch forward and try to yank it off too, but I can't. Something is keeping it down. I try to let the dragon dematerialize back into me, but that doesn't work either. It remains solid and trapped.

My limbs pulse with furious adrenaline.

Auren starts flooding her magic out at the same time that my rage expels from me. Rot cracks through the ground, ready to kill everyone here, when I see the flash of a shadow. I whip my head up, eyes widening when I see another net—the same kind on my dragon—suddenly dropping over *our* heads.

I snarl, my hands flinging forward to push Auren out of the way. She stumbles out of its trajectory a second before it crashes over me and takes me to my knees.

I try to stand, try to tear it off, but the gray bindings aren't rope or fabric. The net is made from something else less pliant, something with grains that move beneath the clear overlays, making my skin itch. A strange weight presses over me that makes my muscles strain and my chest flare with panic.

"Slade!" Auren yells, her tone cracking with alarm.

She leaps back to her feet and races to my side to try and tear the webbing off with her hands and her ribbons, but she can't. It's holding me down as much as the other net holds my dragon.

When she realizes she can't physically remove it, Auren lets magic flow from her instead. But the molten metal slips right off like beads of oil over water.

"I can't gild it," she exclaims, her eyes wide. "I can't gild it!"

My rot isn't affecting it either, nor can my power spread past it, no matter how fucking hard I try. The ground beneath me won't soak in with rot.

This net isn't just holding me down. It's suppressing my

magic too. Which means it's also suppressing my dragon's. My father is stripping me of my strength and my power all at once.

Crippling fear pummels me, stealing the breath from my chest.

Gritting my teeth, I try to straighten, but I can't stretch up past my knees. There's not enough give for me to stand. I'm trapped beneath this thing like a rabbit in a snare, and still, my father won't show his cowardly fucking face.

Fury catches hold like an inferno, burning straight through me.

My eyes flash around at the soldiers. One of them must be responsible for using magic to hold down these nets, but they're being discreet enough that I can't pick out who it is.

Auren whirls, no doubt having the same thought about someone controlling them. She sends her gold at the soldiers, gilding them where they stand, freezing every organ and muscle and trapping them within the gleam. Her magic sludges out and spreads past the first lines.

But a scream gushes out from the palace doors.

I whip my head in that direction while Auren whirls, and there stands my mother.

Looking pale and terrified, her wide green eyes shine with fear. She's trussed up like a hunter's kill, bound with ropes and being held at sword point.

Her gaze connects with mine, and I see the clarity there. Clarity like I haven't seen in her face for so long. As if she remembers everything, mind whole and intact, and not the muddled mess she became after falling through the rip. It's cruel that these are the circumstances in which she'd be fully coherent.

"Elore!" Auren shouts.

She starts to rush toward my mother but only takes a single step before I see her leg suddenly *snap*. Just like the dragon's, I hear the bone breaking a second before she crumples to the ground with a scream.

My bellow of terror rips my throat raw. "*Auren*!"

Her scream cuts directly into my heart. It claws down our bond, pushing every feral fae instinct in me to get to her. To protect her.

I roar rabidly against my restraints, pumped full of fury.

All of this, from the moment we crashed to right now, has only been a matter of seconds. Just seconds, when everything went from right to utterly wrong.

Now, Auren's hurt, my mother is in danger, my dragon is pinned and in agony, and I'm fucking powerless and *trapped*.

Catching movement, my gaze flicks up, and my father appears, stepping out from the doorway of the palace.

He stops next to my mother, and she flinches at his nearness, which makes my blood *boil*.

Just as Auren told me, he wears an eye patch, and instead of being completely bald, he has a thin layer of hair on his head. But other than that, he looks just as I remember.

Fucking evil.

"Hello, son."

Teeth bared, I jerk toward him so I can rip him apart, but my surge of strength doesn't break me out of this net. My father's black gaze passes over me dispassionately before his attention latches onto my dragon. "Extraordinary," he says, his expression lighting up with an excitement I haven't seen in a very long time. Not since I first sprouted spikes when I was a boy.

From the ground, Auren struggles to shove her arms under her, making gold puddle between her palms upon the ground.

My stomach drops as I watch my father lift his hand.

"*No!*" I shout, heart beating wildly.

It's too late. He snaps his fingers, instantly breaking Auren's arm too.

Her wail of agony is like a blade to the heart. It steals my breath. My vision. Makes me and my trapped dragon both strain and fight against our bindings and roar even louder when we can't break free and get to her.

My father looks down at her from above. "We've been through this before, haven't we, pet?"

Pet? He dares to call her fucking *pet*?

My rage isn't red hot. It isn't ice cold. It's pitch black. Delved deeper than the pits of hell. Soaked in the ashes of death and the shadows of vengeance that are ready to devour.

Small bubbles of gold pop from beneath her palms where she lies on the ground, face twisted in pain.

"You try to attack me, I break you. It's quite simple," he tells her.

"*You won't break her.*" My voice comes out like a whip, snapping across his face.

He jerks his head to focus on me. He looks at me longer this time, studying me with the same cruel gaze as when I was a boy. Purposely trying to instill his dominance so that I would lower my eyes in fear.

But now, I stare back at him with pure, suffocating hate.

My body shakes with how hard I'm trying to exert my power. I want to kill him. Fucking rot his heart from his chest and make him writhe in agony. I want to rip him apart limb by limb and watch his blood sully the soil.

I push and push, straining to burst my magic free, but my rot only leaches a few inches past the netting, killing the grass in a circle around me.

"You've grown stronger," he muses, almost gratified. "I knew you had to be capable of manifesting. You were holding back all those years ago."

My jaw clenches like a wolf that wants to snap its opponent's neck between its teeth. My dragon is doing the same thing, eyes locked onto my father, growl scouring its throat.

"I saw her bond solidifying. Saw her using your rot," he says evenly, though his voice grates down my ears. "I knew you'd come for her. And then when she came here, when the king wanted to kill her, I saw that spot." He taps the back of his own neck, and my stomach drops in realization.

*He saw Auren's golden scale.*

"I knew what it meant," he says smugly as he gestures toward my dragon. "Your power is strong for your manifestation to bleed through into your bonded, but it showed me the truth. Showed me that you actually manifested one. And *look at it*," he says with a fanatic gleam in his eye as he watches the snarling creature. "Just as large and fierce as the first dragons of our blood, when Culls were kings of the skies."

"I'm going to crush your skull and piss on your fucking corpse," I snarl.

His eye narrows on me, and I feel sick satisfaction to know he only has use of the one. That for all these years, he's had to bear proof that I wounded him and rendered his other eye useless.

He snaps his fingers again, and I see Auren's finger snap unnaturally. This time when she screams, it cuts off as she slumps into unconsciousness, succumbing to the piling pain.

I roar as I lurch forward, teeth bared like an animal, but the net snags into me, not budging an inch.

My father smirks coldly. "Still unworthy and *weak*." Then he turns his head, looking at someone else. "Do it."

Several of his guards march forward. They pass their dead comrades, while I continue to fight against the net, muscles bunching, rage boiling through my black veins as my spikes surge up. "Don't fucking touch her!"

But the guards walk past Auren.

I tense as they head straight for my dragon. When it lets out a vicious growl at their nearness, several of them flinch away despite it being held down.

Still, they surround the beast while it snarls and spits. With its leg and wing broken, it lies partially on its uninjured side, breathing heavily, pupils dilated.

There is no lead-up. I have no idea what's about to happen. One of them just moves forward, and I don't notice the ax until it's buried in my dragon's chest.

The creature lets out a chilling, bone-grinding shriek. A sound full of agony and shock, one that blares through my head and snaps against my eardrums.

My entire body jerks with blinding pain.

Through tunneled vision, I see black blood seeping between its golden scales and streaking down the toughened exterior. The soldier yanks out the ax and then swings it down again in the same spot, hacking at my dragon's chest, trying to drive the blade in deeper.

Breath gasps out of me. Fucking chokes me. I feel blood crawling up the back of my throat, either phantom or real, I can't tell which. The pain that seeps from the dragon into me is enough to make me sway. My knuckles hit the ground, but I force myself not to fall in a heap or let bile spew from my throat.

"*Stop!*"

I snap my head up at Auren's shout and see her sitting up. She's melted down the armor on her chest to use it to shoot at my father. It streams toward him like a giant spear…

But he moves faster, quicker than a blink, and yanks it from the air.

Then, he takes the sharp weapon and stabs it right into my mother's stomach.

# CHAPTER 59

## SLADE

A hoarse bellow shreds my chest and tears through Auren's throat. I look on in helpless horror as my mother's face contorts with shock and pain, eyes swiveling down to look at the weapon stabbed into her.

This isn't fucking happening. This isn't—

Auren falls to the ground. "No! *No!*"

My mother crumples to her knees, blood draining from her face, blood spilling through the front of her dress in terrifying blotches.

"That was your fault," my father sneers at Auren. "Now you can either try to attack me or save Elore. Your choice."

My heart falls right through my stomach.

Then my attention cracks as the soldier lands another blow to my dragon, and it feels like my own chest is being cleaved open.

A pained snarl rends the air and shakes the ground,

bleating from the beast's throat as it thrashes. Its blood starts to heap onto the grass as soldiers rush forward and start ripping away gold-plated scales from its chest, like plucking leaves from a stem.

Adrenaline, pain, rage, and fear, it all floods me, my arms and hands so riddled with veins that I can't see the skin. Power tries to pump out, ready to rot the entire fucking world, but I'm rendered useless.

I snarl like a rabid animal as my father crouches next to Auren. When his hand wraps around her throat, my dragon and I rage. Fight. Even against the hacking at the beast's chest. Even as pain consumes and the net traps, we fucking rage because how *dare he touch her*.

"A broken-winged bird is *nothing* compared to a Cull dragon," he tells her. "Remember that. All winged creatures will bow to *me*. I'm looking forward to putting you in a pretty birdcage for all to see."

He tosses her aside, making her cry out before she tries to crawl toward my mother who's collapsed on the palace's steps.

My father is doing to Auren what he did to me as a child— breaking her bone by bone, emotion by emotion. Making her feel helpless. Powerless.

And he just threatened to *cage* her, just like Midas did.

Fury makes my spikes tremble. My breath heave.

I will tear his head from his *fucking spine*.

My father walks away while Auren drags herself toward my mother with the use of only one arm and one leg. Misery chokes me as I watch her pull herself forward, inch by painful inch. Stains of gold smear beneath her, her sobs a mix of agony and anger and fear.

And I'm trapped, unable to help. To get to them.

I have never felt so fucking helpless in all my life.

The dragon cries out again, and I look over with a stippled

consciousness, and I finally see what these soldiers were after. Why they've been hacking at it.

Its heart now lies open and vulnerable in its gaping chest. The black, beating organ wrapped with gilded veins.

My father's boots stop in front of me. I look up through the netting, meeting his cold, callous gaze. He stares at me where I'm crouched on my knees, knuckles dug into the deadened dirt, arms shaking, veins leaking.

"Still too weak," he says with a shake of his head. "This is why I knew as soon as you sprouted those spikes and scales that you could never be a true king, even with a dragon."

"You are already dead," I pant out with dark menace. With vicious promise. "The second you touched her. The second you hurt Auren and my mother, you were *done*."

"No, son. *You* are." He rolls up one of his sleeves and drags the dagger down his own arm, opening a vein.

"Culls cull the weak," he goes on. "*I* will be king of the skies. *I* will be king of Annwyn."

He crouches down in front of me then, his dark eye boring into mine as my mind spins. "I will take your dragon the same way our ancestors did when they knew another Cull didn't deserve the manifestation. And by doing so, I will finally divest you of your greatest weakness. Your heart."

I try to surge up, to launch myself at him, but I can't.

My dragon is dying, unable to even roar anymore. My mother bleeding, Auren threatened.

And I'm trapped. Fucking *trapped*.

His soldiers wait around my tortured dragon, while my father watches the blood seep from his arm before deigning to look back at me. "*Pour the heartblood of the ward and its dragon into the veins of the victor…and the victor shall manifest anew*," he intones, his expression eager. The words sound like he's repeated them thousands of times to himself.

Cold realization freezes me and makes my stomach roil.

This is what he'd always planned. This is why he pushed me so hard as a boy. He wanted me to manifest a dragon…so that he could murder me and take it for himself.

"You've finally fulfilled your purpose," he tells me with a biting edge.

From my peripheral, I see soldiers pinning down my dragon's feet. See one of them positioning a sword right in front of its pulsing heart, ready to pierce it through.

And then my father lifts his dagger and arcs it up, aiming it straight at my heart.

Terror freezes me.

Clamorous anguish rips through my soul as I realize I'm about to die. There's nothing I can do but watch the killing strike come for me.

I couldn't protect her. Couldn't save my mother. And now I'm going to be killed at the hand of my father.

And I'm helpless to fucking stop it.

My father's blade comes for my heart at the same time that the soldier starts to plunge his blade into my dragon's heart too.

My dragon *screams*.

It's a horrifying sound that fractures the air as the soldier's blade pierces into its organ. I feel our shared agony, and then I feel our connection sever.

Feel my dragon *die*.

My father's blade swings down.

A split second before my heart is pierced too, there's a flash of gold.

With the help of her ribbons, Auren suddenly flings herself in front of me.

And I watch in horror as the blade meant for me stabs into *her* chest instead.

She cries out, body slamming into me as the weapon sinks fully in, her ribbons collapsing. I lurch up and catch her clumsily through the net, holding her jerking body as shock courses through me.

I can't breathe.

I can't fucking breathe.

I can't fucking—

"*You useless nuisance*," my father grinds out with aggravation. He grabs Auren and tears her away from me, tossing her aside like she's nothing, when she is fucking *everything*.

When he flings her viciously away, it makes the edge of my net lift. Just an inch.

But it's *enough*.

I exploit that single second of weakness, and my power blasts out like an eruption.

My rot seeps past the net's edge, and as soon as I have a foothold, the soil dissolves. Latching onto that gap with a frantic grip, I shove my hand under the weakened space.

Instantly, I feel my power strengthen, surging up from the breach.

The net can't pin me down anymore. My pulse blares in my ears as I tear it off before tossing it away. Its absence is like surging out from the ground after being buried alive.

My father doesn't even have time to blink.

I lunge and have him by the throat in an instant. Rot pours into his body, trapping him in rancid rage. My fury dominates every other thought as my hatred floods into him with vicious intent.

I rot his hands from his wrists, making the skin wither, the muscles melt, both limbs falling off to the ground. He screams in pain and tries to grapple at my hold, but his feet can't touch the ground, and he can no longer call up his power at the snap of his fingers.

I seethe into his face with bared teeth and dark hostility. Within my shaking, wrathful hold, his skin molders and greens, peeling away in painful strips. His teeth go black. His one good eye widens in fear as black veins leach into the white.

I fucking told him. He was done. He was *dead*.

There's so much savagery in me that his soldiers can't do a thing. They fall as one, starting with the one who stabbed my dragon's heart. I rot him through first, making him gasp with decomposing lungs as poisoned blood pours from his every orifice.

The other soldiers try to run, but their bones fester and crumble, death taking them to the ground with choked-off screams.

I squeeze my father's throat, trying to squeeze out every fucking inch of fear and pain that he's capable of. I want him to feel it. To suffer. To die in agony and terror.

"Culling the weak," I snarl as his tongue dries out, the blackened husk breaking off. "You spineless, heartless, evil *piece of shit*. May you rot for fucking eternity and know that you are *nothing*."

His breath spills out with the shit and piss that seeps from his festering body. The last of his skin flakes away and his bones begin to decay. His nose shrinks into his skull, while muffled, tongueless screams scrape up his shredding throat as his useless heart blackens with its final beats.

I drop him to the ground, and his one eye follows me even as the lids peel back. Then I put one boot over his splintering skull, and I *stomp*. I grind his death into the yellowed soil like a killing sacrifice given to the land. Letting Annwyn soak up his poison, letting it digest him down so it can rid this world of him completely. Until he is nothing but dust and ash to forever be consumed by the earth.

I shake all over with fury. With hate. My body heaving with it.

And then, I hear her.

The smallest gasp that blares past my pounding rage and stabs me through.

In an instant, the violence and savagery is replaced with panic.

I spin around and run to Auren's side, instantly kneeling next to her, horror slashing through my insides and making my eyes go wide.

She's lying in a heap, with golden blood circling around her like a leaking star. The dagger is still pinned into her chest. Her eyes are wide as I pick her up to cradle her in my arms, my soul raging with defiance. With denial.

With utter fucking despair.

"Why did you do that?" I sob out. "You shouldn't have done that. It should've been *me*."

Auren's gaze swings up to me, and her face crumples. Her ribbons jerk around the ground like writhing rays of fallen sunlight. "Slade...I'm s-sorry."

Misery wraps its hold around my throat and squeezes.

"No," I say.

One word, over and over again. Over and over.

Over and over.

No, don't be sorry.

No, don't let this be happening.

No, don't take her from me.

*No.*

"No, baby," I cry as I press my lips against her clammy forehead even as her head lolls.

I'm in shock. Shaking all over with it. Unable to stop this.

Gold blood seeps out, her heart clogging with every labored beat. "You're okay," I tell her, my voice fucking ravaged. "You're okay."

No.

But her bottom lip wobbles and she shakes her head. Admitting what I can't.

*No.*

Her aura is fading. Her lips paling, pulse slowing. With wild desperation, I look around, as if I can do something—*anything*—to make this not happen.

*This can't fucking happen.*

My mother crouches beside me. Her wound is plugged with gold, hand held over the spot, her face tracked with tears.

"Help her," I plead.

To her, to Annwyn, to the goddesses. *Anybody.*

Help her.

"Slade…" Auren whispers, and my eyes lock on hers. My heart locked on too. "I…love you."

Her ribbons drift against my arms limply. Barely able to hold themselves up.

"You can't leave," I plead again, but this time, to her.

Because she is the only prayer I ever needed answered.

But her aura darkens more. The black tendrils muting, her shining gold fading. I want to wrap my fist around it and keep it here. Keep it glowing. But I can't.

I *can't.*

My heart is breaking while hers bleeds out.

And there's nothing I can do about it. No trick with rot could ever make her heart repair. I am death—not life.

She is life, and yet…she's dying. Right here in my arms.

Auren looks so scared. So forlorn, and I *hate* it. I have to help her. My pair bond demands that I save her, but all I can do is hold her and try to take away her fear.

Try to protect her in the only way I still can.

"I have to tell you something," I say.

My hands stroke her sweat-slicked hair away from her face, my tone urging her to keep looking at me.

When her eyes focus again, my thumb drags across her wet cheek, though I can't stop my fingers from shaking. "I knew you were my pair even without your aura."

Her brow furrows and she blinks slowly, like she's trying to hold on to my words.

Trying to hold on to her life.

And I need her to, because I fucking need *her*.

"I knew you were mine the second I laid eyes on you. Because someone told me. Someone who hasn't spoken to me ever since," I explain, my confession rattled and grieved. "One word. One single word. Spoken from the lips...of my mother."

Auren's eyes widen ever so slightly.

When I ripped the world and brought my mother with me to Orea, I think I tore her in half just as much as I tore myself. Because she stopped speaking. Her voice went mostly mute. Her mind, mostly muddled.

But it was there and then, beside a poisoned rip, in a foreign cave, where she said the last word she's ever spoken to me.

Just one.

I had been pressing a cool cloth to her fevered forehead, trying to care for her after how sick she became from traveling through the rip. When suddenly, her hand snatched out and gripped my wrist with surprising strength, fingernails digging into my skin.

When I met her gaze, I saw how her green irises disappeared and were replaced with churning milky pools caught in a sightless stare. Saw an ancient scrawl drag across them, the language indecipherable, the size far too small.

That milky gaze held me hostage, and then she opened her mouth and spoke a single word, in a voice that was not entirely her own.

*"Goldfinch."*

That one word, torn from a diviner's lips. And right now, it's pulled from my own mouth and laid at Auren's feet like an offering.

I was fifteen years old when I first heard it, and back then, that word meant nothing to me. It frustrated me. Confused me. It was a word I agonized over. A word I tried to ask my mother about over and over again, to no avail.

But then…after twenty years, I found the meaning.

Found what was foretold.

Auren's breaths saw out of her as I brush away another tear and swallow hard. "With skin of gold and wearing feathers of a finch, I knew right then that you were mine. I realized what that divined word had meant," I tell her, emotion cracking through my constricted throat. "While I was broken and ripped and utterly lost, my mother gifted me with the promise of *you*, Auren. The promise of my päyur."

A tear stabs through the corner of my eye and slices down my cheek, while Auren's eyes overflow. Love and misery carried in each drop and drowning out my existence.

"My foretelling, my life's prophecy, my purpose, my divined was *you*," I choke out. "Always you."

A sob bubbles up with blood that gilds her paling lips.

"Goldfinch," I murmur miserably before I gently place my lips at her cheek, fingers still cradling her face.

Trying to cradle her fading soul.

"You were always mine, and I was always meant to love you with every single part of my existence."

Always.

She weeps as she bleeds. I rock as I hold her. And still, I plead *no*.

*Please, no.*

Auren looks up at me with heartbreak, her expression in agony. "We…we won't g-get our *one days*, Slade," she says with anguish.

My heart fucking disintegrates, but I manage to shake my head. I curl around her, offering her shivering body every ounce of warmth I have.

"Yes we will, baby," I rasp out as I stroke her tortured expression. "Don't you remember? *I will find you in any life.* So just wait for me, okay?" My breath snaps off, but I force my voice to keep working. "I will find you wherever you go, and we will have endless *one days* of happiness. Won't we? Won't we, Auren?"

She nods, though we both know the truth.

No.

Her failing body is fraught with a sob. With heartbreak. With fractured despair.

And I rage against it, but still, the veil of death comes.

"I love you, Goldfinch. In every life," I choke out, my tears falling onto her cheek.

"I love you…in them…all," she says back, her voice a struggled whisper. A shaken breath.

Then her golden eyes close, her aura goes dark, her ribbons fall, and her heart beats no more. Her pulse silences, right beneath my grip.

And my mother opens her mouth and speaks one single word just as my soul shatters.

*"Goldfinch."*

# CHAPTER 60

## SLADE

The world has gone gray.

I have gone numb.

And Auren has gone *still*.

My hands stroke her face, though she no longer feels my touch. My lips press against her eyes, though she no longer cries. My arms cradle her body against mine, though she no longer trembles with cold.

I bury my face against her neck, my tears soaking against her pulse that no longer thrums. Inhaling her scent that's now tinged with the sharp pull of blood. Wrap my fingers around her ribbons that no longer twist.

But I hold her.

Gently. Desperately. Wretchedly.

I thought I knew what it meant to be torn apart when my two sides separated. But no.

No.

This is what it feels like.

To have your soul ripped in half.

My päyur bond has been cut. Like scissors to thread, both pieces left to float in a colorless sea. Drifting further and further away from one another, every wave and gentle lap separating us even more.

I don't know how long I kneel upon the ground with her. I hear nothing but the silence of her body, see nothing but her motionless form.

My mother speaks no more, but I didn't expect her to. That one word seems to be the only thing she's ever able to tell me. The first time, it was my divined promise.

This time, it's my fatal devastation.

She's clutching the wound at her stomach, but then her hand moves to my back. My mother's touch is the only thing that makes me aware of anything else other than Auren. Her tense fingers alert me a second before Wick and a group of Vulmin appear in the courtyard.

"Auren?" Wick calls out. The heavy silence that follows turns his tone urgent. "*Auren*!"

He runs, halting beside her, knees hitting the ground. "No…"

Other Vulmin gather behind him, and I hear their punctuated shock and grief that seems to drive holes through my tattered remains.

I don't turn to look. Don't speak. All my attention stays on her.

My focus will always be her.

"We saw the dragon fall… We brought a healer," Wick says thickly, and one of the Vulmin comes rushing forward.

My mother flinches, but the person gently murmurs something and then puts her hand on the wound. Red shadows drift in, like the magic is sifting through the ghost of the blood my mother has lost.

When the healer pulls away, my mother's face is not quite so pale. Her hands no longer shaky. The two of us share a look, green eyes colliding, knotted together from this horrific scene.

Inside, I'm still denying it all. Still pleading *no*.

But the sky is draped with gray clouds, Auren's aura has gone out like a flame, and I'm left with this gaping rip down my entire being, because she's *gone*.

Gone, and taken all of the light with her.

There's nothing but darkness left.

My dragon lies dead behind me. Its black heart stabbed through with a sword and no longer beating. Decaying corpses pollute the courtyard. My father's disintegrated body still oozes.

And suddenly, I don't want Auren anywhere near this. The dead bodies of the soldiers—my evil, festering father— they don't deserve to be in the same space as her. In this same atmosphere.

I have to take her away from this place. Far away. So I pick her up and I turn from Glassworth Palace, and then, I start to walk.

I don't know where I'm going. I don't care. I'm just following this incessant need to carry Auren away. As if putting distance between her and the place where she was killed will somehow make the claws of death recede from her, to force her from its clutches.

Or maybe I just want to take her from the land that has so utterly betrayed her. The land that let her be stolen away and then let her blood soak the soil when she returned.

I leave behind the death at the palace's courtyard. Trail down the long slope from the plateau. Avoid the river. Bypass the road that forks off toward Lydia.

My gaze stays straight ahead while I keep Auren's body cradled in my arms. Her head is tucked against my shoulder, ribbons gathered at her lap, some of the lengths fallen down to stream below.

People follow.

First, it's just my mother, plus Wick and the other Vulmin from the courtyard. But as we pass Lydia, more join us from the city. They see me carrying Auren, and the whispers and gasps and sobs pull them onto the road. They join in the march, like communing in a parade of a public death rite.

Everyone falls into the fray, walking behind me, keeping a respectful distance. Their quiet crying and steady footsteps are the chorus of a somber song.

My gaze shifts down to Auren's face. I could almost believe she's only sleeping, if I weren't so in tune with her. But I am, so I feel her absence through every thought, every blink, every breath.

When my heart nearly burst with poison and killed me, I thought that was the end. I thought that was the worst thing that could ever happen.

I was wrong.

This—*this* is the worst. For the breeze to still flow and for steps to still tread, and for the world to just keep on going after she's ended.

For me to still live, while she's dead in my arms.

I don't want it. I don't want this life if I can't share it with her.

Thick, horrific emotion clobbers my heart as I look back up at the road. I know I'm in shock, know that numbness hasn't released me from its grip, and I don't want it to. Because I know what follows will be something I can't bear.

The reality that I exist in a world where she does not.

I clutch her tighter against me, long after the sun sets and night clutches us in its grip, and still, I walk.

When Auren came here, she had to remember who she was. But I've always known exactly who she is. Light and life. Love and warmth. A gleaming vibrancy that I never deserved but never would have given up. She is mine and I am hers, for all of eternity.

In every life.

But in this one, she has been taken from me.

And it's my fault.

If only I had been stronger when I was young. If only I had snuck into my father's bedchamber one night while he slept, and rotted him through. If only I'd been faster, more powerful today, been able to kill him before he could hurt her.

Instead, the person I hated the most...killed the one I love the most.

The severed pair bond keeps tearing me to shreds. Crevices spreading, gouging, deepening into the pits of my innermost self. All while the song of the grieving follows me.

I failed her.

My shame clings. Sticking to my breaths with hot blame and fusing with my every thought. A paired should never fail their bonded, and yet, I have. Fatally so. I tore the world open and made her come here alone and unprotected.

Every bad thing has happened because my rip brought her here in the first place.

Maybe that's why I realize I'm walking toward the bridge. I blame Annwyn as much as I blame myself. This land and I, we were supposed to be her home.

Instead, we became her end.

I walk us through the deadlands, realizing they were a terrible omen right from the start. And when the long night gives way to a weak, gray morning, I still don't stop.

None of the other fae do either. They continue with me in this quiet vigil, trailing behind like gathering shadows.

But one of those shadows finally comes up to me and places a hand at my shoulder. My storming silence and unfailing pace bursts open with the touch.

I snarl and whirl, feeling like a fae beast ready to rip apart anyone who dares come too close to Auren.

Wick instantly holds up his hands and takes a step back. "I just…where are you taking her?" he asks thickly, his eyes bloodshot.

"To the bridge," I growl, panting hard. "Back to Orea with me."

Wick's eyes falter. "But this is her home, Ravinger."

"And it fucking failed her, didn't it?" I shout back in his face.

Wick grimaces in the leaden dawn, and his eyes go watery. "Fae will want to be able to pay their respects. To honor her here," he says, his expression strained. "*Please*. I know she's your paired, but she's their Lyäri," he tells me, gesturing to the throng of people who have stopped behind us. "She's my family."

"And yet, *we all failed her too*, didn't we?"

Grief tightens his face.

"Yes," he finally answers with a hard swallow. "We did. She was supposed to be our rising dawn, and we let darkness fall upon her."

And that darkness will never end.

Even now, the sun hides behind a swathe of wrinkled clouds, as if it doesn't dare show its face. As if it's draped itself in a veil of mourning.

"Please don't take her," Wick says again, his voice low and pleading. "Let her stay here, in the world she was born."

I glance away, teeth grinding.

I gnaw on grief and anger and emptiness, though I'm unable to swallow any of it down. Unable to digest it.

Indecision wars through me. I want to go down the bridge. To take her back to Fourth. Back to Digby. The Wrath. Keep her close for as long as I can.

I look back at the large group of fae that have followed.

See flashes of their mournful eyes, their grieving faces all turned toward me. Toward her.

My jaw aches, throat closing. *"I can't."*

My confession constricts. I wait for Wick to argue, maybe even beg, but he doesn't. Instead, silence spreads between us for several long moments until he breaks it with a quiet offering. "I can carry her for a while, if you need."

The first instinct I have is to clutch her tighter, to lash out with anger. But I stop myself, because I know his intention isn't to take her from me. It's a gesture. One that offers to help me carry this monumental loss.

But he can't. No one can.

Though I know they grieve, it will never be the same for them as it is for me.

Carrying her is the last gift I'll ever get. The last chance I'll ever have to feel her. I'm not ready to give that up.

*How can I?*

So I simply shake my head and turn, and I keep walking. Toward the bridge. Toward the end of Annwyn.

Toward the place where I know I will need to stop and make a choice.

But for now, I hold her.

The new day is held beneath a warped sky. No lavender light, no birdsong or fresh breeze. Just gray clouds above that match the gray ground below, as the silt of the deadlands' soil dusts me from knees to boots.

The fae still trail behind us, while my mother walks to my left and Wick to my right. He hasn't spoken again since he asked me to not take her.

And I don't know what's right. I don't know if the right answer is to lay her to rest here in her homeland or if it's better to take her back to Orea. But I'm still walking toward the bridge. Still refusing to make a decision.

Unable to.

Because if I choose and that decision lands here, then I have to stop walking that much sooner. I will have to set her body down and give her to the earth. And when I do that...

I will have to let her go.

I suddenly stop. The tread of my boots sinks into the ashen ground just as much as my stomach, while the sharp scrape of realization flays me open.

Because this is it.

After this, I will never hold her again. Never be able to look upon her.

I will never be able to feel the satiny lengths of her ribbons or brush away a lock of her hair. I will never hear her laugh or see the way her expression brightens with joy. I'll never hear her say my name or feel her heartbeat thrumming against my touch.

I won't feel the curve of her waist or be able to tuck her against my shoulder. Never see the way the sunlight glistens against her skin or how the moon dapples her burnished cheeks.

Thousands of nevers that will stack, one by one, and suffocate me.

The moment I let Auren go, I lose her forever.

Souls are eternal. It's why the finality of death feels so wrong. Why our hearts break and grief strikes. So while death may be common, it isn't *right*. It isn't *natural*.

Her soul is supposed to be with mine for all of eternity.

I swallow hard, eyes burning as I look down at her. My heart was rotted before, but now it lies split and ruptured. Just a gaping organ in a useless chest, the golden scale over it nothing but a torturous taunt.

One glance at the horizon, and I know when I climb this

slope, the bridge will be in view, and I will have to decide. Here or there. Annwyn or Orea.

My knees hit the ground. It cripples me and holds me in place, right here on the dead soil.

"Slade?" Wick says carefully at my side. He doesn't come too close. Doesn't risk my severed pair bond lashing out at him.

"I can't," I say again, the same thick confession that I spoke hours ago.

My mother crouches down beside me. Slender hand stroking my hair. I look over at her with burning eyes and a scoured throat. "How can I?" I ask, though I know she won't talk back, even though I'm desperate for the answer.

*How can I possibly let Auren go?*

"What was the point?" I demand, my voice a furious sob. "What was the point of any of it, if I was just going to lose her?"

Her lips turn down. Her eyes fill up.

"*What was the fucking point?*" I heave out.

My mother lifts her hands, placing one at my heart and one at Auren's. Over one that's split, and one that's still. She doesn't speak, but her eyes and touch say plenty.

*This. This was the point.*

To love her.

The tension in my shoulders finally rolls out, and I slump, my head hanging in heavy misery.

I can't let her go…

But it isn't about me.

It's about honoring Auren. It's about respecting what *she'd* want.

And despite what Annwyn has done, I saw it with my own eyes in Lydia. The way people looked at her with reverence and loyalty. The way she moved through the streets, with a surety of herself.

Annwyn is Auren's home, and I cannot take her from it.

When I look up again with eyes that drip, my mother nods and drops her hands. I get to my feet, clutching Auren with a trembling hold.

I swallow hard, though this lump in my throat will never leave.

"She'll stay here," I tell Wick quietly, the promise rasping out.

I see the relief as it drains out the stiffness of his posture. "Thank you."

The breath I heave in is hard-won, like hands grappling a rope to pull a ship through a storm. "But there are people who care about her in Orea too. People who need to see her. To say…" I have to force the last word out. "Goodbye."

Wick nods. "I—"

A loud noise abruptly tears through the air, making us startle.

"What was that?" Wick says.

We both take one look at each other and then race up the slope. When we reach the top, I'm able to look out toward Annwyn's edge. To where the deadlands drop off and the world ends in nothing but haze and void.

There, the small bridge is tucked in the fog.

But…the bridge is flooded with soldiers clad in red armor. More fae invading into Orea. Except, no, they're not invading, they're—

"They're running away from the bridge…" Wick says, and then his eyes widen. "*Gore.*" He suddenly whirls around to the group at the bottom of the slope. "Run!"

Our group doesn't hesitate to listen to his command. They instantly scatter, including my mother.

"Those aren't Stone Swords," Wick explains as we watch everyone's hurried steps kick up dust. Then our attention turns back to the soldiers. "We need to run."

"But why are *they* running?" I ask.

Wick doesn't get to answer.

That crack of noise we first heard is *nothing* compared to this. Sound splits, making us stagger, and I watch as the fog around the bridge seems to collide, aftershocks folding the air.

Then, in the next instant, the bridge erupts. With a flash of power and bright blue light, it blasts out of existence.

Gone. Just...fucking *gone*.

The way back to Orea, destroyed.

My legs nearly give out from the shock of it as I stare, and beside me, Wick gapes. But a moment later, the land right next to the bridge starts to collapse and give way. The land falling and sucking the fleeing soldiers down with it.

Fear stabs through my chest as Wick and I both realize what's happening at the same moment.

We turn and run.

The land crumbles, falling away in huge chunks, shaking the entire earth while it roars like thunder. "Go, go!" I shout at Wick, and his arms pump, sprinting harder and gaining speed.

Wick looks over his shoulder, sees me falling behind, and his brown eyes widen. "*Faster!*"

I can feel the earth quake. Hear it roaring down at me as it falls away. But I clutch Auren to me and run as fast as I fucking can.

But I'm not fast enough.

Wick makes it over the slope right as the dirt gives way beneath me.

I have a split second to look at Wick, and then Auren and I...

*Fall.*

# CHAPTER 61

There was a ripple in the ether.

It made the stars turn to look.

There, suspended in the void, a river flowing. One of many. Channels branching off, leading to seas and skies.

Yet the ripple comes from one small stream—a stream bridging two rivers together.

The ripple grows, intensifies, the stream splashes, and then…it dries up. Connection lost.

The stars look away.

For junctions and worlds come and they go. The ether ebbs and it flows.

There are so many rivers and connecting streams, one going dry hardly makes any difference.

After all, what are streams to stars?

And yet.

One star hovers high, high above. Far away from the

has gone dark. Cradled in the hands of the void, its fire blown out, it sits with dozens of the dark and doused.

But when all the stars have turned their attention back to basking in their brightness, this one begins to tremble.

The shake swells in the air, billowing down, down to those stars that burn. Reaching even the waters of the rivers, until the tremble breaks against their starshine surfaces.

The stars turn up their illuminated faces. Watching.

Waiting.

Until the core of the dark one *flickers*.

A single flame at first. Then, the fire catches. Burns. Casting off light and then growing. Bigger. Brighter.

Far bigger than the rest. Far more golden.

*Fall*, the others beckon, the voices of a thousand goddesses melded into the echo of one. *Fall, and exist down here with us, amongst the rivers and the realms, where we burn and warm, watch and bestow. Where we rule over life and death, and see all.*

But a filament floats from the golden star's surface. A cut root, pointing down toward those waters.

Reaching.

*Fall*, they say. *You are now one of us.*

But the gilded star feels that root, still growing from its core.

*What if I do not want to fall?*

The others go quiet.

The star burns hotter. Larger. Brighter. Not just a star, but a *sun*. With light that touches the streams.

It beckons again. *What if I do not want to fall?*

And this time, a voice answers. One familiar echo.

*Then, little sun…don't.*

# CHAPTER 62

## AUREN TURLEY

I hatched out of a star.

I blinked away death because he called to me. I didn't want to fall. Didn't want to drift down to that place where I would forever hover above the waters in divinity.

I wanted to go *back*.

So I had to burst free.

I was in the core of a burning light. Except, I *was* the light. Golden and shining. Pure life and warmth. I didn't need to descend, just as I didn't have to stay dark and dead, hanging forlorn in the void. This light that I burned with, it had always been in me.

The gilded light of a goddess-touched.

So I used that power and I gave up the gift of the stars.

Because some are not meant to burn in the dark.

With a push of my will, I cracked the star open. Its splintered shell fell away, and I spilled out from the light.

I knew where to go, even there, in the abyss. Because that root—the one still caught in my core, it *reached*. Pointing the way toward its other half. Toward *my* other half.

I passed by the other stars, saw the goddesses' faces, and I smiled. Then I leaped into the river's current, and I let it sweep me away toward my home.

Toward *him*.

And though I couldn't see, one of those stars smiled back. Then it tossed in a droplet of light to follow after me.

I went through the river and I became myself again. Healed from the cruelty of living, restored from the thievery of death.

I went through the river in the void, and I was reborn.

# CHAPTER 63

## AUREN TURLEY

A flare of breath burns away the cold as life pours back into me. I'm dropped down from the river, past soil and air, and then contained in the confines of my familiar body. Gold drips down my figure and gilds every thread on the fabric of my clothes as I suck in a gasp.

Slade is holding me.

Wind blowing around us, fog so thick I can hardly see.

Only, it's not wind. We're plummeting through the air.

Slade's clutching me tightly with his hand on the back of my head, keeping me tucked against his neck while his other arm is banded around my waist. My ribbons are snapping in the air as we free-fall.

There's a flash of fear that goes through me, but then warmth sparks down my spine.

*What if I do not want to fall?*

*Then, little sun…don't.*

Don't.

Those sparks catch. Melt. Like candle wax, it overflows and drips down the lengths of every ribbon. Each strip melding together with gold and warmth.

Because I don't want to fall anymore. I have been falling my entire life.

So this time, I don't.

My ribbons combine in a searing burst of light, and suddenly, they're not strips anymore. They're not streaming uselessly. No, they come together. Forming into something else.

Forming into *wings*.

Slade wrenches me back as they stretch behind me. "*Auren?*"

I hear him, even with the rushing wind. I smile as tears are torn from my lids.

He quakes around me. "What—"

"It's okay," I tell him.

Because this time, it really is.

I clutch onto him as tightly as he's clutching me, and then, I let instinct take over. He blinks in awe as my wings flare, spreading to their full length. It makes Slade and me snap up in the air from the shift, but I grit my teeth and hold on.

I echo those words Slade first said to me, so long ago.

Don't fall. *Fly.*

And I do.

I move my wings as I've moved my ribbons, with an innate familiarity and ease. They beat against the rushing air of the void, pulling at the muscles in my back, clawing at the grip of gravity.

Until finally, instead of going down, Slade and I start to rise *up*.

Up.

Up.

My stomach bottoms out from the change in direction, but I tilt my head to look above with razor-sharp focus. Every limb is tense, each muscle along my back straining.

Invisible, greedy hands seem to try to swipe at us from the void.

But the void can't have us.

With determination locking my jaw and stiffening my spine, I angle us faster, speeding through cloying fog, eyes stinging, fingers grasping Slade with a steely grip.

And then, we burst out of the haze.

Like the arc of a shooting star, we launch up and then curve back down before we crash into the land. Our bodies roll to a stop, with Slade below and me above.

My breathing is labored, my back muscles screaming, but none of it matters.

Slade grips my face between his trembling hands, eyes so wide I can see my reflection in his green irises. "Am I dead?" he whispers hoarsely.

I shake my head and grip his face too, relishing the stubble that scratches my fingertips. "No. I came back to find you."

He pulls in a shredded breath, in strips and pieces from a tattered heart. His eyes grow wet, his expression fracturing. And then he speaks with the most devoted, heartbreaking tone. "You flew, Goldfinch."

My own heart seems to fill up, every inch that's ever been pinched or prodded or drained. "I did."

And then we're up on our feet, and we're clutching each other. Holding on so tight. He spins me around, making a smile spread across my face—spread across my entire soul.

When we stop, we clash into a desperate kiss. I kiss him with devotion and need. He kisses me with awe and adoration.

I don't need the divinity of the goddesses.

Because with him, I have what I've always wanted.

*Love.*

Whole. Unconditional. Healing. Beautiful. Pure. Love.

When we pull away, our eyes still locked together, I can feel our pair bond singing. Can see his dark aura drifting off his body, with tendrils of gold.

But I can also see the devastation stabbed into him.

A tear escapes the corner of my eye because I can see his hurt. His grief. I want to take all his pain away.

"I'm sorry," I whisper. "I'm so sorry I left you for a little while."

He smiles softly, hand cupping my cheek, gaze intense over my face. "You came back to me."

I nod, lashes wet, chest full. "I'll always choose you."

"I'll always choose you too, Auren," he says before kissing me again. My wings curl around us like they want to hold us in a cocoon, cloistered and safe.

We cling to each other, our heartbeats in tune, our love spilling over. When he pulls back to look at me, his gaze crawls over every inch of my face, trembling fingers stroking over my skin.

His forehead presses against mine, and I hear his ragged breath. "Don't leave me again."

My heart squeezes.

"I won't," I promise.

After another devastating kiss that he presses to my lips, his gaze casts behind me, and I look over my shoulder at my wings.

They've folded together against my spine, but I spread them out again, turning around so we can both get a better look. His hand skates over the smooth curve of the top, and I shiver slightly.

"Your ribbons…" he says, and I nod.

My wings drift open and close slightly, like a butterfly resting on a flower. They've clearly been formed by twelve strips of ribbons on each side, each piece melded together. At the bottom and the very ends, the ribbons are long and stretched out, looking just like…feathers.

Instantly, I remember the story Slade told me as I was dying. About what that nickname really meant for him. For us.

As if to punctuate its meaningfulness, Elore suddenly appears, her face wet, expression joyful. "Goldfinch," she utters as she cries through a smile. "Goldfinch."

I surge forward and wrap my arms around her in a hug. "Thank you," I whisper into her hair.

Thank you for leading him to me.

Thank you for leading me to *myself*.

When she pulls away, she gestures to the ground. "Goldfinch."

I look around, noticing for the first time that the land is gray and dead. Wrong.

Something comes over me then. A presence, a sense of intuition. Like the stars themselves are beckoning… *encouraging*.

I kneel down, pressing my hands against the silt.

"Auren?" Slade questions.

I don't answer at first, because I'm too busy listening to the land and the sky. To Annwyn, as she whispers her secrets. As she calls to me.

Then, I feel it—that piece from the ether. The droplet that the goddess tossed down with me. And with a sense of divine *knowing*, I immediately understand what it is. A gift to stem the curse.

"I can fix it," I whisper.

Slade steps closer to me.

My eyes flutter closed as I feel that droplet drift up to the surface of my body, and then I let it pour out through my gold-touch.

To heal. To restore.

To bring back life and warmth with this goddess-touched light of a cracked-open sun.

With my palms pressed to the land, the light of the goddesses streams, making the entire deadlands *flare*.

The Vulmin were right, this land was cursed. Because a long time ago, a willing connection was made by Orean and fae. A sacred path forged from love and unity.

When fae betrayed that and broke the bridge, it cursed the land. Left it leeched with sickness that spread with death, sucking it dry of all power.

But the stars have been watching, and the goddesses have gifted us another chance.

The drop of power instantly soaks into the land and surges through. It's so potent, so raw and pure, all my nerves and senses seem to ignite. My entire body is wrapped in warmth and light, wings trembling as this unfathomable, otherworldly magic flows out of me.

I nearly pass out, nearly crumple to the ground, but Slade catches me, with my name shouted from his worried lips.

He holds me while my hands are stuck against the soil like a magnet, unable to break away. I can't—not until every part of the gifted magic is used.

My hands shake and glow, veins showing through. Light continues to pour, making sweat bead on my skin and heat flare from every direction.

I feel the power banishing the curse. Feel it burning away the poison. Shockwaves spread over the ground, and I hear people cry out as the blinding light pulses, making me squeeze my eyes shut as my body jerks and my wings flare with one last seizing tug that nearly buckles me, and then…

It's done.

Slade grips me as I fling back, hands released from my duty, his arms catching me as I fall. I breathe heavily as I lift my head, feeling utterly spent.

As the last of the blinding light dims, my gasp joins in with the others who are gathered around us. Tears spring to my eyes, and I blink, looking out at the incredible sight.

My gaze skims over the rolling hills and dappled meadows, past trees that sway against the lavender sky. There's a city woven through the river, with white buildings and rooftops that seem to bloom with gilded vines. In the distance, mountaintops peak with caps of snow, and forests spread out for miles.

Everything is vibrant and alive.

Ecstatic joy lifts me up, pulling me to my feet as I spin around to look at it all. It's *beautiful*. The landscape now ripples with lush grass and sparkling waters and bursting life.

The deadlands are no longer dead. The curse has been broken.

Annwyn has been restored.

I turn to look at the crust of the world that's now smoothed and green, where it tapers off with a beveled edge. Beyond it, fog flows down the void in streams of endless white and glacial blue like a waterfall of vapor.

I smile at it all, feeling the rightness of Annwyn humming through me, but then, my smile slowly falls, a frown forming between my brows.

I turn to look at Slade. "Wait, the bridge of Lemuria. Where is it?"

Slade's eyes meet mine, and his answer makes my stomach drop. "It's gone."

# CHAPTER 64

## SLADE

I clutch Auren's hand tightly, unwilling to let go. Unable. I'm dizzy with the reality that she's okay. More than okay. I can't yet fathom everything that happened, and my cleaved-apart soul is still raw and aching.

But the pair bond sings and her aura twists in a reassuring glow that helps me to breathe.

Though I don't let go of her hand.

I'm not sure if I'll ever be able to again.

Together, we walk to the new, bright city in the valley below. It's sprouted right where the dead city used to be. Now the ruins are gone, and unblemished buildings shine in their place. The white walls are polished and smooth, standing alongside a winding road of moss-soaked cobbles that cushion my every footfall.

The road overlooks the river to our left, and the waters are so full and crystal clear that I can see the colorful pebbles glittering at the river's floor. Trees line the walkway we tread upon, their branches heavy with fruit and sweet-smelling blossoms.

Auren didn't just heal the deadlands. She poured pure, vibrant life into it.

I still can't believe what I saw. The golden sunlight streamed from her and into the earth, stripping away the wrongness and making it reborn.

Just as she was reborn.

Not as many people are still with us. Most of them fled when the land started to crumble, but there are still a few dozen who witnessed what happened.

They followed us here, into this new city, their demeanors shocked and quiet. Everyone keeps turning their heads, taking in the sights. They're in awe of this place—but they're in awe of Auren even more.

Who could blame them?

I can't stop looking at her.

Her clothes have gone gilded, her skin and hair gleaming. She has a glow about her, emanating from even more than the aura that shines from her skin.

She's radiant.

She's *alive*.

My hands still shake, the tremors of my despair sneaking through.

To say I was devastated can't encompass the wreckage I was. With her dead in my arms, I was nothing but ruin and anguish.

To have her here beside me now, real and warm and bright with life…it makes me flounder with both shock and marvel.

Inside my head, I have to keep reassuring myself, have to keep squeezing her hand to feel her squeeze back.

*She's alive.*

GOLDFINCH

Auren looks over with excitement that lights up her eyes, and it makes my tremors go still. "It's beautiful here," she breathes. "Do you think this is what it looked like before?"

"I don't know," I admit, though we both seem to turn to look at the building to our right at the same time. My eyes drift over the golden vines that sprout from its pitched rooftop before trailing down the rest of the way to hang over the eaves. "But I'm fairly certain these at least are new additions."

Auren laughs, and the sound makes chills raise on my skin. Makes me so fucking thankful to hear it.

"Did you notice the vines themselves sort of look like my ribbons?"

I nod. "And the leaves look a bit like…"

"Feathers," she finishes with a widening smile.

I lift our joined hands and press a kiss against her skin. "Goldfinch," I murmur, my heart constricting.

Her voice and eyes go soft, no doubt picking up on the echoes of my torment. "I'm okay," she tells me again. "We're together."

My throat bobs as I nod, and she squeezes my hand again to comfort me.

Her wings stretch out slightly from where they're tucked against her back, and the one closest to me reaches out to stroke my arm, just like her ribbons did. I release her hand so I can drag my fingers over it, and the ends curl around me as if trying to hold on.

My lips curve and I rub it between my fingers. The surface feels satiny smooth and supple, but there's also an underlying core that's strong and sturdy. It bends and sways, each individual ribboned strip spanning the length of the forged wing. But it looks like liquid gold dripped down, forming feathers up and down the lengths.

"Gorgeous," I purr.

The wing brushes over me again, but this time…lower.

Auren's head snaps over with a blush branding her cheek. "Stop that," she hisses beneath her breath as it caresses my ass.

I chuckle as the wing snaps back into place against her. "They're quite handsy," I say through a smile.

"They're new," she says with teasing flippancy. "They just don't know how to move yet."

Her wings fluff up, making my grin widen. "I don't think they agree with that statement."

Auren looks back at them, her eyes crinkling at the corners as she smiles, which makes my heart melt. She loves them. I can see it in her expression. And they fit her perfectly. She doesn't look strange, doesn't walk as if they burden her or feel awkward. They flow with her effortlessly, as if they were always there, just waiting to come out.

Maybe they were.

Maybe it was similar to how I felt when I manifested the dragon.

As soon as that thought crosses my mind, a pang goes through me, though I try to keep the despondency from my face.

"You okay?" Auren asks, so in tune with me that she can sense my shift in mood.

The mourning stretches inside of me, emanating from the place where the dragon slept, right at the core of my healed selves. The spot now lies empty.

I've lost my dragon. But I have her.

I reach down and thread my fingers through hers. "So long as I have you, I will always be okay."

So long as I have her, I can bear anything.

"How do your wings feel?" I ask.

Auren considers my question as she glances over at them. "They feel...like my ribbons. Like there aren't just two, but still all twenty-four."

I hum in thought. "Can you separate them again?"

Her steps falter slightly as she thinks about it, but then she turns focused. Her eyes flutter closed for a moment, and then, her wings stretch out and ripple.

I watch as her wings split apart into all two dozen ribbons again. They twist and flick like they're excited.

Auren beams. "Did you see?"

"Beautiful," I say as one of the strips comes over to stroke against my arm.

Auren pulls in her ribbons, and the lengths fuse into wings again, pouring down with dripping gold that forms the feathers.

She presses a hand to her chest and nearly skips in excitement. "I can have them both," she says with wonder. "Wings *and* ribbons."

Behind us, the people look on with amazement, whispers breaking out between them.

"You're extraordinary," I murmur, and I relish the blush that casts across her cheeks.

As we walk, Auren has them morph from wings to ribbons and back again a few more times, delighting with every transition. I can't get enough of watching her.

And inwardly, I'm still reassuring myself.

*She's alive.*

Soon, the moss-covered cobblestones of the road bring us to what looks like the center of the new city. They curve around a water well like a halo of green, while bigger buildings are set further out. Behind the well, the sight opens up to the river and a thicket of greenery.

When we finally stop, the group stops with us.

"Now what?" someone murmurs.

The question seems to catch onto the faces of every watching fae. As if now that we've stopped walking, they're able to stop reeling.

But I don't know if I'll ever be able to stop reeling.

In truth, my heart hasn't stopped racing since the ground gave way beneath my feet. Once the air hooked around Auren and me and we were dragged down into a free-fall, I thought it was over. That it was all done.

And a part of me was relieved.

Because Auren was gone, and I didn't want to exist without her. I clutched her as we fell, and I was okay with it, because it meant I wasn't going to have to let her go after all. It meant we could stay together.

But then, she started clutching me back, and instead of falling, we flew.

*She* flew. In more ways than one. And she's here. Not lifeless in my arms, but here with me again.

I don't understand it. Don't know how it's possible. But somehow, Auren denied death. Somehow, she came back to me.

So even though I don't know all the explanations behind it, my heart hasn't stopped racing. Not once. So I can understand this question that's being lobbed back and forth as it travels further down the crowd, because I feel it too.

What next?

I turn to look at Auren, just as Wick and my mother step closer to us.

Wick still hasn't quite lost that edge of shocked stupor.

My mother, though, she wears a quiet smile. Who knows, maybe as a diviner, the goddesses whisper in her ear. Her lips may be quiet, but perhaps her head is full of words. And while I'll always wish I could hear her speak to me more, the one word she did bless me with changed everything.

That one word was all I needed.

But that isn't true for this parade of fae who've followed us. Who look expectantly in our direction, waiting for words and explanations.

A Vulmin moves through the crowd to get to the front,

his collar exposing the embroidered sigil of the broken-winged bird. I wonder if some of the Vulmin will change it now. If the symbol will shift with the appearance of Auren's wings.

"Yes, what happens next?" he asks with anticipation, his gaze moving back and forth between Auren and Wick.

Auren shifts on her feet, and I know she's slightly uncomfortable to be the center of all this attention. "Well..." she begins, with a glance darted to Wick. "We can rest here in the city. There seems to be food..."

"The bridge is gone," the Vulmin says. "And the Stone Swords said that Carrick went to Orea. So if that's true, he's gone too."

The thought of the Stone King being in Orea makes worry tighten my shoulders. I hope King Thold unleashes his serpents on the bastard until he's nothing but a constricted corpse riddled with venom. I hope they defeat him and that my brother and my Wrath are okay.

But the bridge is gone.

And Brennur, the only fae who had the power to transport between realms is gone too.

Which means we will never get answers, and I will never get to see my brother or Lu or Os or Judd again. My Premiers. My people. I'll never know if Orea suffers at the fae king's hand, and I can't get there to help them if they do.

Guilt weighs on me like an arm slung over my shoulders, intent on pulling me down.

"The king fled, and Annwyn is finally free of his tyranny," another Vulmin says. "Now's the time to take up the reins!"

"Yes!" several of them call out in response.

"Yes," Wick repeats quietly, and then he turns to look at Auren. His expression weighty.

Everyone quiets. Watching.

"They're right, Auren," Wick tells her. "You made

Carrick flee. You healed Annwyn. You saved countless lives. You were *reborn*. Our broken-winged bird flew, rising like the dawn."

Auren sucks in a breath.

Then he lowers on one knee.

"We bow," he says, face intent on her. "We bow to the new Queen of Annwyn. The last-birthed Turley heir."

Shock courses through her, while excitement travels through the onlookers.

*"We bow to Queen Auren Turley!"*

*"We bow to our Lyäri!"*

*"The golden one rules!"*

*"The golden one rules!"*

Auren blinks at them all, and I know just what she's thinking. Can see every thought as it plays over her features.

She swallows hard at the chanting and then looks back to Wick. "Please stand up."

He does, and then everyone quiets again, waiting to see what she'll say. She shakes her head as she looks around at everyone. "I'm honored that you would call me your queen, but I do not want to rule."

It takes a moment for her words to land, but once they do, everyone goes still. Eyes widen in disbelief, and some expressions twist up in confusion or dispute.

"I was kidnapped from Annwyn as a little girl," she tells them, looking out at the small crowd. "I was trapped and used and manipulated. For years—for *decades*—my life was never my own." Her eyes flick over to me for a second as a small smile tips her lips. "That changed once I met my pair, but we've had to face constant threats, danger, and obstacles. And now…for once, all of that is done."

I see the empathy start to spread, see understanding lighting the eyes of those who watch her.

"A queen's entire life has to be for her kingdom," she

goes on. "But I would like to finally have the chance to live my life...for *me*."

My eyes and heart burn for her. My mother dashes away a tear.

Auren's eyes carry a sheen too, but her voice stays strong. "And though I don't want to be queen, Annwyn can still turn a new page. We can be peaceful and prosperous. You don't need to bow to me for that. We can do it together."

Her head turns, gaze locking onto Wick, who's looking at her in shock.

"We have the perfect person right here to help lead the way," she tells them. "Someone who has been fighting for the rights of fae and Oreans all his life. Someone who understands far more about the nuances of this world and its history and politics than I do. He's been a Vulmin leader, an Orean advocate, and he's..." She pauses, looking at him expectantly.

Asking a silent question.

Wick's throat bobs as he swallows hard, but then he gives her the smallest nod of his head.

"And he's also family," Auren finishes. "Wickum Almon Turley."

Surprised mutters break out, and the Vulmin's eyes go wide.

"With his help, we can figure out what's next," she tells them. "And we'll do it together."

# CHAPTER 65

## COMMANDER RYATT

My adrenaline hasn't stopped spiking.

I know I'm still in a state of shock, but it's because death was certain. I stared into its eyes and ran straight for it. Expecting to crash into it with everyone else.

So when the bridge suddenly exploded and collapsed a chunk of the world with it, my mind struggled to keep up.

I'm *still* struggling. Just like Lu, Os, Digby, and Rissa are. Even Argo keeps whining and scraping his talons through the snow in agitation.

Head turning again, my gaze casts toward the space where the bridge was. My eyes not wanting to accept the sights of the gaping air.

With my heart pounding in my chest, I glance back at the unconscious soldier from Second. I tie off the bandage over the wicked gash on his leg and then slip the supplies into the pack on the ground.

Everyone else has been treating wounds too. We're lucky some of the timberwings kept their packs on them, because we had just enough mender supplies to treat the most serious injuries.

As soon as I finish, Osrik lifts the man I helped onto the back of a timberwing where another Second soldier is already waiting, ready to secure him.

King Thold comes walking over just as I clean my hands in the snow. "That's the last one?"

I nod. "Last one."

Although, even now that we've tended to everyone, I don't know if they'll all make it. We did the best we could. All I can hope is that they survive the flight home and get to a skilled mender.

He nods and brushes snow off his cloak, his own hand wrapped in a bandage too. "You fought well. Orea owes you a great debt."

Maybe I'd feel pride at his words if I didn't feel so shocked. If my pulse weren't still racing.

*It can't be gone.*

"Orea could not have done it without you, King Thold," I manage to say. But really, all I want to do is fly over the crumbled land. To search the space where the explosion happened.

The need is like a fist against the door of my soul, knocking relentlessly.

The snowy snake wrapped around Thold's neck flicks its pale pink tongue in my direction as if it's sensing my agitation. It's as unnerving as its pink eyes that stare at me.

Queen Kaila comes striding over to Thold. Tendrils of her black hair have been ripped from her braid, and her timberwing suffered a minor wound on its leg, but other than that, she came away from this battle unscathed. She managed to stay in the air the entire time.

Her face is lit up in a satisfied smile. "The war is officially over. We won."

A couple of soldiers behind her call out in joined celebration, rejoicing in this inconceivable triumph—and they *should* celebrate. Because this means Orea will survive. That Oreans won't be massacred and wiped off the face of our world.

But this victory came with a price.

"The bridge," Kaila says, nodding to where it once stood. "There was a moment, just before it was destroyed…I believe I saw Queen Malina standing on it."

I blink, remembering that I also saw someone there. "I think I did too."

"Queen Malina?" Thold asks in shock before a thick silence spreads. "Do you think she was somehow responsible for destroying it?"

Kaila lifts a shoulder. "Who knows?"

"If that's true, then she saved our world," Thold says.

"*We* saved our world," Kaila retorts. "We fought for it, and we prevailed. Now, we can alert the rest of Orea. Let people know the danger is gone and that we've defeated the fae once and for all."

I take in Kaila's demeanor. Beside me, Osrik tenses, and I can see Lu pause where she's wrapping a timberwing's leg, her head turning to look at the queen with a hint of distrust.

"Orea is in disarray," Kaila says to Thold. "We may find ourselves no longer at war, but it's still been devastated. Fifth and Sixth have fallen, and with Malina and the new King Fulke gone, these kingdoms need leadership."

The king's mouth presses into a hard line, but I grit my teeth. "We're not even off the battlefield, and you're already vying to claim more kingdoms?" I growl out.

Her shrewd brown eyes flick over to me, dragging from gauntlet to glare. "You have fought well, Commander," she says, though she somehow manages to make it sound patronizing. "But now is the time for monarchs. Thold and I will take it from here. Unless Ravinger is around to join us?" she asks pointedly.

Red-hot anger melts away the chill in the air.

Her brow arches at my silence. "That's what I thought."

"The Premiers have rule of Fourth in lieu of King Ravinger's absence," I bite out, my head turning to look at Thold. "They will need to be included in discussions."

The king looks between the two of us, and I can see the wheels turning behind his eyes. He's formidable, but I have hope that he has enough honor to ultimately do what's right for Orea.

Still, I hope the Premiers are ready to hold their own, because it seems a different sort of battle is about to begin. One fought behind closed doors during diplomatic meetings.

"We will meet at Fourth immediately and call a council to come up with a united plan," Thold says.

Kaila's lips press together, eyes seeming to swirl with plans of her own.

"Orea needs to rebuild and make everyone feel safe again," I state, my words insistent. "We've just experienced devastating losses. We need to come *together*, not grow further divided."

Kaila gives me a dismissive look and then ignores me completely when she turns to Thold. "I will meet you in Fourth," she says before she turns and walks toward her timberwing and mounts it.

I share a look with Lu and Osrik, and I know we're all thinking the same thing. We almost died saving Orea, and before the dust can even fucking settle, Kaila is up to her old antics with her thirst for power.

Maybe I shouldn't be surprised, but it feels like a punch to the fucking gut. I can only hope that her brother can knock some sense into her. He seems to be the only one she listens to.

King Thold looks at me, his astute gaze casting over my tense face. "Do not worry yourself, Commander. The war is over. Your duty is done. Now, leave the politics to us. Queen

Kaila can only reach so far before that grasping hand of hers gets caught."

We watch as Kaila and her group take flight, their timberwings pointed in the direction of Sixth Kingdom.

"I thank you all for Fourth's sacrifice," the king says, drawing my eyes back to him.

My jaw tightens as I think of how much blood was spilled. "We all made sacrifices."

"War always requires them," he rumbles out in reply.

And he's right. But hopefully, greed doesn't ruin what we've won.

Only time will tell.

He walks off, addressing the soldiers of Second who are still left. "Return to your kingdom and tell your prince what has transpired. Tell him that he's called to council in Fourth Kingdom. I will meet him there."

The soldiers tip their heads, and their captain readies their group to leave.

Only four of our own Elites still live, and all of them wear the stricken faces of the after-battle. Their eyes are haunted from the loss and carnage, while both relief and guilt fill the creases of their grimaces.

Tyde walks over, and I notice his middle has been re-bandaged, but it doesn't appear to be bleeding. "Your stitches hold up?"

"Yes, Commander."

His magic has been incredibly beneficial, and he's kept a cool head the entire time, never once wavering.

"Should we all mount and ready to leave?" he asks.

My head turns of its own volition to look at the void again before I answer. "You all leave now. Head straight for Fourth. We need to tell the Premiers everything that's happened. They'll have to prepare for the monarchs to come for the council meeting that will determine Orea's fate."

Tyde nods but looks from me to the Wrath, snow gathered in his blond hair and his eyes bloodshot. "And what should we tell them about King Ravinger?"

A jab goes through my heart. It takes great effort not to let my voice waver. "Tell them that it appears he can't return. That they must rule Fourth in his stead." I swallow thickly.

Tyde pauses. "And you, Commander?"

"I'll be behind you," I say. "*Captain* Tyde."

His eyes widen at the new title. "Me?" he asks in shock.

I nod. "You've earned it."

With his black helmet tucked under his arm, he shifts on his feet for a moment before clearing his throat. "Thank you, Commander."

He offers me a salute and then turns to Lu and Os, offering a deferential nod as he presses a fist to his heart. "We honor the fallen," he murmurs. "Captain Judd will be missed."

Lu sucks in a breath at his name, and Osrik seems to pale. My throat feels like someone is clawing it.

As soon as Tyde turns and walks away, Lu appears at my side. "What are you doing? Why did you tell them to go ahead?"

"Because I can't just leave," I say, the words ripping out more harshly than I intended. It's been a rush of collapsing earth and tending to our wounded, but now that everyone is leaving, I can finally focus on the bridge. On what happened.

Slade left us proof that he came through Sixth and Seventh. I know he crossed the bridge. I know he's there. Just like my mother.

So this bridge can't be just fucking *gone*.

I glare at the fog that rolls and presses like kneading dough beneath unrelenting fists. It used to be only gray, but now, the fog is as white as the snow, with streaks of ice-blue swirling through it.

"I just don't understand what the fuck *happened*..." Lu says, seeming to pick up on my thoughts. "If it was Queen

Malina, *how*?" Sweat coats the dagger shapes shaved into the sides of her head, and her eyes are drawn with exhaustion.

"Good fucking question," Osrik growls. He has his hand clamped around Rissa's, whose face is half-buried behind a thick scarf, her blue eyes haunted. She hasn't said much since it all ended, but she's been practically stuck to Osrik's side.

Digby too stares straight ahead at the bleak emptiness, his brown and silver stubble peppered with frost.

Behind us, Argo whines.

A lump the size of my heart gets stuck in my throat as my molars gnash together. I know this was a good thing for Orea, but for me…for us…it's a disaster.

Why couldn't the bridge have exploded *after* Slade returned with my mother and Auren?

It's not right, and I don't fucking accept it.

"You all go catch up with the Elites, but I'm going to go look," I bite out as I turn and start walking.

Maybe there's still a piece of it. Maybe there's *something* there.

"The bridge is gone, Ryatt," Lu argues as she flings out her hand in that direction. "It's not broken, it's *obliterated*. There's nothing there anymore."

"I know," I snap as I halt beside Argo. I let out a sigh before looking at her over my shoulder. "I know, okay? But I *have* to check."

She studies my face. I can see the devastation in her expression, and the stretched-out breath that spills out of her says everything. "Fine. I'll go with you."

"I want to see too," Rissa declares, and everyone looks over at her, making her shoulders lift defensively. "What? If Auren really is stuck in the fae realm, I want to be certain that she has no way of coming here before we just leave."

Osrik moves his gaze from her to me. "We'll fly over there where it was. Just to check."

Digby stares, and I can see the acceptance of misery tightened around his eyes and mouth. He has championed Auren, insisted on staying by her side, wanting nothing more than to protect her, and with the bridge now gone, he can't.

He's a cut-and-dry sort of man, accepting hard truths. But even he nods. "Let's check."

Because hope, however false, does something for a trodden soul. Sometimes false hope is all you have, so you cling to it for as long as you can.

And I'm going to fucking cling. Because it's not over until I check. Until I see with my own eyes that it's gone.

Osrik and Rissa get on one bird, Lu and Digby on the other, and me on the third. I grip Argo's feathers, my leather gloves creaking with how stiff my grip is. Probably because I'm trying to keep hold of this false hope in a way that feels a lot like trying to strangle flowing water.

But I try anyway.

We lift into the sky, and my gaze drops as soon as we start flying over the broken land. The triangle-shaped break grows wider the longer we fly over it, though the fog still hugs the crevices.

I direct Argo to keep straight, following the path of the new wound in the ground until we reach the spot where the bridge once existed.

Now, there's nothing but this icy, white and blue fog. No pillars, no gray path. No land that once led to it.

No piece of bridge still left.

Tears burn my eyes as we all pull up, timberwings hovering at the edge of the world where the fog rises up like a wall.

Frustration and grief crack open my chest as I stare at it. As reality hammers into me.

*I'm never going to see them again.*

A surge of anger comes over me, because how could this be it? How could this be the culmination of everything that's happened? We won. Orea won. But I lost anyway.

Anger and denial hack into me. I tap my heel and jerk forward, and Argo jolts ahead at my wordless command, his wings flapping.

"Wait!" Osrik shouts, his gruff voice scraping toward me.

"Ryatt, no!" Lu yells.

I ignore them as Argo and I push into the fog, and we immediately get swallowed in its dense depths. My nerves drench me in cold sweat as soon as I'm surrounded by the cloying vapor, and Argo screeches, but I push him to keep going.

Every Orean knows better than to go into this void. There are many old stories about Seventh Kingdom doing trials when their kingdom still existed.

Three things were always made clear from those histories: if someone walked the bridge to nowhere, they wouldn't come back. If someone fell down over the edge of the world, they'd just keep falling. And no one should ever fly into the fog, or they wouldn't be able to fly back out.

Except maybe there's a part of the bridge that still exists in all this murk. And if there's a part, then there's a chance.

A chance is all I need.

But my last false hope is kicked aside, because there is no bridge still suspended in the air. No piece left. No chance.

There's nothing here, except *nothing*.

Only a thick haze of white and blue and an empty void that seems to stretch forever.

Just like that, my false hope breaks apart, pieces of it scraping at the backs of my eyes and making them sting.

I'll never see my family again.

As if sensing my change in mood, Argo slows, hovering as my throat clogs with grief.

Grief for my mother and brother.

For Judd.

For Kitt and all my soldiers—for Finley and Maston.

For every innocent who died.

I feel the losses press against me even more than this suffocating fog.

But then I hear whispers.

Instantly, I stiffen on Argo's back, and my head whips around. Argo turns his head too, his movements jerky.

"Who's there?" I call.

My own voice sounds trapped, like I'm inside a tiny closet. The whispers though, they sound like they're being spoken through a canyon. Echoing and stretching. I can't tell what they're saying.

"Is someone there?" I shout, looking around wildly as I lean in, as if the disembodied voices will clear up.

But it's only wordless ramblings.

"What?"

The whispers suddenly stop. No tapering off, no fading. They just cut out.

Eerie silence follows that makes my stomach churn with nausea because I get hit with a sudden sense that I shouldn't be here.

Fear drenches me like I've stepped beneath a rushing waterfall.

*What the fuck was I thinking?*

Argo lets out a panicked screech like he feels it too, and then he abruptly turns and starts flying as fast as he can, back the way we came.

Only…*is* this the way we came?

Gripping his feathers, I swing my head in every direction. I'm all turned around, confused, and there's no sight of reference, because the fog is so thick I can barely even see Argo.

Worry spreads through me, making me feel lightheaded. Argo's wings flap frantically, head jerking side to side as he goes faster. But dread sticks to my quickening breaths, because we should've reached the land by now.

This isn't right.

I pull on Argo's feathers, and he circles, flying up and then down, left and right, screeching in alarm.

We're stuck. We're fucking stuck in this fog. I shouldn't have forced us in here. I shouldn't have—

Argo abruptly turns and *bolts*. I wasn't expecting it, so I jerk back and start to slip off. My heart lurches right up into my throat as I start to fall back.

My hands fling out at the last second to grip his feathers, keeping me seated. I shove my weight forward and lean in against the rushing air. Wind tears at my face, the fingers of the fog feeling like they're reaching out, trying to grip hold of me and drag me back…

But suddenly, we burst through the wall.

I have a split second of relief when I realize we're out of the fog before we hit the ground in a skid, and I go flying off Argo's back. I tumble through the air and land in a heap of snow, my heart nearly knocked right out of me.

My pulse pounds as I shove myself up, chest rising and falling with rapid breaths as I stare at the wall of fog ahead.

I hear Lu and Osrik shouting my name, and I immediately put my hands around my mouth and call back. "Here! I'm over here!"

A few seconds later, I see the others flying toward me. I wave my arms so they spot me, and they land right at my side.

Osrik jumps down from his bird, stomps over, and then punches me right in the chest. I have armor on, but the hit still knocks me back.

"You fucking idiot!" he snarls at me.

"I'm sorry!" I say, holding up my hands. "I don't know what I was thinking."

"You *weren't* thinking," Lu seethes as she comes over. "You're lucky you made it out of that! We already lost Judd and Slade and Auren. You think we wanna lose you too?"

Shame slips down my back, making my shoulders slump. "No. I'm sorry," I say again before sighing. "I just…I wanted to make sure."

Her sharp eyes meet mine. "And?"

I shake my head. "No bridge. It's all gone."

"So that's it, then," Rissa says as she slips down off of Osrik's timberwing. She sniffs and swipes beneath her eye. "They're stuck in Annwyn."

My voice feels as hollow as my chest. "Yes."

Digby swallows hard and dismounts before starting to pace through the snow like he doesn't know what else to do with himself.

"Did you see anything else?" Lu asks.

I open my mouth and then close it again, my gaze drifting behind her toward the fog. "No, but I heard voices. I tried to call back to them, but I think it was a trick. It didn't seem right."

"*Voices?*" Lu repeats, looking horrified. "You heard bodiless voices in a void, and you thought you'd just stick around in there to listen to them? That it was a good idea to *call back?*" She lets out a sigh before muttering something about me being an idiot.

I don't disagree.

"Believe me, I'm not going in there again."

"You're lucky you came out," Digby says, eyes creased with stress.

I don't disagree with that either.

We stand around in a circle, and I know we're going to have to return to Fourth now, even if it feels so wrong.

I drag a trembling hand down my face, like grief is shaking me where I stand.

But then I hear voices again, and I go rigid. My eyes swing around to the others. "Is that in my head from the fog, or can you hear that too?" I demand.

"Hear wh—" Lu's reply abruptly cuts off when the breeze

carries the sound again. Her eyes go wide. "That's not the fog. Someone's here."

I whirl around, but Lu is quicker. She starts hurrying forward and we quickly follow her through the snow. It's so thick that it nearly reaches our knees.

Lu reaches a snowbank that's formed into more of a hill. When she disappears around it, my panic spikes. What if this *is* the fog? What if there's some sort of curse in there and I brought it out with me? What if these voices are tricking us and Lu just up and vanishes?

*Shit.*

I surge forward with a burst of panic and speed. I'm ready to start shouting her name, but as soon as I get around the bank, I spot her, and relief bursts through me. But then I grind to a halt next to where she's stopped.

Because it wasn't the fog playing tricks on us. There is someone here. Two people, in fact.

One of them is a man with straight black hair and a murderous look on his face, while the other is a beaten and bloodied woman on the ground.

When I see his foot pull back like he's about to kick her, I surge forward without thought.

It's not until I grip him by the arm and toss him away, not until I look over at the woman that I realize…

They're fae.

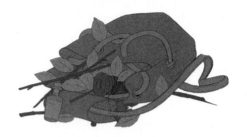

# CHAPTER 66

### EMONIE

I'm lying in a pitiful heap in the snow.

I passed out for a little while, right around the time I saw the bridge explode. I think my heart might have exploded with it, so my body just crumpled. As if no part of me was capable of facing the fact that the bridge was destroyed.

Because that means I'm trapped in Orea forever.

I'm lucky that I was already hobbling away when the land started disintegrating. If I'd still been in that fortress where the Orean came back and tried to convince me to go with him...I'd be swallowed down Orea's gullet right about now.

There were a few close calls.

My body is so battered that I keep going in and out of awareness. I'm in a daze, staring up at the chunky sky while the snow numbs me.

The gray clouds are all thick and bitten off. Like a pack

of wild dogs got into the rising dough and started chomping bits off. Those clouds keep spitting off chunks of frost too, like a lathered tongue that won't stop dripping.

Just like my eyes.

I have no way to get home. Everyone and everything I know and love is back in Annwyn, and I'm here, with no way to get back.

A shudder goes through me, either from sadness or the freezing cold. Even though the numbness is nice, I know if I don't move soon, I'm in danger of never moving again.

I still don't try to get up.

But then, I'm jerked into sharp awareness when a face suddenly appears over me.

"*You*," he spits, and I squint, only to realize with a jolt that it's one of the twins. Not the one I impersonated, but the other... What was his name?

Friano.

Seeing him makes the new antler sprouting from my ear flare with pain. Makes *all* of my pains flare, actually.

"Thanks for ordering that I get beaten within an inch of my life, you ass," I garble out. I can still taste blood.

"How did you get over here?" he shouts, his dark eyes wild, shiny black hair now damp and stringy like he rolled around in the snow. "My brother fell with all the others, but *you* survived? You don't deserve to breathe."

He sounds furious. I don't really care. "Fuck. Off."

His hand lashes out, grabbing me by the ankle, and he starts to drag me. A gasp tears free, pain popping punctures into my vision as his grip digs into my brutalized body.

I try to flip over on instinct to scrabble away from him, but he tosses me aside, making my body roll a few times before stopping. My ribs scream as I try not to puke.

"Did you touch it?" he demands, though it takes me a couple seconds to respond.

"Touch...*what*?" I pant out.

He looks crazed. "If you ruined it, I will *ruin you*!"

At this point, I'm already pretty ruined, but I think I'll keep that to myself.

"I don't know what you're talking about," I say as I try to sit up.

Gnashing his teeth, he swings his foot back, and I flinch automatically, bracing for the kick that's headed right for my face.

But it never comes.

There's a noise, and then I rear back in surprise when I see Friano getting tossed into the snow by someone. I stare in shock when I realize it's a soldier.

An *Orean* soldier.

He's wearing black armor that matches his short hair and the stubble across his jaw. His skin is paler than mine, and his face is twisted in hate as he glares down at the twin.

He yanks a sword from the scabbard at his waist. "You've just breathed your last," he vows darkly.

Friano raises his arm to ward him off, legs scrabbling in the snow, but that's when I notice something on the ground just behind him.

Something green.

My eyes widen, and right when the Orean starts to cut his sword toward Friano, I yell, "*Wait!*"

The soldier pauses and turns to look over his shoulder at me. I start to crawl forward. "Don't kill him!" I call desperately, my frozen limbs making it hard to move.

He narrows his eyes. "He was just about to knock your teeth in, and you're defending him?"

"I need him," I say as I force myself to push up to a stand, my ribs protesting, legs ready to snap.

Though as soon as I'm upright, I realize that he isn't the only Orean here. I freeze as I take in their group. Two women, two men. All of them in armor except for the blonde woman.

Why am I always so outnumbered?

Dizziness cyclones through my head, and I start to pitch sideways, bracing myself to fall again. But the soldier threatening Friano moves in a blink and grabs hold of me before I do.

"Wow," I say, the word slightly slurred as my brain spins. "You move fast."

I can't help but notice that he's grabbed me by the collar so that he's not actually touching me. Either because he can see I'm battered and bruised everywhere...or he just hates fae so much he doesn't want to touch one.

Probably that last option, based on the glare he's giving me.

And that guess is confirmed when he presses the edge of his blade to my neck.

My heart skips a beat, but my mouth takes two more and runs away with it. "That's a very forward introduction. Usually I take a male on a few special outings before I let him jab his pointy thing at me."

There's a pause. Maybe Oreans don't like jokes.

*Great skies, my head hurts.*

"Tell me who you are, *fae*," he demands.

My eyes trail over him as my sluggish consciousness tries to get a handle on this entire situation. "Black armor looks better than stone," I say appreciatively. Maybe I can get on his good side? "You win best uniform."

"We won the *war*," he counters.

"Cheers," I say, trying to lift a hand up. Nope. That hurts. Not going to do that again.

"Did this fae do this to you?" the Orean soldier demands, his eyes roving over my many injuries.

"Umm...sort of."

He narrows his eyes. "What does that mean?"

I quite like the sound of his voice. And he's handsome

too. Sure, he's threatening me at sword point, but we all have our faults.

"Are you going to answer me?"

Honestly, I hadn't decided, but he seems a bit impatient, so…"No."

The sword disappears, which I take as a good sign, until I'm abruptly yanked forward a few steps. "*Iffik*," I cry out, the old fae curse spitting past my split lips. "That hurt!"

I have to breathe through the pain, but that doesn't work so well considering breathing hurts too.

He stops moving me forward, and as soon as I no longer feel like I'm about to vomit, I manage to glare at him. "I liked the queen better. Where is she? I helped her. She'll vouch for me."

I'm not sure the man she was with would sing my praises though, even if I *did* let them free. He didn't seem too fond of me.

Although, he did come back and try to get me to come with them. But while I was turning him down, he had to fight off two Stone Swords before he could get away again. He didn't look pleased about that.

And, if I'm being honest, he didn't try *that* hard to get me to come with him. It was grudgingly at best. Not that I blame him.

"The queen?" the soldier asks in surprise. "You mean Queen Malina?"

"That's the one."

"You helped the Cold Queen *escape*?" Friano snarls behind him on the ground. "It's your fault she went to the bridge?"

*The bridge?*

Friano tries to launch himself at me, but he's intercepted by the woman soldier darting forward. She moves fast, foot sweeping out as she knocks Friano onto the ground again. She has her own sword pulled free, and it's pointed at his face in a blink.

She wears the same armor, and she has dark brown skin, with black hair that's shaved short against her scalp with designs of blades all the way around. My hands itch to collect that look so I can use that hair glamour later.

"I suggest you don't move," she tells Friano in a hard tone. Then she looks up to the soldier still holding onto me. "Ryatt?"

My head swings up. "Ryatt?" I repeat. "As in causing a riot…or you're so funny you're a riot?"

He glares at me, so I'm going to confidently say it's not the second option. It's startling just how green his eyes are, though. Distracts me a bit.

I blame the concussion.

He points his sword down to the green spot in all that snow. "What is that?"

My gaze swings to the ground, but I don't dare show any expression on my face. I lift a shoulder. "What's what?" I ask breezily before I spit out a little blood. I really hope that's just from my mangled tongue.

Impatient anger flashes through his eyes, just as the other soldier, the huge one with the messy beard starts stomping forward to the spot.

Panic flares through me. "Don't touch it!" Friano and I both yell at the same time.

Luckily, the bearded soldier stops and cocks a bushy brow. "Yeah. That's what I thought," he rumbles out.

Ryatt's grip tightens on my collar. He pulls me down slightly, making me hiss in pain as I'm forced to bend toward the ground. "Last chance to explain what this is and what you're hiding, fae."

My heart thumps wildly, nervousness gripping my thoughts. I lift my gaze to Friano. He's got a boot to the chest by the woman soldier, but he's staring at me, and he shakes his head with a clear threat in his dark eyes.

Ryatt notices. He drags me up so we're face-to-face again, making me yelp.

And sure, he's *mad*, but he's also a bit mesmerizing for some reason. I can't *not* notice—not from this close up.

"You will tell me right now, or I will kill you both," he says, his tone low and threatening.

I still like it though.

*Great goddess, how hard did my head get kicked?*

"We will tell you *nothing*, Orean scum," Friano hisses.

I wrinkle my nose, anger lashing toward the twin. "Don't say *we*. You and I are not on the same side."

His attention lands on me with utter loathing. "Shut your mouth, you Orean-loving traitor whore!"

I ignore his jab. "Did you and your twin do this somehow?"

He doesn't answer. Just stares at me with all the hate and pain from me mentioning his brother, but I don't care. I hate him right back, and this is more important.

Because that swipe of green that rests against the snow? That spot that's making my pulse race and my mind spin? It's a patch of grass.

Grass that's grown in the perfect circle of a *fairy ring*.

And it carries familiar sweet-smelling air.

"Where does it lead?" I ask desperately, my gaze hinging on his. "*Where?*"

Friano refuses to answer, but my stomach flips, because his gaze gives me all the confirmation I need.

I still have a chance to get home.

Because this fairy ring…it's connected to *Annwyn*.

# CHAPTER 67

## AUREN TURLEY

When we return to Lydia, I help make repairs to some of the buildings that were partially burned from the Stone Swords setting fire to the city. My gold now envelops some of them, corners swathed and doors patched with gleaming metal. The trees weren't burned too badly, though some are charred, branches stripped or fallen away.

The Lydians settle back into their homes, while the Vulmin and Oreans try to determine their next steps.

And Slade and I determine ours.

We're sitting at one of the outdoor tables along the street, in front of a pretty servette that reminds me of Estelia and Thursil back in Geisel.

Slade, Elore, Wick, and I sit together. The tables look like they've been hewn out of some sort of pale blue gemstone that's been polished and smoothed. The matching chairs are surprisingly light, their backs wickered like a woven basket, with plump cushions on the seats. Every time the breeze blows in, the little glowing blue bulbs that hang above us at the building's eave tinkle together.

Slade is relaxed back in his chair beside me, hand clasped around a steaming drink. His mother sits at his left, and he's ordered every single thing from the display window for her. Every fruit-topped tart, every rolled and sugared bun. Her eyes went wide as saucers, but she's since sampled every plate, and she looks so content that my heart squeezes for her.

I sip on my own warm and bubbled drink, watching people walk by or stop at the market carts across the street. Boats drift along in the canal just ahead, while birds sing above us in the trees.

My wings are slightly stretched out, and every so often, Slade runs a finger down them, making me shiver.

A couple of fae walk past us, and they smile at me with a wave. I smile back, my lips still curved even after they've disappeared from view. "This is so peaceful, isn't it?" I say, turning to look at everyone. "To just sit here in the sun with food and drink, and watch everyone go by."

"It is," Slade says as he places a hand on my leg and squeezes gently.

He hasn't stopped touching me, and I haven't stopped touching him either. The both of us are constantly reaching out in comforting caresses to help settle the aftershocks of the horrors that happened. To reassure each other that we're no longer cleaved apart by death.

"The trick is to *keep* it peaceful," Wick says as he sets down his own drink and looks between us. He's been quiet. Chewing on something more than the food, and when he glances at me, I know he's ready to divulge.

"I'm going to propose that Annwyn do away with the monarchy. That we form an assemblage instead," he says, straightening in his chair.

His expression is serious but impassioned, and I can tell he's probably been thinking of nothing but Annwyn's future since I abdicated taking the crown.

"We can spread the word all over Annwyn. Invite fae to come to Lydia and help create new laws. Anyone who wishes to put themself forward as a member of the assemblage can formally insert their name, and we'll put it to the people for a vote. We'll put everything to vote."

I smile. "I think that's a very good idea."

"It will take time," Slade cautions.

"That's okay," Wick replies. "We need to get it right. That's why the assemblage will be so important. It will allow for both fae and Orean voices to be heard. Vulmin and non-Vulmin. And not just nobles. It will be fair—and full of passionate people who can help us solve the issues and keep an eye on every corner of Annwyn. No more tyranny and the risk of one person with all control. We all know that having too much power can turn even those with the best intentions into a glutton for more. So we restore the old territory lines. Let the people have a say in their lives. We do better."

"We do better." I nod in agreement, happiness warming my chest. "I'm proud of you, Wick."

He shifts in his chair, like he's surprised but pleased at my response.

It would've been easy for him to just claim the throne. After all, he has the Turley name and blood. He has the Vulmin following. But for him to recognize Annwyn needs to try a different way shows me that he really does have Annwyn's best interest at heart instead of his own play for power. I couldn't be prouder.

"Yes, well...I've learned some things. From a certain broken-winged bird who learned how to fly."

That warmth in me spreads, and I can see tentative hope in his own expression. His russet skin is still bruised, but healing. His muddy eyes are illuminated, as if he's already looking toward a brighter future.

"Peace can be difficult to enact," Slade says as he sets down his drink. "But it's also difficult to keep. Eventually, peace always deteriorates."

Wick nods. "It does. And one day, someone like the Carricks may emerge again—someone who will attempt to take control. But in the meantime, we do better and hope that for generations and generations, we *keep* doing better. We make Annwyn peaceful...for as long as we can."

I pick up my drink. "Here's to keeping the peace."

All four of us clink our cups together before setting them down, and then Wick looks to me. He seems relieved now that he's told us his plans, like he's ready to take on the world. "I also want to formally ask that you and Slade become the first members of the assemblage."

I suck in a breath, indecision warring through me as I glance at Slade for a second. "I don't know..."

"You don't have to give me an answer now," Wick hurries to say. "But I want you to have a voice. There won't be any requirement to do anything you don't wish. But when you *do* want to give input or address concerns, being on the assemblage gives you that opportunity. It's because of you and Slade that Annwyn is getting this second chance in the first place. So just...think about it."

Slade and I exchange another look before I answer. "Okay. We'll think about it."

Wick nods and gets up from the table. "I'll catch up with you later," he says before he turns and leaves.

"What do you think?" I ask Elore.

Her gaze moves from Wick's retreating form, back to me, and then she gives the smallest nod, her lips curling in a smile.

"Yeah," I reply. "I think so too."

Just then, one of the Orean women I released from the

dungeon cells walks up along the road beside us. She's one of the Drollard villagers that Slade and I are taking care of, making sure they have everything they need as they recover. Slade is incredibly attentive to them all.

Her eyes light up as she stops. "Elore!" she says in greeting. "We're going down to the river for a boat ride. Would you like to come?" Her face is still healing from the whip mark across her cheek, but it's already looking so much better.

Elore nods and gets up from her chair. She leans over to pop a kiss on top of Slade's head before she walks away. The woman smiles at me, and the two of them head for the water.

"You think she'll be okay?" I ask Slade quietly.

He watches his mother as she and the woman stroll down the street. "She's strong," he says, though I can hear the underlying layer of regret. "We're here now, and he's gone. I hope, with enough time, she can heal. Be happy."

I nod, but my chest constricts. "It's hard though, isn't it?" I say softly. "We're sitting here surrounded by sunshine and beauty, without danger or problems breathing down our necks for once. But how can we even really enjoy it when we don't know if the others are okay?"

Slade stays quiet, but I see his own worry tangled in the shadows of his green eyes.

"I can't imagine how you and your poor mother must be feeling about being cut off from Ryatt," I say, sadness wetting my eyes. "Your Wrath are your family, and we're cut off from them too. Cut off from your whole kingdom. I mean…you're a *king* in Orea, and here…"

"My Premiers will lead. Fourth is better off without me. Once I found you, my priorities changed," he says with a lift of his shoulder. "I'm not saying I regret that, I'm just stating a truth. Fourth is in good hands—*better* hands—with Isalee and Warken."

"I miss everyone so much," I confess as I look at him, my stomach twisting with the bitter taste of separation. "And we'll never know—any of it. If they're okay. If they defeated Carrick." I sniff, like I'm trying to pull my sadness right back in. "We'll never get to see them again. Your brother, Lu, Osrik, Judd, Digby, Rissa...none of them. And I'll never know what happened to Emonie either. We're just...cut off." I press my fingers to my eyes, wiping at the tears. "It's a grim side to this peace."

"It is," Slade replies quietly, his eyes drawn. "It's a hard reality to swallow." His gaze moves through the trees and focuses on the plateau we can see in the distance. Glassworth Palace sits there, empty and full of color.

Color, and smoke.

Wick sent a large group of Vulmin to deal with the dead soldiers and Cull's rotting corpse...and also Slade's dragon.

That beautiful, formidable creature that felt exactly like Slade. That flew us through the sky. It was taken from him after he'd only just gotten it.

"I'm sorry," I say quietly, and his eyes come back to mine.

I hate that he lost his dragon, especially because I know what it's like to lose a part of yourself like that. For someone to come in and take it away from you.

Slade leans forward and takes my hand between both of his. "You are the most important part of myself. So long as I have you, I'm whole."

My eyes tear up and threaten to spill over, while his fingers bracket mine, surrounding me with his warmth.

"We're going to savor each other, okay?" he says softly. "We're going to tell ourselves that everyone in Orea is alright, because we have to. And they'll be doing the very same thing with us. That's how we'll get through the separation. That's how we keep going."

I nod. "You're right."

There's always going to be this bitter to our sweet. A sharp edge to our smoothed surface. I'm going to miss them all. Desperately. But Slade is right. We'll just have to have faith that they're okay, and savor each other.

Because we've lost so much, and we've been given so much.

Sometimes, that's just how life is. Sacrifice in grace, loss within the victory, scar after the heal.

But we have each other.

I press a kiss against his knuckles before settling our hands down on my lap. We sit here for a while in the quiet, our thoughts gathering like strings that drift around our heads and stick together like webs.

"So, I guess we have to figure out what's next for us," I say as I reach for my cup and swirl it around, watching the bubbles rise in perfect streams. "You're not a king, I'm not a queen, and we're here in the fae realm together. But...what now?"

Slade props his elbow on the arm of the chair, thumb dragging against his bottom lip as he watches me. The spikes on his arm are on display, though he's pulled in the ones at his back. Instead of wearing army leathers or the ill-fitting trousers, he has a deep green jerkin and black pants on that actually fit him.

He looks so wickedly handsome it makes my pulse jump.

"Well, you gave an answer to that for Annwyn. Now, I think it's time you give an answer for *you*," he finally says.

"Us," I correct.

"Always us," he agrees. "But I told you before, Goldfinch. I want you to have whatever life you want," he tells me, his voice dropping lower. "Whether that's to travel the world or hide away in a cabin in the woods..."

My breath catches in my chest as I recognize the words

we spoke before, inside the walls of a carriage. Right before we did *very* inappropriate things right there along the street in Fourth Kingdom.

"If you want to climb a mountain or build something with your own hands or sit in a pub or play music or spend all day making love…" His low tone drags against my heated skin. "But I am yours and you are mine, and I will always make sure that you get what you need."

My heart skips, my cheeks warmed by far more than the sun. "So the question isn't *what now*. The question is…what do *you* want now?" he asks.

"I want…" I swallow hard.

Slade reaches forward to brush a lock of my hair away from my face. "Tell me."

My truth sits right there, so I let it spill out. "I want to take you to Geisel. I want to introduce you to the fae there who helped me. Want to show you the field of flowers where Saira Turley and I both fell."

His lips curve, following the slow drag of his finger against my neck, nearly touching my scale. "What else, Goldfinch?"

"I want to eat Estelia's puff cakes. At least a dozen of them."

He breaks out into a full grin. "At least," he says with a nod. "What else?"

"I want to…"

"Tell me," he says again, urging me on.

"I want to go back to Bryol," I admit quietly with a tremor in my voice. "I want to see if there's a way we can rebuild it. I hate that it's just left there in ruins. I know it will probably take a lot, and I'm sure we'll have to talk to someone, and maybe it's stupid, but—"

Slade grips my chin, stopping me. "That's not stupid, Auren. If you want to rebuild the city where you grew up, where you last saw your parents, then that's what we'll do. Brick by brick if we have to." His touch moves to clasp the side of my face. "We have all the time in the world. Every day is going to be our *one day*. Spending it however we want. Okay?"

A tear drips down my cheek in both relief and gratitude. I'm not sure why I'd been so nervous telling him about Bryol. I should know better than that. Because Slade always reacts exactly how I need him to. He's my other half—he knows the direction my heart beats. He always has.

"I love you," I murmur.

"I love you more than all the stars in the sky, Goldfinch." He presses a kiss against my lips. "So let's go to Geisel and Bryol. When do you want to leave?"

A happy smile takes over my face. "As soon as we can."

# CHAPTER 68

## COMMANDER RYATT

I stare between the two fae, all my senses prickling. They're obviously keeping something from us, and I don't like it one bit.

When I first saw the man about to kick the woman, I just burst into action and raced over to rip him away from her.

For a flash, it reminded me of all the times I saw Slade's father hit my mother. All those times I was helpless and far too young to do anything. So seeing that man fling back his foot made my vision go red.

But this woman isn't my mother. She's a fae. A Stone Sword. And if there's one thing that's been made very clear in my life, it's that you can't trust a fae. Save for my brother and Auren, I've hated every other one I've ever known or come across.

I need answers, and it's clear neither fae wants to give them to me. I glare down at the woman's bruised face, eyeing the strange small antler growing out of her left ear and curling around it in thin swoops.

Despite how badly beaten she is, I have to remind myself not to take pity on her. She's a soldier. She marched here with the intention to invade and massacre us.

She and the other fae are having some sort of stare-off. I don't understand the questions she asked him, but he's glaring daggers at her.

But it's *her* expression I'm more interested in. Because there's a gleam in those strange eyes of hers that looks a lot like excited hope. And anything she's excited about can't possibly be good for us.

"You said *where does it lead*," I repeat, looking right at her as I hold her by the collar. "What does that mean? What are you talking about?"

"Say nothing, or I will crush you!" the other fae shouts at her, just as he tries to lash out at Lu.

But he's clearly underestimated her, because when he tries to hit her leg to knock her back, Lu just swings back her foot and kicks him in the temple. Just like he was going to do to the woman, so I don't think Lu did it by coincidence. His brown eyes flare for a split second before he slumps into unconsciousness.

My brows lift, but Lu just glances at me and shrugs.

I look over at the patch of grass. It's grown up from the snow to form a perfect circle, and there are even white and purple flowers blooming through it. Way too strange to be natural.

"What does this mean?" I ask the fae woman. "Did you make this?"

She snorts, though it comes out more like a wheeze. I think her nose may be broken. "Me? Don't be ridiculous. My magic has nothing to do with grass."

"So it's *his* magic?"

She hesitates. "I didn't say that."

I grind my teeth around a growl. "You will start giving me answers, or you will find yourself at the end of my sword again."

"But I *did* give you an answer," she snaps with irritation. "I told you it's not my magic."

"You could be lying."

Her lips press together, and then her hand comes up and slaps the side of my face—not hard, but with enough force that I blink in surprise.

"You—" Whatever I was about to say cuts off as her face suddenly starts to change.

I rear back in shock, watching her skin stretch and pale, her hair darkening, face shape morphing and jawline sharpening. Then I gape even more, because she's somehow turned into…me.

She's still swollen and bruised, but it's definitely *my* face.

I let go like she's on fire, and she goes tumbling back, landing ass-first in the snow.

"What the fuck?" I shout, my pulse whipping around in my ears.

"*What the fuck*," she mocks with a low-pitched voice that apparently is supposed to sound like me.

Behind me, I hear Lu snort under her breath.

The fae screws up her face and rolls her one eye. *My* eye. It's green now instead of the red-orange it was before.

"You tried to say I was lying. Well, this proves I'm not. I have glamour magic," she tells me before she morphs back into herself, feature by feature. "See? That grass has nothing to do with me."

She tries to push herself up as I glare at her. "So you didn't lie, but you're a liar by nature," I counter. "Every time you use your magic, you're lying about who you are."

"Yeah…well…" She pants as she attempts to pivot her body sideways so she can get up, but then she turns pale and presses a hand against her ribs. "I—" She blows out a breath, giving up as she slumps back in the snow. "I can't come up with a witty retort at the moment. Too much pain takes away from one's humor."

"Oh for Divine's sake," I hear Rissa exclaim, and then she comes hurrying over. She skirts past me and kneels down in front of the woman before I can stop her.

"*Rissa*," Osrik growls.

She whips her head around and pins him with a glare, stopping him from following. "Don't *Rissa* me," she tells him before her ire turns on me. "And *you*. What is wrong with you, Commander? Can't you see this woman is hurt?"

"She's a *fae*."

"Yes, well, according to all of you, so is your brother," Rissa seethes. "And so is Auren, so you can—"

"Wait," the fae blurts out, blinking in shock. "Did you say *Auren*?"

Everyone pauses.

"Yes…" Rissa starts carefully, eyes roving over her.

"I know Auren!" she exclaims, making Rissa suck in a surprised breath.

But I shake my head in disgust. "Enough," I growl before looking at Rissa. "She's tricking you. Don't fall for it."

"I am not!"

What a little liar.

"Fine." I cross my arms in front of me. "Then how do you know Auren?"

Her gaze darts around as if to gauge everyone's expressions.

Digby steps forward. "What does she look like?" His face is creased in distrust, but there's a flicker of hope there in his eyes that I want to shake my head at. He should know better.

"Yeah," Lu challenges. "If you know her, you can easily describe her."

I watch this play out, and unsurprisingly, the fae hesitates. I can practically see her thoughts spinning a web of lies to wrap us in.

"See?" I say, pointing at her face. "She's trying to deceive us. She latched onto the first piece of information that slipped out. Nothing but fae trickery."

She narrows her eyes on me, though the effect doesn't do much because they're nearly swollen shut anyway. "It's not a trick," she snaps. "And I don't like you. You have bad tones. Tone. A bad tone." She blinks and sways where she sits, but Rissa's grip keeps her upright. "I'll prove I'm not lying."

The fae drags a hand from brow to chin, and suddenly, her face seems to drip with a waterless deluge. Then, shiny, glittering gold skin appears in its wake, cheeks glistening, irises the same gold as Auren's.

My eyes widen. I hear Digby suck in a breath.

"Great Divine, she *does* know her!" Rissa exclaims.

The fae rubs at her face like she's wiping sweat away, and the glamour magic dissolves, her skin returning to her normal tone again. "There," she says with haughty triumph. "Now how do *you* know Auren?"

"We know her," I say before anyone else can give this fae more information to use against us. "That's all you need to know."

Rissa shakes her head at me, two pink spots appearing at her cheeks that mark her irritation. "What is wrong with you?"

"Yeah, what's wrong with you?" the fae repeats.

My molars grind together in irritation, but I keep my attention on Rissa. "That only proved that she's seen Auren. We don't know if she's friend or foe."

Rissa doesn't look impressed. "Come on, let's get you up," she says to the woman. "Nice and easy."

With Rissa's help, the fae manages to stand. She breathes hard, expression morphing into pain as the blood drains from her face. She sways slightly on her feet, but Rissa keeps hold of her.

"Thanks," she grits out. Then her eyes latch onto something behind us, and she goes still. "Great skies, what is *that*?"

We all turn to see Argo land next to us. His head swings in the direction of the unconscious fae, and he lets out a growl.

"Timberwing," Rissa says dismissively. "Can you tell me if Auren is okay? Is she still in the fae realm? Did King Ravinger find her?"

"*Rissa*—" I growl, just as Osrik comes stomping over.

"I don't know anything about a Ravinger king, but she's there. Last I saw her, she was fighting the Stone King, and then he fled—grabbed me with him."

My thoughts churn with her answers, but I can't help but notice how perfectly worded they are. Just enough information to make it seem like she knows a lot, without actually telling us much of anything.

Lu and I exchange a wary look.

When Osrik moves to grab hold of Rissa's arm, she shrugs him off, refusing him. I hear him curse under his breath.

"What's your name?" she asks the fae.

"Emonie."

I blink incredulously. "Your name rhymes with *enemy*?"

She makes a sound that's something between a snort and a scoff. It wheezes either way. "It's actually a bit funny if you think about it," she says, but when we all just keep staring at her, she sighs. "Oreans need better senses of humor. Look, I know you don't trust fae right now because of the whole *we invaded your world and tried to kill you* thing, but I'm not a Stone Sword. I'm on your side."

I lift a brow. "We might be more inclined to believe you if you weren't *wearing* Stone Sword armor," I point out through gritted teeth.

She glances down at the pebbled chest plate like she forgot she was wearing it. "Oh, this. I had to be in disguise to fit in with the soldiers."

"Convenient."

A sharp breath comes out of her. "Look, you don't trust me, and I understand that. But I *am* on your side, and Auren is my friend."

I stare at her for a few seconds. "Alright then, if she's your friend, if you're really here to help, then prove it to us. Tell me what that circle of grass is."

Her gaze wavers over everyone, including the still passed-out fae.

When she continues to stay silent, I shake my head. "We should just toss her over the fucking edge."

"It's a fairy ring!" Emonie blurts out.

I go still. "A…fairy ring?"

But I've heard that term before. A long time ago.

Lu's brows dip. Osrik and Digby glance toward the grass.

"What's a fairy ring?" Rissa asks curiously.

"Shit in a stew, I better not regret this…" Emonie mumbles beneath her breath before she seems to shore herself up, looking right at me. "A fairy ring is a foothold. Ringers make them by tapping into Annwyn's vein."

"That was a lot of words to speak to not say anything," Lu drawls.

"Said simply, it's a way to transport you. If you go into a fairy ring, you're taken somewhere else."

My breath freezes. Everyone's eyes dart around, like we're all looking to see how each of us take in this information.

But then her previous question to the other fae pops in my head. "Wait a second… You asked the other fae where it leads." My pulse starts racing. "Where does this ring lead?" I ask carefully, my question suspended.

"Well…" she begins slowly. "I think it connects to Annwyn."

I'm riddled with shock.

With possibilities.

With *hope*.

"Are you saying…we can get to Annwyn?" Lu asks incredulously.

Emonie glances over at the other fae. "I think so. He's not a ringer though—his magic worked with his twin, who died in the collapse. But still, I think they were using it somehow."

"We can go to Annwyn to find them," Digby says, gaze darting to me.

My heart knocks its fists against my chest, threatening to punch through.

But Lu comes over and grips my arm, turning me away from the fae. "I know what you're thinking," she whispers, her serious eyes locked on me. "But we don't know if we can trust this."

I drag a hand over my hair in frustration. "I know."

Thoughts whirl, and I keep seeing my brother's face before he left Fourth. Keep remembering what he said to me.

*Orea has a chance because of you.*

He believed in me. Trusted me. And now that Orea is safe, all I want to do is make sure that *he's* safe. That our mother is, and Auren too.

I shake my head, looking at Lu. "We have to."

It's probably a trick. These fae are probably setting up a trap. But we have to try to find them.

I look from her to Osrik. To Digby. To Rissa.

"I'll go," I finally say.

"No."

The reply comes from all four of them at once. Even Argo makes a noise.

Os shakes his head. "We do this? Then we fucking do it together. All or none."

"Wait, you all actually want to go into Annwyn?" Emonie asks in surprise.

"We need to find Auren and the others," Rissa explains.

The fae shoves her orange-tipped hair away from her face. "You all care about her?"

Digby answers simply. "Yes."

No other elaboration, just that one word, but it's spoken so true that she doesn't question it.

"Fine. We can try. But you have to let me go through too," Emonie says, wetting her dried, cracked lips, eyes rounded in desperation. "I don't belong here."

"On that we can agree," I say. "Tell us how it works."

"I dunno," she says, wincing as she presses at her ribs again. "It's not my magic, remember? But that's a fairy ring, even if it is about three times bigger than I've ever seen. All I know is we stand in it. The ringer does the rest. I suggest waking up Friano over there for more details. He was way too twitchy about it."

"If you're lying…"

"Yeah, yeah. Threats and such," she slurs with a sigh. "You think I want to stick around here? No offense, but Orea stinks. Terrible air quality."

My jaw tightens. This fae is getting under my skin.

I turn away. "Os?"

"Yep," he says before he strides over to Friano.

Without preamble, he yanks the unconscious fae up from the snow, holding him by the front of his jerkin until his feet dangle in the air. With his other hand, Os punches him in the gut.

A strangled noise tears from Friano's throat as he springs awake, body jerking. When he realizes he's being held up, he tries to claw Osrik's hand away, which does nothing.

I walk over and point my sword at his eye. He freezes.

"Listen to me very carefully," I say quietly, my tone colder than the snow I stand on. "I don't give a fuck about your life, but *you* do. And if you want to keep it, you will take us through this fairy ring into Annwyn right now."

His eyes flare and then he flicks his attention to lock onto Emonie. "You traitorous little wench! I will kill you!"

"The only one who will be killed is you. Unless you take us through."

Fury hardens his face. "*Fine.*"

I put my sword away and turn.

"Everyone stand around it. We'll step in at the same time," I direct.

Rissa helps Emonie hobble over, while the rest of us circle around the ring. Argo whines and scrapes his talons as he paces just outside the circle. "Go back to Fourth, Argo," I call to him, but he snarls at me, snapping his teeth.

Friano starts to struggle again, legs kicking out, but Osrik doesn't budge. "Let me go, you Orean filth," the fae spits.

"Nope," Os replies before reaching out to grab Rissa with his free hand.

I look around at my group, my muscles stiffening, pulse pounding.

Now or never.

"On three," I murmur. "One, two, *three…*"

Everyone steps inside the ring at the same time, and I hold my breath. We barely fit, arms pressing in together, everyone tense and waiting.

But…nothing happens.

My eyes swing to Emonie, but she's looking at Friano.

"Make it work," she demands, with an edge of desperation. "Take us back to Annwyn right now."

Friano glares at her in silent refusal.

In a blink, Osrik has him by the throat and shoves him down until the fae is forced to kneel. "Make it work, fae," he growls.

When all Friano does is continue to glare, Lu whips out

her dagger and starts cutting across his throat. Her blade drags, making his blood drip. Making it clear she'll just slice his Divine-damned throat here and now.

The fae instantly panics.

His head jerks, eyes nearly popping out of his skull. "Okay!" he screams.

"Last chance at life," I snap. "Because guess what? If we kill you, it doesn't fucking matter to me. I don't actually believe this ring is going to take us anywhere. I think you're full of shit."

The hatred that pours off Friano is so heated I can feel the temperature rising.

"Our soldiers on the other side are going to tear you apart. *All* of you," he threatens, burning his gaze into Emonie. "I'll enjoy watching."

He slams his hand down. Instantly, a flare ignites beneath his palm, and I hear Argo let out a shrill cry.

The light burns white and spreads from his hand, jutting up from the grassy circle. I hear gasps of surprise as the whole ring lights up. My body braces for an attack, my hand gripped around the hilt of my sword.

Out of the corner of my eye, I see Argo launch into the air, flying toward us in a panic. A roar tumbles out of his throat just as he crosses into the illuminated ring.

Then the world dissolves in fracturing light.

I suck in a breath as something seems to lash out and grab hold of me. It wraps around me with invisible, spindly fingers that have no true touch and yet keep me hostage anyway.

Nausea roils through me, and my panic makes me break out into a cold sweat. I try to call out to the others, but I can't breathe. I feel like I'm being squeezed. Like I'm tipping over an edge.

Anger rushes into me.

This *is* a fucking trick. This fae is *killing* us.

I can't take in a breath. I can't see anything but this blinding light. We're going to die grasped in this constricting magic that won't let go.

Suddenly, hard ground slams against my side as I land, no more bodiless fingers squeezing, and I'm able to yank in a breath.

We all topple over each other, just a tangle of limbs, and my eyes swing around.

Then, I hear a *scream*.

# CHAPTER 69

## COMMANDER RYATT

I don't even have a chance to get my bearings.

At the sound of her scream, I instantly leap to my feet, head still spinning from the vertigo. My eyes find Friano, and I see that he's somehow snatched a dagger and is swinging it down at Emonie.

My body moves so fast even *I* don't track what I'm doing. Pure wrath has taken over.

Just before the blade can plunge into her, I slam into Friano's side with all my strength and tackle him to the ground. There's a shout as the fae and I roll. Teeth bared, I yank the dagger out of his clutches and then stab *him* in the chest. His shocked face stares up at me for a second, and then his entire body goes lax.

Dead. In an instant.

I stare in shock, looking down at the blade and his unblinking eyes, breathing hard.

*Shit.*

I lurch around and see Osrik yanking Rissa out of the ring…just as the circle of grass withers and dies.

Everyone looks at me as I race over. "Fuck," I whisper as I stare at the ring. Then I tear my hand through my hair, voice rising. "Fuck!"

My shout echoes, and I flinch when I hear Argo let out a growl in response.

*He got through.*

I spin, gaze frantic. But I see everyone. Os and Rissa, Lu, Digby, Emonie. Everyone made it here.

*Here…*

I take in the sights. Just ahead of us is a sheer cliff, and at the top of the flat plateau is a colorful, glittering palace looking down at us. The surrounding landscape is lavish greenery, and above us is a purple sky.

"Is this…" Lu begins shakily.

Emonie nods with a relieved smile through swollen and split lips. "Annwyn."

We're here, it worked, but…

"I didn't even fucking think," I say, shaking my head at myself. "I just killed him."

Turning, I stride over to Emonie and pull her up from the ground. She hisses from my rough grasp. "The ring died. Can we get back?" I ask desperately. When she hesitates, I shake her. "Can we fucking get back?"

"I don't know," she admits. "I've never heard of a ringer who could make a fairy ring appear in another realm. I don't know how Friano manipulated it."

Realization pours over me with a sobering sluice. We're *trapped* here. The place I despise more than anything.

Emonie swallows hard, paling at my grip, and I scrape together enough wherewithal to release her. She stumbles back but manages to stay standing as I start to pace.

"We can try to find the ringer, Brennur. See if the Vulmin have him captured. Maybe he can do it…" Emonie ventures, but she sounds doubtful. "Then again, maybe it had to do with the twins," she says, tipping her head in the direction of the dead fae. "I don't know."

I curse myself for being such a fucking idiot. Anger churns inside me, making me pivot and point at her. "This is your fault."

She rears back, her red eyes flashing. "Me? I didn't tell you to kill him!"

I let out a snarl, but Lu steps in front of me. "Calm down," she snaps. "It's done. We'll find another ringer to make it back to Orea, okay? Get your fucking head on. Focus on what's important. We can find your mother. Can find Slade and Auren."

Breaths heave in and out of me. She's right. I'm furious, but I know I'm furious at *myself*. That I'm lashing out in panic because I hate this place. I despise the thought of being stuck here.

"We're here to find them," Lu repeats. "So we do that first."

My jaw is locked so hard my teeth threaten to crack, but I take a deep breath and nod. "Yeah."

"You good?" she asks pointedly. "Because we're in the fucking *fae realm*. We need to have our shit together, Ry."

Guilt douses me. "You're right." I swallow hard before looking at everyone. "I'm sorry. I don't know what I was thinking."

"You just reacted," Lu says with a sigh. "It's not the first time we've seen you take a man out for trying to hurt a woman."

"Nope," Os says, looking at me. "And he would've stabbed us in the back the second he had the chance anyway. Better him than us."

"Where should we go now?" Digby questions as he stands beside a very aggravated Argo.

Emonie keeps eyeing the beast with wariness, but she looks over at Digby's question. "Well…that's the capital." She points a finger, though she can't lift her arm very high. "Lydia," she says, directing our gazes to the city. I can see a river winding into the forest just beside it and catch glimpses of buildings amongst the tall trees. "That's the last place I saw Auren."

I only have a small sliver of faith that she's telling the truth. But even a single sliver can catch flame.

"Let's go," I say.

Our group walks down the dirt road through the valley while Argo flies low to the ground, circling over us, unwilling to stray further. We head away from the plateau and palace, away from the waterfall that pours down the side of the cliff.

"Stay on alert," I say over my shoulder. "We don't know what to expect."

I make sure to keep Emonie with me as we lead the way. My eyes keep darting to her as she grimaces with every step. "You gonna tell me who beat the shit out of you?"

"Why? You want to thank them?" she retorts, derision dripping off her words.

My jaw tightens. I try my best to ignore her as my attention sharpens on the city.

"You're going to feel *soooo* bad once you see I was telling the truth," she singsongs before she sways again, nearly tipping right off the road.

My hand lashes out to grab her arm to steady her, fingers instantly gentling when she sucks in a pained gasp.

"You need to learn to have a gentler touch, Commander," she says with a choppy giggle.

"Stop talking."

"Ohh. Silent type, huh? I like them usually. Fewer words

GOLDFINCH

from a male, the better. Doesn't seem to be working for you, though. Maybe try to be *more* silent?"

Irritation jumps in my jaw. "You are aggravating."

She tugs her arm out of my grip as she limps forward. "If it weren't for me, you wouldn't be here," she lobs back. "So maybe have a little gratitude."

"Sure," I reply smoothly. "Unless we're about to walk into an ambush or I confirm that you've lied. Then gratitude will be last on the list."

"But still on the list. That's good."

Annoyance makes my eyes tighten. I can't wait to be rid of this fae.

"Auren is going to be so mad at you," she says before pausing and muttering under her breath. "Unless she's mad at me."

I whip my head toward her as we turn left onto the road that leads toward the city. "Why would she be mad at you?"

I don't miss the way her lips tilt down at the corners. "Well..." She suddenly stops and frowns. "What in the realms?"

Following her line of sight, I stop in my tracks when I see what she's looking at.

"Is that..." I hear Osrik rumble as everyone comes to a stop next to us.

"Oh, shit," Lu exclaims. "It is!"

"What is wrong with the ground?" Emonie asks, her face scrunched up in confusion. "I know they sent soldiers to burn the city, but this isn't from flames."

"No," I say, feeling a smile break through my face. "It's *rot*."

"Rot?" She glances around at all of us. "And that's...a *good* thing?"

"Yep," I say as I start walking again, quicker this time,

filled with rushing relief that's pushing me to hurry. "Because that means my brother was here."

My heart isn't only pounding with apprehension and worry. It pounds with new, leaping hope.

He was here. The evidence is clear as day, with every rotted line singed into the ground.

*Please be here.*

*Please, fucking be here…*

We approach an arch made of some sort of purple stone, and then there's another sight that makes my chest tighten.

Gold. Right there, solidified into parts of the buildings.

"Look," I tell everyone.

"I see it," Lu breathes, breaking out into a smile. "Two out of two."

Rot and gold.

My hope feels even closer now. Like I can almost reach out and grab hold of it. Make it real.

As soon as we get within ten feet of the arch and the tall trees that pillar it, a fae comes walking out. He's wearing a long robe and has a beard down to his stomach. "Residents?" he asks, but then he looks us over, gaze casting over our ears. "Oh, Oreans? You can—"

He stops and looks at me, words cutting off. "Great Goddess. I thought you were someone else."

My pulse surges as I take a step forward. "*Who?*" I ask, all my anticipation riding on the question.

The fae starts to answer, but then his attention diverts. He makes a choking noise, nearly swallowing his tongue when he sees Argo swoop in front of him. "What is *that?*"

"Don't worry. It's just their monster bird thing. It's harmless." Emonie shuffles forward. "Actually…I'm not really sure that it *is* harmless, but it's probably fine."

The fae does a double take. "*Emonie?*"

"Hi, Karth," she says with a small wave.

He shakes his head in disbelief. "Everyone saw the king take you. What the hell happened?" he asks, paling as he takes in her appearance. "Who did this to you?" His gaze instantly moves to us with open accusation.

"Not them, and not important right now," she says dismissively. "How are you here in the city? Where are the Stone Swords?"

The fae seems like he doesn't know quite where to look, his gaze bouncing around from between Emonie's beaten body, Argo, and me. "Wick called all the Vulmin in. We have Lydia. We have…Annwyn, actually."

Emonie rears back. "*What*? What do you mean?"

"Come in, Emonie," he insists. "We need to get you to Parta. She can heal you."

"I will, but first, where's the Lyäri?"

I exchange a look with the others. *Lyäri*?

"And…" Emonie turns to look at me. "What was his name?"

"Slade. Slade Ravinger," I say, stepping forward.

The fae blinks. "You his brother? You look just like him."

I suck in a breath. I don't know how I stay on my fucking feet. "*Yes*. Yes. I'm his brother," I say in a rush. "Where is he?"

He pauses as all of us crowd around him, waiting for his answer with bated breath.

"Karth," Emonie urges. "Where?"

"I'm sorry, Oreans," he says with a shake of his head. "They left. Just a few hours ago, I think."

The disappointment is so buckling that I stumble back. I hear Lu let out a sigh, and see Digby's whole body slump.

They were here, and they left. We *just* missed them…

"Left? Where did they go?" Emonie asks desperately. "I need to talk to the Lyäri!"

"Ryatt?"

My head jerks to the left. Then my eyes widen.

Slade halts in the middle of the street in front of me,

mouth dropped open in surprise. His spikes are on his arms, rot lines crawling up his neck and scales along both his cheeks. He looks really, *really* fae. Pointed ears on display, all his features out at once.

My vision tunnels on him.

We both just stare at each other. Shocked into place. I blink over and over again to make sure I'm not seeing things.

Then he surges forward.

I'm barely able to take a few steps before Slade practically tackles me in a hug. I hug him back, arms constricting around him just to make sure he's actually real.

"How the fuck are you here?" he asks with astonishment as he pounds me on the back before pulling away. "How are you all here?" he says before he turns to grip Lu in a hug too.

"Put those spikes away before you take out an eye," she chastises, but she's smiling, beaming with happiness.

His spikes disappear as he claps Osrik on the back next, his own face broken out into a smile.

When he sees Digby, he pauses.

"Where is she?" Digby asks. His voice is strained, face sharper with all the edges of hope as his emotion pierces through. "Where's Lady Auren?" His voice cracks down the middle. "Is she okay?"

All I see is a blur of gold.

One second, I'm staring at Digby as he barely keeps it together, and then Auren has launched herself into his arms.

He staggers back from the shock and her hold. But when he realizes who's hugging him, when he realizes it's real, he wraps his arms around her, and his face crumples as the old guard cries.

*Cries*.

Clutching her as tightly as she's clutching him. "Hi, Dig," she whispers.

I notice he lets out a scattered sob.

But I also notice that she has *wings*.

"Umm. Where the hell did those come from?" Lu asks.

Auren pulls away with a laugh, her face wet with tears and wonder. "It's a long story," she says as she fluffs them out. They look like they're made from both metal and the soft texture of her ribbons.

"What are you all doing here?" she says as she goes over to Lu next and hugs her fiercely as tears drip down her face. "How is this possible?"

When she turns, she stops short at the blonde tucked into Osrik's side. Shock slackens her face. "Rissa?" she whispers, voice splintering as her hand covers her mouth. "I thought... you..."

Rissa tentatively steps away from Osrik, her blue eyes gone wet. "I almost did."

Then she walks right over to Auren and pulls her into her arms. Auren looks as shocked as everyone else, because other than with Osrik, Rissa is pretty standoffish. Not the hugging type.

But she's certainly hugging now.

Auren stalls for a couple seconds before she hugs the woman back. "I knew we were friends," she says through a smile.

"Yes, well..." Rissa pulls away with a sniff and tries to wave off her emotion. "I figured you needed me. None of these people know how to wear anything other than armor. It's barbaric."

Auren snorts, and then she comes over and gives me a hug. "Hey, Fake Rip," she murmurs.

I smile, my emotions still choking my throat. "Hi, Gildy."

Argo chooses to swoop down just then, knocking right into Slade. My brother goes flying back, landing with an *oof* in the grass. Then he erupts into laughter, jumping back to his feet. "Beast, you crazy fucker, I told you to go back to Fourth!"

The timberwing chuffs at him, nudging at his arm as Slade runs his hand down his neck. "Fuck, am I glad to see all of you," my brother says, looking around at us as he scratches Argo at the jaw. "Where's Judd?"

And just like that, all the happiness empties out.

Disquiet spreads, thick and jagged.

Raw.

Auren and Slade instantly tense, picking up on our reactions.

Slade's head whips over. "Lu?" he questions.

Her eyes fill, bottom lip trembling as she shakes her head.

My brother's face goes lax with shock, face turning pale. "No..."

"I'm sorry," I gasp out, feeling the loss of Judd all over again. My brother turns reddened eyes to me. "He... There was a battle, and he came to help me, and...I'm fucking sorry, Slade."

Auren covers her face with her hands, shoulders shaking as she sobs.

Slade looks fucking devastated. Argo whines low in his throat.

Like he feels the weight of Judd's fall, Osrik's head hangs down. I feel it too. Notched around my shoulders and pinning me in place.

Auren comes over to Slade's side and wraps her arm around his back. He holds her, dragging a hand down his face, wiping away the moisture from his eyes. "Oh, Judd," Slade says with a shake of his head, his tone full of misery. "Fuck."

The grief is too close for us to get a good look at it yet. The wound too fresh. None of us know what to do with it. None of us know how to move around the empty space he's left in our group.

Maybe we never will.

Maybe sometimes, time doesn't help. It just...stretches. Widens the gap between the loss and the after.

Slade takes in a shaky breath and looks around at us. "I'm fucking glad to see you all," he says before clearing his throat. "Come into the city. Let's talk."

"We thought you left."

"We were going to," Auren tells us as she wipes at her eyes. "But we got held up. We were going to leave tomorrow instead."

Thank the Divine for that.

"How in the world did you get here?" Auren asks. "The bridge…"

"Yeah, it exploded," Rissa says. "But then, we found someone." She gestures behind her pointedly, and then Auren turns just as a limping figure shifts out from behind Argo.

"Hi, Lyäri," Emonie says quietly. Her expression looks unsure, her smile nervous.

Auren's eyes go wide. "Emonie! How did you? What— *What happened to you?*"

"I'm so sorry about what I did on the stage," she rushes to say. "I know how it must have looked, but—"

"Stop," Auren says as she hurries over and hugs her, though she does it gently so as not to hurt her. "You had to. I don't blame you one bit. I'm just sorry I couldn't get to you before the king took you away with him. I'm so sorry you were hurt."

Emonie slumps in relief. "I'm sorry *you* were hurt." She sniffs as they pull away, and then her swollen eyes find me. She perks up with a bit of good old-fashioned smugness. "See?" she says with a smirk. "Told you." She looks at Auren. "You got the better brother, I think, because this one is rude."

My lips press together in both irritation and guilt. "I had to be cautious," I defend.

She rolls her eyes. I think. Still too swollen to really tell.

"Let's get you to a healer," Auren says to her.

Slade nods. "We obviously have a lot to talk about."

We start walking into the city with Argo in tow. I look around the stone buildings, the arched rooftops and the glittering waterways. Some fae are rowing skinny boats down the water while people pass over the bridges above. There are some buildings that stretch up into the twisting trees themselves, and glass orbs that hang from branches, glittering with magical light.

Osrik whistles under his breath. "We're definitely not in Orea anymore."

Fae stop and gasp, staring at Argo wide-eyed as we pass. He puffs up a bit, as if he likes the attention.

But what I can't help but notice is that nearly every single person turns around and smiles or waves or even tips their heads in Auren's direction. And all of them are murmuring the same thing.

"Lyäri," I say to Slade. "Why do they call her that?"

He takes in a breath like he doesn't even know where to start. Then, he simply says, "Because…they love her."

I can see the truth of that in every face.

As we walk, I try to settle into the fact that we're actually here with Slade and Auren…in the fae realm. Where I haven't been since I was a child.

I turn to my brother. "Did you find her?" I ask, the question coming out fearful. I'm almost too scared to ask, too scared to hear his reply. Because what if the answer is bad?

I don't fucking know if I can bear it.

But Slade juts up his chin and moves his eyes, and I follow his line of sight. "I found her," he tells me, and I feel my heart stop and start all at once.

My mother stands there.

She looks happy. Safe. Smiling with a group of fae and even some of the Drollard villagers right here on the street. In the sunshine. Not in a horrible freezing mountain in the middle of nowhere.

I immediately race forward, breaking away from the group. People turn to look at me as I run down the brick road, and the commotion makes my mother turn and lock eyes on me.

I see her gasp just before I reach her. I fling my arms around her, wrapping her in a hug as I hold her close. "Mother," I say as I squeeze her, heart spilling over with my tears.

I've been so fucking afraid.

But I was so relieved to see her that I forgot to be cautious. To not scare her.

Shaking, I force myself to pull away. "I'm sorry," I quickly say, because if she's having a bad day, if her memories are more jumbled than usual…

But no. My mother looks at me, and her green depths are clear. Her smile beaming and watery with overflowing joy.

I gasp out a sob, and she smooths a hand lovingly over my cheek as I shake in relief. "Are you alright?"

She nods, and finally, I'm able to breathe right. Able to exhale all that wringing worry I've been strangled with since the moment I discovered she was gone.

The two of us turn as the rest of our group catches up. We all stand here on the street together, while fae watch us curiously, most of them giving Argo a wide berth. I see Slade reassuring them that he won't attack, watch Auren and Digby and Rissa talking.

I shake my head, almost dumbfounded at it all.

"How the hell did we find ourselves here?" I say to Lu.

She snorts. "No clue. But…we're together. That's what matters."

I know she's thinking of Judd, that we all will feel the loss of him in the empty space where he would've normally stood. That we'll feel his absence in every pause between people speaking, where he would've cracked a joke.

"I fucking miss him," Lu confesses, her voice tortured.

"Me too."

She takes in a deep breath and blows it back out as she glances up at the purple sky through the trees. "He would've liked it here, I think."

He would've been ecstatic to see this place, no doubt about it.

"I think we should celebrate finding each other over some fae wine," she says, drawing everyone's attention. "For Judd."

So we do exactly that.

We sit around a table with wine and words, and we celebrate and grieve.

But like Lu said, we're together.

And that's what matters.

# CHAPTER 70

## AUREN TURLEY

*Two months later*

I lift the cup to my lips as I watch the sun begin to dip over the horizon.

The light is dimming with its deliberate quell, the last golden sun rays beginning to drift away. I sit here with my back against my golden tree, watching the sun lower to sleep. Feel my own magic tingle in response, like a banked fire left to cool for the night.

I breathe in the blue steam from my cup before setting it beside me. Tali, the Orean villager who lives in the home just across the street, always comes out to bring me a cup of the flowery brew each time she sees me come to sit here and soak up the last minutes of the day.

Everything here on the street looks renewed. The golden

tree I made when I first visited Bryol is now a sort of landmark, and the ground is cleared and even, with a patch of new grass springing up around the metallic roots. The rest of the road behind me has been smoothed, no longer left in chunks of scorched rubble. Instead, fresh oat-toned bricks have been laid, and they edge behind the tree, lifting up into a short decorative wall that semicircles around it.

This is my favorite spot. I like to sit here in the grass and look out past the flowering plants, toward the view of the rolling meadows that bend against the horizon.

"There you are," Slade says as he comes walking up.

Smiling, I look over my shoulder as he approaches, and take his offered hand to let him pull me to my feet.

"I just wanted to watch the sun set," I tell him as my ribbons flick forward, drifting over his arms in flirtatious greeting. One of them curls around to his ass.

"Absolutely shameless," I say with a shake of my head before tugging it away.

Slade grins and leans down to kiss me.

"Did you and Argo enjoy your flight?" I ask, leaning into his touch as he cups my cheek.

"We did," he says quietly before he takes my hand. "But I have something I want to show you."

My brows lift. "What is it?"

He tilts his head. "Come on."

We turn, and I get the view of the newly built townhouses along the road. They all stand at least two stories tall, with bright colored doors adorning each house.

Except for right here, in this open space, where my parents' house used to stand. I decided I didn't want to build over this spot. So we turned it into a garden instead. A notch in the street where my golden tree stands to watch over it. And if you walk through the garden, you'll see a hundred or so Vulmin charms and pins and buttons left to gleam in tribute.

For my parents. For Wick's parents. For all those who lived and died in Bryol.

I walk with Slade back to the street, just as the first of the night's veil begins to drape.

"It's incredible, isn't it?" I ask as I look around.

No longer is this place charred and left in piles of wreckage. As soon as the Vulmin heard I wanted to rebuild it, they came in swarms and in trickles. Fae from all over Annwyn arriving to help with might and magic.

In just a couple of months, we've managed to rebuild this entire street.

And the village just outside the city's walls—the Clamor of the Blaze—they were the first to show up, ready to help. Ready to raise their sounds for a fresh start and to finally mute the reign of the Carricks and all it represented.

Starting right here.

As Slade and I walk back toward our own house, we pass by fae and Oreans walking, and they wave and smile at us. This city is no longer just cluttered ruin and painful grief. It's promise and healing.

I take a deep breath as the first coos of the nightbirds swoop up toward the sky, their shimmering underbellies glinting like stars.

Up ahead, I see Osrik and Rissa walking down the street, hand in hand, and my heart squeezes at the sight of them. They've settled in well. I think, because they have each other, they don't really care about the where.

They're just happy to be together—though the constant bickering might confuse some, but not me. They're perfect for each other.

Lu doesn't have much trouble either, so long as she stays busy. Which she does, because she's taken on the role of city captain, training new recruits to be Bryol's guard.

Speaking of guard…

I smile when I spot Digby.

He's walking this way with Elore, and I can't help but notice how her hand is draped in the crook of his arm and how she's smiling over at him as he says something. A tinge of color blots his cheeks, making my brows lift in surprise.

My stoic guard is *blushing*. I never thought I'd see the day.

Digby and Elore. I never thought I'd see that either, but my quiet guard and Slade's mother both have a calming presence. I think they've been able to find comfort in each other.

It's nice that they're spending time together. Digby wouldn't be the sort of man who would get frustrated at Elore's muteness, since he's a man of few words himself. And clearly, based on his blush and Elore's sparkling eyes, they're communicating just fine.

I steal a look over at Slade, but he doesn't seem bothered in the slightest.

"Hi, Dig," I call, alerting them of our presence.

Digby's attention pulls to me. "Lady Auren," he greets, looking a bit shy.

I can't help but smile.

"Dig, how many times do I have to tell you that you don't have to call me Lady?"

The stubborn man shrugs, and Elore smiles and shoots me a wink.

Slade goes over to his mother and presses a kiss to her cheek. "Are you alright?" he asks.

She nods with a smile and pats him on the shoulder before shooing us away.

He snorts. "Okay, we're going."

"Have a good night you two," I say as we keep walking, leaving them to go the other way.

We walk in silence for a few moments, my ribbons trailing on the street behind me. Night descends, and the first peeks of stars begin to glitter. The faces of the goddesses high above, looking down with their twinkling eyes.

"Everyone has settled in so well," I murmur.

Slade's thumb strokes over my hand. "They have— everyone except for…"

"Ryatt."

He nods, and a troubled look comes over his face.

Ever since Ryatt had to come to terms with the fact that Brennur was dead, that there were no other fae with the ability to create fairy rings in another realm, he's been…struggling.

He tries to hide it, but I can see how uncomfortable he is, and I know Slade notices more than I do. Mostly, Ryatt has just kept to himself, inside the house he's sharing with Lu and Digby.

"He'll adjust," I say, though it's more with hope than certainty.

Slade gives me a soft smile. "Only time will tell."

"Only time will tell."

Time tells a lot of secrets, passing off the words day by day.

"So?" I venture. "What did you want to show me?"

Instead of Slade taking us further up to our house that the Vulmin built for us, he veers us off the road and toward the field. There's a path here that I made, where the black-streaked gold will take us all the way to the flowing creek.

It's another one of my favorite spots, but instead of watching the sunset, the creek is best for the stars.

After a few minutes, we reach the water. Trees and rocks nestle against it, creating a private little nook. Slade helps me down, my hand clasped in his, and I stop in my tracks just as we come to the spot we often come to sit. There are dozens of blue bulb lights strung up in the trees, and even more of them flickering upon the rocks that surround our patch of grass.

I look over at him in surprise. "What's all this?"

"Come sit with me," he murmurs, pulling me ahead.

I look up at the dim glow of the bulbs in the branches as we settle onto the grass. Slade sits first and pulls me into his lap, my back to his front. His arms wrap around me as we look out past the water to the stars that brighten in the darkening sky.

We sit for several minutes as the balm of night spreads over Annwyn, and I relax into Slade's chest as he leans against the tree trunk behind him. We listen to the twilight crickets as they string together a soothing song like they're baying to the babbling creek. The center of the water glitters with the reflection of the stars, making the sky and land seem endless.

Slade presses a kiss to the top of my head. I look up at his face, gaze skimming over his pointed ears and the patch of scales at the side of his cheeks that lead up to his temples. My ribbons curl around us lazily, drifting over the grass, twirling around Slade's back and arms. I lift a hand over the stubble at his jaw to trace my fingers along the black roots that delve through it.

"How was your *one day* today, Goldfinch?" he asks, and I smile, because he asks me this every day.

My answer is always the same.

"It was the best, because I'm with you."

He cups the side of my face, and I turn in his arms so I'm straddling him, my hands twisting around the back of his neck and tangling into his hair.

"Are you happy?" he asks, another question I get each night.

I look into his deep green eyes. "Unfathomably," I whisper. "Are *you* happy?"

"Immeasurably."

I smile. "We're having all of our *one days*."

"We are." He braces one hand against my back, and my ribbons instantly tangle around his arm while his other hand plays with my hair until I have shivers that scatter down my skin. I feel his thumb stroke over the golden scale at my neck.

He shifts, reaching down, and then he hands me something. I pull back, glancing down in surprise at the book. It's small, its length fitting my hand, and I suck in a breath as soon as I look at it. It's familiar.

Red binding, golden filigree, ancient writing, and the word *Fae* scrolled on the spine. While it's not as worn as the other book, everything else is exactly the same.

"A replica?" I ask as I peel open the cover, eyes lighting up over the painted illustrations inside. "Where did you find this?"

"I had help," he says as he watches me flip through the pages. "Wick was able to track it down."

My heart swells as I look through it, and then I notice the strip of gold tucked at the last page. My eyes dart up, recognizing my ribbon that Slade always carries in his pocket. I flip to the page it's holding and see the two fae embracing. That same illustration I'd been so mesmerized with before, and the single fae word beneath them.

Päyur.

"It's Saira Turley, isn't it?" I say.

"Yes. And the prince." He points to their auras that glow around them. "I've heard from some of the Vulmin that they were one of the strongest pairs to have ever bonded." He pauses, finger hooking over the page. "Like us."

He flips it over, and I blink in surprise, because that wasn't the last page. There's one more. And this one is newer. The tiny brushstrokes are still visible where someone painted.

My breath catches as I stare. "Is this…"

"Us," he finishes, voice caught against my ear.

My watering eyes rove over every inch, taking in every detail.

There we are. Slade and I standing together in each other's arms. Me with ribboned wings, him with spikes and scales. Our auras are aglow around us, tendrils of gold and black that wrap around our figures like a halo of light and dark. And behind us, nearly flying right off the page, a goldfinch and a dragon.

Below it are three words. *Lyäri wyl Betuläria.*

"The golden one and the deathly flight," Slade quietly explains.

A tear tracks down my cheek, my heart filled with swirling emotions. "No tears," he tells me before gently closing the book and setting it aside. "You've had to cry too many already."

"These are mostly happy," I say as he wipes them away.

"Mostly," he murmurs, though I know he understands.

There will always be a piece of sadness for all that we've lost. For what we've endured. But the happy takes up the most space.

And that's a gift I'll never stop being grateful for.

"I love you," I tell him, watching his aura drift off his body, the black and the gold flowing together in gentle wisps.

"Oh, Goldfinch," he murmurs. "If ever there was a person for whom love was created, it was for you."

He presses a kiss against my lips, and I clasp his face with both my hands and kiss him back. Our mouths meet with devotion. Bonds pulsing in sync with our singing hearts that only play for us.

My ribbons come forward, strips plucking open the ties at his pants and loosening the ones at his collar. I peel open his shirt so my palms can smooth over the defined muscles of his chest before my mouth comes down to pepper kisses up his neck.

"My beloved paired," he purrs with a tipping smirk. "I do believe you're trying to seduce me."

I smile against his skin. "Is it working?"

"Flawlessly," he says against me as his hands come down to slip the straps of my dress off my shoulders.

The material easily gives—mostly because my ribbons help him.

He chuckles darkly as a couple of them tug at the front of his pants again, and I shrug. "They know what they want."

"So do I." Then his words rumble with command that makes me want to catch flame. "Stand up, Goldfinch."

# CHAPTER 71

## AUREN TURLEY

My stomach flutters in anticipation, skin heating with want.

I carefully stand, and Slade gets to his feet in front of me. With one hand raised, he tugs his shirt off and tosses it away, baring his chest. My eyes feast, drifting over every defined muscle and vein, along the scales that spread from his heart in a bloom of gold and silver.

"You're beautiful," I tell him.

"You're glorious," he replies instantly. "Undress for me, Auren."

I pull down my dress the rest of the way, letting the silky fabric pool at my feet while my ribbons twirl. I step out of it, and his eyes flare, tracking over my form with rapt attention.

"The rest," he orders, throat bobbing.

Two ribbons hook over the edges of my panties and drag them down inch by inch, while my fingers come up to undo the pretty ties at the front of my bodice. Both garments are slipped off and tossed away, and then I'm bare to him beneath the starlight.

"Your turn," I say as I step forward.

He watches me hungrily as I stop in front of him, hands clenching and muscles bunching like he's trying to hold himself back. My eyes flick up to his face before I focus on the waistband of his pants. My fingers flick out the laces at the top, and then my ribbons spring forward and yank down his pants as soon as they're able, making another chuckle roll out of him and scrape tantalizingly across my skin.

"Eager?" he teases.

I don't even attempt to be coy. My body is wound tight, and I can already feel myself getting wet just by standing here looking at him. Feeling the heat of his attention as he devours me with his gaze. "Yes."

His cock is already hard, and when he reaches down and slowly starts to stroke it, my mouth waters. I surge forward, shoving away his grip to replace it with my own.

He hisses beneath his breath as I squeeze my fist around him. The sounds he makes spur me on, and I drag my thumb over the drop of precum, smearing it over the head.

"Have I ever told you that you have a magnificent cock?"

His fangs flash in the night from his grin. "Have I ever told you that you're utter fucking perfection?"

"So are you," I reply before letting go to back up a few steps, my eyes locked on his.

I lower myself to the soft patch of grass that tickles my skin as I lie down. My legs rub against each other, my fingers and ribbons trailing up my naked torso to tease at my nipples. They harden beneath the touch and the air, and Slade watches me like he's starving, his aura thickening as much as his cock.

I crook my finger in invitation, and he comes down over me, our bodies meeting, skin pressing. Hands and ribbons drag over his back and ass, while his mouth comes down to nip at my lips.

His fingers slide down to stroke between my legs and make me gasp. An appreciative groan escapes him. "Already wet. Already wanting."

"I always want you."

He hums and his touch grazes over my clit. He starts stroking me there, circling, pressing with just the right amount of pressure, not letting up. My nerves start to tighten, my body even more heated than before.

The sweet scent of Annwyn mixes with our own heady mix of arousal, feeding into my need. I tremble, not from the cool night air, but from him. From our bond that keeps us coiled and tied, so wrapped up in one another that our desire flows back and forth.

Slade continues to stroke me, making me writhe on the grass, while my body gushes with slick like it's salivating for him. Demanding him.

My pussy tightens as he slides two fingers inside of me, dragging in and out, spreading my wetness. "I don't want to come unless you're inside me," I pant out.

I reach down and grip him again, stroking him up and down, feeling every inch as I watch his face, watch him react to my touch.

His fingers keep playing, keep making me climb higher with need. "*Slade…*" I beg.

He curses beneath his breath. "Fuck, I love when you say my name like that."

"I want you inside of me. I need it."

He pulls his fingers out and brings them to his mouth, licking off my arousal as he watches me with his glinting gaze. "Delicious," he purrs, making me tighten all over.

His mouth comes down and presses a kiss against my jaw. Teeth dragging over to place another one at my mouth. Our tongues tangle as tightly as our souls are bound, and we kiss with the fervor of our devotion for each other.

"You want me to make love to you?" he says quietly against my ear before his tongue darts out, licking over my pulse. "You want me to take you right here, under the stars?"

"*Yes*," I breathe.

He braces his arms over me, legs bracketing mine, and then slowly feeds his cock into me. My back arches, eyes closing as I revel in the feel of him stretching me.

"Goddess…"

"Look at us," he says.

I peel my eyes open, gaze darting down to where he watches his dick slide in and out of me with a languid stroke. I can see the slight sheen of my wetness coating him, can see how my pussy stretches around his thick shaft. The erotic sight makes my stomach tighten and my skin tingle.

His fingers slip between my legs once more, stirring my desire. I gasp up at the night sky, eyes full of starlight as my own orgasm bursts through me.

"Your perfect pussy is gushing around my cock," he praises in a guttural tone that only excites me more. "Trying to milk me until I come deep inside you. Trying to squeeze me so… fucking…*tight*." The last words are gritted out as the last waves of my orgasm fade.

He leans over me, feeding my breasts into his waiting mouth, making me whimper as his hot tongue flicks and drags. He feasts, sucking and nipping and licking, while he tilts up my hips and drags in and out of me.

But his slow movements are driving me wild.

I brace my ribbons behind me and sit up, pushing him down so I'm on top. Then I start fucking him, moving over his length as hard and fast as I want.

He groans, his hands sliding down to my ass, fingers digging in as he helps lift me up and down. "Look at you, fucking yourself over me," he growls. "Bouncing on my cock, wanting more."

"Yes, *more*," I moan greedily.

I grind and sway, chills scattering over my skin as he strokes me. My ribbons run down his arms and torso, touching him all over.

And still, I say, "*More.*"

Slade flips us, so fast that I gasp in surprise when I suddenly find myself on my side, knees curled up. He kneels on the ground, hand coming down to lightly smack the side of my ass that's exposed.

With me curled on my side and him kneeling, he grasps my thigh to hold one leg up, and hooks my calf over his shoulder. Then he reaches forward and feeds his fingers through my hair before making a fist. Not painful, but forceful. In delicious control, he lifts my head up to watch as he thrusts his cock back into me.

This position makes my eyes roll to the back of my head with pleasure.

He starts fucking me harder, making my breasts bounce with every punch of his hips. This angle makes moans tear past my lips and gather with the babbles of the creek.

"Slade…*fuck*…" I whimper.

His grip at my scalp tightens, and he holds me in place as he fucks up into me hard.

The breath gets blown out of my chest.

"Fuck, look at you," he snarls with hunger, his features sharpening with lust. "Legs spread, cunt gaping around my cock… your tits bouncing. You're magnificent."

His hand leaves my hair so he can tap his fingers against my lips. "Open," he orders roughly.

I immediately comply, and he shoves two fingers in. Thrusts them into my mouth in time with his cock. When I suck, he growls and pulls them back out.

Then he seems to snap, giving in to his animalistic lust. He pulls out of me and grabs my hips to swing me onto all fours, facing him toward his jutting cock.

"Tongue out," he commands, dark eyes flashing where he kneels above me.

I tremble with exhilaration from the look in his eye, watching him as I open my mouth and stick out my tongue.

With his hand gripping the back of my neck, he uses the other to grab hold of his dick. He taps his cock on my flattened tongue, slapping the hard length over my taste buds before shoving his length in until the head hits the back of my throat.

I gag, but he drags back out and does it again. And again. And again.

Making me wind tighter and tighter, making my thighs press together as my clit throbs with need.

"Suck."

I swallow his cock, savoring the taste of our joined moisture. He keeps hold of my neck the entire time and never once looks away. Hardly even blinks.

My cheeks hollow as I suck him, eyes watering every time he hits the back of my throat. He starts to fuck my mouth, fingers tensing around my neck as he takes me until I'm whimpering with need.

He pulls me off, and then I'm on my back, knees pressed to my chest, head spinning. Then he drives into me so hard that I let out his name with a rasping shout.

Slade starts fucking me like a fae possessed, hands and mouth everywhere, and I'm lost. Lost in every single frantic kiss and thrust and stroke. He thrusts into me so hard I wouldn't be surprised if my body leaves an imprint on the ground.

My burning desire reaches a fervor of red-hot pleasure, and I beg in wordless moans as I writhe. His fingers circle over my clit hard, unrelenting, making me swell and burn.

"Come with me, Auren," he orders as he presses our chests together. Fucking me with our heartbeats and panting breaths squeezed between us. "We go together, don't we, baby? Me and you."

GOLDFINCH

I thrash around the ground as he pinches my clit. "Always together."

"Come for me, you gorgeous goddess."

He squeezes my ass with one hand, tilting my hips up, and I ignite around him, fire cracking open and pouring out its molten heat. My orgasm floods me, floods him, and I hear him roar out his release into the night, slaking our lusts and drinking in every drop as our pleasure bursts.

Together.

We lie in a tangle until our breaths even out, and then Slade pulls me into the creek, where we wash each other with reverent hands and pebbled skin. We dry off upon the grass, with heated kisses and blazing eyes, and I know, I will never have enough of him.

Slade pulls me to my feet and helps me dress, his every movement tender and adoring.

"Should we go home to bed?" I ask as I take his hand.

But instead of letting me pull him in the direction of the gilded path, he moves his hand to stroke down the base of my ribbons. "Let your wings out, Goldfinch."

I blink in surprise, but I give in to his words. Glancing over my shoulder, I make my ribbons change. They ripple as they fuse together one by one, the end of the layers forming into feathers until two wings bracket my spine. I stretch them out with a smile, letting them fluff in the air.

Slade looks at me, eyes taking in every inch. "You are stunning."

My stomach dips, heart spilling over. Every time this male looks at me like this, every time he purrs out these words of adoration, it makes me melt all over again.

"Close your eyes," he says quietly. I tilt my head in question, and he smirks. "Go on."

With a smile, I let my eyes flutter closed.

I hear him move forward, and then his hand grasps mine. He lifts it to his chest. I feel his scale beneath my palm, feel his steady heartbeat thrumming.

675

"Our pair bond fixed me," he murmurs as I feel his warm breath skim along my cheek. "*You* fixed me, Auren."

My heart starts thumping harder. I don't know where he's going with this, but I can feel something stirring. My skin prickles in response.

"Every day the sun rises, it rises for you," he says quietly as he brushes a finger gently down my brow, over my cheek, before settling his hand against my own heart. "Every day I wake, I wake for you."

A tear slides from the corner of my closed lid, and he leans down and kisses it like he's accepting an offering. My fingers tighten over his heart, my touch warming through.

"And every time my heart beats, it beats with yours."

I suck in a breath.

"Open your eyes, baby."

His hands drop as he steps away, and I blink in the dark, refocusing on him as he stands in front of me, watching. Waiting.

My brows lower in question, but then my eyes widen as I watch shadows pull out of his aura, out of his body, swirling beside him.

"What is that?" I whisper raggedly.

He doesn't answer, but I stand in shock as those shadows fuse and form.

My hand flies to my mouth, and my eyes fly to his. "Slade. Your *dragon*."

He nods, looking over at the creature with a smile that reaches his eyes. With wonderment that beats through his soul.

The dragon isn't solid, it's made up of that shadowy vapor, and it's much, much smaller than before.

But it's here.

"Look, Auren," Slade says.

I glance down to the wings at its back. Wings that are now edged with a ribbon of gold.

"I don't know how," he says with a shake of his head as he

looks back at me. "But somehow...I think you brought my dragon back to life."

A sob chokes out of me as I stumble forward. The creature is only as tall as me, but it's unmistakably the same one. Spikes down its back and above its brows, golden scales upon its chest.

It looks at me with a knowing gleam. With a familiar pull of its mouth.

"Shadows," I whisper as I graze my hand over its vaporous body.

"I don't know if it will ever get bigger or if I can even manifest anything but a splintered form, but it doesn't matter. That hollow part of me where the dragon was missing? It's filled again," Slade says with a smile as he takes my hands in his. "Thank you."

My head shakes. "I don't know that I actually had anything to do with this," I tell him. "Maybe you just needed time to heal."

"I do know," he counters, tapping at his heart. "I can feel it."

My chest warms and I wrap my arms around him. "I'm so happy for you," I breathe against his skin.

He tilts my head up and kisses me, just as the dragon's form drifts away, fading like mist.

"Come on," he says before reaching down to clasp my hand in his. "Let's go home, Goldfinch."

*Home.*

Hand in hand, we walk in the dark, guided by the gilded path that leads us back to the street. The night whispers, the city sparkles, and inside, my heart sings.

Slade and I look at each other, and the stars look at us.

My wings flutter, my heart soars, and I know.

That after everything. After all of it.

*This* was what I was always fighting for. This was why I kept going even in the bleakest of times. Even with every stumbling fall.

Because this love?

This is what it feels like...

to fly.

# LITTLE SUN

There was a star above and a root below.
And a world somewhere in between.


And for a time, that's all it was.
Space, and death, and gleam.


But that star began to glow,
she began to burn with heat.
And that root, it looked above,
fought from soil then to seek.


The star that burned, it beckoned him.
And the root, it knew to lift.
For that warmth that bled into the void,
it was an ordained gift.


So, from the ground unburied,
it looked up to see afar.
But that was when the root then saw,
it wasn't just a star.

This light that burned and gave its warmth,
it was a little sun.
Gilt tendrils that reached across the dark,
with ribbons twist and spun.


And that root, it knew right then.
Right there, it saw the heart.
For that sun that grew so beautifully,
it couldn't be apart.


So out they stretched—above, below,
and somewhere in between.
And through the space, and death, and time,
branches tied with beams.


There they are, and there they stay,
Paired and tied to core.
Dark and light, through realms, they hold.
And to Time, they whisper, *more*.

# ACKNOWLEDGMENTS

I actually can't believe I'm here. That it's the end.

Auren's journey has been a part of me every day for over five years, and writing her has changed my life.

This is definitely the book that has broken me and put me back together again.
I'm just so proud of her. Proud of Malina too. These women mean so much to me, and it's been an honor to tell their story.

It's been an honor that you've read it.

I have received so many beautiful letters and messages, had so many impactful one-on-one encounters with some of you, and I will never forget it.

I would like to thank all of you from the bottom of my heart for reading, and for coming with me on this walk. For trusting me to tell this story.

I want to thank my family for getting me to the end, because I couldn't have done it without all of you. Writing these last two books with a baby not even a year and a half old has been really hard, but it was possible because of your continuous support and all your help.

To my husband for being my rock. To my girls, for being my little suns. I love you more than all the stars in the sky.

To my parents, thank you for staying and helping, giving me all the encouragement and always being so proud. I love you so much.

To Skylar for being here to see me through to the very end. I absolutely could not have done it without you. Having you here helped me in so many ways, and I am grateful for you.

To the only sister I'll ever have, thank you for always being there for me. Thank you for believing in me.
To my doulas, thank you so much for helping my family and being here without fail, for getting us through every milestone and supporting me whenever I needed it.

To my best friends and amazing authors: Ann Denton, C.R. Jane, Ivy Asher, and Sarah A. Parker, this book would have crashed and burned without you. (And I would have too.) But you kept me going, kept me on track, and turned me back around whenever I took a wrong turn. (And I did that a lot.) Thank you for helping me make sure that this finale was everything it needed to be. Thank you for all the messages, all the sprinting, all the encouragement and advice. You are the best.

To Helayna, I could never trust someone like I trust you. Thank you for all the long hours, the thorough edits, and for making sure I'm not screwing everything up. And I promise to stop shoving 7-chapter clumps at you from now on. Maybe. I'll try. If it works out. And if it suits me. (Lol.)

To Amy, thank you for all your hard work and the rushed time. You make these books actually look like books, planning months in advance, and I'm so thankful for you. Thanks for taking my jumbled notes and making everything look so awesome.

To Aubrey, these covers are breathtaking. Every little detail you've put into them is so amazing. I told you the last one was going to be *Gold* and then messed everything up when I had to add another book (hello, liquid gold spines), but you just turned around with *Goldfinch* and made it absolutely epic without missing a beat.

To my agent Kim, this series wouldn't be the same without you. You've taken an indie and swept it out into the world. I'm in awe of all that you do. You've always done everything in your power to do what's best for me and this series, and I'm so thankful for you.

To my publishers, I want to say a huge thank-you for taking these books and launching them to a stratosphere I never could've reached on my own.

There are so many BookTokers and Bookstagrammers I want to thank, and I wish I could name you all. Honestly, you are a huge reason that anybody reads these books. I am so thankful for your support and love. Just know that I love you right back and I adore each and every one of you. You are the best hype team ever.

So this is it. After six books, Auren has her happy. She gets all her *one days*.

And I'm left with the bittersweet realization that it's over.

But you can bet that I'll keep looking up to smile at the sun, and I hope you will too.

And maybe in the future, I'll write something else that's pulled from the void and that cracks open the stars, and we'll meet again on those pages.

One day.

XOXO—Raven

# About the Author

Raven Kennedy is a California girl born and raised, whose love for books pushed her into creating her own worlds.

Her debut series was a romcom fantasy about a cupid looking for love. She has since gone on to write in a range of genres, including the adult dark fantasy romance: The Plated Prisoner Series, which has become a #1 international bestseller with over three million books sold worldwide.
Whether she makes you laugh or cry, or whether the series is about a cupid or a gold-touched woman in a castle, she hopes to create characters that readers can root for.

When Raven isn't writing, she's reading or spending time with her husband and daughters.

You can connect with Raven on her social media, and visit her website: ravenkennedybooks.com